Cedar Ridge
Chronicles #2

DATE DUE

OCT 0 5 2016	
OCT 2 4 2016	
NOV 0 2 2016	
NOV 1 4 2016	
DEC 2 0 2016	
JAN 0 3 2016	
FEB 1 5 2017	
MAR 2 7 2017	
APR 0 3 2017	

JOE STORM NO LONGER A COWBOY
Cedar Ridge Chronicles 2

A J Hawke

Mountain Quest Publishing
ISBN: 978-0-9834505-7-3
Copyright © 2012 Barbara A Kee
Cover copyright © Barbara A Kee
Layout design © by Barbara A Kee

ISBN: 978-0-9834505-7-3
ISBN-13: 978-0-9834505-7-3

ACKNOWLEDGMENTS

Many thanks for the editing done by Teresa Hanger at A-1 Editing Services. Also thanks for the help of Russell Schoof, Tina Dee, and Janet Grimes as they gave of their time and effort to make this a better book.

Reuben Rog designed the cover. www. Rogillustrations.com

DEDICATION

To all my readers who enjoy good fiction
As always To God Be The Glory

Table of Contents

Chapter One

Waco, Texas 1874

Where am I? Joe squinted against the pale light. The lamp on a small table next to the bed brightened a room he did not recognize. The walls and ceiling were whitewashed boards. He could see a bureau and a wooden straight-backed chair. There was a door leading somewhere.

He tried to shift his hips to turn over in the bed but he couldn't move them. A fire of pain streaked up from that part of his body. When he lifted his head and shoulders, another wave of pain washed through his right hip and up through his left ribs. He clenched his teeth to suppress a groan, but failed. In agony, he dropped back against the pillow—waiting—hoping someone would come, while the throbs radiated throughout his body. After a while, he discovered that if he remained perfectly still, the agony subsided a little.

Vague memories stirred in the corner of his mind...

Joe Storm. Cowhand. That's who, and what, he was but why couldn't he remember anything else?

The door opened and a moment later, a plump gray-haired woman with a soft smile bent over the bed and straightened the covers. She had kind, sparkling blue eyes. "Well, hello there." Her voice held a note of cheer and comfort. "It's good to see you awake."

"Where am I?" The croak in Joe's voice brought more questions. What had happened to him?

"You're at Dr. Rupert's house in Waco, Texas. I'm his sister, Mrs. Mildred Purdy. I help take care of sick folks." She tucked in the sheet around his shoulders with great care.

"When is it? I mean, what day is it?" He fought the fog of confusion that overlaid the pain radiating from his body.

"It's Tuesday." Her voice was soft and low, what he imagined a grandmother's would sound like. But he had never had a grandmother. How did he know that? His thoughts were wandering and he struggle to keep one long enough to understand what was happening.

"Tuesday? What date?" Why couldn't he think? He tried to grab onto his thoughts. Last time he had a headache like this was when he and Tom had fought. Who was Tom? He couldn't remember.

"Today is September 18, 1874. What do you remember?"

Suddenly an image of cattle and men was vivid. "Being on the trail heading toward Waco to sell some cattle with other cowhands. But how did I get here?" And where were the other fellows?

She straightened from tucking in the sheet. "I guess it's close to three days since those cowhand friends of yours brought you in off the trail. Your friends said you saved a cowhand's life from an angry bull, but in the doing of so, you got thrown off your horse and trampled. This was over across the river west of town. They said you were a hero." She smiled brightly. "You're doing much better now."

Joe swallowed the lump of panic in his throat, tried to keep his voice calm. "Lady, what's wrong with me?" He wasn't sure he wanted an answer.

The smile faded from her soft rounded face. Her caring eyes locked with his as she patted his arm. "Dr. Rupert will come in a minute. He best tell you." She picked up a plain white china cup from the table. "See if you can swallow some of this soup. Doc wants me to get as much liquid down you as possible." She placed the rim of the cup to his lips.

Joe swallowed a small amount of the warm broth, but pulled back and shook his head. The effort and the pain drained away what little energy he had.

A thin, baldheaded man in a worn black broadcloth suit strode into the room. "How's our patient, Mildred?" His raspy voice gave away his advanced years.

The woman stepped back from the bed. "You can ask him yourself. He's awake."

The man put one hand on Joe's forehead and then picked up the cowhand's limp wrist. "I'm Dr. Rupert, by the way, but everyone calls me Doc. Glad you're awake. How're you feeling?"

"I'm not sure. I can't seem to move. What's wrong with my legs?" This doctor had to tell him he would be all right. He bit his tongue against the pain—and waited.

"It'd surprise me if you could move. Where do you feel pain?" Doc pulled back the covers.

Joe looked down. Bandages covered his body from his hips to his armpits. He was strapped to a board, which explained why he could not move. His breathing quickened and his heart thumped so hard it surely could be heard by this elderly man.

Doc's fingers pulled and tugged on the bindings.

Excruciating pain seared through Joe like a hot fire. He sucked in a breath to resist the scream that filled his mind, but a moan still escaped.

"Sorry, Joe, but I want these bandages tight. Now, tell me where it hurts most."

Joe gasped for breath and spoke through clenched teeth. "It seems to come from my right hip, and across and up to my chest, but across the hips is bad. My head is also pounding." He could barely breathe, let alone answer clearly.

Doc gently pushed the sides of Joe's hipbones, pressing them inward.

The pain became so excruciating that Joe nearly passed out, but a fellow didn't ever seem to do that when it would be most useful. Instead, he gritted his teeth again and sucked in a deep breath, afraid to exhale for fear the agony would worsen. He was just a breath away from screaming. Sweat broke out over his whole body.

Doc finished his exam and then pulled the sheet and quilt up to Joe's chest. The intensity of the pain eased off.

"Well, you've a bad break in your right hipbone—perhaps several breaks in your pelvis, that's the big bone structure that hold your legs in place. I'm not sure of the possible damage in your back and abdomen. You've got at least two broken ribs. A bump on your head." Doc's low, raspy voice made the bad news sound worse. "Your worst injury is your right hip."

"How long will I be laid up?" Joe cleared his throat and drew in a shallow breath. Pelvis? He didn't even know he had one.

A look passed between Dr. Rupert and Mrs. Purdy. Doc glanced back at Joe. "You want the truth?"

Joe hesitated unsure he wanted to hear what Doc was about to say. Taking a breath to shore up his courage, he said, "Yes. I want the truth."

"You've got as bad a break on your right side as one can have of the hip and pelvis. It's going to be a long time repairing. I suspect you have several breaks in there. There is no way for me to know for sure, but if so, then several pieces of bone have to mend back—and mend right. With time, your ribs will be fine. The healing of the head wound is almost complete. But for the rest ...." Dr. Rupert looked down and shook his head.

"When you say a long time, exactly what do you mean?"

"Well, we're at the middle of September now. I expect we can have you up and out of bed in three or four months." Doc spoke in a calm voice, as though he delivered such news every day. "Hopefully," his voice brightened, "we'll have you up and walking by Christmas."

Three or four months! Joe didn't know what to say. A healthy twenty-four-year-old cowhand who had worked out of doors all his life, he could not envision months of lying in bed.

Doc cleared his throat. "I know it sounds bad, Joe, but believe me, it could've been worse. That bull's full weight could have killed you."

Joe's mind scrambled in a dozen different directions as he tried to see a way to survive the coming months until he could get back to the ranch and to work. How would he earn money?

He looked at the doctor and then at the older woman standing at the end of the bed. "I don't have much right now to pay you."

"Your boss, Mr. Jake, told me to send him the bill. Now, if you're to heal at all, we have to keep that hip and pelvis from moving, so the bones can heal back together. Mrs. Purdy here has agreed to take care of you." He gave a nod in her direction. "She's a good nurse. I'll be checking on you too. But you have to listen to me if you want to ever walk again."

Ever walk again! Please Lord, what's Doc saying? Fear crawled through his gut.

Of course, he would walk again, but for the first time his chest squeezed in a new kind of fear. Not fear of dying, he'd dealt with that many times out on the range. The fear of being helpless, of not walking—he just couldn't face that.

If being still was what it took, he wouldn't move a muscle. "All right, Doc, you tell me what to do and I'll do it." The words left his mouth with more courage than he felt.

Dr. Rupert patted him on the arm as if he were reassuring a child. "I'll do what I can. But I can't promise what the results will be. Joe, do you have family that you want me to write? Someone who might want to come be with you?"

Joe thought of his father. He wanted his father to come, he needed him, but he couldn't ask him. "No sir, no one."

Doc turned to Mrs. Purdy. "Keep him still and get him to eat something. We got us a long haul here, but you're the key to Joe's recovery, Mildred."

"I'll do my best, Doc. Don't you worry about Joe here. He and I are going to work together and get him healed." She smiled at Joe, and then turned to walk with Doc toward the door.

The sound of crickets drew Joe's eyes to the open window and the darkness outside. Their chirping seemed to be in rhythm with the throbbing of the pain

Mrs. Purdy came back into the bedroom, stood by the bed, and brushed back the hair from his brow. "Now, Joe, I know you're hurting and Doc's news is distressful. He left something for you to take if the pain gets bad."

Her kind words were almost more than he could bear. "It's bad," he whispered.

"I'll be right back with some medicine." She bustled out of the room.

Joe stared at the plain cut white washed lumber ceiling. Three to four months of looking at that ceiling. Could he do it?

"Here we go." Mrs. Purdy stood next to his bed, holding a small blue bottle. "Doc knew there'd be a lot of pain." She measured out a tablespoon of brownish liquid, then put the spoon to his lips.

Joe swallowed the bitter stuff, almost gagging. He gulped the water she offered to wash the horrid taste out of his mouth.

"That should work quickly and you'll drift off to sleep. When the pain comes back, we'll give you more if you need it. There isn't anything useful to come from you lying there suffering."

Her kindly face made him glad she was there. The medicine soon did its work and the pain eased. His eyes closed, his body grew limp, the sounds around him seemed to disappear into the distance, and Joe slipped into a peaceful vagueness.

~

The next few weeks were a blur filled with pain from his broken bones and a grogginess from the medicine. Every time he woke, Mrs. Purdy attended him with cool cloths on his forehead, massaged his legs, arms, and back with liniment to prevent sores, and took care of his other essential needs.

Doc came in everyday to keep the bandages wrapped tight.

With the torment that even the slightest movement caused, the temptation to move went away. The bandages were a prison. At times he wasn't sure he would even be able to breathe. He'd never been so scared in his life. Joe's world quickly narrowed down to one room, one bed.

~

Early one morning three weeks later, when the doctor came in to check the bandages, Joe asked, "Doc, could you maybe undo the dressings holding me down?"

The older man adjusted his spectacles. "Do you want to walk again, Joe?"

He nodded. Please God, yes he wanted to walk again.

Doc patted his shoulder, as if he understood the turmoil in Joe's mind. "I know it is hard but bear with it, son. You will get better."

Over the past few weeks, Joe's muscles turned flabby and his body lost what fat it had. He watched as he went from being a well-muscled man, proud of his physical ability, to all skin and bone with barely enough strength to hold the books Mrs. Purdy brought him.

When she first offered to read to him, he almost refused. He hadn't much to do with books, but he was so bored he would have listened to someone read a calendar. He soon held the books himself and he would read while Mrs. Purdy went about her work.

Other than talk to Mrs. Purdy, and a daily five-minute visit from Dr. Rupert, he had nothing to do but lie there and think.

Christmas, when it came, was just another day, except Mrs. Purdy took pity on him and made a cake. She tried to cheer things up, but Joe didn't feel very cheerful. It reminded him too much of the fun he'd had with the other cowhands. He remembered the impromptu riding and roping contests they would have to liven up a poor Christmas on an isolated ranch. Loneliness and memories were his constant companions as he lay and stared at the ceiling.

One morning in late January, after Mrs. Purdy had helped him wash and shave, Dr. Rupert came in. "Joe, I want to remove the bandages and the board. You need to go slow. If I unstrap you, will you promise not to try and stand until I tell you?"

"You know what's best, Doc." Joe longed to be released from the prison of the bandages and to see what his body would do. The agonizing pain had gradually lessened until now there were only dull aches. He sensed that if he could just move around it would feel so much better.

The air felt cool on his bare legs as Doc pulled the covers back. With tugs and snips of the scissors, he cut the wrappings. With a grunt, the older man pulled the board out from under Joe and then released his body to rest back on the soft sheet and mattress. Joe had expected it to be painful, but except for a few aches through his hip, it felt fine.

Doc tucked the covers in under Joe's chin. "There, that should start to feel better. I noticed that you've got a lot of old scarring on your back."

Joe didn't say anything, as there was no way he wanted to tell them who had caused those scars. He had been hiding them for ten years and he intended to keep on doing it.

Doc took off his glasses, wiped them clean with his handkerchief. "You can start to move your legs around a bit, but stop if it hurts. No getting out of bed, yet."

"Yes sir."

When they left him alone, he tentatively moved his legs about four inches before his knees and hips protested with pain. At least he had bent his knees. That was a start. Now to regain his strength, and get back on a horse.

~

In February, almost five months after his injury, the day Joe had waited for finally came.

Doc hurried into the room followed by Mrs. Purdy. He always seemed to do things in a hurry. "Let's see if you can sit on the side of the bed."

Mrs. Purdy held out her arm. "Grab hold and pull yourself up."

Doc slid his arm around Joe's shoulders and gave support as Joe struggled to sit up for the first time since he had been injured.

Then Doc swung Joe's legs over the edge of the bed.

Joe's head spun and his feet throbbed from the blood rushing into them. If Mrs. Purdy and Doc hadn't been there to catch him, he would have fallen off the bed.

"That's enough for the first time. It'll get better. Mildred, let's lower Joe back down." Gently, they settled him back on the bed.

He gasped for breath, as if he had done a day's work. His fists curled at his side. He'd drive them into the wall if he had strength. Instead, he was no better than a weak wobbling baby.

Doc squeezed his shoulder. "I know it's hard, but you'll be up and about in a couple of weeks. Just be patient."

Joe nodded. "Thanks, Doc." Up and about ... and then what? How long would it take to get enough strength to get back to work?

For the next three days, Joe struggled to sit up and hang his feet over the edge of the bed without the help of Mrs. Purdy.

On the fourth day, Doc said, "Let's get you up on your feet today."

Joe stared at the older man. "You mean walk?" He wasn't sure he could do it.

"No, not walk. You need to get used to just standing and putting weight on that hip."

With Mrs. Purdy on one side and Doc on the other, they lifted Joe to his feet. With his arms around their shoulders as support he towered over them.

Pain shot up through his legs. Joe grit his teeth, as he gave thanks for Mrs. Purdy's gentle hold and Doc's firm grasp around his waist. Without their support, he would have dropped like a log.

"Don't look so down, Joe. This is the first step. It'll get easier."

"Thanks, Doc." They lowered him onto the bed, then eased him back on the pillows. If this was just the first step, what was it going to take to get back to riding? His legs trembled under a body engulfed with exhaustion. Would he ever have his strength again?

It took three days more before he walked to the chair five feet away.

From that point, Joe continued to make slow painful progress until he could get himself out of bed without help. Using a cane, he shuffled slowly around the bed.

Mrs. Purdy brought him a shaving kit. She laid a comb on the bureau. He had to lie propped up in bed to shave because he still could not stand long enough to finish the job. Getting up to retrieve the comb on the bureau was too much effort. How was he going to work cattle if he could not even get to the bureau? His impatience was like an open wound, festering.

Determined to push himself, Joe slowly got up and shuffled over to the bureau. He glanced at the figure in the mirror and almost didn't recognize his own image. His skin was stretched tight over the bones in his face, giving a sharp edge to his cheeks and jaw. Sunken eyes stared back at him in the mirror. Long dark brown hair, curled at the ends, framed his face. His normal bronzed tone, from his work in the sun, had faded to a ghostly pale, leaving him with a pallid look. His shirt hung in folds, and if he had not tightened his belt to the last notch, his pants would have dropped to his ankles.

Who was this stranger looking out at him from the mirror? The cowhands used to tease him about him being the handsome one of the bunch. And there had been girls through the years who had told him they found him comely to look at. But now? This man with lines of suffering in his face was what he had become. Could he hope ever to retrieve his strength and the image of who he had been?

He turned back to the bed, not wanting to look at the wreck of a man he had become. Where had the man he had once been gone? And would he ever get back to being himself?

He had spent five months in this bedroom. Winter had passed. Joe walked slowly to the kitchen and stepped out onto the back porch. If it hadn't taken so much energy, he'd have been elated. He wanted to get moving, get back in the saddle and work. He just couldn't make it happen fast enough.

He dreamed at night of riding his horse and following the cattle. Always of riding a horse—fast.

Chapter Two

Six months after his accident, Joe lay watching the sky through the open window. He saw trees with leaves budding out on the branches. Spring had arrived. He sighed. He challenged himself to get out of bed and make his way to the breakfast table. Mrs. Purdy would bring the food to him but he was trying to decrease his burden on her. But still he laid there.

Doc came into the bedroom. "Good, you're still in bed. I want to check on your hip before you get dressed, if you don't mind."

He pulled the covers down to the foot of the bed, revealing Joe's skinny torso and legs. Doc checked his range of movement of the left leg. "That leg is fine. Now let's check the right leg." He took the weight of Joe's right leg in his hands and pulled it to the side, except that the leg would not move sideways.

And it hurt, a sharp piercing pain every time Doc tried to move it any direction but back and forth.

Doc then tried to swing Joe's right leg in a circle. Again, it would not move normally. Instead, the doctor could only move the hip in a forward and backward movement. Without a word, Dr. Rupert laid Joe's leg back on the bed.

"What is it, Doc?" Joe asked with hesitation. He didn't like the look on Doc's face.

"I'd hoped I was wrong." Doc rubbed his hand over his face. "I've been watching you walk around here."

Joe braced himself for what was to come.

"When that bull hit you, tossed you over that ledge, and then fell on you, the weight broke your bones in several places around your right hip. I've no way of knowing why, but for some reason you don't have full movement in your right hip." He paused, as if he searched for the right words. "You'll be able to walk and you'll be able to sit." He paused again. "I'm just going to say it, Joe ... there's no easy way. I've my doubts that you'll ever be able to sit on a horse again. That hip has somehow healed in a way that you can't swing your leg away from your body. And you'll not be able to sit in a saddle normally without some sideway give of the hip. I'm as sorry as I can be about it." Doc rubbed his hand across his eyes again, as if he could not look at the face of such disaster. "I'd hoped with all my heart that was I wrong."

Joe stared at him. He heard the words, but not the meaning. He was a rider. A cowhand. It was all he knew. *If I can't ride a horse, I ain't nothing.*

"You got to be wrong, Doc." He could work and get his legs strong. He would ride again. Doc has to be wrong ...

"But if I can't ride, what am I going to do?"

Doc shook his head. "I don't know, Joe, but you're a young man. For now, continue to take it easy and get your strength back. You got a place here for as long as you need."

"I know I'm not ready to go it alone yet, but one day I'll be able to get out of your hair." His heart filled with gratitude toward both Doc and Mrs. Purdy. He owed them his life and his sanity.

"Well, I have to get on with the day. I'll see you this evening." Doc left the room with a slow tread.

Joe lay on the bed, too emotionally battered to move.

He had often felt alone these last eleven years since leaving home, but nothing like he did at this moment. His gut felt like he'd been kicked by a horse.

If he couldn't ride, he didn't have a job. And no place else to go.

Chapter Three

Sunlight streamed through the windows on a warm Sunday in early April. Mrs. Purdy and Doc had gone out for the afternoon. Now would be the perfect time for a short ride on Doc's old brown mare. Joe hobbled to the barn. His hands shook as he pulled open the barn door where he was greeted by the sweet smell of hay. He stumbled as he retrieved a saddle and horse blanket from the tack room as it weighed three times as much as he remembered.

After smoothing on the blanket, he grunted as he threw the saddle up on the old horse's back. His hands still gripped it, even after he had it on the mare. Joe leaned his forehead against the leather. After catching his breath, he reached under the horse's belly to cinch the girth. Then he led the mare out into the corral.

Preparing to mount, Joe leaned his weight on his right leg. Pain shot through his hip and his leg almost gave out from under him. He kept a firm grip on the saddle horn, slid his left foot into the stirrup, and pulled himself up, but his right leg would not swing up over the horse's back. Over and over—he willed his right leg up over the saddle, but to no avail. He could not swing his right leg far enough to sit in the saddle.

Joe reached down, grabbed the cloth of his right pants leg, and tried to yank his leg up over the saddle by pulling on the cloth, but still, his leg would not swing. He tried to mount from the other side, but his right leg froze and there was not enough room to swing his other leg up and over the saddle. His foot slipped out of the stirrup and he almost fell. Intense pain shot through his body. The world blurred and seemed to swim in front of him. Tears filled his eyes, rolled down his cheeks, and he cried out in pain and frustration.

When the sun's last rays turned the sky a brilliant pink and orange, Joe finally gave up.

"Come on, old girl. You've been patient with me long enough." He forced himself to unsaddle the mare. Joe pushed through the pain every movement brought. After leading the horse back into the stall, he patted the horse on the shoulder then gave her some water and oats.

The walk from the barn to the house was a short one, but for Joe, it was the longest of his life. He struggled to keep control and not let the disintegration within push him into a total black hole of despair. All he could do was get one foot in front of the other. Just get back to the house. There, he could crawl into the womb his room had become, and let go.

He recoiled at walking the long hallway to his bedroom at the back of the house, but did it anyway. When he reached the end of the hall, he fell back against the wall and grimaced. His hip throbbed.

Pushing off the wall, with a heavy, uneven gait, he cleared the threshold to his room. He cast a sideways glance at the window. The last glimmer of twilight faded into darkness—a mirror of his heart. Dragging himself the last few feet, he collapsed on his bed. More alone than he had ever been—the full extent of hope lost engulfed him—and he sobbed.

Chapter Four

The next morning Joe faced the question of what was he going to do with the rest of his life? Waco was a fair-sized town. How many jobs would there be for a crippled ex-cowhand? And how did a fella go about getting such a job?

Joe continued to walk and gained some strength, but he wasn't his old muscular self and didn't know if he'd ever be again. He never mentioned his experiment of trying to mount a horse to Doc or Mrs. Purdy. Shame that he couldn't ride rode him.

On a Tuesday morning, he finally forced himself to walk down the street. After he had only walked four blocks and passed the Ed Flower's Livery Stable, his legs started trembling from exhaustion. He could go no farther and sat down on a bench outside Hughes General Merchandise store.

He watched several women pass by and enter the store, and then leave carrying packages. The light breeze brought the smell of the horse traffic from the street, and the clop, clop sound of the horses' hooves matched the beat of his heart. It tore at him to watch the men ride down the street on horseback. He would just have to get used to it, but the unfamiliar envy ate at him.

A gray-haired man, who looked to be in his fifties, came from inside the mercantile store, broom in hand.

Joe watched him sweep. Sweeping a store out. That's what women did. No self-respecting man would choose a job like that if he could help it.

"Morning, young man." He smiled and the lines around his blue eyes deepened.

Joe nodded. "Morning, sir."

"Nice day, isn't it?" The man stood by the bench where Joe sat.

Joe looked up at the man leaning on his broom. "Yes, it is."

The man turned and met Joe's gaze. "You live around here?"

"I'm staying over at the Doc's place." Joe jerked his head in the direction of the house.

"Oh ... are you the rider who broke his leg last fall?

"Yes. I'm Joe Storm."

"Well, I'm Cliff Hughes and this is my store. I heard you had a bull fall on you. Amazing that you survived it. So, how are you doing?"

Joe sighed. "Yes, sir. You heard right." How could he answer? He knew he was better physically, but inside he was having a hard time dealing with what had happened. However, he guessed that folks didn't want to hear that. "I'm doing all right."

"Good, glad to hear it." Mr. Hughes moved his broom over a bit of the porch without really making an effort to get on with his work.

Joe glanced up at the man. "You don't know of a job around town for someone getting back on his feet, do you?" Although getting a job was not the reason for Joe's walk, it was one that has been on the back burner of his mind.

"Are you particular about what kind of work?" Mr. Hughes took a handkerchief out of his back pocket and wiped his forehead.

"I'm not particular, except I'm not sure what I can do yet. But I hope to get stronger soon." It seemed best to be truthful.

"It's not much of a job, but I need some help here at the store. Just sweeping, dusting, and helping keep things straight on the shelves. I can't pay much, but it might be a start for you."

Sweeping out a store was not a job. But then, what was a job for someone in his shape? The storekeeper was right—it was a place to start.

"How much would you pay?"

The man scratched his head. "Well, I'll give you fifty cents a day and feed you the noon meal, but that's all I can do."

Joe nodded. Was he even worth that? He hated to say it but he needed to be honest with the man.

"I'll take the job. If you decide I'm not pulling my weight, you tell me. I'll try to do a full day's work, but I don't know whether I can yet."

Mr. Hughes nodded. "I'll agree to that and I respect you for saying it. You can start in the morning. Be here at six when I open."

Joe walked back to Doc's house and went into his bedroom. He lay on the bed until suppertime, relieved to have any job. He sighed as a blackness encompassed his being. Had he really taken a job sweeping out a store? If it wasn't riding on a horse, it couldn't be a real job. He had to get over his hatred of any job that did not entail riding a horse if he wanted to survive. No, he had to stop thinking like a cowhand. He needed a job and he had to start somewhere.

~

Joe was aware that Doc was always up at five each morning and spent a couple of hours reading his Bible. Joe asked him to knock on his door and wake him. The next morning, moving his stiff limbs as fast as he could, Joe washed up, dressed, and made it to the store ten minutes before six. Mr. Hughes greeted him with a smile.

"Morning, Joe. You're here in good time. Go into the back and put these on." He handed Joe a blue shirt and a black cotton apron identical to his own. "This way folks will know that you're working here and you'll look official. The apron will help keep your clothes from getting so dirty."

Joe exchanged his shirt for the new one, then put on the long, black-bibbed apron that came below his knees and left him feeling as if he was wearing a dress. What would some of his old pards say now if they saw him in this getup? Joe sensed a final stamp on the end of his life as a cowhand.

When Joe went back into the front of the store, Mr. Hughes handed him a broom. "The first thing I need is for the porch and store to be swept. After that, start dusting the whole store. You won't get it finished today, but at least it'll be a start."

"Yes sir." Joe took the broom. Well, if he was going to be a store sweeper, he was going to be the best one ever. He went out to the porch with broom in hand.

People came and went throughout the morning, but he did not talk to anyone. He kept his head down and worked, sweeping the entire store.

Just before noon, a short, plump woman about Mr. Hughes's age came into the store carrying a big basket. She walked into the back room.

Mr. Hughes waved at Joe. "Come on back and eat. My wife has brought enough for both of us."

Joe went into the back room glad for an opportunity to get off his feet and give his hip a rest. Would the pain and fatigue always be this bad?

"This is my wife. This is the fellow I told you about, Joe Storm." Mr. Hughes sat at the small table where his wife unloaded a full meal from her basket.

She put out three plates and filled them with food. "Sit down, Joe. I'm glad to meet you. Mr. Hughes has been needing help for a long time. I hope you like fried chicken, collard greens, cornbread, and apple pie."

Joe sat down and tucked the red and white checked napkin in his shirt, matching Mr. Hughes. "Yes, ma'am. That looks delicious."

She placed three glasses on the table and then poured tea from a gallon jug.

"Well, go ahead and dig in before it gets too cold." She picked up the glass and sipped her tea.

After the noon meal, Joe dusted the shelves, half of which were too high to reach without climbing the rolling ladder. He found it awkward and tiring and his hip throbbed, but he kept at it, determined to make it through the day, without complaint. Every hour or so, he would sit for a few minutes, or just lean against a counter to take the weight off his hip. By the time it was six o'clock, he had only dusted a fourth of the store.

Mr. Hughes stood behind the counter. "Go on home now, Joe. You did good work, and if you keep it up I'll not have a complaint."

Joe released a breath of relief. Thank the Lord. His limbs were about to give out. He took the apron and blue shirt off, hung them on a nail in the back storeroom, and put his old shirt back on.

He plodded back to Doc's house, wincing with every step and ate supper with Mrs. Purdy, Doc being out on a call. Then he went into the bedroom, undressed, and fell into bed, exhausted, his hip aching in time with his heartbeat.

Crawling out of bed before daylight was a chore. In addition to the pains he had come to expect, his legs, back, and shoulders all ached from the previous day's labors. Nevertheless, he still made it to the store by six. Now that he had a job, he intended to keep it.

Joe dusted, cleaned windows, swept the porch, and straightened the merchandise. Mr. Hughes instructed him about the prices and the ledger accounting book. He was soon helping customers with their purchases. It was what he could do and what was needed. There was not much to occupy his mind so he thought about his situation. Maybe helping people made it honorable work, even if it was menial. After a month, he received his first pay, fifteen dollars.

That evening, he spoke to Doc. "I got paid today. I want you to have it." Joe handed over the money.

"I appreciate that, but I don't want your pay. And Mr. Jake, your old boss, has paid plenty for your keep." The old man pushed the money back across the table to Joe. "You save it. Here's something you could do for me. I need help in the yard and out in the barn. I just don't have the time."

"Sure, I can do that for you, Doc." Why didn't he see that for himself? Joe gritted his teeth, determined to do the barn chores to help Doc out. He would just have to get up earlier to have time.

The people around him did not demand more than he could manage, which he appreciated. He stayed busy and got stronger. Eventually, he could get through each day without as much pain or fatigue.

It wasn't the life he wanted. All he could see in his future was more of the same. He brooded about the loss of his life as a rider. Some days it took everything he had to keep control of his misery. He tried to keep a grip on himself and make it through one day at a time.

Truth was he just wanted to sit down and die. He missed the feel of the wind on his face as he rode his horse out on the range, sharing the work with a good bunch of riders. He had spent almost ten years riding the range and taking herds up the trail. He missed his life and knew of no way to get it back.

So each morning, he got up, went to work, put on the blue shirt, put on the apron, and swept the porch.

~

One hot day toward the end of May warned of the summer heat to come. Joe shelved shirts, pants, and fabric with the feel of sweat running down his back. He stopped often to wipe his face with his handkerchief.

A man came into the store and looked around, as if to search out his goods from a list he kept in his gray-haired head. Joe gauged the man a few inches taller than the store shelves that stood at five foot. With a face seamed and tanned, a sure sign of spending many hours in the sun and wind, the man looked up at Joe, who stood six feet and two inches in his stocking feet, and gave a nod.

The man continued to search his way through the store. His boots were the flat-heeled kind that many riders liked and he was dressed in a shirt, pants, vest, and an old gray, battered Stetson. Hard to tell the man's age because of the lines etched deep on his face.

Joe waited behind the counter for the man to choose what he wanted.

Finally, the man approached him. "You the boss here?"

"Mr. Hughes owns the store. He'll be back shortly. Can I help you find something?"

With sharp blue eyes, he looked at Joe. "Well, I have a long list. I need to know if I can get it here."

"I stock the store. Let me see your list and I can tell you if we got what you need."

"All right." He pulled several pieces of paper out of his vest pocket and laid them on the counter. "I'm purchasing supplies for Matthew Barnes' trail herd. I got chuck and supply wagons to fill. We got twenty riders and three months traveling ahead of us. My name is Malcolm Smith, but everyone calls me Cookie."

A cook for a trail herd! Joe knew what it took to be a cook for a twenty-rider outfit from Texas to Kansas.

"I'm Joe Storm. Which trail you taking?" He gathered up the pages of lists.

"Well, the boss thinks we'll run into less Indians up the Chisholm. Don't suppose you've been up any trails? You look like a town fellow."

"I've been up all the trails, spent near ten years on them at different times."

The man's eyes widened and then narrowed with a look of doubt. "You don't look like no rider."

Joe dropped his gaze. "I used to be a rider, but not anymore." He lowered his head and focused on the list. "We got most all of these things on your list. Want for me to put your supplies together?"

"Sure, if you all got what I need. I'm pulling out day after tomorrow to meet up with the herd before they start up the trail, so I need to be loaded by tomorrow night."

Joe could visualize the herd and the chuck wagon heading out on the trail. He pushed down a twinge of envy toward this man who was still a part of a world Joe had lost.

A few moments later, Mr. Hughes returned from his trip to the bank.

Joe introduced the storekeeper to their customer, then got started on the list while Mr. Hughes talked to the man about the details of pick up and payment for the man's large purchase.

Joe gathered the supplies and stacked them by the front door for loading. Two hundred pounds of flour; a hundred pounds of rice; a hundred pounds of dried beans; five gallons of molasses; twenty pounds of baking powder; twenty pounds of salt; one hundred pounds of Arbuckle coffee...and on and on. Memories assailed him. Struggling to carry the fifty-pound crate of coffee reminded him of cold days and a hot cup of the brew after a night spent riding the herd. He set the crate down, then glanced back at the older man as he left the store.

Wish I could ride out with him.

The rest of the afternoon, Joe collected supplies, but still had a ways to go to complete the lists.

Mr. Hughes stood looking at the growing stack of goods by the front door of the store. "It's time to close. Where are you at with that order?"

Joe looked at the list and scratched his head. "I've got about a fourth of it still to fill."

"Well, go on home. You can fill the rest of the order in the morning as the man is coming back tomorrow afternoon to load up."

That night, Joe dreamed of riding. He woke to the sound of bawling cows, but it was only leftover bits of his dream. Dreams could seem so real. Sometimes too real.

He beat his fist on the bed. Why did he have to dream of what he couldn't have? He hated his present life and was desperate to find a way out of it.

His thoughts shifted to the man in the store yesterday. Many of the large trail herds had a cook, his helper, and a wrangler to handle the second wagon. Cookie had arrived at the store alone...

Wonder if Cookie needs a helper?

Chapter Five

Joe was at the mercantile early to finish collecting goods from the list for the chuck wagon with a plan half formed in his mind. Could he get the job of helper to the cook on the cattle drive? It was a crazy idea to think he could do such work. The more he thought on it, the crazier it seemed.

Mr. Hughes arrived and his brows lifted as he greeted Joe for the morning. "You're here early."

"Morning." Joe stopped long enough to yank out his handkerchief from his back pocket and wipe the sweat from the back of his neck. He'd been working for some time now, and wasn't about to slow down.

While Mr. Hughes assisted customers, Joe finished the lists, and then readied everything to load into the wagons by moving the supplies out onto the porch in front of the store. About three in the afternoon, thunder seem to roll across the ground and Joe stepped out of the store to investigate. His eyebrows rose at the sight of Cookie driving up in one of the biggest chuck wagons Joe had ever laid eyes on. A second wagon, driven by a boy maybe all of fourteen years old, rolled up behind.

Mr. Hughes stepped out beside Joe. "You show Mr. Smith the supplies you've got ready to load."

Mr. Smith? Joe chuckled to himself. To him the man was just: Cookie. He walked over to the wagon and greeted the man. "Morning, sir. Let's go over everything." They headed toward the stacked supplies and he handed the lists to Cookie, each item checked off.

Joe scratched the back of his neck. "I added a few more things I thought you might need and have them over there." He nodded over to the other items he had stacked on the porch. "You can decide whether you want them or not."

"Well, let's have a look." Cookie laughed when he glanced over the items Joe had gathered. "More rope, lanterns, buckets, two more Dutch ovens, another large skillet, cinnamon...Well, you amaze me." Cookie eyed Joe. "Maybe you have been up the trail."

"Hey, Billy," Cookie yelled out to the boy in the second wagon. "Get over here, let's start loading up."

"Mr. Smith, why don't you decide where you want the supplies stowed? You tell Billy and me where to load it. That way you won't have to reorganize it later."

Once again, Cookie narrowed his eyes at Joe. "Good idea." He dragged the words out thoughtfully.

As the afternoon wore on, Joe carried items to the chuck wagon with as much vigor as he could muster, so Cookie would see he was in fair shape and capable of hard work. By five o'clock, they had the wagons loaded and Cookie stepped back into the store to settle the bill with Mr. Hughes.

Joe stretched out his back, then walked to the second wagon where Billy sat ready to follow the chuck wagon. "Hey, Billy," Joe looked up at the ordinary-looking kid with brown eyes and mousey brown hair. "How long you been working with the trail herd?"

"I only got hired last week. I've never been up the trail before, but I can handle horses."

Joe leaned against the wheel. "When is the herd starting out?"

Billy shrugged. "I guess when we get there. They're waiting on the grub."

Trying to sound casual Joe asked, "Has Cookie got his helper waiting there?"

"He hasn't found a helper and he's mad about it. Had someone lined up, but the fellow got drunk and put in jail."

Joe stood, afraid to move. His heart seemed to be beating against his ribs as he waited.

Cookie came out of the store and turned toward the wrangler wagon. "You ready, Billy?"

"Yes, sir." The boy sat up straighter on the wagon seat and tightened his hands on the reins.

Cookie turned to get up on his own wagon.

Joe blocked his way. His heart thumped against his chest and he licked his dry lips. "Mr. Smith, could I ask you a question?" He spoke quickly to keep the man's attention.

"Sure, ask away." Cookie looked at him with a frown.

"I heard you needed a cook's helper for the drive. I want to apply for the job." He didn't dare breathe as he waited for the older man's answer.

"Call me Cookie. Everyone does." He inclined his head to stare at Joe's right leg. "You got something wrong with your leg? I noticed that you seem to favor it."

Joe slowly let out a long, deep breath. So the man had seen the slight limp that he tried to hide. He hated to tell him. He hated that he even had the problem. Cookie's question was reasonable, though. He looked directly at the man. "I got trampled on by a bull last year and got my leg hurt permanent. I'll be honest with you. I can't ride anymore. I can't sit in a saddle because my right hip is all messed up." Joe continued to look the man in the eyes. "I can work, though and I understand trail herding and what's needed to feed riders."

Cookie stared at Joe. "You got a comfortable job here. A lot easier than trail herding, and yet you say you want to leave it?"

"I grew up on a ranch. It's all I know. I'd give anything to be back out on the range with a herd. If being a helper to the cook is how I can do it, then I'm asking for a job." He drew a breath and held it.

Cookie stared into Joe's eyes for what seemed like several moments. "The pay is good, and I expect a lot from my helper. You sure you're up to it?"

"You saw me work today. You'll have to decide." His calm voice belied the turmoil of his gut.

"Well, you did do a full day's work." Cookie rubbed his chin. "I tell you what. If you have your own bedroll and can be ready to leave at daybreak, I'll give you a try. But if you can't cut it, we'll leave you at the first town we come to."

"Thank you, Mr. Smith. You won't regret it. Where should I meet you?" He swallowed and tried to slow his breathing but he couldn't slow his heart.

"Billy and I'll be camped down below the bridge. I plan to start out at first light, so be there, or get left. It's your choice." He climbed up on the wagon seat and took up the reins.

Joe grinned and stepped aside. "I'll be there. And thank you again."

Cookie snapped the reins, and the wagons trailed off toward the Brazos River, kicking up dust in their wake.

Joe hurried into the store where Mr. Hughes worked on his ledgers. He hesitated, not sure how his boss would take his quitting. "Mr. Hughes ... I got something to tell you."

The storekeeper looked up after a moment. "You're leaving."

Joe's brows shot up. "Yes, sir. Mr. Smith offered me the job as his helper on the chuck wagon. I took it."

Mr. Hughes chuckled. "I'm not surprised. You're not a town kind of fellow. I realize that. You've been pining to get back out to the range for weeks. But are you sure you're up to the hard work and travel of a chuck wagon?"

"I'll find out soon enough. It'll be tough, I know. I've been on the trail too many times not to know what the cook and his helper do. But I got to do it."

"Let's get you outfitted and settle your pay. I assume you're heading out in the morning?" He put away his account book.

Joe collected two pair of work pants, a shirt, couple of bandanas, a rain slick, and an extra blanket.

Mr. Hughes added a pair of flat-heeled boots, two blue shirts, two aprons, and a carryall. "A cook's helper will need an apron," he said. Then he totaled up the bill. "It looks like I'll owe you about ten dollars. Does that sound about right?"

Joe gave a nod. Mr. Hughes had been more than generous with his prices. With the ten dollars, and the fifty he had saved already, he would start out with a small nest egg, which did not hurt his pride.

Joe shook the storeowner's hand. "Thanks Mr. Hughes, for everything."

He slung the carryall over his back and headed for Doc's house. He was free. And so exhausted from loading the wagons that he wondered what he had gotten himself into.

For a change, both Mrs. Purdy and Dr. Rupert were home for supper. He enjoyed their company as much as Mrs. Purdy's potpie. When Mrs. Purdy brought out the coffee afterwards, Joe cleared his throat. "I quit my job at the store today. I took another one as a helper on a chuck wagon." He spoke quickly wanting to get it said. "I know it's kind of sudden, but the chance was there, so I took it." He looked down at his empty plate; the next few words would be the hardest to say. "I leave in the morning."

"But Joe," Mrs. Purdy spoke first, concern heavy in her voice. "Are you ready to leave here? What exactly will you do as a helper on a chuck wagon?"

Doc patted her hand. "Don't you worry, Mildred. Joe knows what he's about. He has to test his strength, see what he's capable of. He may as well do it now." Doc turned to Joe. "My question is, will you be called upon to ride a horse if you're with a trail herd?"

He hadn't told Doc about his efforts. "I've tried to ride several times on the old mare. About once a week." Joe dropped his gaze. "But I can't sit a saddle." He hated saying it.

"I wondered if you had tried. In fact, I couldn't imagine that you hadn't. But what if they expect you to ride?"

"I told Mr. Smith that I couldn't. They'll expect me to drive the chuck wagon. That I can do. If anyone else expects me to ride, he'll have to keep on expecting."

"We'll hate to lose you. Mrs. Purdy and I have enjoyed having you here. You've always got a place here, Joe. Don't you ever doubt it." Doc's raspy voice caught, but he and Joe held one another's gaze, man to man.

Mrs. Purdy wiped her eyes on her apron.

Joe got up and kissed her on the cheek. "I have to thank both of you for this last year. I wouldn't have made it if it hadn't been for you both. I hope I wasn't too much work for you, Mrs. Purdy."

Doc stood and put his arm around Joe's shoulder. "There's one thing I ask, Joe. Write to us and let us know how you're doing. We'll wonder, you know."

"I promise, but only if you'll write back." These people had been good to him, but Joe wanted to get back to the world he once knew and longed to be a part of again.

Later that evening, he packed his gear and readied it for the early morning rendezvous with Cookie. Then, he fell into bed and sleep came as soon as he closed his eyes.

At four-thirty the next morning, Joe woke to a light tap on his door and Doc's voice, "Joe, time to get up."

Joe dragged himself out of bed, dressed, and then shaved at the washstand. When he went into the kitchen, Mrs. Purdy had breakfast on the table. Joe shoveled down his food and then went into the bedroom and gathered his bedroll and carryall. When he returned to the kitchen with his things, Mrs. Purdy handed him a packet of beef sandwiches and oatmeal cookies.

Doc came out from his office with a small black leather bag and a buffalo robe.

"I made up a medicine kit with packets of powder for pain. If your hip gets to hurting too bad, you take it. A patient paid me with this buffalo robe. It'll help make your bedroll a lot more comfortable."

Joe took the buffalo robe and rolled it with his bedroll, thankful, as his was thin with only two blankets and a piece of canvas for a ground cover. The small medicine kit went into his carryall. He wished he had something to give them in return, but could only kiss Mrs. Purdy on her cheek. As he turned to say goodbye, he saw Doc taking his bag out the back door.

Outside, Joe found Doc seated in his buggy that was hitched up to the mare.

"Get in. I'll drive you out to the river."

Grateful for the ride, Joe climbed in the other side. He swallowed hard and his eyes watered. Their kindness touched him and he deeply appreciated the ways they showed they cared.

"Giddy up." Doc flicked the reins against the horse's rump, and the buggy lurched forward out onto the street. "Joe, I want to give you some advice, if I may."

"Sure, I can use all the advice I can get." He turned to look at the older man.

"Well, advice about two things. First, you need to watch yourself with your hip. I don't know how fragile it is. If you get to hurting too bad, don't try to tough it out. When possible do things the easy way. Have a blanket on the wagon seat as you sit on it all day. Just realize that you got a problem with that leg. It isn't going away and only you can watch out for you.

"Second, you're going back to a work you know well, but nobody there is going to believe you know anything. You'll be the cook's helper. I'd guess that's about as low as you can get in the camp. You got more experience and knowledge than they'll want to hear about. Keep your head down and don't get into any fights," Doc tipped his head at Joe's leg. "Your leg won't hold up for it. It may mean you have to bite your tongue. Let them get to know you before you reveal the depth of your knowledge and experience with horses and cattle. You probably don't need my advice, but I wanted to give it."

He had put into words what Joe had already supposed. "So you're saying I see myself as a cowhand with ten years' experience on the trail plus growing up on a ranch. But these men will only see me as a cook's helper, and if I say different, I'm either lying or crazy."

"That's about it, Joe. May not be fair, but it's human nature."

"Thanks for the advice—and for the medicine."

Joe saw a few lights in a couple of houses, otherwise the streets were dark except for the lantern hanging on the frame of the buggy. Then he spotted a glow of a campfire and the chuck wagon with several lanterns hanging from it.

Cookie was stowing gear in chuck box at the back of the wagon.

Billy was hitching four horses to the wrangler wagon with the horses already hitched to the chuck wagon. For now the wrangler wagon was half full of food supplies but once on the trail it would carry the gear and bed rolls of the cowhands.

When they drew up beside the camp, Joe climbed down from the buggy and introduced Cookie to Dr. Rupert.

"Dr. Rupert, meet Malcolm Smith. Where should I stow my stuff?" he asked his new boss.

"Toss your bedroll and bag behind the seat in the chuck wagon."

As the two older men got acquainted, Joe grabbed his carryall and bedroll from the back of the buggy and moved to the front of the chuck wagon. He stepped up to the spring seat and stowed his gear behind the wagon seat.

Doc's voice carried from where he spoke with Cookie. "Oh, Joe can handle a day's work, so long as you realize what he can and can't do. He's a good solid worker for sure."

Joe had already told Cookie, but it was just as well that he heard it again from Doc. He joined the two men, so he could shake Doc's hand goodbye.

Doc grabbed the new cook's helper in a bear hug. "You take care, Joe, and don't forget to write."

"I won't forget, Doc, and take care of Mrs. Purdy."

Doc got onto his buggy and, with a last wave, drove away.

Cookie turned to Joe. "Nice family you got there."

"Thanks." He didn't correct his new boss, as Doc and Mrs. Purdy had become family. He followed Cookie to the fire, helped gather the last of the camp gear, and then stomped out the flames.

Cookie stepped up on the front wheel. "Let's load up and start out. I like to sit on the left hand side of the seat."

"No problem. I can sit on either side." Joe climbed up onto the right side of the wagon seat. He tried not to breathe in gasps from the effort it took. He quickly figured out that if he stepped up on the wheel hub and the swung his left leg up and over, he could drag his right leg up. First chance he got he was going to put more steps and hand holds on that side of the wagon.

Cookie clucked and slapped the reins. The four-horse team pulled the chuck wagon across the bridge over the Brazos River, followed by Billy driving the wrangler wagon, as they headed west.

Joe was almost dizzy with the war of feelings within: nervous fear at the thought he might not be able to do the work and the giddy excitement of leaving Waco for the range.

Chapter Six

The sway of the almost new Moline chuck wagon was rough, as Joe had expected. He leaned against the short back of the seat and sensed the springs underneath doing their job. Watching the trail, he anticipated the bigger bounces and braced himself for the sharp pains that shot through his hip.

After a couple of hours, Cookie handed Joe the reins. "Wake me in an hour." He climbed back onto the sacks of food and bedrolls in the bed of the wagon and went to sleep.

Joe had no problem keeping the four horses on the track. Occasionally, he waved back at Billy driving the wrangler wagon that was loaded with food supplies. When they joined the herd, the wrangler wagon would hold the extra saddles, tools, riders' bedrolls, and other gear. It was topped by bows and a waterproof canvas, as was the chuck wagon.

Lifting his face to the pleasantly warm breeze, Joe's spirits rose as the expanse of the land opened before him. The hopeless feelings of the last several months receded with every mile he drove. He hoped that this new adventure would relieve some of the sadness and regret that had been his constant companion for the last seven months. He did not even mind the dust the horses' hooves kicked up, or the pungent, sweaty smell of the animals. At least it was something familiar.

They made eight miles down the dusty trail before Cookie woke. Lumbering back over the seat he pointed toward some oak trees by a creek. "Pull up over there and we'll give the horses a breather and some water. Joe, you build a fire and we'll have some hot coffee."

"Yes, sir." Joe guided the horses under the trees to leave the seat of the chuck wagon in the shade, and then he carefully climbed down. His hip was stiff and uncomfortable from the morning's ride, which was just a beginning of the pain he could expect.

He had the fire going and coffee brewing within minutes. Without Cookie telling him, he helped Billy take the two teams of four down to the creek, and after the horses had drunk sufficiently, hitch them back to the wagons.

When he and Billy had finished their tasks, he found that Cookie had set out a crusty loft of bread and a wedge of yellow cheese on the tongue of the wagon.

Remembering the food from Mrs. Purdy, Joe climbed up into the wagon and pulled out his carryall. Inside the packet she'd made for him, he found beef sandwiches, cookies, and a leather-bound book with a note in it. He read the note.

Dear Joe, This belonged to my brother, Tom Gardner, who spent years working as a cook for ranches. In this book are all of his recipes and ways of doing for cooking on the trail. I thought you might like to have it, and I cannot think of anyone I would rather give it to. God bless you, Mrs. Purdy.

He thought of the kind older woman who had served him so completely in his time of need. Swallowing hard, he opened the book. In a fine spidery handwriting were recipes, and even drawings of how to fix up a cook fire around a chuck wagon. He put the book back in his carryall to look over later and joined the other two by the fire. "My folks sent this with me and I'll be glad to share."

Cookie's face wrinkled up even more with a huge smile. "Thanks, these are a lot better than what I got out. Billy, put that cookie down. There's only two apiece."

Joe grinned at the boy who had grabbed up a cookie, broke the last cookie in half, and shared it.

They gave the horses a thirty-minute rest, then headed out to meet up with the trail herd. That night, Cookie wasn't in the mood to cook, so they made a dry camp and ate out of cans. Joe didn't mind, as Cookie would be deep in meal preparations for the next few months.

Billy was quick to get the horses picketed and fetched them water from the barrel of water strapped onto the side of the wrangler wagon. The barrel of water strapped onto the side of the chuck wagon would be reserved for drinking and cooking. One of Billy's tasks was to refill the barrels whenever they stopped by a creek or river.

Cookie slept in the chuck wagon. Billy and Joe spread a tarp over the ground, unrolled their bedrolls, and then bedded down. Joe gazed up at the stars. He hadn't slept out in the open since before his injury.

It brought back memories of times on the trail with other riders. He shook his head. It didn't help to think too much about what his life had been. Making it through each day was going to be hard enough. In the months to come, he just wanted to be able to do his job without thinking too much of what the future would bring. The end of the trail was as far as he could see. The rest of his life was darkness and he couldn't see into it.

Joe woke in the dark to stiff muscles and a sore right leg, hip, and back. He guessed it was the first of many such mornings.

Cookie stretched and got a fire going. "We'll let Billy sleep until I have breakfast cooked. He won't have many more chances to sleep late. You water the horses. We can eat and be on the trail by daylight."

"Yes, sir." Joe carried one bucket of water at a time and let each horse have a good long drink. He then led them back to the wagons and hitched them up. His mouth watered at the smell of the ham frying in the skillet and biscuits baking in the Dutch ovens. That mingling with the coffee and the early morning smell of the cool mist coming across the prairie was enough to bring back the memories of the countless mornings on the trail. Joe sighed with contentment.

"Come on Billy, wake up. Breakfast is ready." Cookie prodded Billy's bedroll and the boy sat up and put on his hat then his boots. Ready for the day.

Joe took his time eating the hot food as Cookie didn't seem to be in a rush to get started.

They broke camp and by daylight had the wagons moving. By early afternoon, Cookie stopped the chuck wagon close to a creek. Over to the southwest he could see the dust of the herd a half mile down along the wandering creek.

"Joe, get three fires going. I need two off to the side here, and the other one further out for the coffee." Cookie climbed down and looked around. "Be sure to clear the grass away from the fire. We don't need to start a prairie fire."

While Billy tended to the horses, Joe built the fires with the hardwood they had collected and carried in the hide cradles hanging under the wagons. When the fires were blazing, Joe hammered the iron stakes into the ground around the fires, then he placed iron rods and fire hooks on the rods, so they could hang the cooking vessels over the fires. Finally, he set Cookie's collection of pothooks nearby ready to lift the hot lids off the pots.

"Joe, help Billy get this fly up over the tailgate of the chuck wagon to shade my work table." Cookie pointed to the canvas sheet with ties on the corners.

They attached the corners to a couple of poles and the bow at the back of the chuck wagon, thus providing shade. Cookie lowered and secured the lid of the chuck box to form his worktable. He pulled out the Dutch ovens, coffee pots, and pans from the box under the chuck box at the back end of the wagon.

He turned to Joe. "Here, take these coffee pots and fill them with water. Can you make the coffee well enough so the riders don't lynch you?"

"Sure, Cookie, I can do that." Joe chuckled to himself, remembering the many times he'd made coffee out on the range.

"Well, I want the coffee handy for the cowhands, but away from the cooking area. I try to keep as much dust out of the food as possible."

Joe took the three five-quart coffee pots over to the water barrel, filled each within two inches of the top, and placed them on the fire furthest from the chuck wagon. He guessed that as time passed he would get used to the weight of the full pots, but for now it taxed his muscles. Joe spooned in the ground coffee from a bag of Arbuckle. He would keep the fires tended and the coffee made until the chuck wagon pulled out the next morning.

After Joe got the coffee going, he checked with his boss. "What's my next chore?"

"Get two of the bigger pots," Cookie instructed. "Fill them, and heat the water. Then get six cups of pinto beans, sort through for stones and such, rinse them, put three cups of beans, and pieces of salt pork into each pot to soak."

"Right away, Cookie." Joe was careful to do exactly what Cookie directed. Sloppy work now would just mean more work later. He figured he had about all the work he needed.

Joe checked the pots of coffee. He wanted to keep them hot, but not boiling, so he moved them onto small stones, just off to the side of the coals. Then he added a cup of cold water to each to help the coffee grounds to settle to the bottom.

"Joe."

He went over to where Cookie prepared biscuits at the worktable. "Yes, sir?"

"Tied to the underside of the wagon, you'll find some tripods. Set one up over each of the cooking fires and hang the pots of beans you started earlier. Remember how they were tied because you'll have to put them back there in the morning before we pull out. Get a hot fire going under the beans and get them cooked by supper."

"Yes, sir."

"Joe, don't sir me. I'm just Cookie, you hear?"

"Yes, Cookie." He grinned at the cook.

Joe turned at the sound of a rider who rode up and dismounted about forty feet downwind of the chuck wagon. The tall rider tied his horse to a mesquite tree, took off his chaps, dusted off his hat, and then walked over to the coffee fire.

Joe nodded in approval. A seasoned cowhand knew not to get dust stirred up too close to the chuck wagon. The strong build of this cowboy, who looked to be about forty years old from the leathered look of his face, stirred a moment of envy in Joe.

"Howdy, young fellow. I'm Henry Thursgood, trail boss." He looked Joe over. "I don't know you."

"Joe Storm, cook's helper. Cookie hired me couple of days ago out of Waco. Here, let me pour you a cup of coffee."

"Cookie needs a good helper if he's going to keep all these cowhands fed." Henry accepted the cup from Joe and sipped on the fresh, hot brew as he gave Cookie a nod of greeting. He ignored Billy who was returning from picketing the last of the horses.

Joe added a couple of more sticks of wood to the fire. "How's the coffee, sir?"

Henry glanced down at his cup and then back to Joe. "This is good. Did you make it?"

"Yes, sir. I expect that'll be one of my jobs as the herd moves north."

"Welcome to the crew." After another cup and a little more conversation, the trail boss returned to the herd.

Joe got the washtub down from the side of the chuck wagon. He filled it half full of water then sat it on the edge of the coffee fire ready for the crew's dirty dishes. Fortunately, Billy had the washing up duty. Joe would do a lot of work in the next few months that he ordinarily might have considered beneath his status as a cowhand. However, washing up the dishes was something he hoped he didn't have to get used to doing.

"Joe."

He'd heard his name called a least a hundred times today. Better get used to it. "Yes, Cookie."

"Get the other two big Dutch ovens out and fill them about a fourth full of lard out of the big crock. Put them on the fire to get them hot and melt the lard. And then come help me flour these steaks."

Joe soon had two Dutch ovens ready. He quickly floured a dozen steaks then started them frying. The smell of the steaks cooking even got Joe's mouth watering.

"Joe," Cookie called. "Go check on Billy. Make sure he's doing what I told him."

Joe found the boy near the supply wagon peeling potatoes, cutting them into small pieces, and dumping them into a pot of water.

"Good job. Holler when you have them ready and I'll help carry the pot to the fire."

Billy ducked his head and turned red. "Thanks."

Joe didn't know if he was being thanked for his complement or for his offer to help carry the heavy cast iron pot. He guessed Billy wasn't used to either a kind word or an offer of help.

Several of the hands came by and got a cup of coffee. They were careful to dismount, tie up their horses downwind, and take off their chaps.

Keeping Cookie happy was important, and dust in the food didn't make anyone happy.

After helping Billy place the big pot of potatoes on a hook over one of the hot cooking fires, he stood and watched the older man, impressed with his sure way of working.

"Turn those steaks over. Be careful not to slop grease out onto the flames. We don't want burned meat. Causes too much complaining."

"Yes, Cookie."

Joe didn't have a moment to spare to greet the cowhands. He offered a nod, but kept working. They got their coffee, drank it, and went back to the herd, taking very little time.

It felt odd to look at these strong, capable riders as they went about their normal activities. And to think, only a year ago he'd been one of them. In his spirit, he still was one with them, but Joe told himself to be realistic—they didn't see him as a part of their world anymore.

Joe glanced at the sun low on the horizon and estimated it was close to six o'clock.

Cookie looked around at the food preparation. "We don't have a dessert—and that isn't good. But there's no time if we're going to serve supper by seven o'clock." Cookie fed more flour and milk to the sourdough starter he kept in a five-gallon crockpot. "I'm the only one that'll feed that sourdough. It's too important to take a chance of messing it up."

"What did you plan to feed the cowhands that's sweet?" Joe leaned against the side of the chuck wagon to take some pressure off his aching hip.

"I planned to bake a cake, but we don't have time before we serve the supper."

"I saw some raisins with the goods in the wagon. I could have raisin dumplings made by the time the hands finish their supper."

"Raisin dumplings? How do you make those?" Cookie frowned.

"You dump flour, sugar, baking powder, and a little salt together with a little water. Heat some raisons, lard, and water together until it is boiling and then drop the flour mixture in a spoonful at a time and let it simmer until it's thick." He had learned the recipe from the cook at the J Bar C, his father's ranch in Colorado.

Cookie shrugged. "If you can get it going and then help me serve, go ahead."

Joe pulled the raisins out of the chuck wagon, dumped them into a big Dutch oven half filled with water, and hung it on a tripod over the fire next to where the beans boiled. While waiting for that to boil, he measured lard, flour, sugar, baking powder, and salt into a yellow crockery bowl. He hand mixed the flour mixture and then dropped tablespoon-sized lumps in to the boiling water with the raison. After he had all of the flour mixture in the pot, he set it to the side of the fire to simmer. Then, he got the crates of enamel plates and the box of eating utensils set out, while he watched the various pots bubbling on the two fires.

Cookie placed the baked biscuits on the chuck wagon table and the last of the steaks were cooked and stacked on a platter. Joe watched as Cookie scrapped the drippings away from the bottom of the pan and poured milk made from dried milk with flour added for thickening into the pan, added some salt and pepper, and made gravy. The gravy set quickly over the hot fire.

Fifteen cowhands sat or stood around waiting to eat. A few of the hands were still out getting the herd bedded down and would be relieved later.

"Come and get it." Cookie slapped a steak and a big serving spoon of beans onto each sixteen-inch blue enamel plate.

Joe served potatoes, gravy, and dropped three biscuits on each plate that passed in front of him.

The cowhands joked and greeted Cookie, their plates full to overflowing with food. They also spoke with Joe and introduced themselves.

Joe concentrated on filling their plates and barely spoke beyond a howdy. By the time the men had their plates of food and moved on to eat, Joe checked the raisin dumplings. The pleasant sweet fruity smell filled the air. He sneaked a taste. Not the best sweet he'd ever eaten but at least they had one to serve. He sat the big Dutch oven, filled with raisin dumplings, on the worktable.

"Come on back you riders and get your sweet," Cookie shouted.

The men wandered back to the table and got a helping of the raisin dumplings.

"I don't remember you serving this before," a young redheaded rider said.

"I never cooked raisin dumplings." Cookie pointed over to Joe. "This is one of Joe's recipes."

Several of the riders nodded their thanks toward him.

The redheaded rider reached over and shook Joe's hand. "I'm Jefferson Kingston. Thanks for the sweet."

"You're welcome," Joe said with a nod.

Joe appreciated Cookie giving him due credit. Most cookies would have taken it for themselves. He respected Cookie the more he worked with him. It wasn't necessary for him to like his boss, but it sure made it easier to work with him.

He got the coffee pots refilled and ready for those riding nighthawk, who would come in throughout the night wanting coffee.

Billy washed and stacked the dishes so they were ready for breakfast. He'd get firewood ready and refill the water barrel before bed. With the night wrangler minding the remuda, Billy didn't need to tend to the horses until he hitched up the teams in the morning, with the help of a couple of cowhands. Always handy around the chuck wagon, cowhands helped hitch up, or snaked fallen hardwood trees for firewood. Joe was glad Billy was there, otherwise he would have had his chores.

Cookie cleaned off the chuck wagon table. "Joe, go ahead and get your bedroll and bed down under the wagon on the tarp. I'll need you up by four o'clock to help get breakfast ready."

"Yes, Cookie." He checked the coals under the coffee pots. They'd last the night and keep the coffee hot. He pulled his bedroll out of the wagon then spread it on the ground next to the chuck wagon. It took an effort to ease himself to his bedroll as his hip protested. His pain increased as he pulled off his boots. He set his hat on top of them, grateful finally to lie down. Relief escaped him by way of a small groan, along with a deep breath he had no awareness he'd sucked in.

The exhaustion of the day hit him. He had been too busy throughout the afternoon and evening to stop. He had even forgotten to eat any supper. Now that he could relax, the hardness of the day weighed on him. No more difficult than days he had experienced as a cowhand. Trail driving was hard on everyone.

Shifting his weight on his bedroll, he tried to find some ease from the throbbing of his hip. There were the packets of powder Doc had given him. However, he needed to save the medication for more severe pain. He would cope for now with the pain in his hip, but it took a few minutes for it to calm down enough for him to fall asleep. When he did, he slept without dreaming.

Chapter Seven

Joe woke with a sense of just having gone to sleep. His eyes were heavy and his limbs did not want to move. He could make out faint shadows from the light of the stars and a half moon. A metal clank and a murmuring came from the back of the chuck wagon.

"Hey, Joe, rise and shine." A boot poked his bedroll. "Move quiet so you won't disturb the sleeping riders."

"I'm up." Joe crawled out of his bedroll. He threw on his hat and pulled on his boots. After he tucked his bedroll into the chuck wagon, he stroked the fire and put on fresh pots of coffee to brew. He built up the other two fires, making them ready for Cookie to place the biscuits to bake.

Joe set a bucket of water onto the coals. When the water was hot, he put the bucket next to the basin on the tailgate of the wrangler wagon. He fetched his shaving kit with its shaving mug, brush, and straight razor. From the bucket he splashed water into the tin basin and washed up, and shaved. After he finished, he set the empty basin next to the bucket of hot water ready for the next man.

Washing up and shaving helped him wake up. A sense of fatigue lingered, and his hip already had a dull throbbing. If only he could get used to the work and not let any of the men see how hard it was for him. He wished he didn't care what these men thought of him. But he did.

Ready for a full day's work, Joe found Cookie humming to himself and working at the table at the back of the chuck wagon.

The boss already had the biscuit dough resting in a pan on the table. "Well, you don't look as peaked as you did last night." The cook spoke quietly. "You must have slept well."

"I did. What should I do first?"

"What you did. The first thing every morning will always be the coffee. Make sure the coffee pots are full. Even if one of them has a little left from the night before, throw it out. Get fresh made in all three pots. We start north tomorrow morning, so we need to get cooking done and organize the wagons today. Go wake Billy. Get him to gather more wood and top off the water barrel."

Joe shook Billy, still asleep under the wrangler wagon. As Billy staggered up, yawning and stretching, Joe checked the fire under the coffee pots.

He watched as lard melted in the Dutch ovens, and Cookie rolled up a small ball of dough, dipped the biscuit in the hot grease, and then placed the biscuits in the pan with the dipped side up. Joe liked the flaky, crusty top and bottom that this produced. He helped stack the Dutch ovens in the coals and watched as Cookie put a thick layer of coals on top of each.

"Joe, watch these biscuits for me. In about ten minutes, turn the ovens around so the biscuits will brown more evenly. I'll make some pies for dinner and get a couple of roasts started this morning. And we need to get the beans going." Cookie looked toward the wrangler wagon. "Set Billy to peeling potatoes to fry for breakfast. You get a ham out of the wagon, slice, and fry it up." He told Joe the menu for the day. "When I'm busy cooking, I need you to keep Billy at his chores. He's pretty good about getting things done, but the boy's got no imagination. If you don't tell him the same things every day, by the next day he's done forgot what his chores were."

"Sure thing." He walked over to the biscuits and turned them, using the pothook. He glanced around at the first fire with three large stacked Dutch ovens filled with biscuits and a large skillet with frying potatoes. Cookie worked at the second fire with two skillets of ham slices browning, as well as another skillet of frying potatoes. Sure seemed like a lot of food. Joe counted how many men would be fed and with the cook crew, there were twenty-three hungry men. On other trail drives, all Joe had worried about was whether he could get an extra biscuit. Now he wondered if he could even find time to eat.

The aroma of boiling coffee filled the air with its bitter scent, so Joe moved the pots just off the flames. Cowhands liked their coffee hot. He poured a little cold water in the pots to settle the grounds. He filled a tin cup and then looked over at Cookie. His boss might like a fresh cup. Joe set the cup of coffee on the table and then filled another for himself.

"Thanks." Cookie reached for the cup of coffee.

Joe took a moment to inhale the fresh aroma and then swallowed the hot brew. He appreciated the thank you even though he had carried the cup of coffee to Cookie without thinking much about it.

As the sun rose, the riders woke, crawled out of their bedrolls, rolled them up, pitched them into the wrangler wagon, and each saddled a horse from the remuda. Then they indulged in the first cup of coffee for the morning as they waited for the call to breakfast after which they would ride out and get the herd moving.

Joe ached to go with them. He could almost feel the motion of his horse as he had when he rode out to check on the herd. He shook off the memories and longings that hurt, the desires that stirred at the sight of something so familiar, yet so far away. With a deep sigh, he turned back to make two big skillets of gravy after dishing up the fried ham.

The riders gathered about twenty feet from the cook fires some sitting on the ground and others squatting on their heels. The men weren't talking much as they waited to be served, they were still waking up. Joe remembered himself doing the same thing on many a cool morning.

A couple at a time came in, poured themselves some coffee, and then stepped away to slug back their first cup of the morning.

Joe lifted his face to the slight breeze that still carried the early morning coolness but would not last long as the heat of the sun drove it away. He listened to the cooing of doves from the cottonwoods along the creek and the distant sound of the lowing of cattle.

It seemed like breakfast had come together quickly. It only took the three of them two and half hours. The sky was light to the east. Time to serve breakfast.

Cookie called the riders. "Come and get it before I throw it out."

Joe slapped the ham steaks, fried potatoes, and gravy on the metal plates as fast as he could with Billy serving the biscuits. He remembered waking up hungry and ready to eat on other trail drives. But back then he been a comrade of the other cowhands. Now, Joe looked around and just hoped he could make a friend or two. As busy as he was he was still wishful for someone to talk with.

As soon as Joe served the last rider, he filled a large plate of food for himself, and leaned against the wagon to eat. Having missed supper, he was hungry and enjoyed his food. He didn't linger over the meal. There was work to do. The rest of the morning, they prepared roast beef, pinto beans, and cornbread for dinner and supper. By the time they served dinner at straight up noon, Joe was dragging, almost too tired to stand.

"Joe, come here." Cookie rested on the wagon tongue, drinking a cup of coffee. "I have to say, you're real handy around the chuck wagon. You've done all this before?"

"I grew up on a ranch. As a boy I helped the cook." Joe yanked his handkerchief from his back pocket and wiped the sweat off the back of his sweltering neck. "Guess I remember more than I thought." He rubbed his stomach at the queasy feeling questions always gave him. His habit of hiding his past was too ingrained.

"Well, it's hard work. Of course, we get paid better than the riders. We earn it, too. Tell you what, you go get an hour or so of sleep. Billy and I'll get on fine until later this afternoon. I'll take a rest then, and you get things ready for supper. Go climb up into the shade of the wagon cover and rest on top of the bedrolls."

Joe didn't wait for Cookie to change his mind. He was dead tired and had another half day of work to do. Waking at four in the morning would take some getting used to.

~

Opening his eyes, Joe took a second to realize it was Billy poking him in the ribs. "Cookie said to wake you. He wants the fires started and the evening meal readied."

Joe squinted, looking at his pocket watch. The two hours of sleep helped. Joe spent the next couple of hours working to get supper ready and filling the riders' plates.

The sense of what was needed to get the meals ready and served was becoming clearer to Joe. He liked that Cookie more and more just gave him directions for work and left it up to Joe to decide how to get it done. Joe took it as Cookie's growing confidence in him. With how bruised he felt mentally at not being able to ride, he would take any nod of admiration.

It was early in the evening but as soon as Cookie gave him the nod, Joe headed to his bedroll, exhausted.

~

Through a fog of sleep, he heard Cookie's deep, quiet voice. "Joe, get up. Get the fires going and make fresh coffee." Joe blinked out at the night sky. What time was it? He pulled out his pocket watch and by the light of the lantern could just make out the dial showing three-thirty. He glanced around. The riders were still asleep.

It was an early start, but Joe didn't argue.

"Make the gravy and drop in the leftover ham. I'll make biscuits and put on the big pot with oatmeal." Cookie flavored it with sugar and canned butter.

One thing Joe could say for the outfit, the riders never went hungry. Not getting enough to eat, at least with this cook, would be a rider's own fault. He had never been with a trail drive that used as much meat.

Cookie didn't seem to eat much, and Joe didn't eat as much as he would have as a rider.

What would Cookie have done if Joe hadn't been there to pull his weight in the work?

With breakfast completed and the wagons almost packed, Cookie looked around at the teams of horses being led up to the wagons by a couple of riders. "We head out in thirty minutes."

Joe only had a few minutes before they pulled out. He grabbed a clean set of clothes, a flour sack towel, and a bar of homemade soap and headed beyond the tree line for a shallow pool in the creek. He shucked his clothes quickly and shivered as he stepped into the pool, but it felt refreshing to his grimy sweaty skin. Working around the cooking fires was hot work.

It was his first chance to be off by himself since he had joined the drive. After spending so many months isolated at Doc's house, being constantly around so many people took some getting used to. Taking a minute to float on his back, he reveled in the sense of calm and relaxation. Then he remembered all the work to do and Cookie waiting for him. It interrupted his moment of freedom and he finished his bath quickly.

When he got back to the wagon, Cookie had already loaded the Dutch ovens and closed the cook box lid at the back. A couple of the cowhands helped Billy finish hitching up the horses to two wagons.

Joe hung the rinsed out clothes and damp flour sack towel to dry on hooks inside the chuck wagon. After three days of working around the fires and in the sun, the cold-water bath in the creek refreshed him. He was ready for another day of travel. Who knew how long until the next chance to bathe?

After climbing onto the wagon, which was difficult with his leg, Joe folded the extra blanket he'd gotten from Mr. Hughes and placed it on the seat to try to relieve some of the pain from the bouncing ride of the day ahead.

"Why, if you don't sure smell purty," Cookie quipped as he climbed up and took the reins. "Don't know why you needed to go for a swim. You haven't even been at work a week, and already you want a bath."

"Well, I didn't want to get as ripe as some of that beef is going to be if this heat keeps up. I wanted the boys to be able to tell the difference between me and your cooking." Joe grinned at his boss feeling more cheerful than he had in a long time.

Cookie roared with laughter as he treaded the reins through his fingers, getting ready to get the horses in motion.

Joe grinned at the deep bass explosion of sound of his boss' laughter. He was content to sit on the wagon seat and watch the rolling prairie, spread out in all directions. The only trees to break up the view were a few cottonwoods and pecan trees along the creeks. He could see fluffs of white cotton float on the breeze. The combined smell of horses, dust, and grass filled his nostrils. The land seemed flat from a distance but had small ridges and gullies, which made for a difficult ride. Even with the enjoyment of the view from up on the wagon seat, he longed for the high mountains of his boyhood home in Colorado.

They soon outdistanced the herd, and he could hear the doves cooing in the distance. He spotted a hawk circling and diving high above. As Joe watched the hawk, he began to feel just as free. His spirit was rising above the difficulties and disappointment he had experienced. It surprised him to be thinking of it. No, he didn't have what he most wanted, but life wasn't bad.

Cookie drove most of the day, but at one point, he handed the reins to Joe.

"You drive a while." Cookie reached under the wagon seat and pulled out a small Bible. "You mind if I read aloud?"

Joe wasn't sure. His memories of the Bible read aloud didn't make him want to experience it again. Nevertheless, this was his boss.

"Sure. Go ahead."

"I try to read the Bible through every year. I'm in the middle of the Psalms." Cookie flipped through the pages until he came to the marker.

Cookie began reading, and Joe was surprised at the sound of the Psalms read in a kind, bass voice. It was sure different from how he had heard it in the past. Maybe this was the way it was supposed to be read.

After reading for the better part of an hour, Cookie put the Bible back under the seat.

"Sakes alive, that's grand. Hope you don't mind, Joe. Reading aloud seems to make it more real. With the evenings so busy, I like to read every day while I'm driving to our next camp."

Cookie was his boss, and so he said nothing, but Joe would have liked to have told the man he didn't want to hear the Bible read at any time.

Chapter Eight

Joe sighed gratefully into the hot mid-afternoon air when Cookie pulled the wagon into the next campground. It had been a long time coming. The spring seat of the chuck wagon still felt strange to him, and the bouncing left his hip with a constant throb. He carefully let himself down over the wheel using mostly his arms and one good leg.

On the solid ground at last, he stood by the stones of former campfires, hands on his hips, as he surveyed the area. Joe noted the way the creek curved and the cottonwood and pecan trees grew alongside it. In all directions, as he looked away from the creek, was the grass-covered prairie, still green with the June rains. He'd been through here before. It brought back faces of other riders from earlier trail drives, so many through the years. Where had they all gone? He shook his head. At least he was with a good crew so far on this trip. Already the time was going too quickly, bringing him to the day when they would reach the end of the trail and he would have to face what to do next.

Joe got busy working with Billy to get the fires going, setting up the irons to hang pots from, and stringing the fly out over the end of the chuck wagon. Cookie let the folding table down and pulled Dutch ovens, skillets, and pots out of the bin under the chuck box.

The breeze from the south carried dust and the bawling of the cattle. In his mind, he could see the cowhands prodding the reluctant cattle. Joe knew the cowhands would be hard-pressed to get the cattle to move the ten miles from the last campground by nightfall.

He cast a glance up the trail they would continue on tomorrow. At this point though, they could travel in a straight line for four or five hours a day and still be ahead of the cattle. Later they would hit dry stretches where water for the cattle would be scarce, and if they encountered Indian trouble, they would have to travel along with the herd for safety.

Joe checked the fires and the coffee brewing before he took a seat on the wagon tongue for a moment of rest. He watched as John Washington, one of the colored riders, rode in ahead of the herd. Joe had ridden with colored riders before and found them to be hard workers and skilled hands.

John dismounted and brushed off the dust. He approached the coffee fire and poured himself a cup. "Cookie, the boss wants a pot of coffee brought to where he's working with Bob Fife. They're going to count the herd as it comes through. Maybe Joe, here, can saddle a horse and carry it to the boss. That way I could get right back to pushing cattle."

Joe felt like a two-week old biscuit had just landed at the pit of his stomach. He stood, looked at the rider, and wondered what Cookie would say. Joe did not want to admit to this cowhand that he could not ride. He felt humiliated enough without having to say it.

"No, John, you carry the coffee pot back to the boss and make sure it gets back to me later. I can't spare Joe if ya'll are going to have supper." Used to his word being the last, Cookie turned his back to the young rider and rolled out pie dough.

Joe grabbed a rag and handed one of the coffee pots half full of hot coffee by the handle to cowhand. John took the pot, gave Joe a sullen look, and then rode off without a word.

Joe poured a cup of coffee and set it on the worktable. "Thanks, Cookie."

The older man dusted the flour off his hands and lifted the cup. He looked Joe in the eyes. "They'll figure out soon enough that you can't ride. You might as well tell them. But I'll leave it up to you."

Joe stared across the prairie at the rolling land, soon to be covered with cattle as the herd moved up. As long as the riders didn't know he couldn't ride he wasn't a part of them, but at least he had the sense of being in a world that used to be his. Once they knew he couldn't sit a horse ... he'd forever be outside their world.

Joe blew out a long breath. "You're probably right, Cookie. But, I'd rather let it ride as long as possible."

"Suit yourself, but you know one of these days the boys will get to bedeviling you to see what you're made of."

Cookie was right. When the time came, he hoped he could deal with it without looking like a fool. He remembered with regret the teasing he had done to weaker riders through the years. Now he understood how they felt. How could he have once been so strong? Now look at him. He remembered the old saying, "Pride goes before a fall." Well, he had fallen.

~

The next morning after breakfast, Cookie called Joe over. "You and Billy empty the wrangler wagon into the chuck wagon. It will be a tight fit but with some of the food stuff used up you can make it fit. Then take the wrangler wagon over to Red River Station, about two miles east of the river crossing. You should get there by the middle of the morning. We'll stock up on as much as we can because it's a long way to the next store. We might as well take advantage." Cookie handed Joe a list. "I'll take the chuck wagon across the river and wait for you boys north of the crossing. It's going to take most of today and part of tomorrow for the cowhands to get the herd across the river."

"Yes, Cookie." Joe took the money and the list his boss handed him.

Red River Station at the little community of Salt Creek was the last store before crossing over into Oklahoma Territory. The store also boasted of a post office. Joe planned to take advantage and send Doc and Mrs. Purdy a letter.

"Billy, you get the horses watered while I get the store owner started on our order. I'm going to scout around for someone to do some add-ons to the wagon."

Joe strolled into the small store that was dark with crowded shelves. From the look of the place, they didn't have anyone dusting and sweeping such as Joe had done for Mr. Hughes in Waco.

"Howdy, young man. What can I do you for?" The skinny old man behind a cluttered counter waited for Joe to speak.

"I need these supplies. I got cash to pay for them. I'm also looking for someone to build a couple of platforms on our wagon for some water barrels."

The man took the list Cookie had written out. "We can fill you order. It'll take a while to get it together. Over at the smithy you'll find Henry. He can build you a platform that will hold a water barrel and he also sells barrels that he makes."

Joe nodded, "Thanks, I'll go talk to him and be back in an hour or so to load up."

Fortunately, Henry wasn't busy and seemed glad for the business. Within a couple of hours, with Joe's help, he had built a small platform on each side of the wrangler wagon and attached a couple of metal rings that they could use to tie on the water barrels and their lids secure. From past trail drives Joe knew that the more water they could carry, the easier the drive for the Cookie and helpers. The weight of the water was a factor, but the load of the wrangler wagon was lighter than what the chuck wagon carried.

Joe also got Henry to add a wooden step and a hand hold on each side of the wagon and to make extras that Joe could take with him to attach to the chuck wagon. With months ahead of climbing into and out of the wagons, he wanted to make it a little easier on himself. He also suspected that even Cookie would find a step up easier.

Joe walked around the store while the storekeeper tallied up his order. Although a much smaller store, it still reminded him of his time working in Waco. Being a helper to Cookie was harder work but he enjoyed being out on the prairie more. He spotted two folding camp chairs. Unfolding one he sat and stretched out his legs. It felt good to sit. On impulse, he set them aside with the supplies. He was tired of eating his meals standing up.

Squatting on his heels wasn't comfortable any more. The truth was, he almost couldn't do it now because of his hip.

To the list of supplies, he added powdered milk, dried vegetables, dried fruit, and another large piece of treated waterproof canvas. After he paid from the money Cookie had given him, Joe wrote a short letter and left it to be mailed back to Dr. Rupert and Mrs. Purdy.

As Joe and Billy finished loading their supplies into the wagon, a short woman, who looked like someone's grandmother dressed in a plain brown dress and a bonnet shading her face, walked up stepping carefully over the rough ground. She carried an Arbuckle coffee crate, obviously full of something delicate.

"You boys from a trail herd?" She looked up at them hopefully.

"Yes, ma'am, we are." Joe took his hat off as he responded to her.

"I've a crate of eggs here I want to sell. I've wrapped each one in newspaper and they were all gathered within the last two days. I'll sell them to you for two dollars."

"Can I break one open to make sure they're fresh enough?" Joe wanted to buy them, but he didn't want to be taken in.

She gingerly set the crate on the ground and let him pick up one of the paper wrapped eggs.

He cracked it open against the wheel of the wagon and careful not to let the egg run out of the shell, smelled it. He also looked at the shape of the yolk, nice and rounded.

"Can I have it?" Billy reached out his hand for the raw egg in the cracked shell.

Joe handed it to him, and watched, as Billy scooped the egg up into his mouth and in one big swallow it was gone. Joe shook his head at the boy. He turned back to the old woman and pulled two dollars from the money Cookie had given him for supplies.

"Thank you, young man." The woman gave a little bow and then turned and went into the store.

He eased the crate into the wagon, making it secure between two sacks of flour.

Joe drove the wagon west along the Red River for about three miles until he came to where the riders were herding the cattle across.

Bob Fife rode up to meet them and guided them down to the best place for them to cross the river with the wagon. Unless there had been some heavy rains, the river was never very high at the crossing. The herd swimming the river made a mess of red mud but Joe was able to drive the lightly loaded wagon across without any problems.

In the late afternoon, Joe drove the wrangler wagon to park it behind the chuck wagon. Cookie waved as if glad to see them back. He already had the fires going and supper started. Scratching his head, he walked around the wrangler wagon, looking at the extra water barrels.

"You think of this all by yourself, Billy?" Cookie asked with a grin.

"No, Cookie. I didn't think of it at all. It was Joe," Billy quickly said.

Joe grinned. The kid didn't realize Cookie was joshing him.

"Well, it's a real good idea. Now we can carry enough water to get the chores done. Did you get all the supplies I asked you to get?"

"Yes, and I got a few extras." Joe took the crate of eggs out of the wagon. "I thought this might make a nice change for the boys."

"Would you look at that!" Cookie peered into the crate. "There must be six dozen eggs there. Come on and bring them to the chuck wagon. And Billy, don't you tell a soul that we have eggs."

Joe took a moment to catch his breath and think about the miles yet to travel. They had the most difficult part of the drive ahead of them, Indian Territory. The distances between water would now be longer. The days were hotter and dryer, as they were in the middle of June. Already the time was going too quickly. Then, he would have to face what to do after they reached the end of the trail.

~

Later that evening, Joe watched as Billy bent over the washtub full of dirty dishes. He'd once been Billy's age. On their trip back from the Red River Station, Billy had told Joe he'd grown up poor in a big town back east, and that he'd run away at age eleven. Joe wondered if Billy was scared.

Joe took out one of the new chairs and eased into it to take a few minutes to rest. He'd had so many dreams of what his own life would be, but he never dreamed he'd end up a cook's helper. His advantage over Billy was his ability to read and write.

Eleven years earlier, he'd run in fear of his life from his own mother and home. Joe had been terrified. No one ever knew just how scared. He had tried to keep it a secret, even from himself. He wasn't as scared now. Back then he had had hope of making a better life for himself, but after the injury to his leg hope was hard to come by. Somewhere along the way he had lost his dreams for his future.

How does a man catch a new dream?

Chapter Nine

After two weeks on the trail, Joe was used to the routine when Cookie handed the reins to him and said, "Getting up at three in the morning makes a mid-morning snooze a treat." He climbed into the wagon bed. "Head north but keep on the lookout for a bit of high ground. We'll camp west of there."

Joe settled the reins through his fingers. "You talking about Monument Hill?"

"That's right. I forget you've been up the trail before." Cookie settled down on the bedrolls atop the sacks of flour, rice, and cornmeal.

Joe focused on the teams of horses and the trail ahead. He remembered the hill. He had climbed it several times and stood on top taking in the sight of the prairie for twenty miles in any direction. Through the years, riders had built two rock monuments on top of the hill. Easily seen, the monuments served as landmarks for cattle drivers, who pointed their herds toward its base. There were several such monuments along the trail. If he could still ride, Joe would have climbed up there for a look-see as he had in the past. It was worth it.

Joe craned his neck around to see the wrangler wagon that followed close behind. Billy always kept close behind the chuck wagon. The boy might not be the brightest star out at night but he proved steadfast for all of his fourteen years.

All morning Monument Hill had been visible. On a clear day, it could be spotted twenty miles away. Joe had heard cowboys argue about how high the hill was. He agreed with the argument that it was just over a thousand feet high. Compared to the mountains in Colorado Territory where Joe had been born, it was a little hill but in the midst of the flat prairie of Oklahoma Territory, it was a small mountain.

Cookie woke from his nap. "Find a likely spot, pull over, and we'll heat some dinner for the drovers. It looks like we've traveled a little east of the main herd. By the time we stop and get food ready, the riders will be coming in to take turns eating."

Joe thought about the food they had cooked after supper the evening before, roast beef, pinto beans, and cornbread. Joe had also made donuts, or bear claws as some called them. The hands had fussed because Cookie wouldn't let them have any after supper. He wanted to save them for dinner at noontime the next day. It was a lot easier on the chuck wagon crew if they could cook food in the morning and evening and have a cold meal at noon.

The hands had been friendly enough, but Joe hadn't talked much. He would have liked the chance to sit and exchange tales with them, but the cook crew worked until bedtime. By the time his work was done, all Joe wanted was to fall into his bedroll.

Over the past couple of weeks, Joe had learned the riders' names. They all seemed to know his name was Joe, but some of them called him Little Cookie. He didn't take it as a put down. It simply meant that they knew Cookie was the boss, and he was Cookie's helper. Most of the riders offered their thanks when he piled food onto their plates.

There were a couple of riders that always stuck together—never said thanks, and even seemed to smirk as he served them. Maybe it was just his imagination and he was too sensitive about the position he found himself. However, he'd seen the like before on other drives. He shoved aside his resentment, got his mind on the things at hand, preparing the meals and getting the hands fed, checking the coffee pots. Too much thinking time wasn't good for his peace of mind.

Curly Brutus and Frank Moffett sauntered over to the coffee fire and poured themselves a cup of the strong hot liquid.

Joe checked the coffee pots to see if he needed to get another one going. Cookie liked to start out the afternoon with a full pot. He kept it at his feet in the wagon, so when riders came up he could give them a cup of coffee even though it was cold.

Joe picked up the pot, and a couple of cups of the hot liquid swished within it as he turned toward the water barrel. A boot hooked Joe's right ankle—his bad leg—it gave way and he went down, dropping the coffee pot. Hot coffee splashed out sending scalding liquid onto his hand and arm. Clenching his jaw against the pain of the burn, he got up awkwardly and shook coffee off his burned hand.

Curly and Frank sniggered into their coffee cups.

Glancing over at the other riders, Joe saw that some of them grinned, while a couple others looked uninterested.

Joe gritted his teeth—not only because of the pain. He felt the rise of the old familiar fury that had caused trouble for him in the past. If he let it loose, he could hurt people. Then he caught himself. That was in the past. If only he had a different position with the trail herd, or the confidence to take on the two cowhands in spite of his hip, but he saw no recourse but keep his anger under control. If he made a fuss, they'd say that he'd been clumsy. So, he'd let it pass, wait for his chance to get back at them in a way that wouldn't lead to a fight.

He brushed himself off, but the burns hurt. Joe picked up the coffee pot and looked at it for a moment. It would do some damage if thrown at a man, but then what? They had their revolvers strapped on and he was unarmed except for a coffee pot.

But as cook's helper, he had some power that Curly and Frank might not have thought of. Joe suppressed a grin.

"Didn't hurt yourself did you, Little Cookie?" Curly dawdled near the fire.

"Oh, look, Curly; he got coffee all over him. Too bad he's so clumsy." Frank sniggered. They tossed their cups to the ground and sauntered off.

"Cups in the wash-up pan!" Cookie roared from where he rolled out pie dough.

Curly and Frank stopped in their tracks, looked at one another, then turned and hurried to place their cups in the wash-up tub, then ran to their horses, racing away from Cookie's displeasure.

As they drove on from the noon stop, Cookie handed Joe a pot of salve. "Here, put this on your hand and it'll take the sting out. It's a mixture of lavender essential oil and honey and some other stuff. Kills the pain and helps with healing. Don't worry about them two riders. We'll take care of them."

"Thanks, Cookie. Sorry I wasn't quick enough to keep out of their way." He rubbed more of the salve on his hand, thankful it relieved most of the pain. It did have a faint scent of lavender and honey.

"You shouldn't have to be quick. I don't appreciate anyone messing with my helper. You know how it is when you get a bunch of men together. Climb on back into the wagon and get some sleep. We may be up late tonight. I want to have several extra things cooked by bedtime." Cookie pulled a small Bible out from under the wagon seat. "Will it bother your sleep if I read aloud to myself?"

"No, it won't keep me awake." He didn't tell Cookie that just seeing the little Bible made him feel as if snakes crawled in his gut. Too many memories of the horrors from his childhood.

Joe stretched out on top of the bedrolls and hundred pound bags of food with a sigh. He was dead tired, but sleep didn't come immediately. He wanted to call Curly and Frank out and beat them to a pulp. Like that was going to happen with his bum leg. Flashes of fights from the past surfaced and he could feel the give of a man's face from his fist. In the past, his hot temper had gotten him into trouble. Like that time in El Paso when the town bully had made a rude remark and Joe had beaten him senseless. The white heat of his fury had been way out of proportion. He'd only landed in jail for a week and lost his job. Now, his temper could get him killed. Joe rubbed his aching hip.

The sound of Cookie's soft bass voice reading his Bible aloud wafted over him. It surprised him that it was actually soothing. He'd have to find another way to deal with Curly and Frank, a way that he'd still feel like a man. He mentally shook himself. He was working harder than he'd ever worked in his life and he enjoyed being a part of the trail drive out on the prairie. No way he'd let the likes of Curly and Frank mess that up. To keep control of his temper would be a big challenge. With that thought, he finally gave in to sleep.

~

Joe sat next to Cookie on the wagon seat as they rounded Monument Hill. To the west, they spotted the creek that Joe remembered. Only a few small oak trees grew alongside it. They'd set up camp there.

He gazed up to the top of Monument Hill and recognized Santo Real, one of the two Spanish riders with the crew. Santo rode point that day, a position ahead of the herd to make sure it headed the right way and stayed along the trail. He waved to the cook crew then turned his mount to ride down.

"Hey, Señor Cookie. You got coffee?" he called as he rode up.

Joe snatched a cup from the crate and filled it. He handed it to the cowhand. "It's not hot." Joe glanced at the solid looking cowhand. Santo was in his late twenties and rode a horse as if born on it. With his gentle smile, soft voice with the lilting Spanish accent, dark snapping eyes, dark skin, and respectful manner, Joe could imagine that he had his pick of the Señoritas. He was one of the riders that always thanked the cooks for his meal.

"That is okay, Señor. It will help the thirst." Santo drank it down and with a smile handed back the empty cup. "Muchas gracias."

"Por nada."

Santo reined his horse around and rode toward the oncoming herd.

Joe held onto the wagon seat as Cookie pulled the team across the ruts in the trail left by the many trail drives before them and came to a halt near a campground. Joe noticed several stone rings already set up which would make his work of getting the cook fires going much easier.

He turned to see Billy bring the wrangler wagon to a stop. Joe couldn't stop his grin. The boy appeared as if he had just awakened. Joe suspected the boy slept as he drove. The horses hitched to the wrangler wagon would follow the chuck wagon without much guidance.

"Come on, let's get these horses unhitched." Joe helped the boy get the two teams unhitched from the chuck wagon

Billy led the animals down to the creek.

Frowning Cookie gave Joe a look up and down. "You're a mess with that dried coffee all over you. Why don't you get the coffee going and then go wash up in the creek before the herd gets here." He let down the worktable from the chuck box.

"Thanks. It won't take me but a few minutes, and then I'll be ready to help cook supper." Joe quickly got the three fires going and set the three coffee pots on one of the fires.

He grabbed some clean clothes, a flour sack as a towel, and soap. He found a small pool, bathed, and washed his hair. He also washed the clothes he'd removed. In less than thirty minutes, he returned to camp. He tied on a clean apron then presented himself to Cookie for instructions.

"All right, Joe. We have that last hunk of beef left from yesterday. Cut it up into steaks, flour them, and fry them. What we don't use will have to be thrown away."

With fifty steaks cut and floured, Joe fried them in two huge, long-handled skillets in two inches of melted, sizzling lard. Once he had the first batch of steaks frying, he filled water halfway in two big pots, and then set them over the other fire. He dumped in the dried carrots, onions, dried squash, potatoes, and dried apples. Later he'd add any leftover beef. He mixed a bowl of dried milk and water, stirred in some flour, salt, and pepper, ready to make gravy in the steaks' drippings. The tantalizing smell of the steaks frying overpowered the aroma of the strong coffee. Joe inhaled the rapturous scent. He surely did love campfire food.

"Billy, go fill all the water barrels and the wash-up tub before the riders get the herd to the creek. They're bedding down a half-mile west of camp," Cookie yelled.

"Yes, sir." The boy ambled off carrying empty water buckets to fill to top off the water barrels.

Joe fixed a place on the tailgate of the wrangler wagon for the men to wash up before eating. Most of the herds he had worked for before had never done this, but it was something he appreciated as a rider. After a day of riding drag at the back of the herd with the heat, sun, and dust, to be able to wash up a bit was refreshing, and then to be able to drink a cup of hot coffee while waiting to eat and let the fatigue wash over one's body was also a blessing. Joe knew the feeling.

The first evening he'd set the bucket of hot water out for the hands to wash, Cookie had looked at him with protest, but then nodded and said nothing. Several of the men had thanked Cookie for having the hot water ready and he had generously told them to thank Joe. Now the cowhands assumed it would be there.

"Let's get ready to serve these riders. You handle the potatoes and gravy. I'll toss on the steak." He looked through the steaks and set two of them aside with a wink at Joe.

Joe lifted an eyebrow. What was his boss up to?

Cookie yelled out, "Come and get it before we throw it out."

The men lined up, and Joe gave them each a helping of potatoes and gravy.

Cookie didn't say anything, but when Curly and Frank put out their plate, he gave them the steaks he had put aside. Joe noticed gristle crisscrossed the steaks making them hardly worth eating.

Following Cookie's example, Joe dished out smaller amounts of potatoes and gravy.

Curly and Frank returned with their empty plates when Cookie served the cobbler.

"No cobbler for you two," the old chuck master said. "Not after you wasted good coffee. Next!"

They opened their mouths as if to protest and then snapped them shut. The sullen stares they shot at Joe weren't friendly. Avoiding them in the future would be his best bet.

Cookie set out the two camp chairs and then filled his plate. He motioned for Joe to sit with him. Joe served himself a nice steak with plenty of gravy and vegetables and joined his boss.

Across from them, the men sat on the ground or squatted on their heels. Joe noticed that a few of them looked thoughtfully at the cooks' camp chairs.

"These were a great idea," Cookie said. "I don't know why I never thought about them before. They don't weigh much and they take no space tied to the side of the wagon. By the way, could you make some cornbread while I get a cake made?" Cookie didn't wait for him to answer. "In the morning, I want to have pancakes, and scrambled eggs. It'll be a surprise for the boys. Course, I'm not sure a couple of the boys will get any eggs. I need to think about that," he said with a grin.

"I'll wait to see what happens," Joe answered with his own grin as he cleaned his plate. "I'll get the stew finished and then get the cornbread made. Anything else you want before I unroll my bedroll tonight?"

"No, we've got things in hand. I'll tell the trail boss that we need another beef by tomorrow night, or the next day for sure."

Joe pulled his bedroll out. Thunder rumbled in the distant skies. The nighthawks, the men doing the night riding, had a long night ahead of them. Any little thing could set off a herd. Thinking about the herd, where it was, and the path the creek took alongside where they were camped, Joe had to say something.

Cookie was at the tailgate table cleaning the last of the dough off.

"Cookie?"

"Yes?" He wiped his hands on his apron.

"You know I've had a little experience with this part of the country. With that storm coming, we may have a problem tonight. If it spooks the herd, they'll head this way because of the bend in the creek."

Cookie surveyed the area. "Sakes alive. We don't want to get caught in the path of a stampede."

Chapter Ten

Joe took his hat off and ran his fingers through his hair as he thought about the possibility of a stampede. He looked at Cookie. "We can't outrun it, that's for sure. But maybe we can do something to protect the wagons. I suggest we pull the wrangler wagon up to the west side of the chuck wagon." Examining the clouds starting to block the light of the stars to the west, Joe said, "The herd would be more likely to divide and go around them. Also, if they did tip over the wrangler wagon it wouldn't be as big a loss as damage to the chuck wagon." Joe appreciated that Cookie was open to hearing his suggestions.

Cookie nodded while he rubbed his chin. "Go wake up Billy and I'll get a couple of hands. We don't need to hitch up, just roll it. After I close this table, we'll get the fly down and stowed away. And think about the coffee fire. I'd hate to lose the coffee pots but maybe we'd have time to grab them."

They stowed the tailgate table and started taking down the fly.

Bob Fife rode in from the herd. He had tied his horse closer than usual to the chuck wagon, removed the saddle, and then poured himself a cup of coffee.

"Hey, Cookie. Why are you taking down the fly tonight?"

Cookie pointed to the west. "You see that storm coming?"

"Yeah, I see it. Sure has a lot of lightning in it. I can hear the thunder too."

"Joe here pointed out that if the cattle stampede, they'll run right through camp. What do you think?" Cookie asked.

Bob lifted his brows and glanced at the cook's helper. "How do you figure where the herd's gonna run? Not many riders can do that."

"Stands to reason. When cows are spooked, they'll run wherever it's easiest to go." Joe turned to finish stowing the fly and put the poles away.

Cookie finished stowing a couple of pots in the storage box. "Bob, I'm going to be ready if anything happens. I want to move the wrangler wagon up next to the chuck wagon. Get a couple of the boys to help."

"Sure, Cookie. That's a good idea. Is that another one of your ideas, Joe?" Bob gave him a searching look.

Joe nodded, but didn't say anything. He continued stowing the campsite items.

Billy was already asleep under his wagon. "Hey." Joe poked him gently in the ribs.

The boy woke up, looking groggy and confused.

"Get up. Help us move the wrangler wagon. We got some bad weather comin' and you need to sleep under cover tonight."

Bob, along with George Healy and Bill Ramsey who got up from where they had spread out their bedrolls, easily rolled the wrangler wagon close to the west side of the chuck wagon.

Several of the men stirred from their sleep. When they were awake, Bob said, "If the herd stampedes tonight, throw your bedrolls in the wagon and climb in if you can't get to your mounts."

Joe hoped the riders would have time to get out of the way if the cattle spooked. He'd helped bury men killed in a stampede before, and never wanted to do it again. Just the thought gave him a queasy feeling. Bone tired and muscles aching, he spread his bedroll on the far side of the chuck wagon. With a deep sigh, he sank to the ground.

Later that night, Joe woke when gusts of wind full of dirt and sand blew into camp ahead of the storm and the canvases flapped loudly. Lightning blazed across the sky followed by earth-shaking claps of thunder.

Henry Thursgood, the trail boss, directed a few of the riders to try to get some sleep in order to take over watching over the herd toward morning. The men saddled their horses and tied them to the trees along the creek. Dave Miller, the night wrangler, drove the remuda around to the other side of Monument Hill with the help of a couple of cowhands. Most everyone else was out with the herd trying to calm the cattle and keep them lying down.

Cookie lay awake on top of the sacks of flour, cornmeal, rice, and other items that made a nice bed. "You think we need to prepare for a stampede?"

Joe put his bedroll in a corner of the chuck wagon. "Hopefully not, but the lightning is mighty close to the herd now. The boys may not be able to hold them. If they do stampede, it'll be within the next thirty minutes."

"Then get the other coffee pot off the fire."

As Joe went to get the last coffee pot, the ground trembled under him. "Stampede! Stampede!" he yelled.

He grabbed the pot and poured the coffee out over the coals. They didn't need a grass fire too. By the time he got back to the wrangler wagon, the drovers had their boots on and had grabbed up their bedrolls. Joe flung the coffee pot up to Billy. As the riders came up, he grabbed their loose bedrolls and tossed these into the wagon, so men could run to their mounts and ride out.

"Get in the wagon!" Cookie waved Joe in.

The rumbling sound of five thousand cattle running at them grew closer. The ground shook.

Joe flung up the last bedroll into the wagon and climbed up after it.

"Go ahead and climb across, Billy. The chuck wagon is safer," Joe yelled, hoping to be heard above the sound of thundering hooves coming toward them.

Billy, the whites of his eyes showing, didn't have to be told twice and scrambled across to the chuck wagon.

Joe followed him and stepped across from the wrangler wagon to the chuck wagon as the first of the cattle rounded the bend of the creek.

In spite of the darkness, flashes of lightning showed thousands of cattle coming toward them while loud booms of thunder blotted out the sound of running hooves. Lightening was hitting so close that it seemed to literally bounce between the cattle's horns. Call St. Elmo's fire it made for an eerie sight.

The herd thundered straight at them. Although the animals parted at the barrier of the two wagons and ran around on both sides, some hit the side of the wrangler wagon, and tried to climb in, jarring it and shoving it into the chuck wagon.

Billy hunched down, covered his ears, and burrowed between the sacks of food. The noise and vibration set Joe's own pulse to racing. He hung onto the seat of the wagon and tried not to think what it would be like to fall into the middle of a thousand stampeding hooves.

The cattle continued their wild run. Rain began to fall in torrential sheets, accompanied by wind gusts that drove the water inside under the canvas and swayed the wagon bonnets.

When the ground stopped shaking, Joe managed to stand and look outside. The lightning had moved further east. Stray cows wandered through after the still racing herd. He hoped that the next herd coming up the trail was far enough behind not to suffer the same fate and run over them. It had happened before.

The rain continued to pour down. In under an hour, five thousand cattle had swarmed past the cook team and wagons.

Lowing from a hurt cow caught Joe's ear as he climbed onto the wrangler wagon. He looked down at the ground where a steer was crumpled in the jarred up mud.

Cookie stood behind the wagon seat but under the protection of the canvas and surveyed the area. "What do you think? Are we okay now?"

"We're safe as long as another herd isn't too close."

"Sakes alive. Wish you hadn't said that. Now you got me worried."

"Well, we'll probably be all right." Joe squinted down at the animal. "I'm not sure how we're going to get that steer out of the way. Hopefully, the others will be by soon. Who knows how far the herd ran. But I don't think we're going anywhere before daybreak and maybe not then with this rain." Joe stopped himself. He was talking out of the nervous relief of surviving the stampede.

Cookie eyed the rain. "The boys will need coffee. Can you and Billy get a fire going?"

Joe wiped his face. Fatigue was setting in but no chance for rest yet. "Let's wait a bit if you don't mind, and see if the rain will let up. Make sure the lightning is far enough away. Then we can rig canvas to the east side of the wagon and build a fire there. That way you can still have the tailgate for morning cooking."

Joe pulled out his pocket watch and tried to check the time in the faint flashes of lightning.

Cookie lit a lantern and held it aloft.

Only one-thirty in the morning. Joe stuffed the watch back into his pocket. He could build a fire and make coffee, and maybe squeeze in another hour of sleep before they needed to get breakfast ready.

By lantern light, Billy and Joe climbed down and rigged the larger piece of canvas they'd purchased in Red River Station to the side of the wagon and two poles to provide a dry place to set up.

Joe gathered stones to make a gourd-shaped ring. The canvas made it possible to get the fire going, using dry wood from the cradle under the wagon. With the protective cover, Joe and Billy kept the fire going in spite of the falling rain. With the fire built, Joe got the coffee made. He sunk a few inches into the mud as he worked.

Billy got the crate with the cups in it and placed it on a stone close to the fire. "Should I get the wash-up tub ready?"

"You might as well." Joe handed the bag of ground coffee back up to Cookie, who still sat on the wagon seat.

Billy returned with the empty tub. Joe noticed that the boy's boots and pant's hem were caked with red mud.

"Just set it outside the canvas on a rock away from the mud and let it fill with rain water. We should be having some riders show up." Almost as soon as Joe said it, three riders rode up out of the darkness. Jeff Kingston held his left arm in an awkward position. George Healy had blood soaking his thigh, and Will Ramsey had a bad cut on his hand, probably from the tip of a cow horn.

Cookie climbed down from the wagon with his medical bag, while Joe set up the two camp chairs under the canvas. Cookie started working on the wound on George's leg.

Joe finished bandaging Will Ramsey's hand. "Keep this dry and clean." The cut was deep, but he could still move his fingers, so he likely suffered no permanent damage.

"Thanks. That feels better. If I could get a cup of that coffee," he gave a nod in the direction of the fire, "I can get back to the herd. We got some rounding up to do."

Joe got him a cup and then handed a cup of coffee each to George and Jeff.

Cookie continued to work on George, who slumped in one of the camp chairs.

Joe settled Jeff in the other chair and gingerly felt along his forearm. The bone wasn't through the skin, but Joe felt where it was broken. He read the pain on the cowhand's face and understood it.

Beads of sweat glistened on Jeff's forehead.

"I'll get some splints and wrappings. That arm is broke and you need it bound up tight. Sit quiet while I get what I need to splint it." A rider with a broken arm was slowed down, but he'd keep riding. Joe had done it in the past and knew how much it hurt. He stood and rubbed his aching hip. He would trade that for a broken arm any day.

"Joe," Cookie called. "I need to sew George up. He's lost a lot of blood. Can you take care of Jeff?"

"Yes, Cookie." Joe answered easily, as if Cookie had asked if he could make the coffee. There were injuries to tend to—two of these men would return back to the herd tonight, and George in the next day or so. But they'd all make it back out, driving cattle. Joe was getting used to his new acquaintance with envy.

"I declare, Joe—" Cookie's voice broke Joe from his thoughts, and he turned to his boss.

"—but you're handy to have around. I don't know what we'd have done without you on this trip."

Joe helped Jeff out of his vest and shirt and then placed the splint on Jeff's arm. Joe turned and glanced over to Will, who was cradling his injured hand, watching him. "Hey, Will, we got a problem here. There's an injured steer on the ground, on the far side of the wrangler wagon. If I get a rope on it, could you snake it away from the camp?"

"Sure." Will finished his coffee.

"Let me get Jeff here fixed up and then I'll help you get a couple of ropes on the steer." Joe looked around at the men. "Do you fellows know if anyone else is hurt?"

"I just happened on George and Will here," Jeff said. "You couldn't see worth anything. We only found the camp by your lantern. I don't know where the other riders were when the stampede started or how far they've run."

"It'll be daylight before we know anything," Will said. "It's amazing that you fellows made out as well as you did. The herd came right through here."

"That was Joe." Cookie finished bandaging George's leg.

"How do you mean?" Jeff winced, positioning his arm to try to relieve some of the pain.

"Well, Joe here knows as much about taking a herd up the trail as anyone on the drive. He took one look at that storm, the bend in the creek, and knew what path those cattle would cut. He had us pull the wrangler wagon up to protect the chuck wagon and even got the riders up and mounted before it hit us." Cookie's nod toward Joe had the look of a proud parent. "Besides saving some of the riders' hides, he saved all the bedrolls and coffee pots too."

The three riders swung their gazes to Joe as he helped Jeff back into his shirt and vest.

"How do you know about trail herds?" Jeff asked him.

George groaned, saving Joe from having to answer.

Joe turned to Billy. "Help Cookie and me get George into the wrangler wagon so he can lie down."

After they settled the cowhand on his bedroll in the wagon, Joe walked in the light rain over to the downed steer. On the way, Joe slipped in the mud and his right foot nearly slid out from under him.

Will mounted his horse and met Joe where the steer lay quietly on the ground. He tossed a couple of ropes to Joe, and kept one end tied to his saddle horn.

Joe got one rope around its horns, and the other around the steer's neck. This animal's going to start bawling as soon as we start pulling it.

They looped the other rope around the pommel of George's saddle.

"Climb up into the saddle of George's horse. It'll make it easier to pull," Will called to Joe.

If only he could. Joe waved his hand and turned to Billy. "Go climb into the saddle. When I tell you, start the horse toward the turn in the hill. Drag the steer until you're around the hill and out of sight of the camp."

Billy climbed into the saddle and with the rope under his leg and tied to the saddle horn, he and Will began to drag the steer away from the wagon. The steer started bawling just as expected.

Joe left it to them and went back to move the coffee pots off the main part of the fire.

Cookie checked Jeff's arm. "That splint is as well done as I could have fixed it. Just don't be bumping it for a few days. I'll get you a sling which will make it easier to ride."

Joe went back to the wrangler wagon to look at the damage. He kicked aside the remains of one of the water barrels and ran his fingers along the deep scrapes and gorges along the side of the wagon. He pulled the broken piece of a spoke from one of the wheels. That could be fixed. Getting the canvas and poles out, Joe put up the fly over the tailgate of the chuck wagon so Cookie would be sheltered from the rain while he worked on breakfast.

The sound of a rifle shot pierced the air. Will had shot the steer. It was the only thing to do. The animal wouldn't survive with a broken leg. Joe's hip throbbed. A picture of the steer in the mud fixed itself in his mind. He leaned on the tailgate and rubbed his hip. Joe wiped the thought from his mind. He wasn't a steer that someone would take out and shoot. He sucked in a breath and pushed off from the tailgate.

Cookie looked at Joe. "You want to butcher the steer or you want me to?"

Joe laughed half-heartedly. "You give me a choice—I'll cook breakfast if you'll do the cutting."

Cookie nodded. "All right then." He took out his big knife, got an axe, a big pot, and walked toward the steer.

Jeff raised an eyebrow as he stared at Joe. "Exactly who is the cookie and who is the helper of this chuck wagon?"

"Cookie's the boss, but he's easy to work with. He doesn't mind sharing the load," Joe replied as he built up another fire.

He decided not to cook scrambled eggs as Cookie had mentioned the evening before. Instead, he put on a big pot of oatmeal with lots of sugar. He stacked the four big Dutch ovens to heat on the fire. The biscuits would not be as light and flaky as Cookie's. Joe had yet to learn the secret. He dipped the balls of dough into the hot grease and got the biscuits going.

Jeff sat watching. "Where did you learn to cook?"

"I grew up on a ranch and used to help out." Spending time in the kitchen with the cooks had been his refuge from his mother's anger. She rarely went into the kitchen. It had been relatively safe, if there were such a place. Nate, their cook, and his helper, Smithy, had been at the ranch since before Joe was born. The old riders had come into the valley with his father when he had started the ranch. They had treated Joe like their own son.

"I'm surprised you're not a rider." Jeff said. "You got the build for it. You're always working, even more than the riders. Why be a cook's helper?"

Joe nodded, but couldn't bring himself to tell Jeff. "I've got to get breakfast cooked."

There was no easy answer for what Jeff asked, although it did feel good that Jeff saw him as being rider material. He remembered asking Dr. Rupert what he could do if he couldn't ride. At least he had a job and earned his keep. Sometimes a man did what had to be done.

Chapter Eleven

The light pushed forward from the east as a wet, bedraggled bunch of tired riders drifted in. They dismounted, unsaddled their horses, and headed for the coffee.

Jim Finely squatted on his heels next Jeff who was lounging in a camp chair. "So here's where you been hiding out while we stopped a stampede. I can't believe you're letting a little ole thing like a broken arm keep you from all the fun we had last night." The grin on Jim's mud spattered face belied the words.

"Well, I figured you fellas needed to learn to handle the herd without me." Jeff retorted back.

Joe saw the obvious friendship between the two riders who were about the same age. A friendship like he had had with the last bunch of cowhands he'd worked with before his injury. While serving breakfast, he considered what the riders had ahead of them. It would take a day to get the herd back on the trail. They needed to move the chuck wagon north and let the herd catch up to them.

Cookie rode in on George's horse, which had been packed with the butchered meat. He dismounted, filled his plate with oatmeal, and two biscuits and started to eat. "Good job. Couldn't have done better myself."

Cookie's praise was better than a pat on the back.

Bob Fife pulled Cookie aside to talk privately and then they called Joe over and discussed where they needed to take the chuck wagon and when.

Joe pushed his hat back. "If we don't move up, the herd will be too far ahead of us when it gets back on the trail. We can leave signs for any stragglers and tell them where they can find the chuck wagon."

"How would you do that?" Bob asked.

"Lay out an arrow made of rocks. Put a stick in between the stones and hang flour sack streamers from it. We can even brand the streamer." Joe frowned. "Has anyone seen the trail boss?"

Bob raised an eyebrow and shook his head. "No one has seen him and I'm worried. Go ahead and load up and head on up the trail. We'll find you when we need to."

Cookie ran his hand through his hair leaving it looking wilder than ever. He crushed his hat back on. "We'll travel a ways north and stop early. We'll need to cook the beef for supper and tomorrow. In this heat that's as long as it will last."

It took the Cookie, Billy, and Joe an hour to get the wagons loaded and the horses hitched. Trying to keep the mud out of the wagons slowed them down. Finally, they were ready to roll.

Joe clucked his tongue and rippled the reins to get the team moving. The air hung thick and steamy as the day wore on, until they crossed over beyond the storm line. Then the cracked ground was hard and dry, which made it easier for the horses to pull the wagons. Cookie and Joe took turns taking a nap as they traveled.

Built-up tension drained from Joe's shoulders that evening as most of the crew found the chuck wagon long enough to eat supper even though the herd was still northeast of the camp.

Bob Fife took over as trail boss. He sent riders out to search for Thursgood. They couldn't stop the herd as another herd was only a couple of days behind them and they needed to stay ahead of it.

Standing next to the fire and lost in thought about Henry Thursgood, Joe stared into the flames and stroked his cheek feeling the stubble as he hadn't shaved for a couple of days. Henry's horse had probably thrown him—he could be injured or dead. They might never know.

It took days to gather the scattered cattle. They passed Duncan's Store, which was off to the east of the trail, and traveled in a northeasterly direction. With the landmarks and markers put up by others ahead of them, it was easy to stay on the trail. A few days later, a rider from a trail herd several miles behind them, rode up to camp and reported that Henry Thursgood had broken his leg when his horse threw him. He was with a herd about five days behind them where his brother was the trail boss. Joe released a pent up breath at hearing Thursgood was all right.

The next morning they had the wagons rolling by daylight. Bob Fife rode alongside the chuck wagon asking questions about the trail. Joe noticed that Bob looked around to make sure they were out of hearing of any of the other riders. It surprised Joe how good it felt that someone wanted his advice.

They stopped at a small creek, faced with the usual work of getting supper ready for the drovers. It was hot, especially around the cooking fires. Sweat dripped into Joe's eyes and he mopped his brow with his sleeve. He picked up the two pots to fill with water.

Will walked up. "Here, let me take this one. You headed to fill them?"

Surprised, but appreciative, Joe responded, "Yeah, even with this heat the hands still want hot coffee."

Will laughed. "Don't make sense, does it?"

It did help to have someone carry one of the five-gallon pots full of water back to the fire. Joe recognized it as an act of friendliness on Will's part.

"Joe."

"Yes, Cookie?"

"We need a sweet for supper. What can you get together?"

Jeff rested close to the chuck wagon, using his saddle as a pillow. "Yeah, Little Cookie, what can you make for a sweet? I like your cooking."

"Well, Jeff, it doesn't take much to sweeten you up, so just about anything will do." Joe couldn't resist the joshing.

Several other riders sitting around chuckled.

"Well, what about it?" Cookie asked.

Joe leaned against the wheel of the chuck wagon. What could he make? "Can I use the last of the canned corn and eggs?"

"Use what you need. Those eggs need to be used before they go bad."

After Joe mixed the ingredients for the corn pudding, he put it to baking in a large Dutch oven. He wasn't worried about the riders liking his dessert. Put enough sugar in anything and they were bound to like it.

"Well, Joe, where's our sweet?" Jeff held out his plate for his serving.

"Have a little patience. It has to bake before we can serve it." Joe grinned.

"Well, see if it's ready. If we don't keep this bunch of cowhands happy, we'll have a riot on our hands," Cookie said.

Joe checked the corn pudding, which had turned a light brown on top. He lifted the big Dutch oven onto the worktable.

Cookie cautiously tasted a bit. A smile broke out on his wrinkled face as he licked the spoon. "Mmmm ... this is good."

"Come on, Cookie, let us have some." Will begged with his plate at the ready.

"Yeah, if it's that good we deserve some." Jeff added.

"What do you think, Joe? Should we let these lazy cowhands have some?" Cookie asked.

"Might as well." Joe grinned at the light banter.

"Come get your portion, you lazy cowpokes." Cookie yelled.

The riders all crowded around the worktable. Within minutes the Dutch oven was almost empty, leaving barely enough for the cook crew to have a serving each.

"Thanks, Joe," Jeff said.

"Appreciate it, Joe," several others hands said.

In the days following, Joe cooked up several recipes Nate and Smithy made back home on the ranch. He mixed up a sourdough funnel cake and let it rise over night, and the next morning they had light fluffy funnel cake, or pancakes, as some called them. Eaten with molasses or honey they were like a sweet. He got proficient at knowing exactly how many coals to put on top of the Dutch oven to get an even baking. His biscuits were now almost as flaky as Cookies'.

When he had time, he read the little book that Mrs. Purdy had given him. It was amazing how many of the things her brother wrote about he was now experiencing in his work. Joe was eager to try more of the recipes.

~

Joe stoked the fire as they prepared a noon meal. They hadn't had any rain since the storm that had caused the stampede. As they were at the end of June and facing July, everyone was irritable with all the heat, dryness, and dust.

"Billy," Cookie bellowed. "What are you doing under that wagon?"

The boy peered up at his boss from underneath the wrangler wagon. "It's shady."

"Your work is not under that wagon." Cookie wiped the sweat off his face with a flour sack. "I know it's hot, boy, but we got to get dinner ready so we can get on up the trail."

Joe felt for the boy. It was over hundred degrees in the shade and they worked at an open flame.

"Cookie—" Joe started.

"What?" Cookie snapped. "Oh, sorry. It's this heat. Go ahead."

"We could wet flour sacks and put them around our heads and necks. It'll help a bit." Joe already had the flour sacks out.

"I'll try anything." Cookie took one of the flour sacks, soaked it with water, and laid it over his head.

Joe did the same, feeling the cool water drizzle down his neck. A wet shirt didn't matter, as it would soon dry. He soaked another flour sack and handed it to Billy.

"We look a little silly but it feels cooler. Let's get this dinner served," Cookie said.

Joe looked forward to every stop at a creek. At least for a few minutes he could cool off.

It was just as hot for the riders out with the trail herd. It was less dusty riding with the chuck wagon but not by much. Joe tried not to be cranky with Billy and Cookie even though he sometimes found himself being impatient with especially Billy.

Cookie was cranky enough for all of them.

~

Bob Fife rode along side of the chuck wagon in the early morning air.

"You look worried, Bob." Cookie observed, as he slapped the reins to keep the horses prodding up the trail.

"Well, I'll tell you how it is. The hands are working but they question my orders. I don't have the authority to be in charge of the trail herd. It makes it hard to keep this crew going."

"Someone has to be in charge and the men know that," Cookie tried to assure him.

"I need to get them behind me." Bob took his hat off and wiped his brow with his shirtsleeve.

Joe shifted in his seat. "Why don't you get a letter of authority from Mr. Barnes?"

"What do you mean?" asked Cookie.

"Send someone on a fast horse to meet Mr. Barnes in Caldwell. I heard he was going to ride ahead and meet his daughter who is coming in by train from somewhere back east," Joe looked from Cookie to Bob.

"That's right." Bob put his hat back on and nodded.

"Wouldn't he want to give you authority to take over as trail boss? A rider with a couple of good horses could travel straight through and be there in four days, meet with Barnes and be back here within a week and a half. You can keep things together until then." Joe shifted again when Bob didn't answer. "Don't mind what I say, I'm just a helper on the chuck wagon."

Bob frowned at Joe, but his gaze remained intense. "Who would you send?"

Joe considered it. "I'd send Jim Finely." Joe liked Jim, a quiet twenty-year old. Short, slender, and wiry, he was the best rider in the outfit.

"Jim Finely?" Bob turned to Cookie. "Do you have a paper and pen?"

Cookie stopped the chuck wagon, found some paper and pen, and Bob wrote a letter, thanked them for their help, and then rode out to the herd to find Jim Finely.

"That was a good idea. What made you think of it?" Cookie asked Joe.

"It seemed reasonable. If there's a question about Bob Fife being in charge then get the question cleared up."

"Too bad you can't ride, Joe. You'd make a good trail boss."

"Thanks, but the truth is a trail boss has to be able to fork a horse." Joe sighed and looked out over the rolling grasslands of the Indian Territory. He had always assumed he would boss a trail herd someday.

"Well, you've become a good cook. You'll never have a problem getting work."

"I never knew it could be enjoyable to prepare food for others," Joe confessed.

"Yeah, a lot of folks think that men like us become cooks because we can't do anything else. What they don't understand is how satisfying it is to cook for a bunch of hard-working men and see them enjoy what you feed them. I don't know of anything I'd rather do."

~

The chuck wagon wheels creaked along. Joe never tired of looking at the countryside, filled with trees along the creeks, and the rolling prairie of tall grass. The route they traveled was rutted and beaten down by the thousands of cattle that had preceded them. Following the trail did not require much effort but guiding the horses with the uneven ground required constant attention.

They camped south of the Rock Creek Crossing on the Canadian River. Eight days after Jim Finely left the herd with the letter, just as the sun was setting, he rode back into camp one tired rider. With him, he carried a letter for Bob Fife from Matthew Barnes, giving Bob authority to be the trail boss.

~

Jeff Kingston rode in early the next day still favoring his arm in a sling. Joe remembered how long it had taken his hip to heal and how it still bothered him. He hoped Jeff didn't suffer the same fate.

Jeff tied his horse downwind from the chuck wagon. "You got any fresh coffee?"

"Just made." Joe got a mug for him.

"It's hot today. It was hot yesterday, and I would guess it'll be hot tomorrow." Jeff sipped the hot liquid.

"I suspect you're right." Joe laughed then went back to the worktable and started cutting the beef slab into steaks to fry up for supper.

"Hey!" Jeff yelled at someone over Joe's shoulder.

Joe turned around.

Curly, standing next to Jeff's horse, hit the horse on the nose. The gelding went wild and bucked in stiff legged jumps over to the men sitting beyond the coffee fire. Men scattered out of way of the flying hooves.

Joe grabbed a rope lying on a saddle beyond the chuck wagon. He threw the loop of the rope around the horse's neck and jerked it tight. The gray horse squealed in fury and tried to pull away. Joe handed the rope over to Will Ramsey, who stood behind him.

"Keep this pulled tight around his neck," Joe called over as he slowly walked toward the horse.

"Get back, you fool. That horse is dangerous," Will yelled.

Joe waved at him to stay back and turned his attention to the horse. He spoke softly and cooed at it.

The horse looked at him and stood shaking from the effort of his fury.

Joe gazed at the horse but avoided looking it directly in the eye. He slowly advanced a few more steps and then turned and started walking away. He looked back over his shoulder as the horse took a couple of steps toward him. Joe stopped, glanced back, and then turned away again. The horse took a couple of more steps toward him and stopped.

Joe turned and walked back to the trembling horse. He again spoke and cooed at the animal softly, reached under his neck, and slowly grabbed the reins. The satisfaction of caressing the horse's muzzle and feeling him calm served as a reminder of days gone by when he had worked hour after hour at training horses as he had worked on various ranches. He patted the horse's neck, handed the reins to Will, and took the rope off.

All of the men in camp stood, staring at him.

Jeff's eyes were wide as he looked from Joe to the horse. "How did you do that?"

"Do what?" Joe took a deep breath to calm down as he walked toward the chuck wagon.

"Talk that horse quiet. I've never seen anything like it." Jeff shook his head.

"He wasn't mad at us." He went back to the worktable to get the steaks ready.

"Most amazing thing I ever saw." Will rolled the rope up and placed it back by the saddle from where Joe had grabbed it.

"Joe didn't even know to be afraid of an enraged horse." Jeff looked at with a measured look as if he was seeing him in a new light.

"Or maybe he wasn't afraid," Jim Finely put in his two cents. "Did you see how he threw that rope? He's done that before."

They all looked back at Joe.

"There's more to our Little Cookie than meets the eye." Jim spoke again with a hint of humor in his voice.

Joe hoped there was still more to him than just being a cook's helper. In a way, he regretted the attention he'd drawn to himself, but he didn't see how he could've let the horse run wild and hurt someone.

"What do you think you were doing, Curly?" Jeff's angry shout caused Joe to turn and see the two men standing toe to toe. "Don't let me ever see you doing anything that stupid again."

Curly had his hand close to his revolver. "Or what? What will you do about it?"

Jeff leaned in almost nose to nose with the cowhand. In a quiet, stern voice, he said, "You don't want to find out, I promise you."

Joe was surprised with the sense of strength and menace that Jeff gave off. He hadn't known that the man had it in him.

Curly stepped back and looked around at the other men that were holding still, as if waiting to see what would happen. "I didn't mean anything by it. The horse bit me." He turned and disappeared among the horses tied up within the rope corral.

As Joe helped serve the dinner, most of the crew made some comment to him about the 'horse incident.'

Curly stepped up in line with his plate. "You had to pretend to be a cowhand, hey, Little Cookie."

"Yeah. Won't even get on a horse but still wants to show off." Frank said as they wandered off, laughing.

"Don't listen to them two." Jeff stepped up next in line. "I appreciate what you did. Someone could have gotten hurt or we might have had to shoot the horse."

"Thanks." Joe dropped an extra biscuit on Jeff's plate.

Joe felt the friendliness of Jeff's comment but had an uneasy feeling at the continued animosity coming from Curly and Frank. Joe wasn't sure just how mean they might get to satisfy their bullying.

The sun had yet to fully crest the horizon and Joe wished for a few more hours sleep as he worked alongside of Cookie to get the breakfast ready for the waiting men.

~

They were soon back on the trail with another hot afternoon in front of them. Cookie started out driving.

"You used to work a lot with horses?" Cookie's voice drew his attention.

"I've always liked working with horses but I guess that's behind me." Joe felt sick at his stomach with the regret of it.

"I don't know, Joe. You still got the gift. All you need is someone else riding for you and you do the training."

"I suppose that's something to think about. I surprised myself when I found I still had the touch. I used to break colts as a boy back on the ranch. My pa encouraged me to work on my ability with the horses, and through the years I've worked with a lot of them at the various ranches I've worked with." Joe had a vision of owning a small ranch where he gave directions and others did the breaking. Now that would be something to work toward.

"You lose your father?" Cookie guided the horse with a light touch on the reins.

"Yes and no. My pa is still alive as far as I know, but I left the ranch eleven years ago and haven't looked back. He's probably glad to be rid of me."

"What makes you think that?"

"It's hard to explain. My ma was always mad at me and my pa was caught in the middle. It was easier for me to leave and go my own way."

"You were young. What could've been so bad that you had to leave and not go back?" Cookie looked to be frowning but it was hard to tell in the midst of his wrinkled face.

How to answer? The truth was so raw. How could someone who hadn't been there understand? Joe didn't even understand and he'd lived it.

"I've never talked about it. I've always been sort of ashamed. I know it wasn't my fault but I still ... "

Cookie didn't say anything. Just listened.

Joe looked out over the prairie and told him about his ma: about the beatings with his pa's belt, that left his back bleeding, the things his ma called him, coming into his room, to sit and read aloud from the Bible about God's wrath for evil little boys. "So I left."

Cookie softly asked, "Where was your father?"

"He was always out on the range working with the cowhands. Pa never lifted a hand against me, it was always her."

"Do you hear from your folks?"

"Not in eleven years, and it's as much my fault as theirs because I never wrote home. I have a little sister. She was almost ten when I left." Hearing himself say it made it sound worse. "I know it's a weakness, but I won't face my ma. But no way will I ever walk back into that house with her there." Just talking about her produced an ache in his chest and a feeling of something repulsive crawling over his skin. No, he wasn't going to face her ever.

"It's been eleven years. Your sister will be almost grown."

Months had passed since Joe had even thought about the ranch up in the mountains, his father, or home. He didn't have a home. Memories made his chest ache. He always assumed he'd go back one day, but now he couldn't ride, so he saw no reason to go back. Or, maybe his reluctance was based on the look he expected to see on his father's face when he heard Joe could no longer ride. No, he wasn't ready for that.

~

At Silver City, they camped south of town, and planned to stay for the two days in order to cross the herd over the Canadian River.

Cookie took Billy into the small town for what supplies he could get at the trading post.

Joe had no desire to go. Instead, he gave some thought to making something special for the crew, and remembered the fritters Nate used to make back on the ranch. Joe mixed up a triple batch and set it aside to rise for an hour. Thinking of the wild greens he had noticed along the trail and having some time, he grabbed a picket and walked back along the trail picking enough for dinner. After washing the greens, he put them into the pot, added salt pork, and brought them to a boil. He placed two big skillets on the fire and put a smidgen of lard in the bottom. When the grease was sizzling, he dropped spoonfuls of dough into the skillets and fried up the ginger fritters. When they were a golden brown, Joe ladled them onto a platter.

Cookie was pleased when he returned. "Good idea to cook the greens. We need to have something green to fight off the scurvies."

"How was the town?" Joe gave Billy a couple of the ginger fritters to save him from sneaking them.

"The trading post didn't have much that we needed." Cookie ate a fritter and sipped coffee. "Mmmm... these are good. The boys will like these." He took another.

Joe grinned. "I thought they'd like something different." Cookie put the fritters in the wagon out of sight.

Cookie and Joe served the cowhands, then they set out the fritters. Cookie set about two dozen back. Within minutes, the platter was empty.

Joe scratched his neck. So much for two hours work, but the riders did seem to appreciate them.

Curly and Frank rode in from the herd that was half on this side and half on the other side of the Canadian river. After they had emptied their plates and had talked to the other boys, they came back up to the chuck wagon.

"The boys said there were cookies." Curly said.

"There was but they're all gone." Cookie frowned.

Joe looked at Cookie with a raised brow. The man didn't usually lie.

"Why didn't you save some back for us still with the herd?" asked Frank.

"Sorry, boys." Cookie didn't sound sorry.

They walked away disappointed. Cookie looked at Joe and winked.

"They need to learn to keep a civil tongue around the chuck wagon help." Cookie had his way of maintaining authority around the chuck wagon. Two more riders came in from the herd. Cookie dished up two plates of food and put three of the fritters on each of their plates. They went beyond the coffee fire and squatted on their heels to eat.

About that time, Curly spotted the fritters on their plates and let out a yell.

He came stomping up to Cookie. "I thought you said there weren't no fritters left!"

"Are you yelling at me?"

"You bet your life I'm yelling at you. You're holding out on me and I want to know why?" Curly's eyes beaded and his lips thinned.

The other riders looked up at Curly and then at Cookie as if waiting for something.

"I'm sure that it's beyond you to see the reasoning behind a lot of things given your unfortunate ability," Cookie said with a straight face.

"What do you mean?" Curly's brow knitted together.

Bob Fife rode up, dismounted, and walked over. "What's wrong Cookie?"

Cookie smiled. "I'm not aware anything is wrong. Is there something wrong, Curly?"

Curly curled his lip, and shook his head then walked back to his bedroll.

Bob watched him. "I heard about some sweet treat we got for supper. Is there any left?"

"Sure, for you." He placed three fritters on Bob's plate of food.

"Thanks." He took a bite of a fritter. "These are great. Why haven't you made these before?"

"Joe made them. It's his recipe."

"Thanks, Joe." Bob walked to the other side of the coffee fire to sit on a rock and eat his supper. Bob talked to the other riders and smiled as he held up one of the fritters before eating it. Curly, who sat close by him, glared at Joe with a look that made him determined not to get in the man's way.

Joe took his bedroll to the other side of the chuck wagon out of sight of Curly and Frank. He had no intention of getting in the middle of a scuffle over something as minor as a ginger fritter.

Chapter Twelve

Joe flicked the reins and clucked to keep the team moving. A slight, cool breeze blew across his face, bringing a welcome relief from the relenting heat.

Cookie climbed onto the seat after his morning nap, combing his thick gray hair with his fingers and carrying his hat. "Where are we?"

"We're just east of Caddo Spring headed toward the Cimarron River." Joe didn't think the effort that Cookie made to control his hair had much effect. He still looked like a wild man.

"The Cimarron can be running pretty full. Hopefully, we'll catch it at a good level for an easy crossing."

Bob rode up, alongside the chuck wagon. "We're less than an hour from the river. Santo just got back from looking it over. There's an Indian with a ferry. Get the wagons over and then set up camp a couple of miles north of the river."

Cookie handed him a cup of lukewarm coffee.

"I know a good campsite about two miles north near a creek that feeds into the river," Joe said.

Bob handed the cup back to Cookie. "Santo said the ferry is a small one, and you might have a problem with the wagons. You'll have to unhitch the horses and swim them over, so you'll have to push the wagons off and on the ferry. Frank and George can help with the horses." Bob rode off toward the herd.

Joe understood why Bob chose George and Frank to help. They weren't the best cowhands, and the trail boss needed plenty of help to keep the herd swimming straight across. If they didn't keep a tight control, the cattle would become a milling circle in the middle of the river.

They made it to the river crossing by mid-afternoon.

"Joe, go tell Billy to unhitch his team and come help us push this wagon onto the ferry."

"Sure thing, Cookie." Joe winced as he awkwardly climbed down from the wagon. He rubbed his aching hip as he limped back to talk to Billy.

Joe turned as George and Frank rode up. "You fellows think you can get both teams across at once or do you need to take them one at a time?"

Frank snarled up the corner of his lip and frowned. "We can handle a couple of teams. Don't you worry any about it, Little Cookie."

Joe ignored the sarcasm in Frank's voice. All he wanted was the teams taken across the river.

Billy stayed with the wrangler wagon while Cookie and Joe rode the chuck wagon across on the ferry. After they got the first wagon hitched and moving up the bank, Joe rode back across on the ferry ready to help get the wrangler wagon rolled onto the ferry and then helped the ferryman pull on the rope to get across the river.

When they got to the other, George and Frank sat on their horses, holding the reins of the horse team they had to swim across the river.

"You fellows want to help push this wagon off the ferry?" Joe called out.

"No, we don't. Just get these horses so we can get going." Frank yelled back.

Joe bit his tongue to hold back an angry retort. With Billy's and the ferryman's help, they got the wagon off the ferry.

George and Frank, with a lot of grumbling and yelling at Billy, shuffled over to the wagon and got the team hitched up. Then they remounted and turned their horses to ride north after the chuck wagon.

"Bob said you fellows were to go back and help get the herd across. That's in the other direction." Joe shouted.

They shot him surly looks, then rode to where the cattle crossed the river.

Billy watched them ride away, concern reflected on his face. "You better watch out for Frank and Curly. They don't like you."

"I will. Thanks for the warning."

When they caught up with Cookie, Joe gave the reins of the wrangler wagon back to Billy, got down, and climbed up beside Cookie. They stopped a couple miles up the trail where a creek flowed toward the Cimarron River. Scrub oaks provided a little shade and lots of firewood. Tall cottonwoods grew around the stream. Their leaves made a soft, comforting sound in the light breeze almost like the sound of a light rain on a forest. The place was excellent for camping and the herd could bed down beyond the creek, downstream from the chuck wagon.

Joe worked without stop to help get the camp set up and supper ready, preparing extra so they'd be ahead for the next day. The cowhands came in for supper in shifts. The clean up was delayed because Billy had to wait for all the hands to eat before he could finish washing the dishes.

Darkness fell by the time Billy was able to go down to the creek and fill the water barrels for the next day's travel. Joe suspected the boy was uneasy about going down to the creek in the dark. "Come on, Billy. I'll help you get the water barrels filled."

After hitching the team back to the wrangler wagon, they hung several lanterns on the sides. With the barrels from the chuck wagon, they had three to fill.

Joe drove as close to the creek as he could without rolling into the water. The lanterns gave them light, along with the full moon. He waded out into the water with a couple of buckets and filled them. Billy took them and emptied the water into the barrels. It took a while, but they were filling the last barrel when Curly and Frank rode up.

"Where's our bedrolls?" Curly yelled at Billy who stood by the wagon in the light of the lantern.

Curly and Frank glared at Billy and didn't seem to be aware of that Joe stood in the shadows.

Swinging down from his mount, Curly climbed into the back of the wagon. "Where's my bedroll?" He bumped the barrel at the back of the wagon and sloshed water onto his bedding.

"Look what you've done now." He stepped down from the wagon, swung at Billy, and knocked him to the ground. Before Joe could get to him, Curly kicked Billy in the stomach, and then in the chest.

Joe hurled the bucket at Curly. "Stop it! Leave him alone." Billy was still a kid and far too inexperienced to leave him in the hands of someone as mean as Curly.

The man turned to Joe, rubbing his arm where the bucket hit him. "Well, well, look what we got here." He stepped toward Joe.

Frank dismounted from his horse.

"Hey, Frank. Don't you think it's time we taught this Little Cookie a thing or two?"

Frank didn't say anything, but Joe sensed that he was the more dangerous of the two. The two of them moved toward him. Joe backed up, staying out of Curly's reach.

Frank stepped in, swung, and landed a solid blow on Joe's jaw, which exploded with pain. Joe tasted blood where his teeth cut the inside of his mouth. He stumbled back, barely saving himself from a fall. A wild fury filled the pit of his stomach, and he vowed to do as much damage as he could.

Frank lunged toward him and pulled his fist back for another blow.

Joe ducked under Frank's arm as he threw another punch at him and drove his fist into Frank's gut. When Frank groaned and doubled over, Joe grinned.

Joe turned toward Curly and managed to lean away from a thick, swinging three-foot long branch. With Curly off balance, Joe slugged him in the face and felt the soft cartilage of Curly's nose give way.

Curly yelled and covered his nose. When he drew his hands away, they were covered in blood.

Joe shook the pain out of his own hand and stared Curly down.

"You'll be sorry you did that." Curly yelled as he lifted the branch again. A scarlet stream ran from one nostril and stained his shirt.

Both men rushed Joe. He tried to scramble back, but a kick to his bad leg landed him on the ground.

Curly swung the tree branch, catching Joe along the side of his head. A blast of pain exploded. Then another blow and another.

Each blow, each kick battered him into a whole mess of pain. Joe's world spun. He tried to scramble away—to get to his feet, but he couldn't. There was no escape.

Somewhere amidst blows and the pain, the ground crunched beneath the wagon wheels as they rolled away. Billy had run off and left him. Joe's heart sank. Would they actually kill him now?

Frank continued to kick him. Pain seared through his body. Joe thanked his lucky stars that their focus was on his leg and not his injured hip.

A blow to his face snapped his attention to Curly who kicked him again. The assault continued. Each blow brought a new jolt of pain. The kicks were continuous and so swift, he couldn't tell whose boots were doing the most damage.

After awhile the attack blurred along with faces of his tormentors. Blissfully, a well of black nothingness beckoned and he surrendered.

~

Joe became aware of lying on the ground. Cloaked in quiet the only thing he could hear was the sound of the flowing creek. With the moonlight, he vaguely made out the branches of the trees overhead. Something was wrong with his eyes. Feeling peaceful and removed from his body, he seemed to float rather than lay on the ground. From a vast distance, he heard voices calling his name and wanted to answer, but couldn't muster the strength.

"Joe, where are you? Joe, answer us." He heard Cookie call.

"I know it was here, Cookie, I know it was." Why was Billy crying? Had Curly and Frank beat on the boy, too?

Someone knelt next to him. "Over here, fellows, over here. He's hurt bad." The voice sounded like Jeff's.

Joe could barely make out the dark figures of several riders standing around him holding lanterns. When strong hands lifted him, Joe screamed in pain and blackness swallowed him again.

~

Joe became aware of the feel of a cool cloth against his skin.

Cookie's voice seemed to be floating at a distance. "Joe, you're in the chuck wagon, so I can get your wounds cleaned up and keep an eye on you."

He was vaguely surprised. Cookie never let anyone sleep in the chuck wagon but him.

"Cookie ..." Joe croaked. He needed water.

"I'm here. You're back at camp now. Don't you worry about anything." Joe could hear the concern in the older man's voice.

"In my carryall there's a black bag . . . with medicine for pain." He managed to whisper.

"Billy, get me Joe's carryall," Cookie yelled.

"I wish you wouldn't yell," Joe s voice was barely audible to even his own ears.

"Why is that, son?" Cookie wiped the blood away from the cuts on Joe's face.

"It makes my head hurt. I can't see very well."

"With that bump on your noggin and these cuts, I see why your head hurts. And with your eyes swollen almost shut, it's no wonder you can't see."

Joe heard someone scrambling over the wagon seat. "Here ya go, Cookie." Billy had returned with the carryall Dr. Rupert had given Joe. Cookie fished through it.

A hand lifted Joe's head. A cup touched his lips. He opened his mouth and drank the familiar, bitter stuff down.

"Now, that will help." Cookie continued to clean the cuts and put on bandages.

Thank the Lord for Dr. Rupert and his pain medicine, and for Cookie .... Joe drifted off as the pain receded.

~

Toward early morning, Joe woke. His throat and tongue were bone dry, and he could barely speak. "Water...water."

"Here you go." Cookie quickly had a cup to his lips.

Joe guessed the older man had been sitting at his side all night. "Thanks, Cookie. Sorry to be a problem," Joe said groggily.

"Don't you worry about it. Curly and Frank have taken off, but if I ever see their sorry faces again, they'll wish I hadn't." He spoke through a clenched jaw. "Billy told us that you got into it because you stopped Curly from beating on the boy. The riders are all angry. They're talking about what to do to Curly and Frank if they see them again."

"Sorry I won't be able to help with breakfast." He didn't see how he could be ready to work by daylight, but he ought to work. It was his job.

"Don't worry about it. I'll manage. Bob will get one of the riders to help. You need to rest."

Joe tried to take a deep breath but the pain in his chest was a vise clamping off the flow of air. He made an effort to stifle a groan, but didn't quite manage it. Cookie got more of the powder from the medicine bag and mixed it in water. "Here, drink this. I can tell you're hurting."

"How bad am I hurt?" Before he heard an answer, the pain went away and he slipped back into the darkness.

Chapter Thirteen

Morning light filtered through the canvas above Joe's head. The riders' voices drifted in from around the wagon as the men began their workday, but Joe didn't care that he wasn't out doing his duty. He hurt, all over, and only wanted to lie there. He feared what new pain he'd feel if he tried to rise.

Bob Fife appeared at the front of the chuck wagon. "You awake?" He pushed his hat back and revealed black curly hair.

"Yeah, sort of." Joe pressed his hands on the bedroll on top of the sacks of beans, oats, and flour and tried to sit up but a pincer grip in his midsection seized him.

"No, don't bother yourself. I just wanted to check on you."

"I'm all right. Just a little bruised and cut." Joe didn't want to admit to Bob how wretched he felt.

"We've looked for Curly and Frank, but they're gone. Can you tell me what happened?"

Joe didn't want to talk about it. He hadn't been able to defend himself and that bothered him more than the pain gripping his body. But Bob was the boss, so he guessed he had a right to know.

Joe told him about Curly and Frank beating Billy. "I might have managed one, but with two of them I didn't do too good." He ended the story there, preferring to forget the next part.

"Then what?" Bob pressed.

"Well, between the tree branch Curly was swinging and Frank's boots, I caved in. I did land one good punch in Frank's gut. And I managed to give Curly a bloody nose, but beyond that I didn't do much damage." Joe shuddered inwardly as heat crept up his neck with the admission that he hadn't been able to hold his own.

He remembered a time before his accident—fights he had been in and how he had done much better. He had taken pride in how well he could handle himself in a fistfight. But he could maneuver on his feet back then. He didn't share with Bob that his bum leg was the reason Curly and Frank were able to get the better of him.

"Give me a day or so, and I'll be able to get back to work." Joe wanted to get Bob off the subject of the beating.

"Don't worry about the work. I can get somebody else to help. Take the time you need to get back on your feet. Cookie says to ask you if you could eat something. He has oatmeal and biscuits for breakfast."

Joe shook his head. "I don't want anything." Just the thought of food made his stomach lurch. The smell from the cook fire didn't help either. The beating Curly and Frank administered had left his stomach bruised and sore to the touch.

"How about some coffee?" Bob asked.

"Water is all I want."

Bob disappeared, but Joe heard him speaking with Cookie.

"He'd like some water," Bob told Cookie. "His face looks bad, and a couple of those cuts look deep. It's his chest and stomach that concern me. I've never seen such bruising, not even on fellows that have been kicked by a horse."

"Yeah, he'll have some scars, I'm afraid."

Joe winced. Cookie must not know that Joe could hear him.

"I don't know how badly he's hurt, but we need to give him a few days to rest. The reason he can't eat is that the kicks to his stomach bruised him all up inside."

"No problem, Cookie. He takes whatever time he needs to get over this beating. I regret we didn't catch Curly and Frank. I can't afford to send any riders after them. We got to keep the cattle moving, but I'm going to send word up and down the trail to the other outfits. I'd be surprised if they can get another job on the trail this year after the drovers hear what they did."

"Joe's the finest helper I've ever had. This is the best-fed bunch of riders because of him. I hate to say it, but he could do my job with no problem," Cookie said. "Let me see if I can get him to eat something and then we'll prepare to pull out."

"I'll have the boys help you get hitched up. Are all the water barrels filled?" Bob asked.

"Jeff helped Billy this morning with the water, and some of the boys filled the cradle with wood. We're in good shape."

In a few minutes, Cookie appeared at the front of the wagon holding a canteen.

"Morning. How are you feeling, besides sore as all get out?"

"Kind of banged up to tell the truth." Joe accepted the canteen of water.

"Keep the canteen with you."

"If I can have a day or so, I'll be all right." After taking a small swallow of water, Joe put the cap back on the canteen and then put it down close to the bedroll.

"We're going to pull out in a few minutes. Can I get you something to eat?"

"No thanks. Let me rest a bit. Maybe by the noon stop I'll feel like I can eat."

"You let me know if you want anything else." The older man disappeared from Joe's view as he climbed down from the wagon.

Beside the cuts and bruises, Joe was sure he had at least a couple of broken ribs. His head throbbed. Being jostled about in a bouncing wagon for the next several hours wouldn't make it any better.

By the time Cookie stopped to get the dinner ready, Joe hurt bad. He wanted to ask Cookie for another dose of white powder, but didn't want to get too used to it. He would just have to ride out the pain, jaw clenched. Still refusing food, he gently rubbed his stomach. The thought of food coming back up made him break out in a sweat. Since he wasn't doing any work, he could manage a day or so without eating.

Joe dozed off and on throughout the hot afternoon. It was hotter to lie on the bedroll on top of the crates and bags of food than to sit on the wagon seat, where at least there was a little breeze as the canvas was billowing, but he wasn't up to sitting yet.

Through the long day, Joe pondered the trip. They'd been on the trail for thirty-eight days and had about three or four more weeks to go to reach the trail's end. He didn't particularly look forward to the end of the drive. He enjoyed the hard work and he had been too busy to consider what he would do after they delivered the herd at the trail's end.

After the trail drive was over, he saw . . . nothing. Maybe he could try to get on with another herd. He'd been extremely fortunate so far. Cookie was a tough boss, but Joe respected him and sensed that Cookie had grown to respect him. If he couldn't get on with another outfit ... he just didn't know.

Joe woke up when the wagon lurched to a stop. Every muscle in his body ached and it hurt too much even to wipe the sweat out of his eyes. Therefore, he lay there listening to the sounds of the camp being set up. Cookie must have stopped the chuck wagon about ten miles north of the Cimarron. He heard the hands drifting by for coffee. The chuck wagon rocked as someone climbed up onto the wagon seat. He looked to the front of the wagon and saw Bob Fife with a stranger.

"How are you doing?" Bob asked.

"I'm making it," Joe answered in a voice that sounded weak even to him.

"I want to you to meet Matthew Barnes. He owns the cattle we've been driving north. He and his daughter arrived from Caldwell with the supply wagon."

Barnes was a short, stocky man in his late fifties with gray hair and a big handlebar mustache that dominated his face. He looked like a solid, intelligent man. His good-looking brown leather jacket and Stetson hat gave an air of prosperity.

"Hello, Joe. I heard what happened and I wanted to see how you're doing."

"Glad to meet you sir." Joe tried not to grimace as he tried to sit up.

"No, don't disturb yourself. Cookie gave me the details of your injuries, and I can see for myself. Anything we can do for you before we go eat?" Mr. Barnes asked.

Joe held up the almost empty canteen. "Maybe you could get Billy to put some fresh water in this."

Bob reached across the wagon seat and took the canteen. "Sure, and Cookie said to tell you he's made some soup for you, and intends that you eat something."

"Thanks for the warning." Joe's answering grin turned into a grimace, as he had a couple of cuts on his lips. "It's good to meet you, Mr. Barnes. You going to stay with us awhile?"

"Yes, we'll stay with the herd for the next couple of weeks, and then I'll ride on to finalize the sale ahead of the herd." Barnes stared at Joe's injuries.

Joe wished they would go away and leave him in peace.

"See you later," Bob said.

Joe waved weakly at them.

Mr. Barnes and Bob climbed down from the wagon.

Again, their conversation drifted in to where Joe rested. He stifled a little guilt because he wasn't normally a person who listened to other's conversations. As he turned on his side to ease the pain, he still hear the men.

"Cookie, I know you told me he'd been beaten up bad, but I'd no idea. His face is a mess. And those bruises on his chest and stomach ... he seemed to be in a lot of pain. You sure he's going to be all right?"

"Well, I'm no doctor, but he seems to just be cut and bruised. The worst is his head, and then probably a couple of broken ribs. He has a bad leg, and they kicked it black and blue hoping that was a way to hurt him. It'll heal in a week or so. He's not been on his feet yet, so I don't know if it'll affect his walking. But until his head clears up some, and those ribs heal a little, he can't do the work he was doing."

"Bob said that Joe has been a real help in getting the herd up the trail after Thursgood got hurt. I'm not sure how a cook's helper has been all that helpful. You have him take the time he needs. Maybe my daughter, Sara, can help some with the chores until he can get back on his feet. She's good in the kitchen."

His daughter Sara! Joe remembered he had said something about his daughter being with him. A little girl taking his job wasn't easy to contemplate. Moreover, what was the man thinking to bring a girl on a cattle drive? They had a good bunch of riders, but to bring his daughter among them after they had been on the trail for almost two months wasn't wise. However, Barnes was the owner and could do what he wanted.

Billy climbed into the wagon with a canteen full of fresh water. "You all right?" The boy stared at him with big, rounded brown eyes.

"Thanks." Joe took the canteen. "I'm okay, a little cut and bruised. Nothing I won't get over." Joe managed a half smile.

Billy dropped his gaze, sighed, and his shoulders slumped. "I didn't know what to do. They were so quick and mean. All I could think was to go get Cookie quick. So I lit out. I thought they kilt you and it was my fault."

Joe understood what the night before had been like for young Billy. He'd not run away scared, leaving him to deal with Curly and Frank. He'd done what he knew to do—get help. Billy would've been no match for Curly and Frank. He just would've got himself hurt bad.

"You done right, Billy. Don't you worry none. I couldn't have handled it any better myself," Joe assured him.

"You know we got a woman in camp?" Billy blurted.

"I heard that Mr. Barnes' daughter was with him. What's she like?" Joe wouldn't have asked any other man on the drive.

"She's real pretty with blond hair and blue eyes. And she smiles a lot."

"How old is she?" Maybe she wasn't such a little girl.

"I don't know for sure. Kinda young but kinda old. I mean she's older than me, but not like as old as my ma."

"You hear anyone say why she's here with Mr. Barnes?"

"She got out of something called a finished school, where she was for three years in a place called Boston." Billy frowned as if trying to remember what he'd heard. "Mr. Barnes sold their ranch in Texas, so they don't have a home, until he buys another place, so I guess she has to stay with him for now."

"You think she might be eighteen years old?" If Sara Barnes had completed a finishing school for young ladies, she was probably about that age.

"I guess so. She's real pretty, Joe. You wait until you see her. Nice pretty clothes and curly blonde hair all gathered in a net at the back of her head ... and a straw hat." Billy's eyes glowed.

Billy had the look of someone already smitten. Joe stifled a smile. It didn't take much when the crew went months without even seeing a woman.

Billy, once he started talking, kept on. "Her ma died when she was just a baby, and she don't have no brothers or sisters. It's been her and Mr. Barnes. She didn't want to go to the school back east, but Mr. Barnes made her. Or, at least that's what I heard her tell Cookie. She and Cookie have met before."

"Billy," Cookie yelled from outside.

Joe cocked his head. "You'd better go help Cookie. With me laid up, he's short-handed and needs your help. Come visit me later."

Billy scrambled down and out of sight.

Joe lay there and wished he could hurry the healing. He dozed on and off, which he'd done most of the day. It was a little easier now that the wagon had stopped and it was cooler. He heard voices outside the chuck wagon, but couldn't keep track of what was said.

"Come and get it," Cookie yelled to the cowhands. After awhile the sounds died down. Joe lay with his face turned toward the back of the wagon and his eyes closed. The wagon rocked as someone climbed up onto the seat. He assumed it was Cookie, come to get something. No one spoke. Suddenly a feather-light touch brushed over his cheek.

"Joe?" a soft female voice spoke.

He opened his eyes and gazed up at the face of the prettiest girl he had ever seen.

Chapter Fourteen

The pretty girl smiled at him. "I'm Sara Barnes. Cookie asked me if I would bring you some soup."

"Hello." He suddenly realized he was lying on the bedroll without shirt or pants. He only had a light blanket pulled up to his waist. Joe was also acutely aware that he was unshaven because of all the bruises and cuts on his face. Here he was a mess and meeting the first young woman he'd seen in two months. He grabbed the blanket to pull it up higher.

She put her free hand over his and stopped him. "Now, Joe. You don't have to be embarrassed. It's too hot for a blanket. Maybe even too hot for Cookie's soup. He told me I wasn't to come back until you ate it because you haven't eaten since day before yesterday. Can you sit up?" She put the bowl of soup down on a crate.

Her voice sounded like music. Joe hadn't heard a young lady's voice in so long. And as he looked at her and listened to the sound of her voice he sensed she was a lady of refinement.

He struggled to sit up but the pain in his ribs made it difficult.

She touched his shoulder, and pushed him back down. "I can see that sitting is too painful. I'll help you eat and try not to spill any hot soup on you."

"I can feed myself. I don't want you to trouble yourself—" He didn't want to admit it, but his body had taken such a beating that he did need help. But, from a pretty girl?

"Of course, you can feed yourself, but for once let someone else have the enjoyment of helping you." She took the bowl and filled the spoon. She gently held it to his lips. He had no choice but to swallow the creamy beef soup.

It was delicious. The best Cookie had made on the trail. Her feeding him gave him a reason to look at her face and hair without seeming rude. Billy was right; she was beautiful with her golden hair and deep blue eyes. The curls escaping from the ribbon holding her hair back tempted him. A fella just needed to push them back, Joe caught himself before he reached up and touched them.

She fed him until the bowl was empty.

"Thanks, I was hungry and didn't realize it." He appreciated her help. He just didn't like needing it.

"Would you like some more?"

"No, thank you, that's plenty."

Billy appeared at the front of the wagon with a basin of hot water and a cloth and handed it to Sara. "Cookie asked me to give this to you, Miss Barnes. The brown jar is the medicine he told you about."

"Thank you, Billy." She sat the basin on the crate and handed the soup bowl to Billy before he disappeared.

"Cookie asked me if I'd wash your cuts as he's so busy. I've worked some as a doctor's helper. And I've helped my father often as he cared for injured ranch hands." Sara wet the cloth in the basin and rubbed it with a piece of lye soap.

He didn't know what to say. He'd not had a woman help take care of him in his memory except for Mrs. Purdy. At the home ranch, as a child, Nate and Smithy took care of cuts and bruises.

"I'm not sure it's proper for you to do that, Miss Barnes." Joe took a deep breath, but stopped abruptly as it hit the pain in his side.

"Proper? Of course, it's proper. You need those cuts cleaned and I'm the only person around with no other chores to do. So no protest, all right?" She gently sponged the cuts and bruises on his face. She took some salve from the brown jar and spread it on the cuts.

She had a softer touch than Cookie. Joe closed his eyes and enjoyed the sensation of the warm wet cloth on his bruised, hurting face. He drew in a breath and caught the faint scent of flowers.

She moved to the cuts on his head.

They must have been more difficult to see because of his hair. Those areas were more sensitive and painful and without thinking, Joe winced and groaned.

She immediately stopped. "I'll try to be gentler."

Joe opened his eyes and looked at her face, so close to his and decided that a little pain was worth having the sight of her beautiful blue eye examining him with such a soft look.

She leaned over to reach the cuts on his head.

"Don't worry. Do what you have to." As she leaned toward him to wash his cuts, he caught the faint scent of soap and flowers, maybe gardenias and hyacinths.

"Well, for now I'll put some of this salve on the cuts on your head and tomorrow give them a better cleaning. Let's look at these cuts and scratches on your arms and chest." She washed a particularly deep cut on his upper chest. She was so matter-of-fact about it that Joe lost his embarrassment, although he clenched his teeth against the sting of the salve.

"What about your legs? Do you have cuts there also?" She turned toward his legs allowing him a silhouette-like view of her form. She was definitely a fine figured young woman.

As he averted his eyes, his embarrassment came back in a hurry at the thought of her touching his legs.

Without waiting for him to answer, she pulled the blanket up to mid thigh.

"Joe, are you aware that your right leg is a solid mass of bruises? I'd heard you had been in a fight, but this looks more like someone repeatedly kicked your leg." She gently washed the bruises and cuts. The cool salve after an initial sting felt good on the cuts.

"Yeah, well, I guess they stomped on that leg pretty good." Should he tell her about his hip now? He might as well get it over with. Joe suspected in her world that would decrease her respect for him.

"I got a bad leg there and they knew it. They thought they could hurt me worse on that leg. They didn't know that the problem is with my hip and not the leg itself." Joe waited for her response.

"How many were there?" She finished washing and doctoring his legs and pulled the blanket back over them.

"Oh, there were only two. Most fellows could have handled them, but I can't maneuver easily and they got me on the ground. The tree branch on the head, that was what won it for them. I had them until then." He grinned wanting to lighten the conversation.

"Oh, a tree branch on the head." She smiled back. "Has your leg always been this way or was it an injury?" Sara frowned. "Oh, I'm sorry. I have no business asking such questions."

"It's all right for you to ask. It happened last year. A bull trampled me, crushed my hipbone, and broke me up inside. The leg didn't heal right. I can't sit a horse. I was a cowhand for the last ten years ... but I can't ride anymore." Joe looked away from her. He didn't want to see pity in her eyes. When he glanced back, he only saw interest. His sore muscles relaxed a bit. He'd told it and it hadn't seemed to make a difference. It just was.

"Can I get you anything else?" She gathered the basin and cloth. "I need to go help Cookie if I can and then get to bed. I'm not used to trail hours yet and morning will come very early for me."

"Thanks for your help. I appreciate it, Miss Barnes."

"If I may call you Joe, you may call me Sara. I hope you sleep well and I'll see you in the morning." In spite of her long dress, she climbed gracefully over the wagon seat, and before she disappeared from view, she waved and smiled.

Joe lay there amazed. It was like a dream. He'd just told one of his most personal secrets to a beautiful woman.

In the middle of the night, someone groaned. He woke to realize it was him. Cookie was there with a lantern on.

"Cookie?" Joe was not sure for moment where he was or what was going on. Then the pain hit. He groaned before he realized it.

"Where are you hurting, Joe?" Cookie mixed some more of the white powder with some water in a cup.

"All over. All my muscles are seizing up all at once." He gasped as another spasm hit him. The pain was so intense that he couldn't breathe for a moment.

"The muscles are reacting to the beating. I've seen this before. It'll pass in a day or two and then you'll get better quickly." He put his big hand gently behind Joe's head and raised it.

Joe drank the bitter medicine that Dr. Rupert had so thoughtfully provided. Good old Doc.

Cookie lowered Joe's head back to the rolled up blanket he used for a pillow.

Joe could only whisper with the pain. "Sorry to keep you up, you need your sleep." The medicine began to take effect.

Cookie rested his hand on Joe's forehead. "Don't you worry. I get all the sleep I need."

The medicine held the pain at bay. With a sigh of relief, Joe fell asleep.

~

He woke to full daylight and the sound of voices outside the wagon.

"I'd rather not wake him. He'd a bad night of it. We can start and then when he wakes up I'll stop and get him to eat something." Cookie's voice carried into the wagon.

"Papa, let me ride with Cookie and then I can help him take care of Joe. It'll give Cookie and me a chance to visit." Sara lilting soft feminine voice drifted to Joe's ears. He could listen to the sound all day.

"All right, Sara, I plan to ride out with the herd anyway so you might as well ride with Cookie." Mr. Barnes' voice held a brusque deep growl almost. It was a voice used to commanding and being obeyed. Once heard, it was not easy to forget.

Joe, shaky and weak, didn't want to move. The spasms from the night before were gone, along with some of the pain. He lost track of time.

The sun burned higher in the sky and the heat of the day was collecting in the bouncing wagon when he woke. The murmur of Sara and Cookie talking drifted softly from the wagon seat, but he couldn't catch what they were saying over the noise of the horses, harnesses, and things in and on the wagon banging and creaking.

He let his gaze roam the wagon as each new sound caught his attention. Shifting, trying to find a position that didn't ache clear to the bone, he heard the canteen fall and he couldn't find it. Thirst was constant with the heat of the day and he supposed a fever, although it was hard to tell.

Sara climbed carefully over the wagon seat and sat down on a hundred pound sack of beans. "Good morning, sleepy head. How are you?" She smiled.

He could get used to waking up to a face like hers. He quickly shoved such a thought back. No use in tormenting himself by going down a hopeless road.

"I'm all right, a little thirsty. Do you see the canteen?"

She found it and took the cap off.

What was she doing? She slid her hand under his head and raised it, so he could drink out of the canteen.

He drank thirstily. "Thanks." He smelled again the fresh soap and a slight fragrance of flowers.

She lowered his head and slid her hand out from under it.

"How's our boy?" Cookie called back to them as he drove the wagon.

"He seems to be better, just weak and maybe a little fever." Sara smiled at Joe.

"Do I need to stop, or can he wait for something to eat until noon?" Cookie asked.

"I can wait." The last thing on Joe's mind at the moment was food.

Sara wet a cloth with water from the canteen and wiped his face and neck with gentle caresses, avoiding the cuts.

Joe noted her slender soft hands. The urge to touch them was powerful. His hands would easily swallow them. He was hot. He didn't know if it was from fever or because it was another hot summer day, or being too close to Sara. "That feels good." He closed his eyes and enjoyed the sense of coolness, if only for a brief time.

"Drink some more water. That will help." She lifted his head again.

He drank as much as he could and then lay, taking shallow breaths to keep the pain from his ribs at bay.

Sara poured the rest of the water from the canteen onto the cloth and then lightly sponged his chest and neck with the sopping cloth. She made no effort to dry his chest, but let the moisture cool the skin.

He again closed his eyes to enjoy the sensation and started to drift off again. Not a polite thing to do to a pretty girl but he couldn't seem to help himself.

The rest of the day passed with heat, pain, and dozing in and out.

At the noon stop, Sara again fed him some soup. She washed the cuts and bruises. "I've never seen such a variety of colors from bruises, but hopefully it means that you're healing."

Evening found them stopped in a dry camp south of springs full of alkaline. Bob had riders stop the herd far enough south that the cattle had not yet smelled the water.

Bob climbed up on the wagon seat and looked back at him. "Hey, Joe. How are you doing?"

That seemed to be everyone's question as they greeted him. He was a little tired of it. "I'm doing better. I hope to be up tomorrow."

"That's great." Bob sounded surprised.

"That's my plan. Now whether I can do it we'll see tomorrow." Joe grinned.

"You mind if I ask you a question?" He looked around as if to see if anyone else was behind him.

"No, ask away."

"Well, we're about four miles south of the alkaline springs and I'm concerned about what to do because the cows are thirsty and as soon as they smell the water it'll be hard to get them past the springs without letting them drink. And you know as well as I do that the alkaline water there is so strong that the results will be that a lot of cattle will die. How would you get the herd around the springs without going a long, dry way around?"

"I don't know if you'll like my idea, but I'd probably stampede the herd right on past the springs. Before they've fully smelled the water you deliberately start the herd running, and keep them running, until you're north of the springs. I was with another trail herd a couple of years back and that's what that trail boss did."

"You're right. I don't like the idea, but it may be the best solution. We'll probably lose some of the herd, but not as many as we'll lose if we let them near that water. How far beyond the springs to we have to keep them running?"

"Far enough so they won't turn back and go back to the springs, at least a couple miles. Have Santo ride ahead and to see if there's water in the creek beyond the springs. If there is then I'd keep the cows moving until I got to the creek."

"There's a creek not too far north of the springs?"

"There's a creek, but it doesn't always have water. Depends on what rain they've had upstream. But if Santo rode ahead and brought word back to you, you could plan better."

"Thanks, Joe. Mr. Barnes expects me to know what to do, and to tell you the truth, I've never had to make decisions like this before. I know how much you have helped on this drive, even if Mr. Barnes doesn't."

Bob's voice held an edge to it. Had he been arguing with his boss? Joe hoped he wasn't the cause of it. Being laid up wasn't a good way to impress the owner of the herd. He had to get back on his feet as soon as possible. Barnes wouldn't put him off the trail drive in the middle of nowhere, but he might at the next settlement if Joe couldn't get back to work.

Joe sighed, "I'm glad to help. It makes me feel more useful, especially now that I'm laid up."

"I'll let you know what Santo comes back with and what we are going to do." Bob promised.

"I'd have the chuck wagon horses watered from the drinking barrels. We can't run as easily with the stampede, and it'll be harder to keep the team from becoming a runaway right to the alkaline springs."

"You're right again. I'll talk to Cookie." Bob climbed out of the wagon.

Joe was tired of being enclosed in the wagon and also tired of hurting. He let himself think about Sara to distract himself. Did she have a fellow somewhere? The way they met was about the worst way for a man to meet a pretty girl and hope to make a good impression. No, he had no hope of impressing her. With that unpleasant thought, he gingerly turned over and stared at the side of the canvas of the wagon. Life wasn't fair, but it wasn't the first time he'd decided that.

Chapter Fifteen

Joe woke to a morning that promised another hot day. He felt rested for the first time in days. The terrible pain and nausea had abated somewhat. After Bob and Santo climbed onto the wagon seat, he waved to them weakly.

"Tell Joe what you found," Bob told Santo.

"Señor Joe, springs is big and cows want to drink there, no? Stampede is good idea so they no drink there. Plenty water for at creek. Make stampede soon por que cows more thirsty, es mas dificil to keep away from springs."

"What if we had a couple of riders at the springs to turn the cows away?" Bob asked.

Joe considered for a moment. "If they're that close to the springs you probably won't be able to turn them. It's better to use all the hands to stampede them and get them running hard and fast past the springs. Cows can't think of two things at once. If they're running with the herd they won't think as hard about getting to the water at the springs."

"Then that's what we'll do," Bob said. "I'll have the horse remuda run on the far side of the herd away from the springs so maybe we won't lose any horses. And the wagons will have to be on their own. So make it past the spring as best you can."

"Who'll be driving Mr. Barnes' wagon?"

"He has a driver named Felipe with him, but I don't know how experienced he is," Bob said.

"You should have Sara Barnes ride with Cookie. He'll keep her safe."

"Good idea. What about Billy?"

"You tell Billy to beat his horses with the reins and stay right behind Cookie and he'll be all right."

Bob scratched at his growing beard. "Tomorrow is going to be rough on you. You're going to bounce all over this wagon. But I don't know any way around it."

Santo nodded and looked sad.

Joe grinned. "I won't die from a little bouncing around." The next day's work was going to be rough on everyone.

After Bob and Santo left, Joe thought of the rough ride the next day. He dreaded it but there was no help for it. What could he do to make the day easier for Sara? Even if she could ride well enough, a cowhand would have to stay with her, and all the riders were needed to keep the herd moving. No, she was as well off on the wagon seat next to Cookie. He still couldn't understand her father bringing her on the trail drive, although Joe didn't mind her being there.

Early the next morning, the riders piled their bedrolls into the chuck wagon rather than the wrangler wagon. Joe wondered if Cookie did it to provide more cushioning for him.

Then Cookie had everything untied from the outside of the vehicles and put into the wrangler wagon. The nighthawk and night wrangler wouldn't get any sleep this day, as they needed to help keep the herd moving. It was going to be a massive job to get five thousand head of cattle to stampede and keep them going on to the creek.

Sara brought Joe a plate of hot biscuits and gravy and drank a cup of coffee while he struggled to feed himself.

"Do you think the cattle will actually run past the alkaline water? How long will it take?" She plucked at her skirt of the light blue cotton dress that fit in all the right places. Modestly high necked, it still drew Joe's gaze.

Joe sat his plate down and rubbed his temple, trying to massage away the last of the headache. He heard a hesitation in her voice and guessed she might be nervous. "Don't worry. We'll stay off to the side and be well out of it. Cookie will trot the horses but he won't gallop them. We'll bounce along and watch the herd run past." He hoped his explanations reassured her. "When you get too tired to hang onto the wagon seat come on back here. There's plenty of room for both of us. This is going to be the smoothest place to ride with all these bedrolls stacked up."

"I hadn't thought about that." She looked around. "I'll keep that in mind. Also you can't see what's happening from back here, so I might not get so scared."

He didn't tell her that it scared him more not to be able to see what was happening. But he would only be a burden to Cookie if he tried to sit on the wagon seat.

Cookie helped Sara climb up on the wagon seat and then climbed up himself. It was full daylight and they were ready to pull out.

"Hang on, Sara. If you get too tired, you crawl back there with Joe. He's safe." Laughing at his own joke, Cookie yelled at the horses and snapped his long driving whip.

The starting lurch jarred Joe's ribs and he grabbed hold of a strap to steady himself. It seemed like each turn of the wheels made the ride more jarring. After awhile all he could do was hang on and try not to let the pain overwhelm him.

Joe became aware of Sara settling on the bedrolls next to him and catching hold of his free arm, her eyes squeezed closed, and her head lay on his shoulder. The distraction of it helped him push the pain away. That she looked to him for comfort and protection filled him with a feeling he couldn't name.

Several hours later, he relaxed a bit with Cookie bringing the chuck wagon to a halt. Joe heard him climb down and then the sounds of harness being checked. Hopefully, they were past the springs and not too far from the stream where they would stop for the night.

Joe looked down to find Sara gazing up at him. "I bet you haven't had this much fun in a long time," he said and grinned at her. He had to fight himself not to smooth back the golden curls, which seemed always to be escaping her hair ribbon.

She laughed and sat up. "If this is your idea of fun then I pity you, Joe Storm. I'm hurting in places I didn't even know I had. I can't imagine how you feel." She offered him water from the canteen.

"I'm sorry, I can't sit up." It wasn't the pain. All his muscles had turned to mush from the effort it took to deal with the bouncing wagon.

"No problem." She slid her hand under his head, and helped him drink from the canteen. After he satisfied his thirst, she slid her hand out from under his head by running it down under the back of his neck. It felt like a caress. The feel of it lingered as he stared into her amazing blue eyes. Suddenly Sara gently pressed her lips to his and then retreated so quickly it was almost as if he imagined it.

Before he could respond, Cookie climbed back up onto the wagon seat and looked back at them. "You folks all right back there?"

Sara broke the lock of their eyes and turned toward Cookie. "How much further until we camp?"

"We only have about two more miles to go. We can walk the horses now. I can see the dust on the right about a mile east of us. I want to camp on the creek upstream from the herd."

Even though every muscle hurt, Joe wasn't in a hurry for the ride to be over. Sara's continued presence was a heady experience. What would her father think if he saw her sitting with him in the wagon? They finally pulled up at the creek and Joe heard Cookie yell at Billy to unhitch the teams. The hard day's ride was over.

"I'll go see if I can help Cookie with supper." Sara climbed down from the wagon.

Joe struggled to find a comfortable spot for his aching body. It was now three days since he'd had the run in with Curly and Frank. He would get out of the wagon the next day, if he could. For now, he needed rest. He dozed and woke to the sound of the cowhands starting to drift in. So they had the herd bedded down by the creek.

Bob climbed up into the wagon. "Hey. You look as beat as I feel." The trail boss ran his hand over his face.

"I've been better." Joe said. "How did the stampede go?"

"Oh, like any good stampede, the cows ran and ran." Bob laughed.

"Glad to hear it." Joe grinned.

"Well, we got them past the alkaline springs and we only lost five head that I know of."

"You could have lost the whole herd. Good job."

"I wouldn't have done it if you hadn't thought it a good idea," Bob said.

"Why is that?"

"I'm doing well as a trail boss because I listen to your advice. You've known what to do every mile of this drive. You're not the usual cook's helper. I'm not sure what you are."

"I used to be a rider. Now I'm just a cook's helper. Things happen in life and sometimes you have to go a different direction."

"But that doesn't mean you stop knowing what you know. Being a trail boss or a rancher isn't only doing the heavy work, it's also knowing what decisions to make and what orders to give. You think about that, because one of these days you may have the chance to use that knowledge. Here, now, I'm going on and on and we're both worn out. I just wanted to thank you."

"You're welcome to any of my ideas." Bob was a good man and the next herd he brought up the trail he wouldn't need Joe.

"How are you doing with getting back on your feet? Not that I want to hurry you, but I get the feeling you've had enough of this wagon."

"I'm aiming on getting out in the morning."

"Well, I plan to stay over for a day and let everyone get rested up. Give the herd a chance to recover. We ran some fat off them today and we need to take it easy for a few days." Bob suggested.

Joe looked at Bob's tired face. "You look like you might like to find your bedroll yourself."

"I plan to get acquainted with it right now." Bob gave a wave and left.

Sara came a few minutes later with a plate of food and a cup of coffee.

Joe wasn't particularly hungry but he needed to eat to get some strength back.

"That ride today was the most difficult wagon ride I've ever been on," she admitted. "I'm glad it's over and we can rest tomorrow."

"What does your father think of stampeding his herd?"

"He said it was an unusual move, but effective. I'm not sure he would have done it on his own, but he admires Bob for making that decision."

"Bob Fife is a good man. Your father is lucky to have had someone who could take over as trail boss."

"Rest well, Joe. Tomorrow we can all take it easy."

"Everyone but Cookie and Billy because their work won't stop." Joe said with regret. "And I'm not holding up my part."

"I hadn't thought about that, but I guess that's true. The riders still have to eat." She smiled. "And now I'm off to bed. Goodnight." She climbed out of the wagon with a wave.

Joe thought about Sara for a long time. Her golden hair and blue eyes were easy to think about. Did she think about him? He had nothing to offer her. Why torment himself? At the end of the drive, she would be gone from his life, anyway.

~

Joe woke at dawn, his head and ribs still aflame with pain. But pain he could deal with if he moved slowly. Carefully rubbing his unshaved jaw, he stiffly got up and found a clean shirt, pants, his boots, and got dressed. A good night's sleep made a difference. Moving carefully, he eased himself down from the wagon with a little help from Cookie.

"You better this morning?" Cookie got one of the camp chairs down and folded it out for him.

"The pain is fading, but I'm weak. Give me a day to rest and I'll be back at work tomorrow morning." Joe promised sinking into the chair as his legs felt as if they would fold under him.

"Yeah, I can see how much better you are." Cookie chuckled. "You want a fresh cup of coffee?"

"Of course, I've wanted a good cup of coffee since I got on this drive."

"If I'm not mistaken, since you been on this drive, you've been making the coffee," Cookie observed with a laugh as he handed Joe the cup of coffee.

"See what I mean?" Joe raised his eyebrows at him.

Joe sat and watched Cookie and Billy work, and the hands coming and going as they came to eat, get coffee, and change out their horses.

Sara was soon up. She nodded a greeting at Joe, went over to the worktable, and helped Cookie serve breakfast. Joe couldn't help but notice how her gingham dress with little red and blue flowers on a yellow background swished and swayed as she moved.

After feeding most of the hands, Cookie brought him a plate full of food. "I expect you to eat all of it."

"Yes, Cookie." Joe grinned.

"You better say, yes, Cookie," he replied, his voice grim.

Sara frowned.

Joe just chuckled, hoping she would realize Cookie was joshing with him.

The day passed in a slow and lazy fashion. Joe sat around and talked to different hands as they came in and out of the campground. As the day ended, all the hands, at one time or another, had been by to let him know that they were glad he was better. Joe was beginning to feel that he'd found a place with the trail drive and that felt good.

Mr. Barnes and Bob Fife rode up as the riders gathered for supper. After they unsaddled their horses and turned them over to the wrangler, they came over to where Joe sat talking to Jeff, Jim, and Will.

Will sat in the other camp chair, but he got up and offered it to Mr. Barnes.

They stayed and talked about cattle and the countryside until Cookie called out for everyone to come eat.

As the others lined up for their grub, Mr. Barnes stayed seated and turned to Joe. "It's been an interesting two days," he said. "I've worked cattle a lot, but I've never taken a herd up the trail. That was the first stampede I ever saw that was intentional. How about you? How many times have you been up the trail?"

"I'll have to think awhile to remember exactly how many. There were several years when I came up the trail with a couple of herds, one in the spring and another in the fall. I'd guess it's about fifteen times that I've been up different trails."

"But not as the cook's helper?"

"No, this is the first time as a cook's helper," Joe admitted.

"And why is that?"

There was an edge to the older man's voice that Joe didn't like. One of the customs of the trail was one didn't ask about a man's past. Joe stared at the man while he considered how to answer.

"Why? Maybe I should ask you. Why do you want to know?" Joe spoke softly, so that none of the riders getting their grub could hear. To respond in such a way might not be the best as Barnes was his boss, but there was something about the man that set Joe on his guard.

"You've a way about you. The riders talk as if you're the top hand here. Bob Fife doesn't make a decision unless he's talked it over with you. Cookie has never respected anyone around a cook fire but himself, and he has nothing but praise for you. And there's my daughter." He paused. "My daughter is very precious to me. When she makes a new friend, I want to know about him." He paused, again. "She tells me that you're becoming a special friend."

"I appreciate hearing that your daughter considers me a friend." Joe said slowly. "She's a lovely lady to have as a friend, and I hope she'll always consider me that."

"But my daughter is too important to me to let her get involved with just anyone. She's meant for a finer life and doesn't need to get sidetracked with a cowhand or a cook's helper." Mr. Barnes' voice had an edge again that grated against Joe.

What did Barnes mean, 'just anyone'? He gripped the arm of the camp chair until his knuckles were white. He might just be a cookie's helper, but he was still somebody.

"Let me set your mind at ease, Mr. Barnes. I've already told your daughter about why I'm working as a cook's helper. Last year I had a run in with a mad bull and I broke my right hip bad. My leg is messed up. However, I can make coffee, fry steaks, make biscuits, and put out a batch of doughnuts that riders will ride miles for. Same as I told your daughter right off." Joe stared grimly at him. As he had talked, he felt a frustration and fury gathering in his chest.

"I just wanted there to be no mistake. You understand that my daughter is not available to anyone on this drive." Barnes's voice held a menacing tone. "Here comes Sara. We won't mention this conversation to her."

It was all Joe could do not to strike the man. "There's no mistake." Joe said without warmth.

"Hey, what are you two talking about so seriously?" Sara carried two plates of food as she approached, smiling.

Joe took a plate of food, gazed at her bright eyes, and then looked away. "Thanks." He stared at the plate of food. He didn't have much of an appetite, but he ate anyway. The sooner he was back at work, the better.

Sara came back in a few minutes with a couple of cups of coffee.

"Sara, you go get your plate. Come back and sit with us." Mr. Barnes told her.

"All right, Papa, I'll be right back."

After she walked back to the worktable to get a plate of food, Joe started to get up, but Mr. Barnes was up first, put a hand on Joe's shoulder, and kept him from rising from his chair.

"No, you finish eating. Sara can have my chair. And Joe, no offense, and thanks for what you did for Billy. I respect a man who'll do that." He then turned and walked over to where Bob Fife sat on the ground.

The man had just told him he wasn't worthy to speak to his daughter and then he says he respects him for aiding Billy? Joe didn't know what to make of it.

Sara returned with her plate of food and sat in the camp chair vacated by her father.

Joe finished his meal in deep thought. Barnes had given him some things to consider, especially concerning what the other men thought of him. The herd owner was probably wrong considering how mistaken he was about what his daughter thought.

"You're awfully quiet all of a sudden. You talked away with my Papa."

"Your papa and I had an interesting conversation. It got me thinking. But I'm tired. It's been a hard couple of days." He didn't trust himself to say more without his anger showing.

"Yes, they've been hard days. Hopefully the next few days will be better." Her voice held an optimism.

Cookie came over. "You look peaked all of a sudden, Joe. Why don't you climb back up into the wagon and get some rest. You've been up all day." He took Joe by the arm and guided him back to the front of the chuck wagon.

"I feel bad about taking your bed again tonight. I can make out in my bedroll on the ground." Joe offered.

"No, you go on and get to bed. I'm fine in the wrangler wagon. In fact, it's more comfortable than the chuck wagon if you want to know the truth. I may sleep there all the time."

"Thanks, Cookie. Thanks for everything."

"Don't know what you're thanking me for. Now go on and get some sleep."

Joe knew why he needed to thank Cookie. He thanked him for accepting him as a man equal to himself. Cookie was boss, but even so, he treated Joe with the respect of equality. That was what had been lacking from Matthew Barnes.

"Good evening, Sara. I hope you sleep well." Joe gazed back at her. She was looking as lovely as ever. A sense of longing twisted in his chest so deep that it left a physical pain. If only he could cross the distance between them, but she was too far away. He trembled slightly as he knew that wasn't likely to change.

"Good night, Joe," she replied.

Cookie gave him a steadying hand and Joe took it. He climbed up the wheel at the front of the wagon. Slowly, and with difficulty, which he tried to hide, he climbed back up over the wagon seat into the chuck wagon. He undressed and lay down on his bedroll with a sigh and tried to get his aching body comfortable. It took awhile to stop the thoughts that went round and round. It had been a while since he'd been that angry at anyone except Curly and Frank. Sara was a lovely, friendly young lady. Her father was overprotective. No way would she ever take a second look at a has-been cowboy.

Chapter Sixteen

Joe turned carefully onto his side trying for a position with the least pain from his broken ribs, but sleep eluded him. The sound of a horse trotting in from the west and then the murmur of two deep male voices slid into the wagon. The herd was east of the trail camp, so who was coming in from the west? Of the two voices next to the chuck wagon, he recognized only Mr. Barnes. The other was a stranger.

"Have a seat in one of these camp chairs and I'll get you a plate of food and some coffee, Thomas," Mr. Barnes said. "You'll enjoy the food that Cookie puts together. We've one of the best fed crews on the trail."

"Call me Josh. I can use a good meal. I've been on the trail for eight days. Elisha Evans had me start out as soon as he got your telegraph."

"I assume since he sent you that he wants the herd?" Joe heard the question in Mr. Barnes' voice.

"He wants the herd if we can agree on a price. But he wants the cattle delivered to Colorado," the man named Josh said. He sounded young to Joe. Intrigued, he kept listening.

"If the cowhands will drive the herd to Colorado, and if Evans will take delivery within six weeks, I'll agree to five dollars a head." Mr. Barnes replied.

"Five dollars a head is a fair price, but I'll want to look over the herd. And I'd want the assurance that all the riders will go the extra miles to Colorado."

"That sounds like something I can agree to. First, I need to make sure that Cookie will go. Without him, I doubt if half the hands would head up the western branch of the trail. If you can stay a day we'll get the details worked out, and then you can start back to let Elisha know of our deal."

"After I inform Elisha of the deal, I suspect he'll want to have a representative with the trail drive, or he may even want to meet you on the trail himself."

Joe heard Mr. Barnes cough and shift in his chair before he answered. "I've no objection to that. I plan to stay with the herd until it's delivered. I'd ask that you to get a couple of wagons of supplies started out from Dodge as you ride through."

"What about your trail boss? Does he know the western trail to Dodge, and then on to Colorado?"

"I'm not sure what experience my trail boss has on that trail. I've another hand that may be familiar with the trail, and he probably knows that part of Colorado. I asked my trail boss about him and was told that's where he grew up," Mr. Barnes said.

Why had Barnes asked Bob about where he had grown up? Joe remembered a talk he and Bob had about a hunt in the mountains. An uneasiness settled over Joe. He would have to be on guard around Barnes.

"What rider is that? I may know him if he's from Colorado."

"His name is Joe Storm, and he's been up and down the trails for more than ten years, I'm told." Barnes' voice had a lift to it, as if he was responsible for Joe's experience on the trails.

"If Joe Storm is riding with you, I don't have to worry. He knows the trails. I haven't heard of him in about a year and was afraid something had happened to him."

"Well, he did have a run in with a bull a year ago, and only a couple of days ago he got hurt bad. He stopped a couple of no accounts from beating up a boy we got as a driver of the wrangler wagon and they ganged up on Joe. Left him banged up, but he's about recovered."

"I'll tell Elisha that you have him with you. He'll be pleased to hear it. Let me find a place to bed down and tomorrow I'll rest up for the day."

"My daughter travels with us and I bed down by my wagon where she sleeps. You're welcome to bed down there. Come on, and I'll show you the way."

Their footsteps faded into the night. For someone who didn't usually listen in on someone else's conversations, he'd sure listened to Barnes and Josh Thomas.

That he was known on the trail even in Colorado surprised him, as he hadn't been back in the state for several years. Mr. Barnes' intention to ask him about the trail came as another surprise. Joe had been over the trail to the west twice. From here to Colorado would make the drive a month longer, and maybe more. Joe didn't mind. But the prospect of going to Colorado left him with a sense of excitement and feeling of dread fighting each other. Joe thought of mountains with a twist in his gut that left a longing. The mountains were home; but he couldn't go home and that brought an empty feeling.

Still, extra time on the trail with Sara wasn't a bad thing.

~

Joe dressed slowly the next morning in the dark with a sense that he had passed a barrier. The overall sick feeling was gone, but he still had a headache, and his ribs would ache for weeks. He climbed out of the wagon with care. To the east, the sky promised daylight. The need to get back to work and earn his keep was pushing him to move past the pain and weakness. He was also curious as to this Josh and the possible change of direction for the herd. What would it mean to him and the end of the trail? Did he want to go with the herd to Colorado? Didn't make much difference whether he wanted it or not, it wasn't his decision. Sighing deeply, he turned toward his work, refusing to acknowledge that the shivery feeling deep in his gut was a fear at the thought of going back to Colorado.

Cookie lit the lanterns around the worktable. He gave Joe a sharp look, nodded, and then began mixing the dough for morning biscuits.

Joe stoked the three fires, filled the coffee pots, and made the coffee. The full coffee pots pulled at his still sore muscles. He had to carry them one at a time, but it was a relief to be back at work. Between thoughts of Sara, Matthew Barnes' attitude, the trail drive ending in Colorado, and the unknown future beyond the end of the trail, Joe would rather be too busy at work than lie around and think.

He went back to the worktable. "What do you want me to do first, Cookie?" He kept his voice low so he wouldn't wake the riders who ringed the campgrounds in their bedrolls.

"Get the water heated for the men to shave. You first, if you feel like it. You look a little scruffy."

"Yes, Cookie." Joe grinned.

"It's good to have you back." Cookie laughed softly.

Joe wanted to tell Cookie about the conversation between Mr. Barnes and Josh, but on second thought had the good sense to keep his mouth shut. The owner of the herd could talk to Cookie in his own time.

Joe poured hot water into a tin bucket, retrieved his kit, and went to the back of the wrangler wagon. He still had several cuts on his face that were only partially healed. These he shaved around with care. The purple of the bruises stood out more with the three-day growth of beard gone. But the swelling was down, especially on his nose and along his jaw. Results would still scare the fox out of the hen house, but it was the best he could do. In a couple of weeks, he'd be able to shave with ease. But he'd probably picked up a couple of permanent scars.

In his shaving mirror, he noticed that his hair was so long it curled over his collar. He'd ask Cookie to cut it. And since they had a day with no travel, he hoped to take a dip in the creek later in the day, if the cuts had healed enough.

When he got back to the chuck wagon, he saw Mr. Barnes, Bob Fife, and Cookie at a distance from the riders, talking. Joe got busy making breakfast.

Sara came up to him as he got the skillets ready to fry the salt pork. "You look better. How do you feel?"

With the effort she had made to help look after him, she deserved an honest answer. "I feel weak as a kitten, and I hurt all over. And I'm not sure I can last the whole day, but other than that I feel a lot better." He grinned at her. What he really wanted to do was pull her into his arms. She was a real temptation.

She laughed softly. "And you're an honest man. What can I do to help?"

Joe liked the sound of her laughter. It reminded him of a bird in the morning air. That was something else he wouldn't mind getting used to on a regular basis. He caught himself. That road was closed.

"If you watch the salt pork, I'll get the biscuits turned and the gravy ready to make." He showed Sara what to do and then left her to it.

He scrapped the hot coals back onto the fire from the lids of the Dutch ovens, set the lids aside to lighten the weight, and heaved the Dutch ovens filled with baked biscuits onto the worktable. His ribs and bruised muscles protested, but if he did his work, there was no way around the pain. He paused a moment by the worktable to catch his breath and hoped that Sara hadn't noticed.

Joe added dried milk, water, and flour to a bowl, ready to make the Texas gravy. "How are you doing, Sara?" He glanced at the pork sizzling in the skillets.

"How can you tell if they're ready to take out of the pan?" She wiped her forehead with an edge of her apron.

"I'm not sure, I just know. Here, let me finish up and you go give the potatoes a stir." The pork sizzled nicely, browning around the edges. The aroma spread out over the camp as the riders stirred. Joe dished up the salt pork onto the large metal platter. He dumped the excess grease, but left enough to flavor the gravy with the meat scrapings in the bottom of the pan.

Joe poured in the flour and milk mixture, stirred the gravy to the right thickness, until it was ready to ladle over the salt pork and biscuits, just the way the riders liked it. Joe called out, "Come and get it!"

The cowhands managed to delay the line. Usually, they couldn't get through quick enough, but with Sara there they dallied.

Joe smiled at the riders' response to Sara. They spoke to her politely while at the same time, they managed to glance at her trim figure and shining bright golden hair. Most of them were red in the face from shyness of being around a pretty girl by the time they got to where Joe was plopping salt pork and gravy onto their plates.

"Let's keep the line moving, fellows." He understood their reaction as he found himself glancing over at Sara. It had been weeks since any of them had seen a woman, much less a pretty girl dressed in a yellow dress that looked like sunshine. This dress was a solid yellow, not like that yellow dress he had seen her in a few days before with the little flowers all over it.

Perhaps yellow was her favorite color. Joe couldn't stop himself from thinking about her. And the bright smile she gave to Joe and the riders didn't make them want to hurry through the line, either.

Joe tapped his serving spoon lightly on the side of the gravy skillet as the last man in line lingered. The usual five minutes to serve twenty men now took well over three times that long. "Let's move along, fellas."

Last in line to be served were Cookie, Mr. Barnes, Bob Fife, and a stranger that Joe guessed was Josh Thomas. The tall solid-built rider was about Joe's height, broad shouldered and lean hips. Josh had a boyish sandy haired good-natured look about him, which gave Joe a friendly feeling.

"Thanks for the way you filled in for me." Cookie said to Joe. "Miss Sara, we'll make a Cookie out of you yet."

"I don't know. I couldn't keep up this morning. I'm amazed how it all came together just at the right moment." Sara filled her own plate and sat on the wagon tongue to eat her breakfast.

"Get your plate filled and come on over here by Mr. Barnes." Cookie told Joe.

He was tempted to refuse. Already tired and aching, he just wanted to eat his breakfast in peace. However, Cookie was the boss.

Joe filled his plate and got a cup of coffee. He walked over to where Mr. Barnes and Josh were seated in the camp chairs.

Mr. Barnes got up and motioned for him to sit. "Like for you to meet Josh Thomas."

"Howdy, I'm Joe Storm." He shook hands with the rider.

Joe appreciated Barnes' gesture, but a part of him was still angry with the man and didn't want to take anything from him. Barnes' treatment of him in front of others didn't match what he had said to him in private. Joe didn't respect a man who would act that way.

Joe looked at Cookie and Cookie nodded. He sat down and turned toward Josh Thomas with his back partially toward Barnes.

"That was a good breakfast. Thanks for getting it ready, Joe." Mr. Barnes leaned against the wheel of the chuck wagon. He methodically ate the food from his plate, swallowing before he spoke. "I asked you to come over here because we're making a change of direction for the herd and wanted to get your ideas about the trail." Barnes took another big bite of biscuit and gravy.

"Yes, sir." Joe set his cup of coffee on the ground by his chair. He continued eating while he waited for what Mr. Barnes wanted to ask him.

"This is Josh Thomas, who represents Elisha Evans. I may sell the herd to Evans with delivery to Colorado." Mr. Barnes sopped up the last of the gravy on his plate with his biscuit and stuffed it into his mouth. "What I need to know is what do you think about us taking the branch trail over to the Western Trail to Dodge. From there we will trail the herd on to Northern Colorado. What I need to know is how long it will take? What water conditions we can expect? How much grass will be available?"

They were all staring at Joe as if he was a rabbit in a cage.

He saw a humorous side of it. Here he was the next to the bottom in status on the drive—Billy being the bottom—and all these leaders wanted his opinion. For some reason this relaxed him. A calm confidence swept through him. He'd been up the western branch two different times, which was two more than anyone else here.

Joe glanced at Josh, and then looked at Mr. Barnes. "We're a little north of where the trail branches off and it'll take a day to get back to it. It follows the Cimarron River most of the way, so there's plenty of water until we have to leave the Cimarron and head north." He sipped his coffee. "You have to be ready for the hundred miles from the Cimarron until you get to the Arkansas River south of Dodge. Depending on how many herds are ahead of you, by the time you meet up with the Western Trail, you may have a problem with enough grass after you leave Dodge. Where in Colorado are you headed?"

"Do you know a small town called Cedar Ridge, southwest of Cheyenne?" Josh asked.

Joe nodded. "I know it well." The town was where his father used to get all the ranch supplies. Cedar Ridge was the only town Joe had seen until he was fourteen and ran away from home.

"Well, you go west about twenty miles to Sam Weathers J Bar C, and then head northwest about thirty miles."

At hearing the name Sam Weathers, Joe felt an icy chill run down his back. He kept his face still.

Josh emptied his cup and then said. "There's a large valley up behind a big ridge north of Pinto Creek. That's were Elisha Evans has his ranch."

"I know where that is. I wouldn't go through Weathers' place." That was the last route Joe wanted to take. "It's easier to go further north from Dodge to Ogallala, and then go west of the mountains north of the ridge about twenty miles north of Pinto Creek. Then you can trail right into the valley from the east." Joe was glad he could tell them the truth. With a large herd of cattle, the way he had told them was the easiest route.

"I haven't been in the valley where Evan's ranch is since I was a kid and used to hunt up through there, but I know where it is." For a moment, Joe was lost in the memory, and then he shifted in his seat to bring himself back to the discussion at hand.

He didn't want to say more and get them to asking questions. Did Mr. Barnes know what he was about to get them into? Joe could think of many things he'd rather do than make a drive over that part of the trail.

"Are you ready for those hundred miles after we'll leave the Cimarron River?" Joe asked, to get them talking about something besides Colorado Territory.

"What do you mean ready?" Mr. Barnes asked.

"There's no water to speak of for the cattle, and you just get the herd through as best you can," Joe explained.

Bob shifted on his feet. "What's the best way to cross that hundred miles?"

The two times he had crossed that hundred miles were not happy memories. The trip took four rough days, but it was the only way.

"I'd do it in a forced drive, move the cows along at double time. You'll lose some, but you can get them through. It's rough on the cows, horses, and the riders. You might get a wagonload of water moved down the trail from Dodge. That might save some of the horses." Joe waited for their response.

Josh glanced over at Mr. Barnes. "You're right. This fellow knows his way over the trail, and the best way to take a herd into the Lazy ES." He turned a friendly grin on Joe.

"How long do you think it'll take us to get to Evan's ranch?" Mr. Barnes asked Joe.

"If all goes well, five or six weeks. You can get there with the cows in good shape if, after Dodge, you take it slow, let them graze, and get back some of the fat they'll lose over the dry trail." Their faces told it all. They really didn't understand just how bad the four days on the dry trail would be and that the cattle would lose a lot of fat.

Mr. Barnes turned to Cookie. "Well, Cookie, what do you think?"

"I want to know if Joe will go with us. I don't want to go unless he goes." Cookie said.

The condition Cookie put on his own decision surprised Joe. Cookie's friendship continued to help him on his road to feeling like a whole man. It felt good to know he had such a friend.

"Joe, what do you think? Will you sign on for an extra month or so?" Mr. Barnes asked.

"If Cookie will, I'll go." He wasn't happy about going into that area of Colorado Territory, as it was too near his father's ranch.

Joe glanced over at Sara where she sat on the wagon tongue talking to Billy as he peeled potatoes. The boy was red faced and had a silly grin on his face.

Sara's kindness to the boy stirred a deep feeling within Joe. He wanted to return such kindness to her. No, he didn't mind a month longer on the trail at all.

"Then that's settled. I can tell the riders that Cookie and Joe are going. Thanks, fellows, that helps. Bob said he'll go, but only if Joe goes." Mr. Barnes said.

Joe was again surprised. He knew that they were friends, but not that Bob had that much confidence in him.

The trail boss shifted from one foot to the other and cleared his throat. "The riders need instructions, and now would be a good time. I told them to wait to ride out."

The men saddled horses from the remuda.

"Let's go talk to them." Mr. Barnes agreed. "We can get reorganized today and pull out early in the morning for the trail to the western branch. What do you think about that, Joe?"

"It won't hurt the cows and horses to have one more day. The cowhands could also use a little time off to go bathe in the creek and get their clothes washed." Joe's throat was getting dry from all the talking. He took a swig of coffee before continuing. "Once we leave the river, it'll take everyone working all out to keep the cows on the move. There'll be no rest or relief and barely enough water for the men and horses. I assume you'll get supplies sent down to us from Dodge. We only have enough for about half the route from here to Dodge."

"Good ideas." Mr. Barnes turned to Bob. "Let's go talk to the riders. You might as well come too, Josh." Mr. Barnes then walked over to where the men waited. Most had already mounted their horses.

Cookie gathered plates from everyone. "Come on, Joe. Let's see where we are for meals."

Joe still was bruised enough that he stiffened from sitting in the chair. He pushed himself up slowly catching his breath as the broken ribs sent a sharp pain through his chest and limped on his bruised leg over to the worktable.

"We got a whole day to cook and organize the wagons. I don't want to waste it." Cookie drummed his fingers on the worktable. "I'll get Bob to round up one of the boys to put some tallow on the wheels."

"Why don't we have the roast you cooked last night for dinner?" Joe poured cups of coffee for Cookie and himself.

"Um. We can do that, and then have steaks with some dried apple cobblers for supper. And you make doughnuts, and maybe some ginger fritters that we can use over the next couple of days." Cookie sipped coffee.

It sounded like a lot of work, but with a day without traveling, they needed to take advantage.

"Any chance I could get you to cut my hair today?"

"This afternoon I'll set up barbering and see if the cowhands want me to cut their hair, too." Cookie grinned at Joe. "Some of them look a little woolly, and that describes you also. Doesn't hurt to spiffy up around a pretty girl."

Joe could feel his blush as he had also thought about wanting to look a little better around Sara. "I'll get busy on sweets if that's what you want me to do. What about some beef jerky to use on the dry trail?"

"Tell you what, you do all the sweets. I'll do the rest." Cookie walked over, put his empty cup in the wash-up tub, and then returned to the worktable where Joe waited. "We'll feed the boys well up until we start the dry run, and that way they'll be the best prepared to face those hard days."

"Do we need to conserve sugar?" Joe considered what he might bake.

"No. We got plenty what with the supply wagon that that arrived with Mr. Barnes. That is, if we get a supply wagon sent to us from Dodge. That reminds me—I better get a list ready for Josh Thomas to take before I start anything else." Cookie went and searched for his tablet of paper and a pencil to start his list.

Joe checked the fires as he decided what to make first. He would start with the dried apple cobblers. After he built up the fires, he returned to the worktable.

Sara stood there, waiting. "Can I help with something?" Sunlight flickered through the leaves and danced across her face.

Joe swallowed before he could speak. He wasn't used to seeing such beauty in the mornings, or any other time of the day out on the trail. "You can make some ginger fritters if you want to." Joe forced himself to turn away and get the ingredients together.

"How do you make them?" She stepped closer as she watched him gather the ingredients.

He stepped back from her, when he really wanted to step closer. Was that hyacinth he could smell from her hair?

Joe pulled out one of the large enamel bowls from the storage box. "Here's a bowl to mix the ingredients. I'll tell you step by step while I make cobblers."

While Joe got three of the Dutch ovens out for the cobblers, he told Sara how to make the fritters. It was fun to work with her, as she was pleasant and lighthearted, and ready to laugh. With Cookie, it was always too much of a rush to allow for much fun.

By the time she had the dough ready to fry the fritters, Joe had the three dried apple cobblers baking. He got the big skillets out and melted some lard in the bottom. When it sizzled, Joe showed her how to drop a spoonful of the fritter dough into the hot lard, mash it down so it was thin, and then before it browned too much to turn it over. He placed a flour sack towel on the worktable, and told her to put the fritters on the towel as she took them out of the skillet.

Bob approached the worktable. "All the hands have agreed to continue the drive to Colorado. Mr. Barnes has promised an extra ten dollars a month for each rider."

Cookie poured Bob a cup of coffee and handed it to him.

"Barnes has also promised a bonus for you two." Bob sipped on the hot coffee.

"That's nice. Course, Joe and I deserve it." Cookie chuckled. "Can you get a cow butchered for us? I want to get some jerky made for the trip up the dry track." Cookie took off his hat and scratched his head. "It would also help if some of the hands would get wood gathered and the water barrels filled. I need Billy here at the chuck wagon."

"Sure, Cookie. Whatever we need to do." Bob emptied his cup.

"This afternoon I'll set up my barbering if any of the fellows want a haircut." Cookie ran his fingers through his own unruly gray hair and put his hat back on.

"Can I be first in line?" Bob took his hat off and ran his fingers through his long black hair that was almost to his shoulders.

"You can be right after Joe. I promised him first."

"Good, you can practice on Joe, and then I'll get a better haircut." Bob laughed as he put his cup in the wash-up tub and went to get the riders started on the chores for Cookie.

Since Joe had the cobblers baking and Sara making the fritters, he mixed the dough for the doughnuts. He used the sourdough bread starter as his leavening, which gave the doughnuts a good flavor. Setting the doughnut dough aside to rise a little, he made the biscuits for dinner.

Cookie got some racks put up over one of the fires, ready to use to dry strips of beef to make jerky.

The riders came for coffee and hung around. With the herd resting, it only took five or six hands to keep watch over the whole herd. Bob rotated the riders every four hours, which meant that most of the riders were in camp at any one time.

The riders were respectful, but they did stare at Sara as she moved around the cook fire. She seemed to be unaware of all the male attention. Joe felt an odd sense of jealousy, as he wanted to keep her to himself.

Several of the men had already been down to the creek and bathed. Washing hung on all the bushes between the camp and the creek.

Joe planned to wait until he got his haircut and then go find a deep pool in the creek to soak in. Between the heat of the day and the heat of the fires, he dripped sweat already. He got his bandana and tied it around his forehead to keep some of the sweat out of his eyes and the cuts on his face, although it didn't help much.

Billy had the potatoes frying and was busy, so Joe went to the coffee fire and checked on the coffee. Two of the pots were almost empty. With more free time, the hands drank more coffee throughout the day.

Jeff appeared, and he offered to help get the coffee pots filled with fresh water. While Joe got a bag of coffee out and emptied the last of it into the two pots of water, Jeff offered to grind the coffee beans and get the coffee bag refilled from the fifty-pound bag in the chuck wagon.

It suddenly dawned on Joe why Jeff was so helpful; Jeff wanted to be introduced to Sara. Joe frowned at the thought, and he got Jeff busy grinding the coffee beans, then he checked on Sara and the fritters.

"How are you doing?" Joe put more wood on the fire.

She wiped her face with her sleeve. "I'm on the last batch. What can I do next?"

"Don't you need to take a break and rest a bit? Bending over that fire is hot, tiring work." Joe wanted to give her a chance to back away from the work, as it wasn't her job.

She simply smiled at him. "I can keep at it as long as you can, Joe Storm." A challenge laced her voice.

"Hey, I'm ready to stop right now." He grinned. "We can leave it to Jeff there. Have you met Jefferson Kingston?"

She turned to Jeff. "I'm Sara Barnes. How do you do, Mr. Kingston?"

Sara cleaned her hands on her apron and shook hands with Jeff.

Jeff turned as red as anyone Joe had ever seen.

"Ma'am, call me ... uh, Jeff." He stammered, going even redder.

"Thanks, Jeff, for grinding the coffee. I know that Joe and Cookie appreciate it."

"You're welcome, uh, Miss Barnes." Jeff ducked his head.

Joe grinned at him and said to Sara, "We're about ready to get things together to serve dinner. You want to help?"

She turned from Jeff back to the worktable. "Sure, what should I serve?"

"First, we need to get this worktable cleaned off. Then get the fritters stored away for tomorrow, and get everything set up," Joe answered.

While Sara washed the worktable, Joe wrapped up the huge stack of fresh-made fritters in a couple of flour sacks and stored them in the wagon. Then he walked back around to where Jeff ground the coffee.

"Put these in your shirt and don't let any of the other hands see them." He spoke quietly, as he slipped Jeff a couple of the fritters.

"Thanks, and for the introduction. That was nice of you." Jeff turned red again.

"You're welcome." Joe grinned.

He got the sliced roast, fried potatoes, gravy, and biscuits onto the worktable, ready to serve. He looked over at Cookie.

With several cowhands working together, they had butchered a cow in record time. Cookie was already putting thinly sliced strips of beef on rods laid over the smoking coals of the fire. It would take about six hours for the meat to cook and dry over the hot, smoky fire. By evening, they would have dried beef ready to pack. The jerky would stay edible for weeks at a time, without worry that it would spoil.

Cookie looked up at Joe and nodded, indicating that he could begin serving the meal. The older man went back to tending his dried meat, and Joe yelled to the riders. "Come and get it."

After Cookie ate, he got one of the camp chairs set up under the canvas shading the side of the chuck wagon. "Take your shirt off and sit so I can get you shorn."

Joe made sure Sara had already gone back to her wagon to rest, and then took his shirt off and sat in the chair.

Cookie cut his hair short with lots of scalp showing above the ears. After a few minutes, he brushed the cut hair off Joe's shoulders and back.

"Go ahead. Get your stuff and head to the creek. And take some time to soak. It'll help with your bruises."

Joe had taken his shirt off without thinking of his bruises. His chest and stomach were all sorts of colors of black, blue, yellow, and even green, from the beating. Joe had to assume his back looked the same, on top of the mass of old scars.

Glancing around, he noticed that the riders who waited for their turn to get a haircut were staring, but trying to pretend they weren't. Joe wished it didn't bother him, but it did. He didn't like the questions that usually followed when someone saw his back covered with scars and he quickly pulled his shirt on.

"You care if Billy comes down to the creek and joins you after I cut his hair?" Cookie asked. "I want him to bathe and wash his clothes. He isn't as finicky as you are about taking a bath, and in this hot weather he's getting a little too ripe."

Joe laughed. "No, I don't mind. Send him on. I'm going upstream a ways to find a clean pool."

As Cookie cut Bob Fife's hair, Joe got his stuff and walked up the creek bank. He wanted to find a clean, deep pool, but he also wanted to be out of sight of the camp. Sara had gone back to her wagon after eating, but he didn't know where she might wander later.

After he had walked about ten minutes alongside the creek, he found a pool shaded by big cottonwoods. Joe scrutinized the ground carefully for snakes before he undressed and waded into the pool. The water was only about five feet deep, but it was cold and clean. He scrubbed his body, careful of the cut places and not wincing too much when the bruises protested. He washed his hair twice and ducked under the water to rinse off. It was a hot end-of-July day. The cool water rinsed away the sweat and heat from his skin, while the refreshing coolness wiped away his fatigue.

Using the bar of lye soap and a rock on the edge of the pool, he washed every stitch of clothes he owned. After he had them all washed, he laid them out on some large, sun-baked rocks on the edge of the creek. He went back into the pool and slowly swam around. It felt good on the muscles that had been abused by the tree branch and Curly and Frank's boots.

Joe caught the sounds of twigs breaking and someone's shuffling footsteps. He glanced up to see Billy stumble up from behind the cottonwood trees that hugged the creek bank.

Billy wore his hat, but even so, his head looked smaller with his brown mop of hair gone.

"Hey, Billy, did you bring soap?" Joe asked as he lazily floated in the pool.

"No, I didn't think about it." Billy put his dirty clothes down on a rock and examined the pool of water. "Is that water real deep? I can't swim."

"It's not deep by the shore and you slowly walk into it until you're as deep as you like." Joe now understood. Billy was afraid of the water. "There's a piece of soap there on the rock."

He told Billy to scrub his clothes and himself with the soap. Sometimes Billy needed directions, and he didn't seem to resent it when Joe told him what to do. It made it easy to work with him. He liked young Billy.

Billy undressed down to his long johns, and then with his hat still on, walked carefully to the edge of the pool.

"Billy, get out of those long johns and take that hat off. You can't bathe proper with your hat on." Joe laughed.

"Oh, I forgot I had it on. I thought I'd scrub me and the long johns at the same time."

"No, that won't work. First, you scrub yourself and then you scrub your clothes." Joe turned and swam upstream and let the current of the stream float him back down.

Billy got about waist deep in the water and scrubbed his head vigorously.

"That's the way. Give your head a good scrubbing." Again, Joe swam upstream and floated back down.

"I've scrubbed all over until I'm rubbed raw," Billy said.

"Great, now go scrub your clothes and rinse them."

Billy dutifully did so.

"We've a whole box of soap bars in the chuck wagon, and whenever we stop by a creek or along the river, you need to get a piece and go bathe and wash your clothes. You'll feel better in this heat and it'll make it nicer to be around you, especially as we have a lady with us." Joe splashed water at him and grinned.

"Yes, sir, I can see that." Billy found a place to spread out his clothes, copying the way Joe had spread his out on the rocks and branches.

"Now come on back into the water and stay cool while our clothes dry." Joe floated on his back and looked at the white clouds drifting overhead.

"Can I ask you something, Joe?"

"Sure."

"I don't mean to be disrespectful, but how does Miss Barnes stay so nice and clean and fresh? She don't never even look hot and she for sure don't sweat like we do." He sat down in the water up to his shoulders.

"Well, I'm not sure, but I think that she bathes in her wagon. Felix, who drives their wagon, is always getting pots of water heated, and he washes clothes for both Miss Barnes and Mr. Barnes. But you and I have to make do with the creek, which is fine with me. This is great." Joe paddled in place in the deeper part of the pool. "I haven't seen in their wagon, but it's probably fixed up like a little bedroom. You realize they aren't carrying all the grub, gear, and bedrolls we're carrying."

Billy nodded. "I didn't think about that. You sure got some fine bruises. Do they hurt?"

"Not much anymore unless I bump them. They look a whole lot worse than they are. Floating around in this water makes it feel a lot better. But I guess we better get going soon, or Cookie will start supper without us."

But Joe didn't make a move toward getting out of the pool. It was the best he'd felt in several days and with the heat of the late afternoon, it would take about five minutes to be sweaty again. He ducked his head under the water one last time, and then made himself head for dry land.

When they got back to the camp, the riders sat around on the ground with their hats off, and enjoying their new shorn heads. Every bush and branch in sight had clothes drying on them. It seemed everyone had taken advantage of the day to bathe and wash clothes.

Chapter Seventeen

After supper, Joe found Bob waiting for him by the chuck wagon. "Joe, take a walk with me out to the remuda."

"Cookie," Joe yelled, "Can you do without me for a while?"

"Sure, go on. Most everything is done here for this evening."

They walked toward the remuda and found a place among the trees, out of sight of the campground. For several minutes, they discussed different aspects of the route that they would take to the hundred miles of dry trail.

Bob lifted his hat and ran his fingers through his short hair. "Anything else you can think of that I need to know before we take off in the morning?"

Joe leaned against a tree and looked out over the horse herd. "I think we've covered everything. But I do have something I would like you to do."

"What's that?" Bob rubbed the back of his neck.

"We have a tough drive for the next couple of weeks. I hate to put Sara through it. Would you ask Mr. Barnes to take her up to Caldwell, catch the train, and meet us in Dodge City?" Joe turned his head toward Bob, and caught his fleeting smile.

"I understand, and I'll speak to him. I wouldn't be too hopeful. He strikes me as sort of stubborn." Bob squatted on his heels. "I know you're concerned for her, but I expect she'll be all right. We'll just have to make sure of it."

"I wish her father was as concerned as we are." Joe couldn't stop himself from speaking his mind.

"I don't think Barnes understands how bad it can be. Or at least, I hope he don't because if he knows and doesn't try to protect his daughter—I'm not sure what to call that." Bob stood up.

"Yeah, I don't either." There were several things he would have liked to call it. "After we leave the Cimarron, we just got to get the herd moving and keep it going. Once we make the Arkansas River we'll be fine."

"I'll go talk to Mr. Barnes. I'll let you know how it turns out." Bob led the way back to the camp.

Joe checked on the coffee pots before climbing up into the chuck wagon. With relief he crawled into his bedroll. He was on the edge of sleep when someone climbed up onto the chuck wagon.

"Joe?" Bob called.

"Yeah?"

"I talked to Barnes. I strongly encouraged him to take Sara up to Caldwell. But he sees no reason to do that. Just wanted to let you know, I've told all the hands that we need to watch out for her and make sure she makes it without a problem. She'll ride with you?"

"I expect so. It'll be the safest place for her." Joe breathed deep to mask his disgust. Although he was not surprised, once more Matthew Barnes had disappointed him.

"Well, I thought you'd like to know I tried."

"I appreciate it."

"See you in the morning."

Joe clenched his fist. He would have to do what he could to be the protection she needed. Did Sara realize her father's lack of effort to protect her?

They started out at daybreak. Josh Thomas pulled out at the same time, riding a fresh horse. He would stop in Dodge City and get two wagons of supplies headed back to meet the trail herd, plus arrange to have a wagonload of barrels filled with water meet them. Hopefully they'd meet up with the supply wagons before they left the Cimarron River. If not, they'd run short of rations.

Joe didn't talk to Mr. Barnes again for several days. He was polite when Barnes came through the chow line, but neither of them initiated conversation.

Sara rode with Cookie and Joe. Squeezing together, the chuck wagon seat accommodated the three of them. Joe had offered to ride with Billy but Cookie wanted him riding the chuck wagon.

It was impossible to sit with Sara in between Cookie and himself without being acutely aware of her. When the wagon gave an extra bounce either her shoulder or arm bumped his and brought his attention back to her. She seemed to sit closer to him than to Cookie, as he didn't notice her bumping into the older man. Joe didn't mind her closeness, but he did have to keep a rein on his thoughts. He wondered if he was in her mind as much as she was in his.

"Well, it's time for me to get my nap." Cookie handed the reins across Sara to Joe, and then climbed into the wagon bed.

"What does he mean, 'his nap'?" The curls that had escaped from the netting that captured her hair caught Joe's attention. The urge to touch her golden locks pulled at him.

"Uh..." With effort, he brought his attention back to the question she'd asked. "We get up so early and work so late that a nap in the middle of the day is a big help." Joe made a clicking sound and slapped the reins to encourage the horses.

She seemed surprised. "Do you take naps?"

"Every day I can. I usually get a couple of hours sleep after dinner." Joe kept the horses at a steady pace, so as to disturb Cookie as little as possible.

"I guess it does make sense. I never thought about it." Sara took a drink from the canteen. "Maybe I can help drive some?"

Joe glanced sideways at her small, petite figure. "You think you can drive a team of four?"

"Yes, I can." Sara reached over and took the reins from Joe's hands.

He leaned back and stretched. "All right. You drive all you want."

Mr. Barnes rode up. "Sara, what are you doing?"

"I'm enjoying myself, Papa. Joe is letting me drive the teams." She gave her father a big grin.

"Well, that's Joe and Cookie's job. Don't get too tired." Mr. Barnes scowled at Joe, turned his horse around, and rode back to the herd.

"I don't think your papa was too happy with you driving." Joe reached and put his hands on top of hers to take over the reins.

But Sara held on.

His work-roughened hands completely covered hers. Touching her soft skin sent a tingling up his arms that ended with a thumping in his chest. There was nothing he could do if he didn't want to jerk the reins out of her hands. Reluctantly, he lightened his touch. After a couple of moments, he slid his hands off hers in a light caress.

She gave him a side-glance and smiled. "Don't you worry about my papa. I'm doing just fine. And I can drive these horses as well as anyone, Mr. Storm. I challenge you to drive these animals any better than I'm doing right now."

"All right, you drive awhile and then I'll drive. When Cookie wakes up we'll ask him which was the smoother ride."

Actually, she handled the teams just fine, he had to admit, but he wasn't about to tell her. Mr. Barnes would just have to get upset. Doing even a small thing that gave Sara enjoyment was a satisfaction.

"Where did you learn to drive a team of four?" Joe was curious about what her life had been.

"At our ranch in Texas. An old cowhand, Ned, who worked around the house and barn, would let me drive the teams when we took grub out to the cowhands during round-up." She sighed and then straightened her shoulders. "I miss the ranch, but Papa sold it. I need to look forward instead of the past."

Joe understood her pain and wished he could take it away. "You didn't want to make this move?"

"No, I thought that when I completed my schooling I would return to the ranch where I grew up. Then I got the letter from Papa that said to meet him in Caldwell, Kansas. That was the first time I knew we were moving to California."

"Did you always live on the Texas ranch?"

Holding the reins in one hand, she straightened her wide-brimmed straw hat and tightened the ribbon that held it securely under her jaw. "I was four when we moved to Texas from back east. My mother died there when I was eight. That's one thing that makes this move so hard. Leaving her buried there makes me feel as if we left her behind." She brushed a tear from her eye. "I didn't get to say good-bye to her. I don't know why that should bother me so. She's in heaven and in my heart. She's with me no matter where I'm at."

Not knowing what to say, Joe put his hand over hers. He was glad not to even think of his own mother. He didn't want his mother anywhere near him.

Sara took a deep breath and asked, "What about your folks? Where did you grow up?"

Joe's chest tightened in panic. He didn't know what to tell her. Cookie saved him by poking his head in between them.

~

Within the next few days, Cookie started riding the wrangler wagon with Billy, which left Sara riding the chuck wagon with Joe. He liked her curiosity and energy, as she asked him questions constantly.

Joe noticed the cowhands watching them as they worked around the cook fires. Outwardly, Joe behaved as a perfect gentleman around her. He had a harder time with his thoughts.

Joe sensed his body getting stronger each day and, with Sara's help, they were finished with the evening cooking at an earlier hour. On the days they pulled into a camp a little early, which they seemed to do more often, Joe cooled off by taking a dip in the nearest creek. Billy usually managed to follow. Joe didn't mind. Of course, he never asked Sara to join then. It would not have been proper. However, it did seem to him that she gazed after them sometimes, as if she wouldn't have minded.

On the north side of the Cimarron River, buffalo skulls marked the trail every half mile, making it easy to follow the trail to the western branch. Plenty of grass covered the land and the camp stops were cleaner and less trampled than those on the main Chisholm Trail. Because of this, the trail was more peaceful to Joe. It also rained several times in the twelve days before the supply wagons met them.

The evening before they left the Cimarron River and faced the hundred miles of dry trail, quiet fell over the camp. Joe looked at the hands resting against their saddles waiting for the call to supper and thought it likely that everyone's mind was on the same thing—the double-time drive, no water, and the possible losses they'd face.

Bob asked to talk with Joe while they ate supper together. "All right. Tell me what you suggest for tomorrow."

Joe swallowed his bite of steak. "Get everyone on the trail by daylight, and push the herd until about noon. Then let the cows and horses rest for about three hours through the heat of the day. Get the herd going about four o'clock and keep 'em moving. That'll be the tough part because the cows won't want to start again. Stop the herd when it gets dark and let them rest until about four or five in the morning."

Bob nodded.

"By the second day, the cows will want water, and there won't be any. Keep them moving. The herd needs to do a hundred miles in four days, and as you know, that'll be tough."

"Is that what you did with the last herd you worked up this way?" Bob asked.

Joe nodded. "That's what we did." No need to tell him it had been miserable for everyone. Bob would find out for himself.

"What should the wagons do?"

"We need to keep up with the herd. We have filled every container we have, so we'll have water for the hands and the coffee. If we lose a horse and have to stop, somebody needs to bring up another one." Joe stopped talking and finished his meal.

"I better go tell the riders to be ready to move out early." Bob gave Joe a pat on the shoulder and then walked over to where several riders where bedded down for the night.

Cookie finished packing the chuck box. "Joe, I'll ride with Billy tomorrow, and you drive the chuck wagon with Sara and take the lead position. Mr. Barnes' wagon will take up the tail. The first day we'll try to get ahead of the herd and have a meal ready for noon. We'll have to make good time if Bob pushes the herd. He wants to make about ten miles by the noon stop. This is going to be a rough few days."

"It'll be tough, but we'll make it. Just need to keep moving."

Joe went down to the river and took a quick dip before the sun set. It would be the last chance to cool off for at least five days. As Joe made his way up the bank, Felix stood down by the river holding his rifle. Joe guessed Sara was also taking a dip.

~

Joe woke to the sound of twigs breaking and the clang of pots and pans. From the shadows on the canvas of the wagon cast by lantern light, he could see that Cookie had started the breakfast preparations.

In the half-light, Joe dressed. He pulled out a clean bandana, as he anticipated a lot of dust in the next few days and then he climbed down from the chuck wagon. He walked into the light of the lantern, pulling out his pocket watch. Just after three in the morning. An early beginning to a day he didn't look forward to.

Memories assailed him reminding him of previous drives along this trail. The coming days would be hard on Sara, and that had him worried. In one way, he wished her father had listened and taken her to catch the train at Caldwell. They could have met them at Dodge City, and saved her from the hardship of the drive; but for himself he was glad her father hadn't listened. He loved having her riding with him on the chuck wagon.

"Morning, Joe. Thanks for getting up so early. We need breakfast cooked and served by five."

"Yes, Cookie." Joe gave a big yawn. "What do you want me to do?"

"I'll do biscuits and peel potatoes. You fry the steaks. What we don't cook of that beef this morning we'll bury. It won't last another day uncooked. Then after you have the steaks done, move on to the gravy." Cookie dumped flour into his big mixing bowl. "Let Billy sleep for a little while longer. He's going to be working hard enough in the next few days."

Joe had cooked so many steaks in the last couple of months that he could do them in his sleep. This would be their last full breakfast for the next few days. He appreciated Cookies' thoughtfulness toward Billy. The older man really did have a good heart.

The riders woke before their normal time. Everyone was tense about the day's drive. Before they even had breakfast, riders had their bedrolls in the wrangler wagon and their horses saddled in the temporary rope corral. When breakfast was ready, the cowhands ate quickly and in silence, then they mounted and rode out to the herd.

Joe filled several Dutch ovens with water, then placed them in the wagons in front of the driver's feet where they might ride smoother. He also placed a pot of hot coffee next to the Dutch ovens.

Felix offered to carry the big pots full of water in the Barnes' wagon, so they filled all of them and placed them inside the wagon. The heavy cast iron pots with lids would ride without water sloshing out.

Joe climbed up on the chuck wagon seat and picked up the reins. Sara sat next to him with a bonnet covering her hair and shading her face. Joe took the lead with the wrangler wagon following, and then Barnes' wagon last. He clucked and slapped the reins to maintain a fast walk, and occasionally a trot. If they wanted to stay ahead of the herd, they needed to keep the pace up. Joe didn't envy the riders their work today.

"You ready for the day?" Joe looked at Sara's pretty, smooth complexion. What would the next few days do to her?

She returned his gaze. "I'm ready."

"Well, hang on tight and drink lots of water when it gets hot. We're in for a rough ride." He wanted to take care of Sara so much that he could barely keep from putting a comforting arm around her.

She leaned toward him and placed a hand on his arm that held the reins. "I'm going to be fine. You're going to make sure of that." The smile she gave him lit up her whole face.

Joe returned her smile and found his voice husky as he spoke. "I'll do my best."

Chapter Eighteen

Jim Finely led the way as he was riding point. A little after noon Joe saw him in the distance waving his hat in a circle. They rolled up to where he indicated, and built a couple of fires. He, Cookie, and Sara had fresh coffee made and a meal ready for the hands who took turns riding in. Each man ate and headed back out to the herd where they waited out the worst of the mid-day sun.

After about three hours of baking under the brutal August heat, they headed out again for another five hours, moving the stock at double the normal pace. The cattle didn't like it, but the riders didn't give them a choice. They stopped sometime after nine that night, got a fire going, coffee made, and managed to put a meal together. As soon as a drover ate, he crawled into his bedroll for a couple of hours. Bob had the hands rotate through the night to keep the herd settled down.

Before dawn, they were on the trail again. They made thirty-miles the first day, but it would be difficult to keep that up for three more days. Each day would get more difficult.

~

Joe noticed Sara wasn't talking much as they headed out ahead of the herd on the second day. "You all right?" He glanced over at her pale face, partly hidden by the bonnet she wore instead of her usual straw hat.

She adjusted the ribbon that tied on her bonnet. "I'm doing fine."

Joe regretted that she covered up her hair which, when free, caught the sun like spun gold. He preferred it when she wore the straw hat, but knew that the bonnet offered more protection from the dust and sun. "I wondered because you're not saying much."

She laid her hand on his arm. "I know, but you need your energy to keep these horses going. This is harder driving than we've had before. You don't need to listen to me chatter."

"I like your chatter. I can handle these horses." He felt a warm glow deep down that she thought about what he needed. The hard drive in the heat of the day wore out the riders and their horses. Each rider could easily go through six to eight horses in a day. They changed out the teams for the wagons every couple of hours and stopped for ten minutes every hour.

"Well, if I have something important to say, I'll let you know. Besides, it's so hot and dry. I need to conserve my energy by not talking so much." She squeezed his arm and then took her hand away as Bob rode to the wagon.

Riders rode to the chuck wagon in a steady stream for coffee and to refill their canteens. Joe notice that Mr. Barnes didn't came to the chuck wagon to ask Sara how she was doing. Was he not concerned for her or did he trust that Joe and Cookie would keep her safe? Joe could barely stand for her to be out of his sight when she left in the evenings to find her bed in her wagon.

As the second day passed, Joe watched as the riders slumped in their saddles. When they came for water, their usual joking was absent. They didn't even try to get a special word from Sara, which told Joe how rough the journey was for them.

They were going through the water fast. Joe hoped the supply from Dodge City was on its way. All was quiet in the camp that night, save for the crackle and popping of the fires. The riders barely had enough energy to eat a bite and get into their bedrolls. But many of them had to be out with the herd to keep it from turning back and scattering.

About two in the morning, thunderstorms swept through and dumped enough rain to bring relief. Bob sent all the riders out to keep the herd quiet, fearing another stampede. Joe got up and uncovered the water barrels to catch some of the rain. He returned to sleep to the sound of the rain on the treated canvas of the wagon.

The next day there were puddles of water along the trail. Joe was more hopeful they'd make it through without a great loss though the cattle and horses were difficult to keep moving, as they wanted to stop feed and drink.

By evening of the third day, they were beyond the area of the previous night's rainfall and once again it was hot and dry. Dust lay thick over everything.

Joe pulled out a clean bandana from his bag. "Here, Sara, let me tie this around your face to help keep some of the dust out of your mouth." He quickly tied the big red bandana around her face. "Now you look like a proper bank robber."

"Thanks." She managed to show her smile through her eyes just above the bandana at his teasing.

Dust-covered riders rode up to the chuck wagon to fill their canteens with water throughout the afternoon. When they lowered their bandanas to swallow some needed water, their faces showed the line where that coverage of the bandanas stopped just below their eyes. All the riders had developed a haunted look from weight loss and lack of sleep, But Joe didn't hear any complaints. Those boys had a job to do and they did it. And Joe knew how hard it was on them, having been there himself.

On the fourth day, they lost their first cows. Some of them stopped and nothing could get them to move again. Others lay down and couldn't get up.

Several horses also went down, and as much as the riders hated it, the kindest thing was to shoot a horse or cow that couldn't get up.

Exhausted, covered with sweat, and smelling from the work, Joe dreaded the day ahead. Even Sara, who sat slumped on the wagon seat, looked small and wilted.

He handed her the canteen. "Here, drink some water." He wanted to protect her from the difficult day ahead but there was nothing to do but keep the wagon moving. Somehow she managed to still appear fresh, even though the fatigue was showing.

"I'm all right. I don't need a drink." Her voice was weak, as if breathing was an effort.

Joe worked to keep his voice soft. "Don't argue with me. Just drink up."

She smiled weakly at him and drank from the canteen. Her not arguing with him showed how badly the drive was affecting her. They had only one water barrel with any water left in it, but Joe kept Sara's canteen filled. Why hadn't Barnes listened and not put her through this?

He slapped the reins and yelled at the horses to keep them moving. Suddenly, the horse on the left of the lead team stumbled, and then stumbled again. "Whoa, easy there." Joe reined back and pulled the brake.

Cookie pulled the wrangler wagon next to them. "What's the problem?"

Joe climbed down and went around to the lead horses. All the horses stood with their heads hanging and their sides heaving. The far lead horse on the left barely stood.

"This horse is about to go down." Joe patted the horse's neck. He hated to see animals suffer and this horse was suffering.

"What do you want to do?" Cookie frowned and looked over the other horses.

"You all go ahead, and as soon as you can send someone back." Joe unhitched the horse and led him off to the side. The horse swayed, ready to collapse.

Will Ramsey rode up and yelled. "What's the problem?"

"We need another horse." Joe told him. "Can you ride over to the remuda and bring us one?"

"Sure, I'll be back quick as I can." He whipped his horse around, and rode toward the remuda in the distance.

"We'll keep going, and you come on as soon as possible." Cookie stood, shaded his eyes, and pointed north. "Wait a minute, Joe. What's that I see ahead there?"

Joe climbed back up on the wagon, and searched in the direction Cookie pointed.

"It's a wagon." Joe sat down on the wagon seat with relief. "Maybe it's the water wagon from Dodge City."

"I hope so."

A rider met up with the wagon in the distance and point toward them. A short time later, a large freight wagon came rolling up.

"Are you the fellows who ordered all this water?" The freighter asked.

"We sure are." Cookie said with a grin. "Let's use some of it to water these horses pulling these wagons."

They all climbed down and gave each horse a half a bucket of water.

Joe took half a bucket to the horse he had unhitched and hoped it was enough to save it. He patted the horse's neck. "Sorry, old fella."

Will Ramsey rode up with a horse in tow to add to the lead team.

"How far are we from the Arkansas River?" Cookie asked the freighter.

"Y'all only have fifteen miles," the freighter said. "Hope them steers don't smell the river and stampede on you."

Joe climbed back up on the wagon seat. "Cookie, you and Felix need to keep up with me. I'm going to keep these horses moving as fast as I can without killing them. We need to reach the river before we camp."

Cookie waved as if in agreement. "You lead the way. We'll be right behind you."

Joe glanced at Sara and gently touched her hand. "You all right, Sara?" He noticed the dark circles under her eyes and the frown lines between her brows. She looked exhausted.

She pushed herself up from her slumped position to a lady-like posture. "I'm fine, although ready to get this day over." Her voice came just above a whisper, and Joe saw no signs of a smile behind the bandana.

He wanted this day over for her sake, as well as the rest of them. She was too small and fragile to put through such rough conditions. "You and me both. Let me have that canteen. Let's both drink up now that we have plenty of water." He swallowed several gulps of water, and then handed the canteen back to her.

The riders came in for water, and Joe and Cookie were able to offer water not only for the riders, but also for their horses.

Joe shouted back at Cookie. "We need to keep the freight wagon away from the remuda and the cattle. We don't want them to smell the water and run over us."

Cookie waved his hat.

Joe took that for agreement as he started the horses moving. He reined the teams to give the herd a wider berth.

They were only about two miles from the Arkansas River by the time darkness fell over the land. Bob told the riders to let the herd head on to the river. Once they smelled the water, they couldn't be held back.

Joe reined the horses under some trees west of the herd on the south side of the river. His arms trembled from the hours of holding the reins. If someone blew on him now he feared he would drop to the ground and not get up for days. Everyone else looked to be in the same shape.

He helped Sara down from the wagon seat and she slumped for a moment against him as if her legs couldn't support her. He put his arms around her to steady her and she leaned her head against his chest.

With a sigh, she straightened. "What do I need to do to help prepare supper?"

Joe looked down into her tired face and noted that her blue eyes had the same sparkle as ever. His arms ached to hold her, but instead he stepped back. "You're not going to do anything. You're going to your wagon and get into bed. I'll bring something for you to eat when we have supper ready."

"But..." She gave a halfhearted protest.

"No buts, go to bed. You're about ready to drop. You've just been through four tough days. Get some rest."

Sara looked up at him and smiled. "Thank you. I am exhausted. If I can get a good night's sleep I'll be fine by tomorrow." She squeezed his arm and then walked toward her wagon.

Joe wished that he could go crawl into his bedroll, but they had a meal to put together.

While Cookie put on some oatmeal to cook, Joe built a couple of fires and made coffee for the boys. It wasn't much of a supper, but it was about all they had the energy to make. The hands wanted coffee, but were too tired to eat much. Until they crossed the river, most of the riders still had to be out with the herd.

After they served breakfast the following morning, they started packing up to move across the Arkansas River on the ferry run by an old Indian. Getting all four wagons across would take all morning. The freighter would go first and then drive on into Dodge City, a few miles north of the river. Jim Finely had located a place to camp and an area where they could bed down the herd for a couple of days to allow the cattle to recover from the dry run. The riders needed the rest as well after they got the herd across the river.

Bob strode over for one last cup of coffee before he rode out. "Joe that was some hard drive, I don't want to do that again."

"Yeah, it's hard on horses, cows, and men." Joe said. "That was my third time through."

"The hands want to go into Dodge. You've been there. What do you think?"

Joe thought a moment. "Let them go into town but only in the daytime, and only a few at a time. Let them go in for about two hours, and then have them get back. That way they won't be as likely to get drunk, or into fights. Also, they will be less likely to quit the drive." Joe cocked his head at Bob. "Is that what you were asking?"

"That's exactly what I was asking. If we're going to get the herd to the Evans' ranch we need them to stay on the job for at least four or five more weeks."

~

Mr. Barnes waited for a response from Elisha Evans while he held the herd outside Dodge City. After two days, they moved the herd north, close to a large creek away from the traffic crossing the Arkansas River, and Cookie took the chuck and wrangler wagon into Dodge City for supplies.

Joe looked north up the trail they would take. They must travel the four hundred mile route up to Nebraska, over to Wyoming, and then back down into northern Colorado territory before they delivered the herd to Elisha Evans' Rocking ES ranch. They had another good thirty to forty days of driving ahead.

As Joe helped pack the supplies they'd bought, he thought it should last until Ogallala, Nebraska. They could buy supplies out of Ogallala, and then again at Cheyenne. For now they were ready to start across Kansas with plenty of supplies for the chuck wagon, and hopefully plenty of water and grass for the cattle.

Cookie bought several freshly killed and plucked chickens near Dodge City from a farmer. He had Billy pick some blackberries from wild bush along the trail.

As they dished out a meal of fried chicken with mashed potatoes, canned green beans, gravy, biscuits, and blackberry cobbler, Joe had to grin at the crew's whoops and hollers.

"Hey, Cookie," Jeff ribbed as he came back for seconds, "just how old is this chicken?"

"Well," Cookie drawled. "Let's just say it had gray feathers."

"It was a chick when we started on the drive," Jim said, his mouth half-full. He started to say something else, and froze mid-speech. Joe's eyes followed his gaze.

Two riders were coming in from the north at a slow jog. The dust from their trail spiraled lazily in the slight breeze.

Josh Thomas dismounted and, throwing his reins to the nearest hand, jerked his chin towards the other rider. "This here's Elisha Evans."

Evans nodded to no one in particular as he dismounted.

Joe had assumed Elisha Evans was close to Mr. Barnes' age of fifty, but the man appeared to be in his early thirties. Evans was a little taller than Joe, with a rider's broad shoulders and narrow hips. Joe guessed the ladies would think him to be a handsome man, given Evans' dark eyes, and the bit of curl to his dark hair. Joe glanced over at Sara and found her staring at the new arrivals.

Joe set out the two camp chairs out under the canvas attached to the side of the chuck wagon. He then checked the bucket of hot water and found plenty for the two men to wash up after their journey. They had the look of riders who had been on the trail for several days.

After they had washed up, they came over to the worktable to pick up a plate of food each.

"Let me introduce Cookie, Joe Storm, and this lovely lady is Mr. Barnes' daughter Sara. You all, meet Elisha Evans of Colorado," Josh said by way of introduction.

"Miss Barnes, I'm happy to meet you. Josh told me about you traveling with the trail drive. That's certainly an adventure for a young lady." Elisha took Sara's hand and briefly held it.

"I'm pleased to meet you, Mr. Evans. And you can imagine that Mr. Thomas has told us about you and your ranch up in the mountains. I believe he said that you're married and have children."

Joe was so busy staring at Sara that he almost missed Elisha Evans' reply. She was such a lovely sight in a simple white dress with little red flowers sprinkled over it. She'd tied her blonde hair back from her pretty face. He was a little uneasy at the color in her cheeks and at how long Evans was holding her hand.

Elisha smiled. "Yes ma'am, my wife Susana and I have a little boy and girl." His voice brightened as he spoke of his family. "I hate that I had to leave them back at the ranch, but it was too fast a trip for them to come with me."

Joe took a deep breath of relief. The man was just being polite. Ouch. Was that jealousy that hit his chest like a hammer? He didn't want any man giving Sara attention but him.

"And I hear you're an exceptional trail cook." Evan shook hands with Cookie.

He then turned to Joe with raised eyebrows.

Joe extended his hand. "Joe Storm, cook's helper."

"Joe Storm, I've heard interesting things about you. Good to make your acquaintance. I understand you are from Colorado and look forward to having some conversations with you." He shook Joe's hand with a firm grip.

Joe liked how Elisha gave each person his full attention, as if each was of equal importance to him. There was something about this man that Joe felt a kinship with. But even so, it wouldn't do to have the man asking questions about himself and his old life back in Colorado.

"Yes, sir, let's go ahead and get you all served," he said, changing the subject. "You look like you've been riding for a couple of days and are ready for a good meal."

After a while, Joe brought the three men servings of cobbler, and then refilled their coffee cups.

Joe listened to their discussion as he worked around the chuck wagon. Barnes and Elisha talked about the sale of the herd. Elisha Evans seemed calm and confident. He didn't insist on anything, but he didn't agree until he had what he wanted.

"Do you think any of your riders might be interested in working through the winter?" Elisha asked Mr. Barnes. "After we get the herd to the ranch, I plan to hire several riders."

"I feel sure several would welcome a chance to stay on. Of course, those with family back in Texas will want to head back as soon as possible." Barnes answered.

Did Elisha have a cook? It was something to consider. Joe could survive the harsh winter conditions having grown up in the mountains. However, some of the riders that had brought the herd up from south Texas had barely seen snow, and much less had the know-how to survive a Northern Colorado winter.

Before they finally went to spread their bedrolls on the ground around Barnes's wagon, Elisha Evans and Matthew Barnes shook hands on a deal. The herd was sold, with payment upon delivery.

Joe had mixed feelings. He longed to see the mountains close to where he had grown up. However, the Rocking ES ranch too close to his father's place.

Later that evening as he lay in his bedroll, Joe comtemplated taking the herd to Colorado. His stomach clenched. Was he afraid to go? The memories of his childhood, and his mother were still too sharp. His heart grew heavy; he didn't want to see his mother and experience her rejection again. He thought back to when he had first been on his own at age fourteen. He had assumed he would eventually learn to deal with his feelings about his mother, and they wouldn't bother him.

He turned over and tried to squeeze the memories back into the box where he tried to hide them in his mind. Since the injury, it seemed to be more difficult to bear than ever and he didn't know how to let it go.

Chapter Nineteen

The next morning was clear and the heat of the day was still slumbering. Bob Fife stood in the middle of the camp as the riders finished their breakfast. "Everyone gather round. This includes the cook crew." Joe noticed that left only Jeff and Santo out riding the herd knowing it would be only for a short time before the other riders would join them.

Mr. Barnes walked up beside Bob and waited for them to gather and to quiet down. "This is Elisha Evans of the Rocking ES of northern Colorado. I've sold the herd dependent on delivery to his ranch. Elisha, you have anything you want to say?"

Elisha looked around slowly at the gathered men and smiled. "I've looked over the herd. You're all to be commended on getting it up the trail in as good a shape as these cattle are in. I've heard about the dry run and that's a hard way to herd cows. It's four hundred miles to my ranch. I want every one of you to stay on all the way there. I'm buying the herd at delivery, so that means Mr. Barnes is still acting owner until we get to my ranch. We'll travel under his trail brand, and then after the cattle are at my ranch, we'll brand them with my Rocking ES brand. Josh Thomas and I'll make the rest of the drive with you and we'll work just like any other hands." Evans turned to Bob. "I'll turn this over to you."

He stepped forward. "I've come up all the way from Texas with you men. You're a good trail crew. We have four hundred more miles to go to deliver these cows. This morning, we'll start out slow. We'll have a count that will be the basis for the sale of the herd. Anyone who doesn't draw his pay now will be expected to drive all the way to the Rocking ES. If no one has any questions, get saddled and let's move out."

John Henry Davies and Harvey Standard drew their pay and left the drive near Dodge City. Both were average riders and had been hard working, but had wives and children back in Texas. Joe wasn't surprised that they wanted to get back. They'd arrive home with some hard cash, and with luck get on with an outfit closer to home.

"Let's get the wagons organized." Cookie sat on the wagon tongue drinking coffee. "We'll have the same number of mouths to feed because Josh and Elisha plan to stay with the herd. Mr. Barnes told me he didn't see a need to replace the two men leaving."

"That makes five gone who started out with us." Billy spoke up from where he was washing dishes.

Joe looked at the boy with a grin. Billy rarely said anything. Maybe he was getting more confidence as the trail drive continued.

Bob rode up and dismounted a ways off. He walked up to the fire and poured a cup of coffee. "Got everyone working and the count underway, although I could have told them as I've kept track of every head."

Cookie glanced at him over his cup of coffee. "So what are your numbers?"

Scratching his head, Bob said, "Although we lost at least twenty head of cattle on the dry run, butchered and have eaten ten head of cattle, when the count is completed they will probably show we've picked up about two hundred head of cattle on the trail."

Joe nodded. He had seen it happen before. As the herd had come up the trail, they'd picked up strays from other herds. "So you're predicting the final count will be five thousand three hundred eight head of cattle. That should make it easy for Mr. Barnes to let us butcher a few to help feed the crew along the rest of the trail."

Joe enjoyed the days on the trail, which fell into the pattern they'd followed before the dry run. The grass was plentiful. They found much-needed water in the creeks. And Sara continued to ride beside him on the chuck wagon. Although they were never out of sight of others, the noise of the wagons and horses made it possible for them to talk without the others hearing. Sara was an educated, intelligent young woman and Joe learned from their far ranging conversations.

As they traveled up the trail, they heard rumors of Indian raids from travelers who passed by the herd and the cowhands were nervous. Some of the cowhands talked to the riders from the herd ahead of them who had also heard the rumors. The one good thing about the rumors was that most of the settlers along the trail had hightailed it to the towns and forts to the east. They didn't have to deal with rancher's protests of the herd passing, nor their demands that the owner pay a toll for crossing their land.

An old Comanche Indian rode up to the chuck wagon at noon one day to ask for food and a couple of cows. He said that his village was hungry. Joe spoke some of his language having learned it from a rider on another trail drive and so talked to him about the rumors.

"Bob, this Comanche tells me that the rumor of trouble with the Wichita Indians is just that, a rumor started by a trail boss to clear out the settlers in front of his trail drive." Joe told him. "You might tell the fellows so they'll sleep better at night."

Bob laughed. "I'd not doubt that at all. Well, if this Indian knows what he's talking about that's a relief to my mind. I'll cut out a couple of cows and send a few other supplies for him to take back to his village."

Joe looked around and made sure no one could hear him but Bob. "We will pass by Oberlin in a day or so. You might get some supplies there, and then drift west until you come to the Plate River, and then follow it toward Wyoming. That'll take you clear of Ogallala. I wouldn't stop near there anyway."

Bob, as usual, was grateful for his advice. "Thanks. That's exactly what I'll do. I've heard about Ogallala. It has the reputation of being a wild town with more saloons that homes."

"You should come up on the Sappa creek tomorrow, and then on north of there you'll cross over into Nebraska, although it's hard to tell exactly where the boundary is between the Indian Territory, Kansas, and Nebraska. In the morning, I can swing over east and go through Oberlin to get supplies and then meet up with you by supper."

"Sounds like a good plan. I'll go tell Mr. Barnes what we're doing. Take Jeff and Jim with you tomorrow."

Sara talked her father into letting her go to Oberlin with them so she could do some shopping, although Joe doubted the little town would have much beyond the one general store.

They piled everything from the wrangler wagon into the chuck wagon and Joe drove the empty wagon toward the little town with Sara next to him and with Jeff and Jim as outriders. Sara kept the drive fun with lively conversation. She teased them with jokes and word games that left them all laughing. Joe had to admit he hadn't felt so contented in a long time.

They reached the little town by noon and pulled up in front of a small, unpainted narrow building that had a sign that drooped from one corner, Kelly's Mercantile. Joe helped Sara down from the wagon and walked into the store with her. The store was surprisingly well stocked and Sara immediately started talking to the older woman behind the counter. Joe gave Cookie's list to the short, rotund, baldheaded man that he assumed was Mr. Kelly.

The man took the list. "You got money to pay for all of this?"

"Yes, sir. Just fill the order and you'll get paid." He had money that Mr. Barnes had given him to purchase the supplies.

Jeff and Jim disappeared with the horses. Joe assumed that they were watering and feeding them at the livery he had seen down the road from the general store.

He started loading the wagon with their purchases as soon as he paid Mr. Kelly. He dumped a hundred pound bag of flour onto the wagon bed when out of the corner of his eye, he saw two men move toward the door of the store. Sara came out of the store burdened with several packages and collided with one of the men. Parcels scattered on the ground.

"We beg your pardon, ma'am." One of the two reached down for one of the fallen packages.

Joe's head jerked toward the sound of the familiar voice, one he had hoped never to hear again. What were they doing here?

"Now what is a pretty little thing like you doing out here in a place like Oberlin?"

Joe moved toward the men that he recognized as Frank and Curly.

"Excuse me, sir. Just let me have my packages and I'll be on my way." Sara's voice sounded unsure.

"No need to be in a hurry. We just want to talk a bit." Joe saw that Curly had a grip on her arm.

"Sara, walk over here to me." Joe put as much steel into his voice as he could.

Curly and Frank both turned to him with raised eyebrows and open mouths.

Sara saw the opening, scooted between the men, and quickly moved to stand behind Joe.

"Go down to the livery and meet Jeff and Jim. Do it now, Sara." Joe stepped away from her and was relieved that she immediately hurried down the road.

"Well, well. If it isn't little Cookie." Curly voice held a menace and asperity that caused the hairs to stand up on the back of Joe's neck.

Joe wore his revolver as he usually did as a defense against snakes— reptile or human. Well, here were two snakes if he had ever met any. "Just get on about your business, Curly." Joe hoped he could talk Curly into moving on, but the cold, black-eyed stare from Frank left his scalp tingling.

"I don't think so, little Cookie. What do you think, Frank? Should we just be done with this now?"

"Yeah, I say let's just be done with this little bug." Frank's lips formed what was his version of a smile, but instead screamed a warning in Joe's brain.

So quickly that it might've happened between heartbeats, Joe threw himself to the side as Frank drew his gun. The split second that Joe hesitated, he felt the impact of the bullet in his left arm and then he fired his own weapon. Bullets thudded into the wagon behind him and gunshots exploded again and again. Then other guns were going off and, as quickly as it had started, the street was quiet except for the sound of dogs barking an alarm in the distance.

Curly and Frank lay on the ground. Blood stained the ground under their crumpled bodies.

Joe could barely put his revolver back into his holster he was shaking so. He couldn't seem to breathe as he stared at the men on the ground. He hadn't meant to kill them. Hadn't wanted to kill anyone. Then Sara ran into his arms.

"Oh, Joe, are you all right? You're bleeding. How bad are you hurt?" Sara's face was white as if all the blood had drained from her body.

He looked at his left arm and the spreading bright red blood on the sleeve of his shirt. His vision blurred a little and the earth swayed under his feet. Blinking and shaking his head, he cleared his vision.

With their revolvers still drawn, Jeff and Jim came into his sight.

Jeff put his hand on Joe's back. "Come on. Let's go into the store and get you fixed up."

The men holstered their weapons and Joe let them lead him, still with Sara wrapped in his right arm, into the store. Mr. Kelly stood with a rifle in his hands and Mrs. Kelly huddled behind him with a stiff face of fear. She shuddered and wiped her face with a lace-trimmed handkerchief.

Sara took a deep breath. "Please, we need some cloth for bandages, hot water, and some alcohol or carbolic acid if you have some."

"Of course, I've got everything we need." Mrs. Kelly recovered quickly and went to get the things needed.

Joe sat down in a chair by a potbellied stove. He couldn't seem to stop trembling. Only now was he feeling the full terror of the last few minutes. What if Sara had been hurt? He didn't want to think about that.

The storekeeper came over and asked, "Did you know them fellers?"

Jeff looked at the others before he spoke up. "Yes, sir. We've had trouble with them before down in Oklahoma Territory."

The older man nodded. "I saw the whole thing. They meant to kill you. I'm amazed you only got one bullet hole in you."

Sara tore Joe's shirt from around the wound, took the cloth from the woman and dipped it into the hot water before beginning to clean the blood from around the wound. "The bullet went in here and out at the back of your upper arm. All I know to do is clean it with some alcohol and carbolic acid and bandage it tight to stop the bleeding." Her voice was low and calm.

Joe clenched his jaw against the burn of the alcohol being poured over the wound. The touch of the cloth soaked in carbolic acid against the still bleeding hole in his upper arm was almost a relief. At least no bones were broken and he could still move his hand and elbow.

Jeff had torn the sleeve off Joe's shirt and was now holding Joe's arm while Sara cleaned up the blood and wrapped a bandage from the strips of cloth Mrs. Kelly had provided tightly around his arm. "Joe, you think you can ride back to the herd?"

Joe wasn't too sure he could even walk to the wagon, but they needed to get back. "Sure, but what about Curly and Frank? Is there a lawman here?"

Mr. Kelly shook his head and looked out at the road where a group of men and boys had gathered around the bodies. "We don't have any law here since our last sheriff left. I guess we just need to bury them and let that be it. It was self-defense for sure. Do you boys know their names?"

No one knew more that their first names. Jeff spoke up. "Bob should have their full names written down and where they are from. We can send that to you and you can mark their graves at least."

Mrs. Kelly came in from the back room with cups of coffee on a tray.

Joe drank the coffee, which was strong enough to give him some relief from the weakness he was feeling in the aftermath of the fight. He guessed it was a fight, although it had happened so fast that if he closed his eyes and shut out the pain in his arm he could almost believe it hadn't happened. He had seen men die violent deaths before but he had never killed. It would take a little getting used to.

"Joe, you all right?" Sara had her hand on his shoulder squeezing as if to bring him back from wherever his thoughts had taken him.

"Yeah, I'm fine." He opened his eyes and looked at the small crowd on the street and the two bodies being placed on boards and taken away. Gripping his left arm close to his body to help ease the pain, he knew it was real.

"Let's finish loading the wagon and start back. If we need to we can stop along the way. You tell us, Joe, what we need to do," Jim said.

"I'll be fine. Let me just sit here until we're ready to go." He leaned back in the chair and felt Sara's body at his back with her hand resting on the back of his neck.

Sara stood behind Joe and moved her hands to his shoulders. "I'll stay with Joe while you all get the horses."

He felt the strength of those hands and felt his insides starting to calm.

It only took Jeff, Jim, and Mr. Kelly a few minutes to finish loading the wagon and get the horses hitched. Jeff insisted that Joe lie down on the sacks of supplies while he drove the wagon. Sara sat beside Jeff but turned often to check on Joe as they made their way the three hours it took them to meet up with the herd. Jim rode alongside the wagon, constantly scanning the countryside as if fearful of another attack.

Joe hurt, but it wasn't something he couldn't handle. The mounting fever was more of a bother. By the time they drove into camp, he felt poorly indeed. His arm blazed with pain and he was sweating profusely. Even though he had not eaten since morning, he feared he would throw up.

Cookie had him sit in a camp chair while he checked his arm. It was red and hot around both the entrance and exit wounds. But Joe was glad to see that there weren't any red streaks and no smell of a wound going bad yet. He could only hope that it would heal clean.

Mr. Barnes' harsh voice was loud and insistent. "What happened? How could you allow Sara to be part of a shooting?"

Jeff started to speak up. "Mr. Barnes, it wasn't—"

Sara interrupted. "Papa, Joe had no choice. The two men were harassing me. Joe told them to stop and sent me to the livery to get Jeff and Jim. The men drew down on Joe and he had no choice but to defend himself. I wasn't anywhere near the shooting."

Joe thought she was stretching the truth a bit. She could have easily been hit by a stray bullet. He knew she had witnessed everything.

Jim, who usually didn't talk much at all, said, "If Joe hadn't jumped in those men might have hurt your daughter. I ain't heard no thank you." Jim's face was still and calm, but his black eyes were a hard glitter as they stared at Matthew Barnes. "He could have just walked away, but of course that's not Joe's way. He stood up like a man."

Barnes seemed to be confused by what, for Jim, was a long speech. "Of course I appreciate that my daughter wasn't hurt. But did he have to kill them in front of her?"

Jim shook his head. "Nobody knows who killed them. All three of us fired at them. Any one of our bullets might have killed them."

Joe looked up at Jim in surprise. He had just assumed it was his bullets that had done the killing. Did it make a difference whether he had killed the men or not? He wasn't sure. The two men were still dead. He hadn't liked Curly and Frank, but he had never wished them dead.

Cookie put his hand on Joe's forehead and turned to Mr. Barnes. "It's done and over. Sara is safe. We need to let Joe rest. He's got a fever now. He needs to lie down if he's going to get better."

Elisha Evans took Mr. Barnes by the arm. "Walk a ways with me, Matt. I need to ask you something." He led them from the chuck wagon. The other men wandered away about their business leaving only Joe and Sara.

Joe was glad to be away from Mr. Barnes. He didn't fault the man for being upset. Joe sighed. He had failed to protect Sara from an ugly scene. But what could he have done differently?

Sara stood by the chair and laid a cool wet cloth on his forehead. "Maybe that will draw some of the fever."

"I'm sorry." He took her hand and looked up into her eyes. "I wish you hadn't had to see that."

"It's not your fault. I don't know how any of us could have stopped what happened. I'm all right, Joe." She squeezed his hand, leaned over, and kissed his forehead. "I'm just so thankful that you're not hurt any worse."

He reached up and pushed back a golden curl that had escaped the ribbon holding her hair back from her face. "I'll try to do better."

"Better at what?" She had hold of his hand again.

"Better at protecting you." He sighed, wanting to pull her head down to his and kiss her. Instead he let go of her hand. "Go change, eat some supper, and forget what happened today."

She looked down at her blood-splattered dress and nodded.

Chapter Twenty

Whether it was the frequent alcohol poured over the wound, which hurt something awful, or the clear air, Joe healed quickly. The arm was painful for a couple of weeks, but the fever only held for three days. However, nightmares of the gunfight continued to plague him.

As they reached the Platte River valley and drove the herd west, toward Wyoming Territory, the land rose until Joe could tell from the plants and trees that they were at an altitude of about four thousand feet. The early September nights were cool, which Joe didn't mind, though the noonday sun shone bright and warm. He was thankful they had left the blistering heat of the lower prairie behind. The evening and nighttime chill, however, spooked some of the South Texas boys, who feared winter had come.

They left the Platte Valley and followed Lodgepole Creek. At the border of Wyoming, they passed through the canyon where pine trees hung on the sides of the cliffs, then the trail ran through the middle of a cluster of buildings, which a sign declared was Pine Bluffs. More a gap through the scarp than a true canyon, it was only about three miles long.

They emerged from the Lodgepole Creek canyon, onto a broad plateau six thousand feet high. There in the distance Joe got what his heart had hungered for, a glimpse of the snow-capped Rocky Mountains shining in the sunlight almost a hundred miles away. For the next several days, they traveled with the sight of the slowly approaching mountains in front of them. Ahead of them, Joe knew, was the town of Cheyenne only about forty miles away.

Elisha rode point every day now, as they approached his range. Mr. Barnes rode into the town and had a couple of freight wagons come out to meet them. Some of the supplies were for the rest of the trip, but some were winter supplies of Elisha Evan's ranch.

They passed about thirty miles north of the cabin on Pinto Creek, which was just south of the huge ridge that was the northern border of his father's ranch. Joe felt the worst pull to turn the chuck wagon that way, as he remembered times as a boy on hunting trips with his father and they would stay at the cabin, which was located at the northern most boundary of his father's ranch. Did his father have cowhands working out of the cabin now, or was it deserted? He wanted to ask Elisha about the ranch and family to the south, but didn't want to get questions started.

As they skirted a couple of the tall peaks of northern Colorado, they finally came to the series of valleys that made up Elisha Evans' ranch. Joe stopped the chuck wagon and took in the beauty of the valley. The ranch buildings were up against the mountain bluffs on the north side of the valley.

Joe guessed they were somewhere between six and eight thousand feet high. The clear, cool mountain air at this altitude refreshed his spirit, and Joe feasted his soul and his eyes with the mountains all around him. Until they'd arrived here, he'd not realized how much he'd missed the mountains' rugged beauty. Even if he couldn't ride the mountain trails, Joe stilled appreciate the inspiring landscape that was his homeland.

His mind flooded with memories of riding with his father through this very valley and tears stung his eyes.

Sara, sitting beside him, looked at him with puzzlement. "Is something wrong."

He wiped his eyes with his shirtsleeves. "Just dust from the cattle." He wanted to tell her his thoughts and share his feelings about being back in the mountains. But he couldn't, not without also telling her about his family, and he wasn't ready to do that.

They were all silent as the cattle slowly drifted into the valley as though they knew they were finally at the end of the trail.

The grass in the thirty miles of valley was chest high on the cattle. In the center of the valley, a large stream flowed toward the east. Elisha had two other valleys where he planned to put part of the herd, and each of the valleys had box canyons that led off as they came up against more of the high mountains.

The north boundary of his father's ranch was about thirty miles south. From the northern boundary the land gradually flowed to lower elevations, into the huge valley that was the ranch headquarters and his father's home. At that point, the elevation was only about three to four thousand feet high. Because of the different altitudes, the two ranches had very different winters. Elisha's Rocking ES would have a severe winter, and Joe wondered at the ability of the Texas bred cattle to survive it. He had to assume that Elisha had taken that into consideration.

Elisha pulled his horse up close to the chuck wagon. "Why have you stopped?"

Joe waved his hand to take in the valley and the mountains. "I'm just looking at it, Mr. Evans. What a great place."

"Yes, isn't it grand? The first time I saw it I knew this was where I'd build my ranch." His rich bass resonated with a sound of satisfaction. "I'm going to ride on to the house and tell my wife that we got a lady with us. She'll be pleased. You see that far edge of the bench beyond the barn by the stream?"

Joe nodded.

"Pull the wagons up there." Evans grinned, and then rode on.

Joe clicked his tongue, slapped the horses' rumps with the reins, and got them moving, passing the large log house.

Evans jumped down from his horse and took a small woman into his arms. He swung her round and round as they both laughed. Peering out the door of the house were two small children, a little girl about two, and a little boy about three or four years old. The children were much younger than Joe had expected.

Joe turned to Sara. "You want me to stop and let you off here?"

Sara shook her head. "No, keep driving to where Mr. Evans indicated. Let's give him time to greet his family before he has to introduce me to her."

He nodded. "That's thoughtful of you and what I would expect you to think of that."

Sara ducked her head. "If the one I loved had just returned home, I would want time to greet them before welcoming unexpected guests."

Joe wondered if he would ever be greeted like that. He glanced sideways at the beautiful woman sitting next to him. Yeah, he would want to greet her first before having to deal with other people.

Sara looked up at him and the sun came out in her smile.

Driving past a big barn and corral, Joe found the spot Evans had indicated. The flat bench had several large trees at one end, trees covered the bluffs rising on the north side, the barn on the east side, and the valley and the stream on the south side. The grass-covered campground looked to him to spread out over about three acres. It was a good place to camp.

Joe drove the chuck wagon up close to the trees, as it would be less windy and not as cold at night in the fall weather as the bluff would block the north wind.

Joe turned to Sara who sat beside him, hesitating for a moment as he watched her gaze out over the valley and toward the high mountains to the southwest.

"Well, Sara, we're finally here. What do you think of Elisha Evans' ranch?" Joe's voice sounded huskier than normal, even to his own ears.

"It's absolutely beautiful. I want to sit here, catch my breath, and look at that view." She smiled at him, and then turned to gaze at the scene before them.

Joe wanted to sit and look at her forever. The rapt expression on her face as she looked out over the valley caused a lump in his throat. He wanted to drink in the sight of her as long as he could. Now that they were at the ranch, their days of riding together on the wagon seat were over. His sense of loss was a piercing pain through his chest, as if he needed to weep. He wanted to say so many things to her. "But unfortunately, the riders expect to be fed." That wasn't what he wanted to say, but he had no right to say what he wanted. Joe wrapped the reins around the brake and climbed down.

She gathered her skirt and readied herself to climb down from the wagon. "I forgot. We may be here at the ranch, but we still have twenty people who are still working and want to eat."

As she started to climb down, he reached up, put his hands around her tiny waist, and lifted her down. Then he kept his hands on her waist longer than necessary.

She looked up into his eyes and he saw an unspoken longing and message there that matched his own.

The lump in his throat was too big to speak over. He took a deep breath, tore his gaze away from hers as he let her go. There was nothing he could say.

Sara rested her hand on his arm a moment, then she too stepped away as if she understood.

Cookie stood by the wrangler wagon and stared off across the valley as the cattle slowly spread out to graze. "Is this what your father's place looks like?"

Joe stood with his hands on his hips, and looked at the mountains with a sense of coming home. "Not as high in elevation, but almost as surrounded by the mountains."

"I can't imagine how you could deal with the plains and prairies after growing up in this area." Cookie gave a nod toward the valley and snow capped peaks beyond.

"It hasn't always been easy to be away, and being back feels good." It did feel good to gaze out on the mountains. Turning he saw Sara leaning against the wagon looking out over the valley and the feeling of the joy in seeing the mountains dissipated into the sadness of having no way to keep her with him.

"Well, let's get some fires going and start some supper. The boys want something hot in this chilly air." Cookie lowered the worktable from the end of the chuck wagon.

"What do you mean chilly air? This is a hot September day for the mountains." Joe closed his eyes and breathed in a lung full of the cool, clear air. For the first time since the beating, he could breathe deeply, without his ribs protesting.

Joe hunted for enough stones to make the fire rings and soon had the fires built. As usual, the one for the coffee was prepared first and he soon had three pots of coffee going.

Elisha came down from the house and asked Mr. Barnes and Sara to come up and meet his wife. Sara gave a smile and a little wave before walking away. Joe watched her walk away with an ache in his chest. In a little while, Mr. Barnes and Elisha returned without Sara. Mr. Barnes spoke to Felipe who was soon carrying luggage up to the big house from the Barnes' wagon.

"Cookie, I hope you don't mind, but I invited Mrs. Evans to eat with us tonight. I figured you'd have plenty and she seems eager to meet the hands." Mr. Barnes said.

"And don't forget my two children." Elisha laughed. "They'll want to see everything that's going on."

"We'd be honored to have you all eat with us," Cookie said.

"Come see the barn, Matt." Elisha led Mr. Barnes off to look through the large barn, made from the same native logs as the house.

"Well, if we're going to have another lady here for supper, what should we fix special?" Cookie asked.

"We have that side of beef we need to cook up, so I guess it's back to steaks. We know how to fix them." Joe chuckled. "We don't have lots of choices for anything fancy."

Cookie scratched his head. "You're right. Let's just do a good hot meal like we know the boys like and maybe she will, too."

"You should make your dried peach cobbler, Cookie. That'll dress it up some." Joe didn't ask Cookie what he wanted done any more. He knew from months of working with him that he preferred to make the biscuits and cobblers.

"Okay. Fried steaks, mashed potatoes, canned corn, gravy, and biscuits, and then we'll have cobbler for dessert." Cookie decided.

"Why don't you get Billy to set up some of the crates for a little table with the two camp chairs on either side for the ladies and children?" Joe suggested.

"First, let's put the old canvas piece on the ground under the awning, so the children can sit on the ground and eat." Cookie directed Billy to set up a dining area under the awning to the side of the chuck wagon, and then peel the potatoes.

Joe got the skillets ready to fry the steaks and a large pot out to boil the potatoes.

It took the three of them a little over an hour to have supper ready. By then, the long shadows of the mountains had filled the valley.

Joe prepared the gravy and became aware of the sound of children's voices. He looked up to the delightful sight of Elisha carrying a little dark-haired boy. The pretty, little woman led a beautiful little blonde girl by the hand.

And Sara walked with them. His heart ached from the longing to someday have a family of his own. Elisha was a blessed man.

Elisha set the little boy down by the camp chairs, but held on to his hand. "Cookie, Joe, Billy, I want you to meet my family. This is my wife, Susana."

Joe couldn't tell whom the children resembled most—their father, or their mother.

Susana smiled. "Hello. So you all are these great cooks I've heard so much about?"

The musical lilt in her voice reminded Joe of the look of sunshine playing on a mountain stream. He liked her immediately. Joe thought she looked young, not much older than himself.

The little girl pulled on her mother's arm and pointed toward the camp chairs.

Elisha had the little boy sit down on the ground cloth near one of the chairs. "Now, son, you sit here until we get ready to eat."

He then turned and picked up the little girl. "Come to papa."

She was still enough of a baby that she immediately laid her head on his shoulder and wrapped her arms around his neck.

Joe thought how safe that must feel to be held so securely in your father's arms.

"This little fellow here is Samuel, named after a wonderful friend. We mostly call him Little Sam. He's three, soon to be four in November."

Joe was so astonished at the name of the little boy that he almost missed the next thing that Elisha said.

"And our daughter is Christine Marie, and she is named after our friend Sam's little girl, and my wife Susana Marie. Christine, by the way, is two." Elisha's chest swelled with obvious pride.

Joe's thoughts whirled. Samuel was his father's name and Christine was his sister's name. Was there that close of a connection between the two families? Somehow, Joe couldn't imagine Susana Evans as a close friend of his mother. He couldn't imagine anyone as a friend of his mother.

Chapter Twenty-One

Cookie waved to the two camp chairs. "Miss Sara and Mrs. Evans, please be seated."

Susana sat down and stroked Little Sam's hair as the child sat quietly waiting as his father had instructed, but with big eyes sparkling as he took in all the new sights of the cattle, horses, and cowboys.

Sara strolled to the worktable. "I'd like to help serve, if that's all right."

"I'll serve the steak and potatoes; Joe, you serve the corn and gravy; and you can serve the biscuits, Miss Sara. That will leave Billy to eat and get going on the washing up."

As the hands got in line to eat, Elisha Evans stepped forward and put up his hand for silence. "We would like to welcome each of you to our home. We're thankful for all the hard work you've done to bring this herd all the way from Texas. Here, we observe the custom of a blessing before the meal. If you all will, bow your heads for a moment with me." He removed his hat and the riders all followed his lead.

"Our heavenly Father, we come before you with hearts brimming over with thanksgiving that you have protected these men and this family. We are thankful that so few were injured. Please bless George, Jeff, and especially Joe as they heal from the most serious injuries.

"We ask that you bless each one here with whatever they need to be people for you. Give them safety in their work, and contentment in their lives. We also ask you to bless all those that we love and care for, whether near or far. You know who they are for each of these men.

"We ask a special blessing on the hands of these three men, who have provided such a wonderful meal for us. Help us to show our appreciation to them. It's in the name of our Lord, Jesus Christ that we ask for your mercies. Amen."

"Ya'll come get it, as we say back in my home state of Texas," Elisha yelled.

The men let out rebel yells and moved in to form the grub line.

Joe grabbed three plates and went through the line first. "These are for Mrs. Evans and the children."

Cookie cut one of the steaks into small pieces and put some on the plates for the children. And Sara dished small helpings of the rest of the food and placed a biscuit on each plate.

Joe handed the children's plates to Evans, and carried the one for Susana Evans to her himself.

"Thank you, Joe. That's very thoughtful." Susana smiled at him and accepted the plate of food.

"You're welcome, ma'am. I'll get you some cups of water for the children. Would you like water, or coffee?"

"I would like to try your coffee. It's been awhile since I've drank camp coffee. And please call me Susana."

"Yes, ma'am." Joe returned her smile.

He placed cups of water and coffee on a crate for Susana and the children, then he went back to help Cookie and Sara serve the hands.

Sara served the riders, and then she filled her plate, and sat down in the other camp chair by Susana Evans. With the two of them seated next to each other, it was easy for Joe to see how close in age they were. Susana Evans must have married young. To Joe, she hardly appeared old enough to have two children.

He leaned against the chuck wagon and ate thinking about the prayer that Evans had given. It sounded so familiar. His father used to pray that way at the beginning of each meal. A shiver traveled up his spine. He saw reminders of his family everywhere he turned. Maybe it had been a mistake to come this close to his father's ranch.

Leaning back with a cup of coffee, Joe enjoyed watching the two little ones. They took in all the cattle and men showing up in their valley as if a circus had showed up. Looking beyond the men seated on the ground around the chuck wagon, Little Sam dodged back and forth hollering with laughter as Billy took off chasing him. Cookie just smiled and didn't call Billy back to his work. Joe was glad, for Billy still had a lot of boy in him and had done a man's work for months.

Putting his empty plate in the washup tub, he took a plate of cobbler over to Susanna. He felt little arms wrapping around his leg. Looking down, he found little Christine grinning up at him.

Surprised, he cocked his head at her inquiringly, and she held up her arms.

Her mother smiled at him. "Go on Joe, pick her up if you want to."

Joe reached down and lifted the little girl who had same name of his little sister. "Hello, Christine, my name is Joe."

She patted his face with her little hand. "Yoe." Then she laid her head on his shoulder and wrapped her arm around his neck, as she did with her father.

The surprise of tears trying to surface caught Joe off guard. Could it be a longing for children of his own?

"That's amazing, Joe. I've never seen Christine take to anyone like that before. Are children usually so drawn to you?" Elisha asked.

Joe didn't answer, but stood gently rocking the child. He couldn't ever remember holding a child before. His mother never let him near his little sister; he'd never held her, even once. The sound of his mother's voice telling him he was too unworthy to touch the child still lingered. He rocked Christine for about five minutes while everyone else chatted and the little girl soon fell asleep.

"My goodness," Susana said, "you've rocked her to sleep, and I thought we'd have quite a time getting her to sleep after all this excitement."

Elisha reached over, gently unwrapped his daughter's arm from around Joe's neck, and then lifted her to his shoulder. "I'll carry her to the house and put her in bed while she's still asleep and maybe she'll stay that way until morning. It's amazing how she instantly took to you. Evidently you have a special touch."

"From what I hear he has the same touch with horses." Mr. Barnes reclined against the wheel of the chuck wagon.

Elisha turned to Joe. "You worked with horses much?"

"I used to work a lot with horses before I hurt my leg. That's one of the ranch chores that I was good at."

"We'll have to talk about that. I've got about eight hundred head of wild horses on my ranch, and I want to do something about them other than shoot them. However, for now I need to get these children to bed. Goodnight, everyone, and thanks for the supper." Elisha and Susana gathered the children to go back to the ranch house.

"Matt, you and Sara come on to the house when you get ready. You know where your rooms are." Elisha told them.

Sara and her father would sleep at the ranch house with the family. Joe was pleased for Sara's sake that she could stay in a proper home with another woman nearby. He also guessed that Susana wanted Sara close by, as he suspected she didn't have a chance to talk to another woman very often. Joe already missed Sara, and she was still there. He feared how it was going to feel when she truly was gone from the valley as she would soon leave with her father.

The next morning was clear and the air held a crisp chill, cool enough for the riders from Texas to pull their coats on. Joe watched as Bob put in place the system that he and Joe discussed out on the trail—an ambitious plan to brand the herd with the Rocking ES within two weeks.

~

Toward the end of their second week at the ranch, Elisha asked Cookie and Joe to come to the house for a talk.

Joe hoped to see a glimpse of Sara as he and Cookie walked to the big rectangular log house. Even at meals he didn't see her now, as Mr. Barnes and Sara took their meals with the Evans family, and Joe was with the cowhands at the chuck wagon. He kept watch but found no opportunity to talk to her without being too forward and Mr. Barnes always seemed to be about at the same time. He missed her constant presence with a deep aching longing. Every where he looked around the chuck wagon and campground he remembered her presence and the constant thinking of her day and night left him edgy and tired.

Joe and Cookie crossed the covered porch, and after knocking entered through the front door in response to Elisha's call for them to come on in. The front room was huge with a fireplace off to the right of the door. Along the back of the room, a central hallway led off to other rooms. A staircase in the corner rose up to the second floor.

Looking around at the front room, Joe was impressed with the welcoming feel of the house. Comfortable upholstered chairs and couches furnished the room, complete with small tables with lamps on them and ladder-backed chairs. Toward the end of the room near to the kitchen was a big desk with shelves of books behind it. Facing the desk were two overstuffed chairs like those Joe remembered from hotel lobbies. There was also a potbellied stove at that end of the room.

Joe and Cookie maneuvered their way across the colorful braided rugs, and stepped gingerly around the toys scattered about. The sounds of the children and Susana talking filtered in from the kitchen. Joe listened but didn't hear Sara's voice. He struggled to keep his disappointment from showing as he had hoped to at least see her.

Elisha waved Cookie and Joe toward the two chairs facing the desk, and he sat in the chair behind the desk.

What seemed so familiar, as Joe walked into the room, was the similarity of the house to the one on his father's ranch. He swallowed and took a deep breath reassuring himself this was not his family's place and that his mother was not going to appear. This house was bigger and obviously newer, possibly built within the last couple of years.

Elisha leaned back, his palms together as if praying. "I appreciate you men coming. I wanted to talk to you about some of my plans here, and see if you all would stay on and work with me. I'll get straight to the point. There's about a month to six weeks before the snow starts, and I want to get a bunkhouse built, and hay cut. If the crew can stay on for some of those projects for another month or two, before they go back to Texas, we can get it all done before winter. I plan to ask about five or six of the men to stay on permanently.

"I want the two of you to stay on permanently as of right now, as cooks for my ranch. Susana is a very able in the kitchen, but she has the children.

By the way, we have just realized that we are expecting another child in about eight months, so you can see her hands are full. I don't want her to cook, clean, and do all the washing, especially if I have six or so cowhands. I know I've sprung this on you, and you probably need to think about it. But what are your first thoughts?"

"Would you want both of us?" Cookie spoke first. "Would there be enough work for both of us?"

Elisha nodded. "Yes, you'd cook for both the crew and the family. We'll all eat together. And Joe, I have some other plans I want to ask you to be a part of beyond the work with Cookie."

"What about Billy?" Cookie leaned forward.

"I see no reason he can't stay also. There'll be plenty of work around here for him to do. If he wants to cowhand that would be fine, or we can have him help with the barn work." Elisha said. "I should probably also tell you that I bought the chuck wagon from Matt, as part of the price of the herd, so it'll stay here."

Joe and Cookie exchanged a glance and they both smiled. "That's great," Joe said. The chuck wagon was a new one and one of the best Joe had ever seen.

"Would you be open for us to work through the winter, and then see how we like it?" Cookie turned to Joe. "What do you think?"

Joe nodded. "I'd go for that."

"That would be a wise condition to set. In the spring we both can reconsider, and if it doesn't work out for either of us, we can say so." Elisha agreed.

Joe cleared his throat. "What are these other things you would want my help on?" If Elisha wanted Joe to do anything with riding, he didn't know how to respond. Would there be a place for him at the ranch if he couldn't ride? Joe's stomach knotted with the thought. He wasn't sure Elisha knew he truly couldn't sit a horse.

"You can help me plan out how to catch and break several hundred horses."

Joe frowned and cocked his head. His mind was fuzzy with was puzzlement. "You mean you want me to break horses for you?"

"No, I understand that you can't ride enough to break horses, but I hope you can teach some of the hands to and supervise that part of the ranch work." Elisha said. "I'd like to get a horse raising business going. There is a possibility of a contract to supply horses to the army. It would be profitable to start with breaking some of the wild horses first while I get a breeding program going."

Joe glanced at Cookie who waited for him to handle it. "I'm not sure you understand. I can't ride. I can't sit a horse at all." Why couldn't he get used to saying it without the physical ache it brought to his chest and the desire to hit someone—though he wasn't sure who.

Chapter Twenty-Two

Elisha rubbed his chin. "Knew you found riding difficult, but I didn't understand that you couldn't sit a horse. I'm sorry, Joe, that must be hard for you. You could actually accomplish what I want done seated from a buggy, or a wagon. I need someone with the expertise to manage that part of the ranch operation and to teach some of the riders to do the work. We could try it, and see if it'd work out. If it doesn't, we can work something else out."

Cookie shifted in his chair. "What would you pay? I'm sure you know that as cook on a trail herd I get good pay."

Elisha laughed. "And I would expect to pay along the same line. What would forty a month sound like? And all you can eat, of course?"

The usual cowhand's pay was twenty, or at the most, thirty a month. But Joe didn't like the idea of Cookie and him making the same wages.

"Joe, I offer you twenty a month plus a bonus for every horse you break. You could take the bonus in money, or in horses and cattle. You can run your stock in with mine, but under your own brand," Elisha offered.

Joe sat up a little straighter. A surprise offer for sure, a chance to start his own herd and build up some horse stock—too good an opportunity to let pass by.

Cookie spoke up. "Let us consider it, and we'll get back to you this afternoon, if that's all right."

"That'll be fine. You let me know. Now, I've a favor to ask. Would you both mind giving me your take on who, from among the riders, I should ask to stay?"

"Well, I'd immediately advise you to ask Bob Fife to stay on as foreman, but you already have Josh Thomas." Cookie said.

Elisha laughed. "I would agree with you, except I don't have Josh Thomas. He doesn't work for me on a regular basis. He comes and spends months at a time with us, but he's more like family. When it gets close to winter, he'll head back down to the J Bar C, if not before. Josh works for the J Bar C mostly."

Joe felt a chill. Josh works for his father? He listened to what Elisha said next.

"Sam Weathers loans him to us whenever Josh gets a notion to go wandering. I'd like for him to be my foreman, but he doesn't want it. So the first on the list is Bob Fife. Who else?"

Joe pushed past the thoughts swirling in his head from what Elisha had said about Josh Thomas; he wouldn't let himself think on them now. He forced his mind to the subject at hand.

"I'd ask Jeff Kingston, Jim Finely, and Will Ramsey. Especially Jim, if you want someone who can ride and break horses. And Santo Real is a good rider," Joe said.

"Jacob Blunfeld is a quiet German man. I'd ask him if you plan on building much. You hardly know he's around, but he can build anything, and he can also blacksmith." Cookie added.

"Most of the others have family back in Texas they'll want to get back to before winter," Joe added.

Elisha read the list he'd written down. "So you recommend Bob Fife, Jeff Kingston, Jim Finely, Will Ramsey, Santo Real, and Jacob Blunfeld."

"Of course, we don't know if they'll stay." Cookie shifted in the chair and ran his fingers through his hair. "They're all good cowhands, and they've have been a congenial crew. One of the best I've ever worked with once we got rid of a couple of rotten apples."

Joe knew exactly whom Cookie referred to, and he agreed.

"Do you have plans for the bunkhouse?" Joe was curious.

"I have a tentative plan, but I'm open to suggestions."

Joe thought a moment. "You know I've lived in the mountains, and if you want to build the bunkhouse to meet the needs for winter time I've some suggestions." Joe also knew that if he stayed, the bunkhouse would be his home. Having it close to the house with adequate heat would make it more comfortable, especially in the harsh winter of the mountains.

"Could you draw out a plan of what you would suggest?" Elisha asked.

"Yes sir, I could."

"Then consider that your first job."

Susana came into the room from the kitchen carrying little Christine who immediately held out her arms to Joe.

Well, of course, there wasn't anything to do, but take her from her mother. Joe stood and reached for her, then returned to his chair.

Christine played with his shirt buttons, undoing them one by one.

It surprised Joe how easily he held the child. It just felt right. Was this what a father felt? He'd like to believe he could be a good parent one day, that his past hadn't robbed him of that.

"Elisha, I have coffee and cake made. Will you come carry it?" Susana smiled at Christine and Joe.

"You boys got time for coffee and some of Susana's blackberry jam cake?" Elisha asked.

Cookie laughed. "You go get it, and we'll show you how much time we got."

As soon as Elisha left the room, Cookie turned to Joe. "What do you think? Should we take him up on his offer?"

"Do you have anything else lined up?" Joe hadn't heard the older man mention any plans for the future.

Cookie shook his head. "No, do you?"

"No, and I say let's take the job while we got the offer." Joe buttoned his shirt, and little Christine proceeded to undo them again.

Elisha came back into the room carrying a large tray with a pot of coffee, cups, small plates, and fork. Susana followed him carrying the cake on a cake stand. After cutting the cake and pouring cups of coffee, Susana placed the coffee and cake for Joe on the desk.

"You want me to take Christine off your hands?" Susana offered.

"As long as she's content, I'm happy to have her company." Careful to keep his cup out of reach of the child, Joe sipped his coffee and ate the cake. He'd have to ask for the recipe, the cake was that good. He settled the little girl on his lap with his arm cradling her and listened to Cookie.

"Well, while you were out of the room, Joe and I talked about it. We would like to accept your offer of a job, on the condition that we reconsider in the spring. If either one of us is not happy with the work, we'd like the option to part at that time with no hurt feelings. Will that work for you, Mr. Evans?" Cookie asked.

"Call me Elisha. That'll work great for us. Now I've more of a chance to get the other hands to stay, if they know that the two of you are staying." Elisha smiled and nodded. He evidently was pleased with their decisions. "Joe, as soon as you can draw me a plan for a bunkhouse, I'd like to see it. I want to start building it within the next couple of days."

"I'm so glad you're staying." Susana gave them both a big smile.

As she took little Christine back into her arms, the child began to complain and say "No, Yoe, Yoe," and held her arms out to Joe.

Joe felt amazed at how good it felt to be liked by a little child. He gave the toddler a kiss on the cheek. "I'll come back and play with you another time, sweetheart."

Elisha and Susana shook their heads, smiling, as if they couldn't believe the child's behavior.

"Horses and children—that says something pretty powerful about you, Joe," Elisha said.

Joe didn't know what to say, especially as he didn't know what it said about him.

"May we come this afternoon to see your kitchen?" Cookie rescued him by asking. "We need to go now and get dinner ready for the cowhands."

"Sure, that's a good idea. You also need to start a list of what we should purchase to feed everyone over the next five months. I'll send you to Cedar Ridge, a town east of here, for supplies. It's closer than Cheyenne. We'll talk about that later." Elisha walked them to the front door. "This afternoon, I'll talk to the hands that I want to stay. I'd like to get it all settled before Matt and Sara leave."

Joe's heart jumped into his throat. They planned to go to on to California, but he hadn't let himself think about it being so soon. Joe would miss her, but there wasn't anything he could offer to get her to stay. Would she even consider staying if he had something to offer? He hated to let her go.

~

After feeding the hands their noon meal, Joe put a pot of beans over an open fire. They left Billy to tend the fires and then he and Cookie strolled to the ranch house to inspect the kitchen.

Elisha and Susana met them on the porch. Elisha waved them through the front door. "Come on in. We were just stepping out when we saw you headed to the house."

Susana led the way into the big kitchen where the sunlight streamed through the many large windows. "You can't imagine how happy I am to turn over the cooking chores." She placed her hand over her stomach. "It's too much for me now."

Cookie stood by the big, fourteen-foot table and surveyed his new domain. "This is really something. Just look at that stove, Joe."

Joe strolled over to the large cook stove, which had four burners and two ovens. Compared to cooking over an open fire, it was a wonder. "How did you get this into the kitchen?"

Elisha laughed. "So you noticed it's bigger than the outside door. We put it in before we finished the door. I hired four men to bring it from the railway and put it in place."

"I thought at the time," Susana said with a smile to her husband, "that we got too big a cook stove. I couldn't imagine needing something so large, but now it'll barely be big enough."

"Don't you worry, ma'am. I'll be able to cook just fine on such a stove." Cookie grinned, his eyes roving over it.

"Please, call me Susana."

"Yes ma'am ... I mean Susana." Cookie opened the tin pie chest, where food could be kept safe from small critters.

Elisha walked over to a door at the backside of the kitchen. "Let me show you my favorite thing about the kitchen." He opened the door and stood aside for them to look in.

It led to a small well room.

"When we first saw the valley and filed on it four years ago, the first thing I did was to dig this well and line it with stones from the creek." Elisha put his hand on the top of the pump that rose above the well cover. "Then we built the kitchen around the well."

Joe rested his thumbs in his belt. "That must've been a lot of work."

Susana walked over to stand beside Joe in front of the well. "It was! But Elisha told me that one chore that he hated was going out in the cold to bring in water. Of course, the other reason was to have water in case we had to defend against Indians, which we have never had to do, thank the Lord." Susana glanced over at Elisha. "Of course, there was that one time Elisha took an arrow in the chest."

"We weren't living here yet. That was when we lived in the cabin on Pinto Creek." Elisha nodded.

Joe looked from Elisha to Susana and back. They had lived in the cabin on his father's ranch?

Elisha led the way back into the kitchen. He pointed at the sturdy ladder that led to a loft that covered two-thirds of the kitchen. "That can be used as a bedroom if you want, Cookie. It's large enough for both of you. It just needs to be cleaned and have some furniture added."

Cookie climbed the ladder and looked at the space. "This will be great. I can be right here to tend to things. And I'm like you, Elisha. Getting up on cold, snowy mornings and walking to work is not something I like. I prefer it nice and convenient."

Joe wanted to laugh. Working as a cookie on a trail drive was as inconvenient a way to live as he could think of. He had never heard Cookie complain.

"When do you want to move in and start using the kitchen for your cooking?" Elisha asked.

Cookie scratched his head. "I'd like to give the loft and kitchen a thorough scrubbing before we move the supplies and pots and pans from the chuck wagon. You got everything real nice now, Susana, but I'll be moving in a lot of stuff and need to think of how to organize it."

"I've tried to keep it in good shape, but I won't mind it having a deep scrub down. You move things around any way you want. I don't mind, really." Susana sat at the table.

Cookie nodded. "Well, why don't we give ourselves a few days to get that done?"

"You let me know when you want to move the supplies from the chuck wagon and I'll have the hands work with you." Elisha took several cups down off a shelf and poured coffee for all of them. "Who do you need to help with the cleaning?"

"Billy and I can do that. When it comes to the actual move, I'll need Joe. He's a good organizer. I suggest we continue to cook out of the chuck wagon as long as we have the full crew of men." Cookie took a sip of coffee. "Good coffee, Susana."

"Thank you. I consider that high praise. I plan to help you out with the cooking and cleaning as I can. I'll also need to prepare some different foods for the children, and later for the new baby. I'll try not to get in your way." Susana patted Cookie's arm.

"Don't you worry about getting in my way. It'll just be a delight to be cooking with a lady."

Joe spoke up. "You realize, Susana, that Cookie is indicating that I'm not as delightful as you."

Cookie let loose his booming laugh. "Well, I don't see anyone arguing with that. You're all right to cook with, but compared to someone as pretty as Susana here, you lose out."

Cookie and Joe took their leave of Elisha and Susana and walked back to the chuck wagon.

"Cookie, I think I'll plan to stay in the bunkhouse after it gets built. For now, Billy and I can use the wrangler wagon so as not to sleep on the ground. You go ahead and fix up the loft for you."

"Suit yourself. That loft is big enough for both of us."

"I know it is, but to tell you the truth, I don't relish going up and down that ladder every day. I could, but it would be easier not to have to." Joe also knew Cookie would rather have a place to himself.

"I hadn't thought about that. I forget about your hip. You don't never complain. You do what you want."

It gave Joe a warm glow for Cookie to say he forgot about the limitations of the hip. That's what Joe wanted. To be treated as if he didn't have a problem.

~

One by one, Elisha talked to the men that afternoon. Every man on his list accepted his offer at once, except for Santo Real, who asked for a day to think about it. Elisha then talked to the other men about staying on for one more month to help with haying and building the bunkhouse.

As Joe predicted, they all agreed to stay for a few more weeks. But they wanted to be headed back to their families in Texas by Christmas and before the snows.

Mr. Barnes offered to have the pay for the men heading back to Texas sent to the bank in Waco, so they would only be taking the trail back with the money Elisha would pay them. Joe knew more of the hard-earned cash would make it back to Texas and their families, and not spent in the towns in between Colorado and Texas.

Mr. Barnes paid those staying to work for Elisha off in gold coins from the money he got from Elisha for the herd. Joe asked Elisha if he would hold his wages for him. Joe's wages came to almost three hundred dollars with the bonus that Mr. Barnes had promised. It wasn't a fortune, but it was a beginning. Maybe toward a ranch of his own someday.

Chapter Twenty-Three

Later that evening, the valley descended into darkness, with only a halo of the setting sun showing above the rim of the snow-capped mountains. Joe stepped up on the hub of the chuck wagon wheel and grabbed his bedroll. Hearing a noise behind him, he turned as Santo strolled up.

"You maybe talk?" Santo asked in a low voice. "Maybe where no one listen?"

Puzzled Joe stepped down and waved toward the back of the chuck wagon. "We can walk this way and have privacy." He had no idea what Santo wanted to talk about, but he liked the soft-spoken Mexican and was willing to give him some time.

"Señor Joe. I want to ask you something. You maybe help me know what to do." He spoke softly in a Spanish accent. "I want to stay. This good job. But my señora, she waits for me. Señora Evans, she need help with babies. My Mara, she help with babies. Maybe Señor Evans, him let me bring Mara here, no?" Worry lines etched Santo's anxious face.

So this is why Santo had not said yes to Elisha's offer. Joe didn't know if Susana and Elisha would agree, or not, but it was a good idea. Another woman on the place would be a blessing.

"How would you get your wife here? Where is she?" Joe glanced at the tall slender man walking beside him.

"She with her family in Texas. I send message and tell her come. Her brother brings her. I meet them in the middle to here."

"Let's go talk to Señor Evans and ask him about it." Joe turned back to the camp. "The only problem is, where would you stay?" He kept his voice low to keep their conversation private as they walked.

Santo fell into step with Joe. "We could stay in barn. It warm with horses. Then I build."

Joe admired the assurance in his friend's voice.

They found Elisha ready to head back to the house. Joe asked him if they could walk with him and ask a question. Joe explained Santo's dilemma and the possible solution.

Elisha stopped and looked at Santo. "How long have you been married?"

"We marry for ten years."

"You have children?"

"We have, but they die when born. We hope, we pray, we wait." Santo said softly.

Joe felt for Santo and Mara. The longing for a child weighed thick in his friend's voice. Santo was a strong man to hold onto hope through all of those years. The love between Santo and Mara had to be tight to hold them together through so much loss.

Joe thought of Sara. He would give anything to be able to have a hope as strong as the one of which Santo spoke.

"I'm sorry to hear that. How is your wife's health?" Elisha asked.

"She strong. Never sick. She care for sister's babies, but better if we no stay there, she want own place." Santo's voice betrayed his need to provide a place for his wife.

Hearing the longing in Santo's voice, Joe wanted to tell Santo to go get his wife, but it was Elisha's decision.

"All right, let me ask Señora Evans. If she agrees, you go and bring your wife back with the understanding that she'll work in the house helping care for the children." Elisha shook Santo's hand, waved at Joe, and went into the house.

Santo turned to Joe with a big grin. "Thank you, Señor Joe. I think maybe he say yes."

"I can't speak for Elisha and Susana, but I think you can be hopeful. It never hurts to ask." Joe thought of the courage it had taken him to ask Cookie for a job back at the store in Waco. Now, look where he was. He slapped Santo on the back as they walked back to the chuck wagon. No, it never hurt to ask.

The next day Elisha told Santo to send for his wife. The man's smile told of his relief and happiness. Elisha gave leave for Santo to ride into Cedar Ridge to send a letter to his wife.

The next morning Elisha asked Joe to meet him in the front room to go over plans for the new addition.

Joe spread out the brown paper that Susana had given him to draw out his plans. "There's plenty of room here on the west end of the house by the kitchen. It would be easier to build by it sharing the wall of the kitchen, but I suggest a large hallway. Double doors at each end would lead to the outside and windows would let in sunlight. The doors can be opened in the summer to make a breezeway that will help cool the kitchen. And in winter they can be closed, so those living in the bunkhouse wing don't have to go out into the weather to go into the kitchen."

Elisha looked over the drawing of the plans. "This will add four rooms, if we count the hallway, to that wing of the house and an attic storage space with a ladder from the hallway. You're talking about extending the original roof?"

Joe nodded. "That way it will look as if the addition was part of the house from the beginning. Also, another door into the well room from the hallway will let the hands draw water without going into the kitchen. So, the front section of the new wing will be the bunkroom for the cowhands, with two doors, one into the hallway and another out onto the covered porch and then into the yard. The middle and north rooms could be for the cowhands with wives. All three areas would open into the hallway." Joe waited with an unsettled feeling in his gut. Would Elisha like the plan or would he think it was too much?

Elisha took several minutes to look the plan carefully. Finally, he glanced at Joe. "This is an excellent plan. It's much more than what I was thinking of building. We'd need to put a potbelly stove in each of the rooms. How long will all of this take to build?"

"It'd depend on how many men work on it. If there were ten men, we could finish it in a week. The first job will be to get timber cut and the logs ready. Once we have the outer walls built above shoulder height, we will need as many men as possible to lift the big logs to finish the walls and get the roof on tight. The more men we have the faster it'll go."

Evans tapped his chin. "I thought about having a few men work on the bunkhouse, and a few men haying. It'd be better to get one thing completed, and then put everyone on the other. The branding is almost done. If Josh will stay around to help, we can get both the building and the haying done in about two weeks. What if you and Jacob find the trees we need? I'll get a couple men to help cut them down to make logs. Then by the time the branding is done, we could start on the building. Since you've drawn the plans, would you organize and direct the building of the bunkhouse? I'll work with you, but if I could hand this off to you, I could check on the other work at the same time."

Joe was surprised to be given so much responsibility. "I could do that for you, especially, if you let Jacob work with me."

"Good, our first chore is for you to find and get cut the trees for the building. I'll see to the branding."

Elisha sent a rider to town and ordered glass for the windows, kegs of nails, and three pot-bellied stoves. They made everything else. Susana sewed together ticking for the cowhands' mattresses on her fancy Singer sewing machine.

~

A sense of mental energy and a strength of will surged through Joe every time he was around Elisha. He wasn't much taller than Joe, but whenever the man walked into a room, Joe knew a force had entered. Elisha

Evans was an easy man to like and respect. He was fun to work with. Now, if Joe could only keep up with him.

Joe admitted to himself, even if to no one else, that he'd never reach that place with Matthew Barnes. That Sara's father planned to leave was almost a relief. Too bad he had to take Sara with him. Barnes' belief that Joe was beneath him still grated on Joe. They had hardly spoken ten words in the last month. Joe avoided Barnes and he was sure Barnes was avoiding him.

It took a while, but Joe finally admitted it to himself. He loved Sara. He yearned to tell her his feelings, but it wouldn't be fair to her. Instead he had to prepare himself to watch her leave.

Sara never tried to hide her feelings that she liked being with Joe and he sensed a link between them. They had a friendship, but Joe feared it could never be anything more. How could he say anything when he had nothing to offer her?

Joe had always wondered if he would ever be able to love a woman. Since leaving home, he much preferred to be working out on the range with the men. He avoided situations that might lead to a relationship with a girl. The visits the other men made to the houses in the back alleys in the trail towns had repulsed him.

He had his chances at the different socials he'd attended through the years. Joe could tell when one of the girls was especially interested. He'd feared that the horror of his relationship with his mother had somehow damaged him, and he was unable to care deeply for a woman. Now he knew different, and even the caring hurt.

Susana planned a special meal for Mr. Barnes and Sara the evening before they were leaving. She asked Cookie and Joe to eat up at the house with them. As he sat across from her at supper, he felt the tension between them. She seemed to want him to say something to her before she left. There wasn't anything he could say. Her father was always there, making sure there was a barrier, and it was obvious to Joe what Barnes was doing. Whether Sara understood what was going on or not, Joe didn't know.

~

The morning finally came for Sara and Matthew Barnes to ride out for Cheyenne and catch the train for California. Joe planned to work with Cookie scrubbing the kitchen that day, and move part of the chuck wagon gear. Everything was in a confusion of activity. Joe's last chance to be alone with Sara was slipping away. Wanting at least to say good-bye, he sought out Susana's help.

Joe found her sitting alone in the front room with some mending she was working on. "Susana, can I talk to you about something?"

"Of course, what can I do for you? I was finishing sewing on this button and then I'll head out to say good-bye to Sara and Matthew." She stopped her stitching and leaned forward.

Joe took the seat across from her. "I have a problem, and need some help. If you think I'm out of line, you tell me." He hadn't been so nervous in a long time.

"Just ask me." She set the sewing aside.

"Sara and her father are leaving within the hour. I need to talk to her without her father around. And I think she wants to talk to me."

"You care for her, don't you, Joe?"

"Yes, I care a lot, but you know my situation. I can't offer her anything. Maybe someday, but not now ...." The starkness of it twisted and turned through him like a knife cutting away strips of skin until he had to own up to the enormity of the coming loss.

Susana reached out and laid her hand on Joe's arm. "What can I do?"

"If you could arrange for me to talk to her alone before she leaves?" Beads of sweat formed at his temples and his breathing became shallow, he scarcely got the words out.

"Everyone is getting ready to leave, so you wait here. I'll find a way to send her into the house alone. You won't have much time, but I don't know what else to do." Susana took his hand. "I know it's hard on you, but you're doing the best thing for her. Just don't put her into a situation where she has to choose between you and her father."

"I don't want to do that to her. But if I could just speak to her alone for a couple of minutes." He could hear the desperation in his voice, or maybe it was despair.

Joe stayed in the front room of the house and waited. He couldn't help pacing, but he had to do something with himself.

A short time later, Sara came through the front door.

"Hello Joe."

Joe drank in the look of her trying to fix it forever in his mind. Her cheeks were rosy, he supposed, from her hurrying up to the house. She had on a dark blue traveling dress and matching hat that tied with a ribbon under her chin. Even with the hat, her blonde curls struggled to escape, begging to be tucked back in where they belonged.

Why was he thinking about her curls when she was about to disappear from his life? Maybe he could put off thinking about her leaving for just another moment. Could she see how hard his heart thumped against his chest?

"Susana sent me to get her shawl for her." She tilted her pretty head to the side. "What are you doing here?"

"Actually, I asked Susana to send you up so we could talk in private." Joe took her hand.

She didn't pull it away. Instead, she tightened her hold on his hand.

"Sara, I got something I want to say to you, and I wanted to have some privacy."

"What do you want to say?" Her directness helped.

"It's been an honor and joy to get to know you. You've no idea what a difference it has made, having you in my life these last few months. I don't know what you think of me, and I'm not asking you to say. I wanted you to know I'm your friend, and if you ever need me, you call on me." He paused and allowed himself to be swallowed up in her blue eyes. "And I guess I want to ask you to remember me."

It wasn't what Joe wanted to say, but it would have to do.

She looked at his face in silence for a several moments, as if trying to memorize each detail. "I could never forget you. I'll always remember you, Joe. Perhaps one day I can come back, and we'll see if we can be more than friends. I can't promise. For now, I know I have a true friend. I'll write to you, and if you care to, please write me back. I'll want to hear from you." Then she took his face between her hands, and kissed him softly on the lips.

Joe wrapped his arms around her and felt hers around his waist. He held her close for several minutes and didn't want to let go. But he had to let her. He stepped back and gently released her from the embrace.

In the distance, Mr. Barnes called her name.

She must have heard him too. "That's why I must go. My father needs me. Goodbye, Joe. Don't you forget me." She rested her palm on his check for a moment, then turned and walked to the door. She reached out for the handle, her hand closed around it, and then she looked back at him.

He thought he saw tears on her cheeks.

She then flung the door open and rushed out, closing the door with a thud.

Although flooded with sunlight, the room was suddenly dark and empty.

Joe wanted to go off by himself, but he wasn't given time to grieve over Sara's leaving. There was too much work to do. Wiping his eyes, he took a deep breath and knew he should head out to work.

Instead, he stayed in the house until the sound of hoof beats and the rolling wagon faded into the distance. He couldn't bear to watch them leave.

Chapter Twenty-Four

Joe finished eating his breakfast and sat a few minutes in the camp chair enjoying a second cup of coffee. "Cookie, you agreeable for me to go out with Jacob and chop down trees for the bunkroom? It leaves you shorthanded with the cooking."

Cookie took an empty bread platter from the worktable and handed it to Billy to be washed. "You don't need to worry about the cooking. Billy and me can handle the kitchen. Elisha wants you to get the logs ready for building."

Joe nodded. "Good, because I'd rather be out and about on these fall days."

Cookie grinned. "I sort of figured that. Just get done what Elisha wants and don't worry about me handling the cooking. With only half the crew that we had, I can get meals together just fine."

Jacob drove the wagon up just as Joe grabbed his jacket and hat. He was content to be out in the open. It wasn't like riding out on a horse, but it was the next best thing. When he had been out on the trail with the chuck wagon, he had felt tied down to it. It had been noisy with all the pots and pans clanging. Now he felt a freedom that was similar to what he used to have as a rider out on the range, with just his horse for company. He still missed those days on horseback.

Joe didn't know if Cookie understood, but Billy wasn't going to be content to be the helper much longer. He'd told Joe he wanted to be a cowhand back on the trail as they headed along the Cimarron River. Joe hadn't been surprised. He hadn't mentioned it to Cookie as it was Billy's business to tell.

By using the Elisha's smaller wagon, Joe was able to explore some of the valley. It would have been easier on a horse, but as that was not an option for him, the wagon worked. Whenever Jacob and Joe went out tree hunting, they came back with the wagon bed full of fallen timber. They needed a lot more firewood for the coming winter than Elisha had been able to cut so far. After two days, they had found all the trees needed to build the bunkhouse addition to the house.

When Jacob and Joe got back to the ranch house just before dark he saw that Santo had arrived. At supper, he was introduced to a pretty, Mexican woman.

"Joe, my friend, this is Mara, my wife." Santo stood tall and proud next to the petit woman with black hair and sparkling black eyes.

"Ma'am, I'm glad to meet you."

She looked over at Santo and then with a small shy smile said, "Hola, Señor Joe."

Santo had told him that she and Santo had married when she was fifteen. Because she had not been able to have children, at twenty-five she still had her girlish figure. Joe saw that Mara was lively, quick, and spoke very little English. Little Sam and Christine didn't seem to mind. They took to her immediately.

"After we get the kitchen cleaned we will meet in the front room for cake and coffee to welcome Mara." Susana shooed the children toward the front room along with Elisha, Santo, and Mara.

Joe got busy clearing the table and then helped Billy wash dishes while Cookie cut the cake.

After everyone was gathered in the front room with cake and coffee, Elisha looked at Susana. "Where are Santo and Mara going to stay?"

Santo looked embarrassed. "We maybe stay in barn?"

Susana smiled at Mara. "You'll do no such thing. You'll stay in the extra bedroom here in the house until the bunkhouse wing is completed. Joe has planned a room just for you all."

Elisha slapped Josh on the shoulder. "Isn't that where you're sleeping?"

"Yeah. Guess I get to go sleep in the barn." He grinned at Susana.

She put her hand to her throat. "I'm sorry, Josh. I didn't mean to be so rude. I thought maybe you could sleep on the couch in the front room."

"Don't worry about it. I'm leaving to head home as soon as the bunkhouse or bunkroom as Joe here calls it, is finished." He turned to Joe. "When do you think that will be?"

"We'll be starting on it in the morning. With all the hands working on it, I figure to finish in a week."

Josh nodded. "Good, as I need to start south soon before the weather snows me in here for the winter. I think that would truly wear out my welcome."

"You're right about that my friend." Elisha's laugh was full and left Joe with a smile on his face. He really enjoyed the easy-going ways of the folks on the Rocking ES Ranch.

~

With the branding completed, the entire crew started on the bunkhouse wing. Jacob was a wonder at building and he did beautiful work, but he didn't like to tell anyone what to do. He would tell Joe, and then Joe directed the hands.

Joe was up every morning at five, helped Cookie get the breakfast ready, and then worked with the crew the rest of the day. When it came to the actual building of the bunkhouse, Joe could hold his own with any of the hands. His leg was not that big a problem. He had to be careful when he climbed up to help put up the rafters, and then when they worked on the final roofing.

The bunks were built according to Joe's specific measurements. He made sure that each bunk was six and a half feet long. For too many years, Joe had slept in bunks that were too short for him because the ranch owners were too stingy with the space and wood. They also built shelves, put up hooks, and built a couple of tables with chairs for the bunkhouse. In the winter, the cowhands would spend a lot of time inside.

They completed the bunkroom addition in eight days, from start to finish, including the flooring, windows, and doors.

Since everyone was in a building mood, Joe had the men build a double bed, a bureau, a couple of small tables, shelves, and two chairs for Santo and his wife to use in their room.

Jacob handled all the fine finishing on the building. The man could have stayed in the east and been a cabinetmaker. He was that good. They benefited from his being there, and he seemed to enjoy it.

There was more Elisha wanted to have built, but it was time to concentrate on the haying.

Joe could swing a sickle if he paced himself, but he couldn't keep at it all day. His hip wouldn't stand up to it. So, he drove the wagon back and forth from the meadows, bringing cut hay to the barn. Everyone that could be spared from watching the herd worked at filling the big loft of the barn and stacked the rest of the hay west of the barn.

They had more haying and wood chopping to do, but Elisha needed to send the men back to Texas if he didn't want to feed them all winter. The early mornings frosted and the first snow could come at any time. They were at the end of October and Joe was surprised they hadn't already had snow.

That evening Elisha called the men into the house who were leaving the next morning. He settled their wages. To each man he gave a horse. Since some of the men had come on the trail drive not owning a horse; it was a nice bonus.

Cookie and Joe packed enough food to last the men at least two weeks on the trail to Texas. If they didn't run into too much trouble, they would be half way home by the time they ran out of food and would need to buy more. Josh also decided it was time to leave and return to the ranch to the south before the snows blocked the passes.

The next morning they saw Josh and nine riders off with a lot of yelling and laughter. Joe looked around at the men that were left, satisfied they had a good crew.

That afternoon, Joe helped Cookie and Billy move the cooking into the kitchen of the ranch house. Supper proved to be a challenge to get ready, but they managed, even if a little later than usual. Memories of Joe's childhood flooded through his mind as the hands jostled and shoved into the kitchen to find a place around the big table.

The end of the table closest to the front room they reserved for Elisha and Susana. Two little high chairs, made by Elisha, were pulled up to the table for the children. Elisha asked everyone to bow their heads and he gave a blessing for the food.

Joe imagined his father at the end of the table saying the prayer, Elisha sounded so much like him.

~

While the weather held, Elisha sent someone into town every week to bring back supplies. Jim, Will, and Jeff tried to be in front of the line to make the trip. Young and single, the fun of going to town had a lot of appeal. Elisha managed to rotate it so everyone who wanted to, got to go to town.

Joe had no desire to go, although he put items on the list if there were things he wanted.

Almost every trip to town brought back a letter for Joe from Sara. He also received letters from Doc whom he had written when first coming to Elisha's ranch. This meant that Joe had letters to write. Since his social life was limited, he wrote of life on the ranch and the people around him. He also wrote Sara stories about the children.

Joe still couldn't figure out why the children seemed to like him so much, but he didn't mind. Actually, he thoroughly enjoyed their attention. They were a continual source of interest and amusement for him.

He was surprised to learn this was the first winter in the valley for Elisha and Susana. They had built the house and barn over the last three summers. In the winter, they'd worked down on the ranch with Sam Weathers. Elisha and Susana talked about Sam, but Joe never heard them mention Sam's wife and he didn't feel free to ask why.

Joe enjoyed life on the ranch. There was always something to do and someone to do it with. Through the years, he had heard people in town talk about the loneliness of ranch life. It puzzled him that they thought such a thing. He looked around the bunkroom at Bob, Jim, Will, Jeff, Jacob, and Billy all sprawled out on their bunks, or at the table playing cards. How anyone could be lonely? There was also Santo, Mara, Cookie, Elisha, Susana, and the two children. That made for a total of fourteen people around the kitchen table for meals.

Elisha had some interesting ways about him. The man intrigued Joe. The ranch owner didn't talk a lot about being a Christian; he lived it. Every Sunday was a day free of work for the hands except for a couple riders that were out with the herds if needed. He and Susana invited anyone who wanted to meet in the front room at ten on Sunday morning for a worship service.

Partly because there wasn't much else to do, and partly because Joe enjoyed them, he always went. Most of the hands attended.

Again, it reminded Joe so much of his father, whom he ached to see again until he reminded himself that would mean also being with his mother. He wasn't ready for that.

Elisha read the Bible aloud and he had a beautiful reading voice. He gave explanations, as good as any preacher, about the verses he read.

Of course, Joe had never heard many preachers, having been neglectful of religion the last eleven years. The few he had heard didn't stand up against Elisha's lessons.

Then when Elisha, Susana, and Cookie sang a hymn, well, all the cowhands listened.

As they met week after week, Joe tried to sing with them. He sat next to Cookie so he could follow his strong bass voice. Most of the hymns were ones he had heard his father sing. Soon, he sang along with the rest of them, most of the cowhands did.

The entire crew along with Elisha worked hard getting up hay, chopping wood, herding the cattle, and all the other chores that a busy ranch required. Joe helped with the breakfast, but the rest of the day, he spent out on the range. He was almost content. If only Sara could have been with him.

~

Elisha had been serious about getting the wild horses under control. They found a box canyon they could use to herd in the horses, and to contain them. Once they had the horses corralled, they could catch one horse at a time and work with it in a smaller pen.

Joe had been right that Jim Finely was good at working with the horses, as was Santo. Bob, Jeff, and Will weren't bad, but they weren't as skilled as Jim and Santo. Jacob was useless on a horse. Of course, Joe couldn't say anything, as he couldn't even ride.

Elisha was an excellent rider, but Susana had privately told Joe not to let him on a bucking horse as he had an old back injury. Elisha never said anything, but he didn't complain that Joe never put him on an unbroken horse when he came and spent time working with the horses.

With the help of the riders, Joe found he could be of use in working with the horses. He helped Jim and Santo become gentler at breaking a horse. Joe wanted to break the horses to ride to the rider's commands, not break them physically and mentally. It took longer, but his way left them with a horse that was teachable and not dangerous. When he first began to approach an unbroken horse, he searched for something that he couldn't describe. It was almost as if he connected mentally in some way with the horse. Some horses, Joe could tell by the look in their eyes, were not teachable. There was no connection between him and the horse.

Elisha rode up to where Joe sat in the small wagon looking over the horses that Santo and Jim had herded into the big box canyon. "What do you think Joe? Do we have any horses worth breaking?"

"Most of these are good horses, but you need to trim the wild horse herd," Joe responded.

"Why is that?"

Joe waved his hand toward the herd. "Some of these are not worth training being too old or sick, or too wild to break. We need just to shot them. It is really a kindness."

Elisha scratched the back of his neck. "I have to confess to you, Joe, I'm not sure I can do that, just shot a horse. I know it is probably the most humane thing to do. And if I can't do it, how can I ask someone who works for me to do it?"

Joe looked at his boss. Being soft hearted toward animals and children didn't make the man any less strong. If anything, it made him stronger in Joe's eyes. "Don't worry about it. This winter the cold and wolves will probably thin out the weaker horses."

Without riding, Joe could do a lot of the breaking. Once the others got the horses rounded up and into the corral, Joe chose which one to work with and worked with it in a smaller pen away from the larger herd. Slowly, step-by-step, he worked with a horse until it would allow a bridle and saddle to be placed on it.

Then he would add a sack of feed onto the saddle to get the horse used to the weight. Joe would put his left foot into the stirrup and let the horse get used to the weight of a rider about to step into the saddle. However, from that point, Joe had to get Jim or Santo, or one of the others to carry through to the last part of riding the horse.

While Joe worked with a horse, he talked to it and made little cooing sounds like a dove. By the time Joe decided a horse was ready for someone to ride, the horse usually followed Joe around the corral. Once it had a rider on its back, it would look around at the rider with what seemed a puzzled look, and then be responsive to the bit. If Joe took his time and stayed patient with a horse, it seldom bucked when a rider first got on it.

Joe corralled several of the mares carrying foals into one of the box canyons away from the rest of the wild horses. He didn't try to break them for riding, but he did work with them to get them gentle enough that he could help them with their foaling should the need arise. Because Joe didn't know when the horses had mated, he had to guess when they might be ready to deliver. The gestation for a horse is 340 days and can vary several days either way.

If they kept the mares corralled, they had a better chance of keeping the foals from being killed by wolves and could better control the next breeding cycle. Joe pointed out to Elisha several mares that would drop a good foal. He also admitted it was all guesswork. If they could control the breeding within the herd, they could have a good herd of horses to sell within the next few years. They needed to have the stallions cover the mares within twenty-one days after the foals were born to ensure a crop of foals for the next year. All of that took getting the animals together at the right place and the right time. Joe made recommendations to Elisha, who now had a group of twenty stallions that were of a good breeding quality. By the next fall, Joe hoped to have a herd of three hundred horses broke to sell. They could have herded the horses, driven them to the railhead, and sold them. They would receive a better price for horses that were ready to ride.

Elisha got the contract from the army to deliver three hundred head of horses, broken to ride by the coming fall. Joe had the job of getting the horses caught, broke, and increasing the herd for the next year. Ten horses a week ready for a rider was the most that Joe could do. He worked from first light to dark that was coming earlier and earlier as November arrived.

Joe enjoyed his work. He spent more and more of his time out with the horses and less in the kitchen. Cookie didn't seem to mind. The kitchen was easy to work in, and Mara and Susana often helped him.

Why couldn't he just live for the day? But too often thoughts of Sara during the day and nightmares of his childhood at night left him feeling edgy and discontented.

Chapter Twenty-Five

Joe and the other hands had been working on the Rocking ES ranch for a month since the others had left for Texas when Jeff and Elisha came back from a trip to town. Jeff drove the big wagon with two teams, but Elisha drove the most amazing little cart with a narrow bed and two big wheels with a large wheelbase. Wide enough for two people to sit on the padded spring seat, if they sat close together, it only needed one horse to pull it.

Elisha pulled up in front of the house where Joe stood on the porch with Susana, Cookie, and the cowhands gathering around.

"Come take a look, Joe. What do you think?" Elisha called out.

"Think about what?" Joe walked around the cart. "I mean, what is it?"

"I'm not sure what to call it either." Elisha got down from the seat. He handed Joe the reins. "I guess it's a cart. Here, try it out. It handles with great ease."

Curious, Joe climbed up on the seat and clucked at the horse. The horse stepped out and the cart glided over the ground. He drove to the barn, spoke the command 'haw' for the horse to turn to the left and the cart seemed to turn in the space of a dime and was amazingly easy to handle. Joe pulled up in from of Elisha.

"Where did you find such a thing?" Joe was curious as to why Elisha had brought the vehicle to the ranch.

"I had it made for you." Elisha gazed intently at Joe.

"What do you mean you had it made for me?"

"Well, you need to get about where you want on the ranch. A horse can pull this almost anywhere. A few of the mountain passes might be too difficult, but otherwise, I figure you can get on this and go anywhere you want to go. The design is based on a sulky. I just had them add the wagon bed to it so you could transport gear with you."

Realizing that everyone was staring at him as if they were holding their breath waiting for his response, Joe looked at Elisha. The rancher was frowning as if he was afraid the gesture might have offended. Joe might have reacted that way a year ago, before he learned some hard lessons. Now, with the reality of his life and the freedom Elisha offered with the little cart, Joe felt quite pleased.

He laughed, breaking the tension. "This is great, Elisha. How did you ever think of such a thing? I'm assuming you're saying this contraption is mine to use."

Elisha and the others smiled and laughed in relief.

"No, it's not yours to use. It's yours to keep."

How could Joe express his appreciation for the thoughtfulness that had gone in the design and making of the cart? "I think I'll call it a cart, but it's also like a wagon. No, it's a cart." Joe decided.

Everyone talked at once and came up to examine the odd contraption.

Joe climbed down and turned to Susana. "You want to try it?"

"Of course." She climbed up on the seat and drove down the track toward the pass and back again. She stopped the cart in front of Joe and grinned. "Oh Joe, this is great. It glides over the ground and the horse doesn't seem to feel the weight at all. Elisha tried to tell me about it, but I couldn't imagine."

The cart made such a difference for Joe. He rode out to the cattle, and up the canyons to look for wild horses with a freedom he hadn't experienced since his horseback riding days. Soon he noticed that the others on the ranch lost interest in his cart and they took it as just what he rode. Joe trained five horses to pull the light cart. By changing horses through a day's work, he could be on the go from morning until dark.

~

By Christmas, snow covered the land and closed the passes in and out of the ranch.

Little Sam stood by the barn door wrapped in a heavy coat, hat over his ears, thick mittens, and with a scarf around his neck. "What'ja doing?"

Joe grinned at the small boy who looked as wide as he was tall in his extra winter clothing. "I took the wheels off the cart and put on runners to make a winter sled. Want to help me try it out?"

"Sure."

A small squeaky voice came from behind Little Sam. "Can I come, too?"

Joe glanced behind Little Sam and there was Christine, equally wrapped up against the snow. He glanced at the tracks they had made in the snow and realized they had wandered out of their normal play area around the front porch.

"Let me ask your ma if it's all right." Joe slugged through the snow to the front porch and stuck his head through the doorway. Susana was in the front room at her sewing machine. "Can the children go out on the cart with me?"

Susana looked up with a bright smile. "If you want to deal with them. They are tired of being cooped up in the house and it's only December."

She grabbed a buffalo rug from the back of the couch. "Here, put this around them and don't go too far."

"I'll have them back in the hour."

Joe hoisted the children into wagon bed of the cart. When he'd bundled them under the rug, only their little faces showed. With a "Walk on!" to the horse, Joe took them across the snow-covered rangeland alongside the creek.

"Whew! Go faster, Uncle Joe!" hollered Sam.

"Faster, horsey." Encouraged Christine.

Joe kept to the steady pace even as he laughed at the little ones. Had he ever had as carefree a moment when he was a child? He couldn't remember any.

"Hang on, it's going to get a little up and down." Joe warned them just as they crossed a section of range with rolling slopes.

Gales of laughter from Sam and Christine kept Joe chuckling at the delight of the children.

When he brought the cart back to the house, Sam said, "Let's go again, Uncle Joe."

Grinning, Joe lifted Christine out of the cart and set her on the porch. "We'll go again tomorrow. For now we need to let this horse get some rest." After depositing Sam on the porch, Joe winked at the boy. "I bet that Cookie might have some hot cocoa for two frozen kids. Why don't you go ask?"

Sam and Christine's faces lit up and they barely waved good-bye as they tumbled into the house.

With a grin of satisfaction for having given the children an hour of pleasure, Joe led the horse and cart to the barn to unhitch.

~

The cowhands from Texas found dealing with the snow different, but compared to a blue northern out on the plains of west Texas, where the wind came out of the north and the temperature could drop forty degrees in twenty minutes, the winter was no worse than what they had faced before. And Elisha and Suzanna had planned well: there were plenty of supplies on hand.

The cowhands had cut plenty of hay and stored it not only at the barn, but in several of the box canyons. By feeding the cattle with snow on the ground, it took less land area to contain them. The horses that Joe worked and broke in the largest box canyon thrived on the hay they were fed.

The cowhands were continually out on the range to make sure the cattle didn't bunch up against a ridge, and that they could get to water. During the cold hard freezes, the hands rode with an axe to chop holes in the creeks for the cattle. The horses would eat the snow, but the Texas cattle didn't seem to connect the white stuff to water at first, but after about three days they started consuming the snow as their water source.

Coming into the house after a day spent in the cold, Joe was grateful for the hot food that Cookie had ready for the crew.

As most were finishing eating their supper, Susana rose from her chair at the table and said, "Let's get the dishes done and then meet in the front room for some fun."

Elisha cocked an eyebrow. "And what do you have planned that is fun?"

"You wait and see, Mr. Evans."

Joe enjoyed watching Elisha and Susana as they poked gentle fun at each other. With several helping with the cleanup, they soon had the kitchen squared away. Joe carried a kitchen chair into the front room, as did several others so everyone would have a seat. "Here, take this chair, Joe. I prefer that kitchen chair for my back." Elisha waved him toward one of the overstuffed chairs by the fireplace.

"Thanks." Joe sighed with relief, as the cushioned chair did feel better on his aching hip and leg.

Santo and Jim came in carrying their guitars and Cookie pulled out his harmonica. And then to everyone's surprise, Jacob walked in with a small case from which he brought out a violin.

"We're going to see how many of the songs these boys can play and we can sing along with. The one who knows the most songs gets to choose what cake I bake tomorrow and will get the biggest piece." Susana announced.

The chill of the cold winter evening receded with the warmth of the fire in the fireplace and the music. Joe joined in the fun of trying to sing as many of the songs as he could but soon was left behind by Bob and Jim who along with Susana who seemed to know all the songs. To everyone's surprise Jim won.

Joe looked around the front room at Little Sam seated next to Billy and Christine snuggled up in Mara's lap. He had never worked for a boss who was so willing to share his family with the ranch hands as did Elisha and Susana. Even with the hard work fighting the elements, times like this almost made up for not having a family.

Elisha clapped his hands and got everyone's attention. "We need to get to bed and be ready for another day of work. I just want to let everyone know that day after tomorrow is Christmas and we'll have a big dinner. Except for the necessary chores, everyone gets the day off. What time do you want to serve the meal, Cookie?"

"Since it will be both dinner and supper let's plan for one o'clock."

Jim Finely had brought in an elk and Cookie planned to serve elk steak, gravy, mashed potatoes, green peas, stewed tomatoes, sweet potatoes, and rolls. For desert they would be baking for the next two days blackberry pie, apple pie, pumpkin pie, chocolate cake, and sugar cookies for the children. Joe looked forward to helping Cookie prepare the special meal for the ranch. This would be a different Christmas than any Joe had experienced in the last few years.

Joe tried to stop himself from remembering what Christmas had been like as a child. His father tried to provide something of a holiday, but his mother's disapproval always spoiled it for everyone. Joe often found himself contrasting Elisha and Susana's home to what he'd had as a child. It didn't do any good to think about a time when there had been only pain, fear, and loneliness.

Actually, Joe was more content than he'd ever been in his life. He tried to think on that, and not let the dark cloud of the past creep in and ruin it. He mostly succeeded.

~

After Christmas and the New Year, everyone on the ranch was eager for spring, especially Susana, as her baby was due in May. She was less patient as her time grew near, and Joe tried to stay out of her way. Often Little Sam rode out with Joe. He added a strap to the seat for both the children and himself. Sometimes the little cart bounced unexpectedly as he took it off the trails and across the range. Joe liked to go fast, and he'd have lost Little Sam several times if he hadn't been strapped in. The little boy always laughed when they hit the bigger bumps and he had to hold onto his hat.

The first of May, Joe was helping get the breakfast on the table when Jim came in.

Elisha looked up from tying an apron on Christina. "What does it look like?"

Jim poured a cup of coffee and took a sip. "The pass through the gap is clear. I think you can get a wagon into town."

Cookie set a platter of biscuits on the table as everyone took their seats. "Good because we only have enough coffee for another week at the most."

"We have to go for supplies, Elisha. I can't do without my coffee." Bob sounded mighty serious.

"Make your lists. Now who wants to go to town in the morning?" Elisha asked with a grin.

Immediately, every one of the hands was talking, volunteering to go. Joe sat quiet. If Elisha wanted him to go, he would, but he didn't really want to make the trip. The only thing he was interested in was the possibility of letters.

"Bob, why don't you take Jeff and Billy. Take both the wagons. We're low on supplies. I can't go because of Susana's condition."

Joe spent the evening writing letters to Sara and Doc, and added them to the bundle of letters the boys took into town to mail. They were loaded up and pulled out by dawn.

During the next few days, Joe searched the trail leading into the valley watching for the supply wagons to return. It wasn't the supplies he waited for, it was letters from Sara. Would she have forgotten him over the winter?

Finally, Joe saw the wagons and riders coming down the trail. They had taken four days to get to town, load up, and return to the ranch which was good time considering the roads.

While Cookie, Joe, and Billy put away the foodstuff, Susana sorted the sack of letters and handed them out to the cowhands. It was the first mail after a long winter.

Joe had several letters from Sara and Doc. He hitched the sorrel horse up to the cart, and drove up to the top of the ridge on the south side where he could see the length of the valley and the high snowcapped mountains beyond. There he opened his letters.

He read the letters from Doc first. They were always short, to the point, and mostly a chronicle of patients he'd treated. Doc always asked about the work Joe did with the horses. He was especially intrigued by Joe's description of the cart. He always ended his letters with the hope Joe was well, and greetings from Mrs. Purdy.

Joe arranged Sara's letters by date, and read them slowly. He could hear the sound of her voice through the written words. She and her father now lived in San Francisco, where he was involved in banking, buying and selling mines, and buying up parts of the San Francisco valley. With a sigh, he came to the last letter in the stack.

Dear Joe,

Well, it is spring here. The nights are cool, but it is warm in the daytime. I keep wondering what it is like in the mountains. Do you still have snow? Has the pass cleared enough for you to get to town? Have you received any of my letters? It has been months since I received one from you. I wait everyday to see if a letter has come. I chose to believe no letter comes because you are still snowed in at the ranch and not because you don't want to write anymore.

I will be going to Natalie Wheater's party tomorrow. It is all so silly. You would not believe what these girls talk about. There will be several young men there from the various rancheros, but they don't want to talk to me of anything serious either. They assume because I'm a girl that I wouldn't be interested in ranching, business, or politics.

How I do miss our talks as we rode along on the chuck wagon. Do you realize what a smart conversationalist you are? You have spoiled me for talking to these young men.

Papa wants to take me to the opera tonight. There will be all sorts of important people there. I don't really want to go, as Papa will spend all his time talking to other men about business. But he likes for me to go with him, so I probably will.

I do enjoy the church I'm attending here. Papa doesn't really like the one I go to. He would rather we went to a bigger one with all the important people. But I prefer to be with a smaller group that wants to come together to worship. We're studying Romans. I so wish you were here. There are so many things I would like to talk about with you. Perhaps, someday, you can come and visit?

Write me about what is happening at the ranch. It is so boring here. You have such a wonderful life there. How I miss it.

Give my love to Elisha, Susana, Little Sam, Christine, Cookie, Billy, Bob, Jeff, Jim, Will, Jacob, Santo and his wife whom I hope to meet someday, and especially to you, my friend.

God's blessings,
Most sincerely, your friend who remembers you,
Sara

Opera, parties, that was her life. Joe found it hard to believe that Sara's life bored her, as her world sounded so much fuller than his. When Joe had written to her, before the valley was snowed in for the winter, he had tried to tell her stories of the life on the ranch. She seemed especially to like the stories Joe told her about the Little Sam and Christine.

He appreciated that Sara considered him her friend, and wrote him long letters every week. Why would she care about him when her world and her life were so interesting? Hers was a world he couldn't enter, nor did he want to. Joe could never offer her what her father did. Maybe he shouldn't keep writing her, let her get on with her life. His chest ached at the thought.

As he looked at the stack of letters in his hands, one for almost every week of the long winter, it touched a part of his being that he tried to keep closed. He had hoped she wouldn't forget him and she hadn't. Joe sniffed the letters and the faint scent of lavender surrounded him. It was like having a bit of Sara with him.

Joe carefully tucked her letters into his jacket pocket to be read again later and climbed onto the seat of the cart. Taking the reins, he headed the sorrel for the barn. He unhitched the rig, rubbed the horse down, and turned him into the corral. Then, he went to the kitchen. Cookie was busy putting supplies away.

Joe walked over to the pegs on the wall, exchanged his hat and jacket for his apron, and turned to help.

"You don't have to do this, Joe." Cookie unloaded a box of canned goods onto the table.

"I know, but I don't have anything else going for the moment. You know, I have to admit that I miss working with you." And Joe did, but not enough to go back to just kitchen work.

Cookie laughed. "What you miss is our talks together. I hope you don't miss the work of cooking on the trail."

"You're right. I miss our time talking as we followed the trail herd. I don't miss all that hard work. This is an easier life."

"You hear from Miss Sara?" Cookie asked as he put sacks of Arbuckle coffee on the high shelf.

"Yep, I got several letters from her. She sends her greetings. No, that's not right. What she said was to give Cookie her love."

Cookie beamed, which made his face even more wrinkled.

"Now, isn't that nice. When you write her back tell her Cookie sends his love also."

"I'll do that." Joe hoped he wouldn't forget.

"Did you hear that we're going to have visitors?"

"Who?"

"You know that rancher, Sam Weathers, the one Elisha and Susana are always going on about?" Cookie stood on a step stool stacking sacks of coffee on an upper shelf, his back to Joe.

Joe held himself still in the middle of the kitchen, glad Cookie couldn't see his face. Or see his hands start to tremble.

Chapter Twenty-Six

Joe had to get away. He had to be anywhere but at the ranch when his parents arrived. He couldn't meet up with them again, he just couldn't.

No. That was wrong. He didn't want to see his mother. But his father—Joe wanted desperately to see him.

"When are they coming?" Joe asked as he didn't trust himself to ask the ones he wanted to.

"It could be any day. Their letter for Elisha and Susana came in the same bundle as your letters. I'm glad we got supplies in so I can cook something decent for them. Maybe you could give me some help with what to cook."

"Is their daughter coming with them?" How old would Christine be now? She was ten when he left, so she'd twenty-two now, a grown woman.

Cookie stopped what he was doing and turned toward him. "No one said anything about a daughter. How did you know they had a daughter?" Cookie waited. "What's the matter, Joe? You look all peculiar."

"Cookie, I want your word you won't tell anyone if I tell you."

"I give my word." Cookie stepped down from the stool then sat at the table. He folded his arms, giving Joe his full attention.

Joe pulled up a chair and sat across from him. "You remember me telling you about my folks having a ranch south of here?"

Cookie nodded.

Joe took a deep breath. "My folks are Sam Weathers and his wife, Myrtle. I thought maybe you'd guessed." Joe let out his breath.

"Your folks!" Cookie's surprised expression revealed he hadn't guessed at all. "Why haven't you told us? Why haven't you told Elisha and Susana?"

"I didn't want to have to give explanations, I guess. In twelve years I haven't told anyone but you about my folks." Joe didn't know why he was telling Cookie now, except that the prospect of them turning up at the ranch had surprised Joe and thrown him into a dilemma.

"Don't you think you ought to tell the Evans' before your folks show up?"

It was a reasonable question but Joe didn't want to face it. "Once I tell them they're going to want all kinds of explanations. Elisha and Susana don't see my folks the same way I do. If I told them why I ran away, I doubt they'd believe me."

Joe didn't look at Cookie, but traced a pattern on the tabletop with his finger. "And in a way, I'm embarrassed by my family. I mean, when you compare my place with my family, and what Elisha and Susana have as a family . . . ." Joe didn't know how to finish what he had tried to say, or what it was he wanted to say.

"Are you afraid to see your folks again?" Cookies' voice was low and gentle.

Joe looked up and saw compassion from his friend. It bothered him to know that he needed Cookie's compassion, but he did.

"I hadn't thought about it as fear, but I guess it is. I'm scared of how I'll react when I see my mother. The thought of her fills me with nothing but dread." Joe swallowed, and then put his hand to his stomach. "I get sick to my stomach when I think of her." Joe took a deep breath that ended in a shudder. "Can you imagine that, Cookie? A grown man who's afraid to see his own mother, but that's the truth."

"I'm sorry, Joe. I can't imagine what it was like for you as a young boy that would leave those kinds of feelings, after so many years. It had to be awful bad."

"Yeah, it was. And then, Cookie, you realize what I got to tell my father. He only knows ranching and riding. Now, here's his son who thought he could make it on his own, can't even ride a horse. What's he going to think of me?" Joe stopped because he couldn't seem to get his breath.

"What are you going to do? They're supposed to visit any day now." Cookie looked concerned.

"I got to face it sometime, and it might as well be now. Otherwise, I need to pack up and leave and I don't want to do that. I got nowhere else to go." Joe wondered if it sounded as pathetic to Cookie as it did to him, but it was the truth.

"You're right. You need to face up to them. Get it over with, and then it won't hang over you so. I'll stand with you. Why, every rider on this ranch will stand with you. And, Joe, if you can't face them, you let me know. I'll leave with you and we'll go find a herd to help bring up the trail. Or, you and me, we could open a restaurant somewhere. Of course, we'd have to take Billy with us."

Joe knew he was serious. It meant a lot to Joe that Cookie would give up a job that he enjoyed for him. Joe saw how rich he was, he had friends.

"Thanks, Cookie. I'll keep that in mind. No, I need to get ready to face them, see what happens. Only to you would I admit this. I am scared." Joe looked at the kind, gruff man that he had come to respect over the last several months. They'd come up a rough trail together.

"I know you are, but you're still willing to face your folks. That's what I call courage. So let's get a plan going. We'll surprise them with your being here, and impress them with our great cooking." Cookie picked up a big ladle and held it up as if he was waving a wand.

They both laughed, and then Joe couldn't stop. If he didn't stop laughing, he'd soon be crying. Joe was that muddled by the prospect of seeing his folks again. He managed to stop laughing by getting up and making a fresh pot of coffee.

As he stood by the cook stove, he said, "They may not recognize me. I've changed a lot in twelve, no, going on thirteen years."

~

The next week dragged as Joe constantly looked down the trail toward the gated pass, expecting his folks to appear. Dreams filled with his childhood haunted his nights. Elisha and Susana, in the meantime, got everyone busy sprucing up the place. Joe wanted to talk to Elisha and Susana about his folks, but put it off.

Joe spent his time in the box canyon, working with the horses. In between gentling a horse, he watched over several of the mares about to foal. Three of the mares had foaled overnight. It had gone well and they now had three more little foals standing on shaky legs nuzzling their mothers. Joe never got over the wonder of it. Each foal was a little miracle to him. After he completed his day's work, he stopped by the creek and took a quick plunge in the cold water. He put on the clean clothes he had with him.

After Joe returned to the ranch house, he put his gear away in the bunkroom, and then went to the kitchen. A cup of coffee to warm up after the bath in the cold water of the creek sounded like a good idea. Cookie was busy with supper preparations.

Joe heard the noise of a team and buggy stop in front of the house. The front door banged open and the sound of excited greetings drifted into the kitchen. Joe, with Cookie behind him moved over to the window and looked out.

A big, solid looking, gray-haired man in his fifties with a weathered and lined face gave Elisha a hug, and then turned to help a woman down from a buggy.

"Is that your folks?" Cookie asked softly as he looked out the window.

"That's my father, but I've never seen that woman before in my life." Joe couldn't take his eyes off the group out in the yard.

The woman was taller than Susana, with brown hair parted in the middle and pulled into a bun at the back of her head. She had an open, pleasant look with a nice smile. She was a fine figure of a woman dressed in a hat and a dark gray coat over a soft blue dress with a lace collar.

"What do you mean?" Cookie looked sharply at Joe.

"That's not my mother. I don't know who that is."

"Well, Joe, get ready. They're coming into the house." He put his hand on Joe's shoulder and squeezed it.

The gesture said much to Joe. He closed his eyes and took a deep breath. Lord, Help me. Was that a prayer? Yes, he guessed it was. Joe only had a couple of minutes, and then Elisha and Susana would bring the visitors into the kitchen to introduce them.

Joe stepped over to the end of the table and waited. He took slow even breaths to calm down. His arms hung loose by his side, but his hands were numb. All he wanted to do was turn and run out the back door . . . like a little boy.

Cookie stepped in close and stood by him.

Elisha walked into the kitchen followed by Susana, Joe's father, and the woman. "Cookie, Joe, let me introduce Sam Weathers and his wife, Vivian. This is our Cookie, and Joe Storm, who handles the horses."

Sam Weathers stepped forward. He shook hands with Cookie, and then with Joe.

Joe felt the firm calloused skin of his father's large hand grasp his own.

"Joe . . . ?" He looked Joe in the eyes. "Do I know you?" He continued to grasp Joe's hand. "You look a lot like someone I used to know."

Joe looked at Cookie, who nodded back at him.

Joe swallowed and turned back to his father. "You do know me."

"Who are you?" The man stared unblinkingly at Joe's face and his hand tightened on Joe's hand.

"I'm Joseph." He gave the name his father had always used for him. Joe's knees felt as if they would buckle from the strain.

"Joseph?" The color drained from the older man's face, and his grip crushed Joe's hand. "My Joseph?" His voice had gone husky with question and hope.

"Yes, Pa, it's me, Joseph." Joe couldn't take his eyes away from his father's face.

"But Elisha called you Joe Storm?"

"That's what I've called myself for the last twelve years." What else could he say?

His father let go of his hand and grabbed Joe in a bear hug.

"My son, my son." He cried now with silent tears running down his face.

Joe didn't know how long they stood there. "Pa?"

His father pulled back and held Joe by the shoulders.

"Let me look at you. You've grown so tall and look so much older." He laughed through his tears. "I guess you are older. You must be twenty-five-years old now."

He turned and pulled the woman toward Joe. "Vivian, I want you to meet my son, Joseph. This is Vivian, my wife."

Joe was having a problem putting meaning to the words his father was saying. They didn't make sense. He looked to Cookie for help.

Cookie nodded, as if to say to Joe, you can handle this.

"Joseph? Is it you?" She took his hand.

Joe didn't know what to say to her. He turned back to his father.

"Pa. Where's Ma? Where's Christine?"

The look of pain on his father's face warned Joe of what was to come.

"You don't know?" The raw edge of emotion spilled into his voice.

"No. I've had no news since I left." Joe tried to brace himself. What was his father trying to say?

"Your mother and sister died in a wagon accident two months after you left." His father said in a quiet voice.

It was as if someone hit Joe in the stomach. They had been dead for almost as long as Joe had been gone. He couldn't take it in.

Cookie put his arm around Joe's shoulders and took his father's arm. "Elisha, these folks need to sit and talk. Let's go into the front room."

With the pressure of Cookie's arm on his shoulder, Joe walked into the front room, and sat on a sofa.

His father sat beside Joe. Vivian took a seat at Sam's other side.

Elisha and Susana, who had not said anything, sat across from them. Concern was heavy in both their faces.

"I'll get everyone a cup of coffee." Cookie went back into the kitchen.

Joe sat with his elbows on his legs, his hands clasped tightly together to keep them from shaking. He looked up at his father. "I can't believe it. Christine, she was only ten."

"I know, son. It was a hard time. I looked for you all over. I looked and looked. Why did you leave?" He shook his head. "No, don't answer. We can talk about that later. For now, tell me how you are today. How long have you worked for Elisha?" Without waiting for Joe to answer, he turned to Elisha. "Did you know? Did you know Joseph was my son?"

Elisha shifted in his seat. "No, Sam, I'd no idea. He told me he was raised in Colorado, but I first met him in Oklahoma Territory on a cattle drive. If I'd known I'd have sent word to you. I knew of your grief over your son being missing." He looked at Joe. "Why didn't you tell me, Joe? You've heard us talk about Sam. You had to know he was our friend."

Joe had a pain in his stomach with a tightening of his muscles.

"I wanted to tell you, but I didn't know how to explain things. I for sure didn't know my mother was dead. That would have made a difference." Joe turned to his father. "If I'd known about her being dead and Christine, I'd have written to you. But as long as she was still there, I couldn't come back."

His father patted Joe's arm and gave him a look of profound sadness. "I understand, Joseph. I don't blame you. If only I'd known how to contact you." He shook his head, and the tears flowed down his seamed face again.

Cookie returned from the kitchen carrying a tray with cups of coffee. He set the tray on a side table, and Susana stood to help serve.

"Here, Joe, drink this down now." He handed Joe a cup of strong, hot coffee.

Cookie sat in one of the chairs. Joe was glad for Cookie's presence. He sipped his coffee, and as he suspected, Cookie had put a lot of sugar and milk in it. Joe drank it down.

"Let me tell you about myself, Joseph. After your mother and sister died, I wanted to find you, in the worst way. I hired people to look for you, contacted all of the sheriffs I could. I searched and searched. After about five years, I decided I had to go on living and gave up the search, but not my hope. I stayed on the ranch in hope that you'd come home. I prayed to the Lord to take care of you, and to bring you back. He has, and in a way, I could never have imagined He would do it. Four years ago, I met Elisha and Susana and they became my family. They even let me be grandpa to their children. Then last year I met Vivian, and the Lord blessed me to be loved, and to love in a way I have never done before." He put his arm around Vivian's shoulder and gave her a hug.

She leaned into him and smiled.

"We came up to try to be of help to Susana with the birth of this new baby. Instead," he turned to Susana, "you've helped me find my son. Praise God."

The image of his mother's face the last time he saw her kept invading Joe's thoughts. It had been such a look of hate and disgust, and now he would never see her again. How sad that the only response he had was relief. He had always imagined his sister growing up, but all during that time, she had been dead. He had a hard time wrapping his mind around the truth of it.

"Joseph . . . Joseph?" His father spoke.

His father's voice dragged Joe's thoughts back to the present.

"Yes, sir?"

"Tell me a little about what you've been doing." His father put his hand on Joe's arm and let it rest there.

The touch of his father's hand helped make what was happening seem real. He was able to focus back on the present.

"I hardly know where to start. After I left home, I traveled to New York and saw the east and the ocean. I went to Texas, and got work on a trail herd going to Wichita. I spent ten years, or so, trailing herds up from Texas and working on ranches. Then ..." Joe drew in a deep breath.

He didn't know if he could tell him.

His father's eyes gazed at Joe with such an expression of love.

Joe released the breath he'd been holding. He'd take the chance, he'd tell his father.

"Last year I got hurt bad. I can't ride anymore. I can't sit a horse . . . . " Joe trailed off and he dropped his gaze. He didn't know what else to say.

Why didn't his father say something? Joe's heart pounded in his chest for several seconds. He couldn't look up, couldn't take the disappointment he'd see in his father's eyes.

"I don't understand, son. Elisha said you work with his horses."

Joe finally forced himself to meet his father's gaze. "I manage the horse business for Elisha. Other riders break them. I can't ride. I can't sit a horse. I use a cart to get around." Joe didn't want to go on. His chest and stomach hurt, and he feared he would throw up. He didn't know how much more he could take.

"You seem to walk fine. You got any other injuries?" His father accepted what Joe had said. However, when his father understood what it meant, would he be as accepting? Would he respect a son who couldn't ride?

"I've about healed. But the damage to my right hip, from it being broken bad, won't ever heal. That's why I can't ride." Joe had to say it again to make sure his father understood. He needed to get past it.

"I don't care if you can ride, or not. I wouldn't care if you could walk or not. I've found you at last. That's all I care about." His grip on Joe's arm tightened with each word.

Cookie stood. "I need to get back to the kitchen if we're going to have any supper. Susana, Vivian probably wouldn't mind seeing their room. I'll send some hot water so you can wash up after your journey."

Joe glanced at Vivian and realized she did look exhausted. He was also thankful to Cookie for helping him to get out from under the gun with his father's questions. It wasn't that he thought his father didn't have a right to ask the questions, but Joe was exhausted from the emotional strain of meeting his father for the first time in almost thirteen years.

"My, yes, Vivian, I'm so sorry. Let me show you to your room." Susana got up, took Vivian by the arm and led her toward the guest bedroom at the back of the house.

Joe stood. "We'll have time to talk later, Pa. Why don't you go on now, and get settled. How long are you staying?"

"We plan to stay a couple of weeks if Elisha and Susana can put up with us."

"Sam," Elisha said, "you know that Susana and I want you to stay as long as you can."

"It's so good to be here with you all." His father hugged Joe again. "Words are beyond me to tell you how I feel right now, son. We'll talk later." He went down the hall toward the bedroom.

Joe waited for Elisha to speak.

Elisha put his arm on Joe's shoulder, and in a kind voice said, "We're going to need to talk later about what all of this means, Joe."

"All right." Joe felt sick. Would Elisha fire him? Joe hadn't thought about that. Elisha might not want him to stay on the ranch now that he knew Joe hadn't told him the whole truth of who he was. What a mess.

Joe went back into the kitchen. "You need my help?" Joe wanted to get somewhere alone, but he owed Cookie.

"No, Joe. You go take a walk or something. Just be here for supper. Your father wouldn't understand if you weren't."

How did he know Joe wanted just to get lost for the evening? "All right." Joe got his hat and jacket from the peg, then stepped out the kitchen door and headed for the barn. He hitched up the cart and drove up the valley. Slapping the reins, he got the sorrel into a full gallop. He wanted to drive as far away as possible to escape that flood of memories.

His heart hurt, and he wasn't sure why. He should have been relieved and happy to be back in touch with his father. He should have been.

He couldn't keep from thinking of his mother and sister being dead.

Then he realized why he was so miserable. He could have gone home that first year. Maybe if he had he'd still be able to ride. It was almost unbearable. But he had to find a way to let it go, because down that path was too much pain and regret. Choices he'd made had been based on the knowledge he had at the time. If only . . . two of the saddest words Joe knew.

Joe noticed how low the sun was on the western horizon, and turned the cart back toward the ranch house. After he unhitched the sorrel, cooled him down, put him into the corral, then put the cart back into the barn, he headed slowly for the kitchen and to supper with his family.

Chapter Twenty-Seven

Joe stepped into the kitchen and closed the door behind him. He turned to find everyone seated around the table. From the frowns and raised eyebrows, some of them must have been fearful he wasn't coming back in to eat. He wasn't sure he wanted to face them but now was as good a time as any. After hanging his hat on a peg by the door, he looked around the crowded table for an empty chair.

"Sorry, folks, I didn't watch the time." He spotted a chair next to Cookie and sat down. With a nod, he acknowledged his father seated across from him.

Elisha looked at Joe. "Should I make the introductions, or will you?"

Joe nodded at Elisha. "I'll make them. Everyone, I want you all to meet my father, Sam Weathers, and his wife, Vivian, of the J Bar C Ranch. Be sure and welcome them to the Rocking ES."

Everyone nodded and gave words of welcome.

Elisha cleared his throat. "Let's bless the food and eat." He bowed his head and began to pray.

Joe closed his eyes as he bowed his head and he slowly released a deep long breath, thankful Elisha said the blessing. Joe wasn't ready to hear his father's prayers. Too much already was bringing up memories of childhood that he had tried to keep securely buried.

For Joe, the meal and the rest of the evening passed as if he was in a dream. He tried to answer people when they spoke to him, but his mind was in turmoil. He couldn't focus. His thoughts went from the present to the past and they wore him out.

With so many people about, especially the children, there was no time, or space in which to talk privately with his father. They had to talk, but it would have to wait.

He finally said goodnight to his father and Vivian. Speaking with Vivian was an awkward experience. He still could not grasp that his mother was gone. Hard to believe this kind, pleasant woman was his father's wife and his own stepmother. He was still unsure what to call her.

Joe ambled out to the barn in the cool crisp air of the night. Doves were cooing in the distance and he could hear the sound of the light wind in the tops of the lodgepole pines. In the barn, he grabbed a couple of horse blankets to make a bedroll and carried them to the chuck wagon. His joints, especially his weak hip ached along with his mind, which felt beat up from too many emotions throughout the day. The other riders were curious as to what was going on but he needed to be alone without questions. Settled into his bedroll and alone in the dark at last, he felt tears rolling down his face. Why was he crying? Surely not for a mother he was relieved was dead. Perhaps for a sister that he had imagined growing up but who would always be a child of ten. Twisting and turning, he struggled to relax and escape into sleep to stop the thoughts that gave him no peace. Toward morning, his exhausted body finally gave in to slumber.

~

"Joe, you in here?" Cookie's voice carried in the dark barn.

Yawning and stretching, Joe responded, "I'm here in the chuck wagon."

Cookie, carrying a lantern, climbed up on the wagon seat. "I was worried. Bob was up early and said you hadn't made it to your bunk. He wants to know what's going on. I told him to wait, and he'd find out in good time. Are you all right?"

"I'm not sure. It's been a lot to take in that my mother and sister are dead. Vivian seems like a nice woman. I'm glad for my father. He deserves some peace, between having my mother for a wife, and me for a son." Joe glanced at Cookie. Did his friend think him weak for saying such things? He seemed to tell the older man things he didn't dare tell anyone else.

"You got a lot to deal with all of a sudden. Take it slow and easy. It's obvious that your Pa loves you but the two of you have got to get reacquainted." Cookie looked intensely at Joe. "He don't know you yet, as a grown man. Give him and yourself some time."

"How'd you get so smart?" Joe sat up. "I don't know my father apart from my mother yet. How do we get acquainted? What do I say to him?"

"Well, the best thing would be to spend time together." Cookies voice was calm and quiet and he had a frown of concentration. "Take your father with you as you work. Let him see what your life is like now, as a grown man. Also, spend some time with Mrs. Weathers, Vivian. Getting to know her will help you to get to know a different side to your father."

Joe saw the wisdom in the old cook master's words. "I'll do that, Cookie." Joe got up and climbed down from the wagon.

Cookie chuckled. "As soon as Bob told me you hadn't gone to the bunkroom, I knew where to look for you."

"Yeah, I don't know why, but it seemed to be comforting." Joe patted the side of the chuck wagon.

"But it's not a very soft bed."

"I didn't sleep much last night anyway, too much to think about." Joe strolled into the kitchen behind Cookie. "I'll get some water heated, and go wash up." He sniffed the strong scent of the fresh brewed coffee.

"Sit down and drink some coffee while you wait for the water to heat. I got the coffee going before I came looking for you." Cookie poured them both a cup and sat across the table from Joe.

Joe took a sip of the hot brew. "What are you fixing for breakfast?"

"Oh, the usual. Fried ham, biscuits, fried potatoes, eggs, gravy, and we got doughnuts left from yesterday," Cookie said, without blinking.

Joe laughed. "Sounds good. I'll go wash up and help you."

"You don't have to if you'd rather not."

"Cookie, with how upside down I'm feeling, working with you and Billy would be sort of steadying."

"I understand, Joe. You do what you need to do to deal with all of this. If I can be of help, you tell me."

"Don't you know that you have already been the best help I could have? You've been a true friend, and a man couldn't ask for more." Joe lifted his cup up in a salute to Cookie.

Cookie looked like he was close to tearing up as his eyes glistened. He got up, and started banging pots and pans. "Well, the water is hot. Go wash up, and get back here, so we can get breakfast cooked."

"Yes, Cookie." Joe squeezed Cookie in a quick sideways hug, the only kind Cookie would accept. He got a rag and picked up the bucket of boiling water by the handle, and walked out to the wash up stand in the hallway by the back door.

He had put on his apron and stirring the gravy when his father and Elisha walked into the kitchen from the front room. Joe nodded. "Morning."

"Morning." Elisha took two of the enamel cups down from the shelf then poured coffee from the pot already sitting on the table.

Cookie lifted a large pan of biscuits out of the oven. "Good morning Elisha, Mr. Weathers."

"My name is Sam, Cookie." Joe's father smiled kindly and then turned his attention to Joe. "What is that you're cooking, Joseph?" He stepped in closer, put his hand on Joe's shoulder, and peered down at the gravy. "Hmmm. Everything smells good. I'm hungry this morning."

Joe looked at his father. "I remember you always liked your ham gravy and biscuits. You'll like Cookie's biscuits."

"I'm sure I will, son." He patted Joe on the shoulder, pulled out a chair, and sat at the table where he could still face Joe.

In a way, Joe was still uneasy with his father, but his father's touch on his shoulder felt comforting. He hoped he would become more relaxed around him in time.

Joe put the large bowl of gravy on the table soon followed with a huge platter the ham, a bowl of three dozen eggs scrambled with cheese, and a bowl of fried potatoes.

Cookie set two huge platters of biscuits on the table, then went to the hallway, and rang the bell hanging by the door.

Vivian Weathers, Susana, and the children flowed into the kitchen at the same time the cowhands stumbled in from the bunkhouse. Santo and Mara followed at a quieter slower pace.

Christine put up a fuss. "Yoe hold me."

He skirted the table, picked her up, and sat at the table with the little girl on his lap. He looked into her eyes and she returned his gaze. The plain truth was that he often ate his meal with the child on his lap, and he flat out enjoyed it. Everyone had gotten used to the attachment the child had for Joe. And he had lost his heart to her.

Christine patted Joe's face. "Yoe, yoe."

"Yes, honey, what do you want?" Joe asked her with a smile. Would she ever be able to say his name correctly?

She eyed his plate and then looked up at him and smiled showing all her baby teeth. She turned to the table, and grabbed the biscuit Joe had put on his plate.

Joe let her have it.

Elisha tapped the side of his cup with his fork and the hands got quiet. "Sam, would you say the blessing for us?"

"Let's pray. Our most gracious, heavenly Father. We thank you for your continued blessings. Thank you for the blessing of family and for keeping them safe. Bless each one around this table today with health and safety as they go about their work. Bless these two precious children and for the child soon to be born. Give a safe birth and good health to both mother and child. Thank you for the rebirth of my son into my life." Sam Weathers prayed in a strong deep voice. "Thank you for the blessing of this food and the hands that prepared it. In the most holy name of Jesus the Christ. Amen."

As Joe listened to his father's prayer, he felt that it helped put words to his emotions. Amid the feelings of regret, love, and hope squeezing about his heart, he realized that his father was being reborn into his life.

The precious three-year-old girl sitting in his lap demanded Joe's attention, so he fed her eggs, biscuit, and gravy.

Vivian Weathers smiled. "Joseph, you look like you've fed little Christine before."

"Yes, ma'am." Joe smiled back. Cookie's suggestion from earlier that day came back to him about talking to his father's wife. "She likes to sit with me."

"We can't understand it." Susana laughed. "The first time Christine saw Joe she took him under her wing, and she hasn't changed her mind since. Horses and children, they all love Joe."

Joe smiled at Susana. These folks had a continuing discussion of why Joe had such influence on the horses, and the children liked him. He had no explanation for either.

"Sir," Joe spoke to his father. "I'm going to work with the horses and check on some mares about to foal. I'd be proud to have you ride along with me."

His father's face brightened and he leaned forward. "I'd be happy to come along. When do you want to go?"

"I'd like to leave as soon as we finish eating and can get hitched up." Joe handed Christine to Elisha. Normally Susana would have taken the little girl, but she was so close to giving birth, that no one allowed her to lift anything.

Elisha nodded. "If that's what you want to do, Sam, I think watching Joe work with the horses will really be interesting for you to see. I'm not going to ride out today. I need to stay close to home." He and Susana shared a look.

Done with their meal, Joe headed out to the corral with Jim and Santo, and picked out a big red gelding for his father to ride. They saddled it up with the saddle Sam Weathers had brought up from his ranch to use while at the ranch.

Joe hitched a roan mare that some called a Cayuse Indian pony. The pony stood about fourteen hands tall and had a sloped back. Joe liked her because she could trot all day and not seem to get tired. Joe could cover more area with the least strain on his hip because the horse's gait was easy for him.

Joe climbed up on the seat of the cart and his father mounted the big red horse, and they started out.

"That's an interesting cart you got there, son." Sam looked it over. "I've never seen anything like it."

"That's because it's the only one like it around. Elisha designed it and had it made for me. It's been great. I can get to about anywhere on the ranch."

Joe drove the cart up to the barrier at the box canyon, got down, and opened the big gate. "Pa, go ahead and lead the cart through, and I'll close the gate."

His father grabbed the headgear on the pony and led it through the gate.

Joe closed the gate and climbed back on the cart. He drove to the far corral where several mares contentedly munched on hay as they waited to foal. Joe climbed down from the cart and tied the pony to the corral rail.

He entered the corral, cooed at the horses, and stroll up to one of the mares. He rubbed her neck with slow strokes. The mare stood and let Joe feel her belly as he checked the placement of the unborn foal. He checked the other mares also. Some foals would be born within the next day. Joe turned and saw his father, by the railings of the corral, watching him. He had forgotten his father was there for a few minutes.

"Those are some good looking mares. Are they from the wild herd?"

"Yes, sir. We corralled them back in the fall. Elisha plans to have them corralled until they're ready to be covered, and then we'll have only the best stallions cover these mares. Next spring we'll have another crop of good foals." Joe tied up the gate to the corral and then climbed into the cart seat.

His father mounted the red horse. "You all have got a good plan here. Elisha told me about the contract with the army. He also said that you would get a percentage of every horse you all break and sell." Sam leaned over on his saddle horn and looked over at Joe. "Good job, son."

"Thank you, sir. It's work, but over time it'll pay almost as much as the cattle." Joe drove over to the big corral, about a half mile up the box canyon. He handed off the reins of the cart to Santo.

Santo led the pony off a ways and unhitched her. He staked the pony out to graze, as they would be there most of the day.

"You want to watch or you want to help, sir?" Joe wasn't sure he wanted to be observed while he was working but he had been the one to invite his father. He wanted his father to see him as capable in spite of his injured hip. Now that his father was there all of the emotions and doubt he had felt over the last year seemed to be coming back. He hoped his fear of failing in front of his father didn't communicate to the horses or he wouldn't be able to get anything done.

His father climbed up on the rail of the corral and made himself comfortable. "Let me watch for a bit and see what you do, and then I'll help anyway that I can."

Jim and Santo drove a group of fifteen horses into the corral where Joe stood in the middle of the corral. With Jim herding the horses into a trotting circle, Joe watched with a practiced eye. When he spotted a horse he wanted to work with, he indicated it to Jim.

Santo stood by the gate to help herd the horse through the passage to the smaller corral.

Joe ambled into the smaller corral, stood quietly, and looked at the horse. The horse nodded his head up and down and pawed the ground with his front hooves. He talked low to the horse and cooed softly, careful not to look the animal in the eye. When the horse moved around the corral, Joe slowly moved with it. The horse settled down, stood with its head down, and looked at Joe.

He took a few steps toward the horse, which backed up. He then turned his back on the horse, and slowly walked away. After about four steps, Joe stopped and glanced back toward the horse over his shoulder. He then looked away, and took another four steps. For over three hours, Joe walked up to the horse, then back. He never took his focus off the horse. By the end of the three hours, the horse followed him, allowing Joe to feed it sugar cubes.

Joe slipped a hackamore on the horse, all the time cooing and speaking in a low tone. He led the horse around the corral several times, and then stood still and talked to the animal. Joe picked up a brush he had earlier laid on the ground at the edge of the corral, and brushed the back and neck of the horse for about thirty minutes, cooing and whispering. By the time he was through brushing the horse, Joe was lying across the back of the horse with his chest and shoulders, and putting his weight on the horse.

The horse looked around at Joe, as if to ask what he thought he was doing. He handed the horse over to Jim after he had worked with it for about four hours.

During that time, Jim and Santo had been working in another corral with horses that were already broken to the saddle but still needed schooling.

Joe left the corral and walked over to the cart watching his father climb stiffly down from the corral rail. He couldn't believe that his father had sat and watched for so long. What did Pa think of his work? Would he discount what he had done because Joe couldn't finish up by riding the horse? For the first time in months, Joe felt a shame that he couldn't mount the horse and complete the job but had to hand it off to someone else. But there was nothing he could do about it.

Joe drank deeply from the canteen, then poured some water on his bandana, and wiped the sweat from his face. As his father walked up, Joe offered the canteen.

After his father drank his fill, he handed the canteen back. "Joseph, I have to say that was the most amazing thing I've ever seen." His father stood shaking his head. "I have to ask. Are you sure that was the first time that horse has ever been worked with?"

"As far as I know. We gathered those horses from among the wild herd here on the ranch. Elisha has never worked them."

"But how did you do that?"

"I can't tell you how I do it. Horses are very curious creatures. I think they get curious and stop being afraid." Joe took another sip from the canteen.

"How many horses do you work with a day?"

"I try to work with two a day, but some days I can't make it. If I get too tired, or my hip hurts too bad, I can't make headway because I can't keep a focus. If I don't focus on the horse, the horse won't focus on me, and it won't respond." Joe wanted his father to understand what he did. "Like today, I'll try a second horse, but I'm not sure I can do it."

"Do you have a lot of pain from your hip?" His father gazed at him with a look of concern.

Joe hated that his hip was even a problem, but it was. He wanted his father to be proud of what he had become as a man. If his physical problem was a barrier, Joe wanted to know now.

"The pain never completely goes away, especially when I'm moving about. The battle is to keep the pain limited to where I can get things done. Some days are better than others. I try not to let the pain decide what I'm going to do." Joe had never told anyone his constant battle with the pain. In a way, he was testing his father.

"How have you managed the disappointment of not being able to ride?" His father's look held concern, but not pity.

Joe didn't want pity from anyone. His father's question was almost too intimate, and too all-encompassing of his life. Joe struggled to find the words to answer. If anyone else had asked such a question, Joe won't have answered, but this was his father.

"At first it was almost more than I could bear. I couldn't see life as anything but being a cowhand. Then I got on with the trail herd, and got to spend a lot of time with Cookie. He never says much, but he helped a lot. I don't think he even knows how much he helped. Now not being able to ride is just something that's a part of me. What would I give to be able to ride again? I don't know, because I don't have that choice." Joe took another drink from the canteen. "I can't say I didn't mind being a Cookie's helper because I did. If I had to do it again, I could do it. Elisha, by giving me the chance to work with the horses, has helped a lot. I like the work with the horses, being out and about a lot more than cooking." Joe grinned at his father. "Although I'm a good cook and won't ever go hungry for lack of knowing how to cook."

"Well, that's something good that has come out of all of this." Sam smiled back at his son. "I can tell it's hard to talk about, and I appreciate you telling me."

Joe gazed into his father's eyes and saw a respect and acceptance. Something he had never thought to see.

Chapter Twenty-Eight

Joe wanted to forestall any more questions. "I'm ready to get going on another horse. You want to watch? You don't have to stay."

Pa leaned against the corral railing. "I want to watch and even help."

Joe whistled at Santo who was beyond the big corral, and waved his hat in a circle above his head. Santo waved back, and drove another group of horses into the big corral for Joe to pick out the next horse to work with. For the next four hours, Joe labored with the second horse, going through the same process as he had that morning.

Pa watched for a while, and then Joe was aware of his moving over to the next corral and talking with Jim and Jeff who were resting between their work of schooling horses that Joe had already gentled. Then Joe turned to see his father riding one of the half-broken horses with Jim and Jeff giving him instructions in their method of schooling the animal. Joe had to admit that Pa was still an exceptional horseman just as he had remembered from when he was a boy.

The day was almost gone when Joe turned the second horse over to Jim, and wearily strolled to catch up his pony to hitch up to the cart.

Pa handed the horse he'd been riding over to Jeff, and walked over to the cart. "You done for the day?"

"Yes, I'm done." Joe answered with a grin. "You ready to head back to the house?"

"Will there be any food there?" His father grinned, and rubbed his stomach.

Joe felt a tinge of guilt. He usually worked through the day without stopping for a meal at noon. He had not thought to ask Pa if he wanted to have something to eat.

"I'm sorry. I forgot that you might have liked to eat dinner."

"Don't worry about it. I often go through a day of work without stopping to eat. I'm a grown man, and could have gone back to the house." His father reassured him.

"I also didn't think to tell you that I usually take a quick dip in the creek before I head back in the evening. I've clean clothes with me. I should have said something." Joe was uncertain of what to do, whether to forego his usual bath in the creek and head directly for the ranch house, or keep to his usual routine.

"Lead on. I can put the same clothes back on. A quick dip won't hurt me either, and I suspect that Vivian would appreciate it if I didn't come back so sweaty."

His father mounted the big red horse, and Joe climbed up on the seat of the cart. They left the box canyon, and Joe took a trail that led down to a bend in the big creek in the middle of the valley. At the deep pool with aspens along the banks, Joe climbed down to the bank of the creek carrying the bundle of towel, soap, and clean clothes.

Pa followed.

Joe undressed and jumped into the pool, as he had found it was better to jump in and deal with the cold water all at once.

Pa jumped in the water. "Whew! Why didn't you warn me this creek would be so cold? This water is freezing."

"I forgot." Joe laughed. "I guess I've gotten used to it. But I don't stay in too long."

"I can see why. After you finish with that piece of soap pitch it over, so I can scrub and get out of this cold creek."

"Here, catch." Joe threw the piece of lye soap at Pa who caught it easily. Joe swam over to the bank, and climbed out of the water. He grabbed up his dirty shirt to dry off, and threw the flour sack towel to his father. "Use the towel, I can use my shirt."

They both shivered from the cold, and Joe hurried to dry off. As he pulled his pants on, he noticed Pa staring at him.

"Didn't mean to be rude and stare, but you realize that I've never seen you as a grown man. I thought you would have scars from your accident. But your leg looks fine. Of course, you still got those old scars on your back."

He could tell it pained Pa to see the old scars. Joe's back was crisscrossed with them. All from the whippings with the belt buckle his mother had left as her legacy.

"As bad a break as I had from the accident there aren't any scars. These other scars are from other times and then the beating I got last year. This one on my arm is from a bullet wound last year." Joe touched the scars on his chest that were faint, but still there—where Curly had cut him with the tree branch.

"You're a fine looking man, Joseph. I remember you as a baby, and a little boy. When you left at age fourteen you only came up to my shoulder and you were skinny as all get out. I don't think you were even shaving then. And now look at you, as tall as me and well built although still skinny. You probably work too hard, and don't eat enough."

"Well, before my accident last year I had a lot more muscle, but I lost so much weight the five months I was laid up in bed that it's taking time to get built up again." Joe was now more at ease talking to his father about such personal things.

"Five months! I had no idea it was that bad. Are you saying you were laid up in bed, and not walking for five months?" His father's voice filled with a concern. "Where was this? Where did you stay?"

"The accident happened outside of Waco, down in Texas. A doctor and his widowed sister took me in, and I spent the winter before last in their home. Doc wouldn't let me get up for months because of the broken bones in my hip and across my pelvis. Until the accident, I didn't even know I had a pelvis, but Doc told me that was what your hipbone is attached to, and evidently, I had a bunch of breaks all across it. I had to lie perfectly still for months, so the bones would grow back together. But somehow, the hip socket on my right leg didn't grow back together normally, and I can't move it sideways. That's why I can't sit a saddle. I don't know if you wanted to know all of that." Joe sat quietly, embarrassed that he had gone on so. There was just something about being with his father. Joe wanted to tell him what his life had been like for the last years.

"Yes, Joseph, I want to know all of that. I want to know everything that has happened to you. We've lost so much time, and I want to get as much back as possible. And son, anything you want to know, you feel free to ask."

"Let's get back and have supper but if you mean it, soon I'd like for us to talk more. I do have questions about mother and Christine." Joe saw a door opening and he hoped he could go through to the relationship he had always longed for with his father.

Joe was relieved that supper was a more relaxed meal with more animated talk. After the meal, Joe sat in the front room with Elisha, Susana, Vivian, Pa, and the children. Elisha, Susana, and Pa got to telling stories of how they had met. Joe heard for the first time the story of how Elisha had gone to spend a winter alone as a line rider in the cabin on Pinto Creek, and had come back in the spring married to Susana.

They told of the terrible time when Elisha had been shot in the chest with an arrow, results of a fight with the Utes, and Susana had almost given birth to little Sam on a wild ride down the mountain to the ranch to get help for Elisha. Joe didn't say much, but listened to the stories of happenings in his father's life.

Susana asked, "Vivian, tell us how you and Sam met."

In a soft cultured voice Vivian said, "I worked in a bookshop in Chicago and Sam came in to look for books to take back to the ranch. He bought enough for the winter, so it took him some time. We got to talking, and he asked me to eat with him at a restaurant. We found that we could talk, and we had the common interest in books. For a week, he came to the shop every day, and then we went out in the evening to eat together, walk along the lake, and talk. At the end of the week, he was due to catch the train back to Cheyenne. I didn't want him to go, and he didn't want to leave me." Vivian looked over at Sam with a smile.

Pa took Vivian's hand. "So I decided that since I didn't want to leave Vivian, I needed to marry her and take her with me. So I asked her and, thank the Lord, she said yes."

"I said yes, but I had no idea what I was saying yes to. You have to understand. I was a city person. I grew up in Chicago and had never even been on a farm. You cannot imagine my amazement at how big the land is out here. For the first month, I was afraid to leave the porch. I still am afraid of horses and cattle. How this kind gentleman can put up with me I'll never know." Vivian flashed a radiate smile at the man next to her.

Joe could guess at how Pa could put up with her. She was so opposite what his mother had been. Everything about Vivian generated a sense of kindness and sweetness. She was soft, not in a weak way, but in a gentle way. Joe could see why Pa didn't want to leave Vivian behind.

"What about you, Joseph? Any girls back down the trail with their hearts broken?" Pa asked.

"Not that I know of." He caught Susana's knowing glance to Elisha. Joe guessed she thought of Sara. "I do have a friend . . . but that's all it is."

"Where is does she live?" Vivian asked.

"She lives in San Francisco with her father. We write from time to time." Susana winked at Joe.

He wondered if he was turning red, but didn't say more.

Susana stood. "I'm not feeling real well. Vivian, let's go to my room, and let me lie down. We can visit and leave these men to talk about horses and cows."

"Are you all right?" Elisha asked anxiously.

"I'm fine. A little tired. Don't worry so, my love." Susana kissed Elisha goodnight.

His father stood and patted Vivian on the shoulder, and she went down the hall with Susana.

Joe envied these men their women.

"Well, this'll give us a chance to talk." Elisha moved over to the chair across from Joe and his father sat back down on the couch. "How'd the work go today, Joe?"

"It went pretty well. I got one horse broke enough that Jim and Santo can finish up. I'm not sure about the second one. I got tired, but I can work with him some more in the morning."

"It was the most amazing thing I have ever seen," Sam said.

"Yes, Joe has a special gift. I'm happy to get the benefit from it. How many does that make now?" Elisha asked Joe.

"I'm not real sure. It probably won't hurt for us to do a count to make sure we're on target for September. I'm thinking we've got about 250 fully broke, and about another fifty that still need work. I could use more of the hands riding the horses that are already broke to make sure the schooling stays solid."

"Okay, we'll start having most of the hands working on it for a while, but by June we'll need to pull most everyone from the horses for the gathering of the herd. I'm hoping to take about two thousand head of cattle to market. How many more horses are you going to try to break this summer?" Elisha asked.

"I'd like to get about fifty more broken, and then the foaling will continue. It's also taking time to get the mares covered with the right stallions at the right time. I could have the horses for the army ready by July. Do you think they would take delivery early?"

"I can always ask them. It would be good to get the horse herd delivered, and save the grass for the horses we have left." Elisha said.

"What do you think you'll get for the horses?" Sam asked.

"Well, the contract calls for hundred fifty dollars a head. So for 300 head of horses we should get close to $45,000. $15,000 of that will go to Joe, here, which is only fair, because he's done the major work." Elisha said.

Joe knew he would make money off the sale of the horses, but to hear Elisha tell him how much was a shock. It was more money than he had made in the last ten years. He had no idea what he would do with the money. Although some of it, he wanted to use to buy some cattle and horses from Elisha.

"That's a good return for your work, Joseph," said his father. "I'm proud of you."

"Thank you, sir." It was the second time he had heard his father tell him he was proud of him. He liked hearing it.

Sam stood. "I'm tired out from watching Joseph work today. I'm going to bed. Is it all right with you if I tag along tomorrow?"

"Of course, although tomorrow I may put you to riding the unbroken horses," Joe said with a grin.

"I'll do what I can. Goodnight, son. Goodnight, Elisha." Sam ambled quietly down the hall to the bedroom.

Joe had stood when his father stood, but now Elisha motioned him to sit back down.

"Let's you and me talk a bit, Joe."

"Yes sir." Joe sat back down. He feared what Elisha wanted to talk about, but now was as good a time as any. Elisha deserved an explanation.

Chapter Twenty-Nine

Elisha's calm, steady gaze fell on him. Joe wanted to be honest with the man, for he respected Elisha. And he wanted Elisha's respect.

"It's been an amazing couple of days. How're you doing with it all, Joe?" Elisha asked.

"It's been a bit of a strain. Learning of my mother and sister's death hit me hard. I imagined them still at the ranch, and my little sister growing up. Vivian, I mean Mrs. Weathers ... I'm not sure what to call her. She seems nice, and my father is happier than I can ever remember."

"I get the sense that there's something more going on. You look like you're barely holding on."

Beads of sweat broke out across Joe forehead and upper lip. He tried to put into words feelings that were so deep. "My heart is full at being with my father again. I hardly know how to express how much I've missed him all these years." He gulped. No matter how he tried, he just couldn't get enough air. The room felt small and warm. He didn't know it would be this hard. "But I have a terrible sense of loss. I'm not sure I can explain it." Elisha was a good boss, and he wanted to talk openly with him, but for the last thirteen years, he hadn't shared—with anyone. Just held it all inside.

"Is it the grief of learning about your mother and sister's death?"

"I grieve at the loss of my sister . . . you're going to think this isn't something a person should say, or think. But, about my mother . . . I'm glad she's dead." Joe waited for the look of disgust from Elisha toward someone who could say such a thing. He surprised himself by saying it, but it was the truth. All he felt about her death was relief that he never had to see her again.

"I can't imagine what your mother did to you for you to feel that way. But it must have been awful because I know you're a good kind man, who would not deliberately hurt anyone. I'm glad you trust me enough to say it, as hard as it is."

He acted as if he didn't find Joe to be anything less than before.

Taking a deep breath, Joe continued, "But the thing I can't seem to get my mind around, is that they died two months after I left. All these years, I could have gone home. And maybe . . . if I had known, I could have gone home . . . and not had my accident. I'd still be able to ride." Joe fought to hold back tears that wanted to ran down his cheeks. "Sorry, Elisha." Joe wiped his eyes with his shirtsleeve.

"Don't be sorry for honest tears. You got reasons. God gave you those tears, and it's a manly thing to use them. I think I understand what you are saying. I think the regret of what might have been is the hardest thing to bear. It's almost as if you have to grieve the loss of what might have been, before you can go on to what comes next in your life."

Joe nodded. "I never meant to be dishonest with you about my father. I've spent so much time running away from my growing up years. I'd gotten used to being Joe Storm, and hiding my past from people. It's like I'd got myself in such a web of hiding that I didn't know how to be honest with you." Joe didn't think he made much sense, but he wanted Elisha to understand.

"I know you didn't set out to lie to me. I let you down somehow. You didn't feel you could come to me. Can you forgive me?"

Joe straightened up, overwhelmed with the idea of Elisha thinking he'd let Joe down. "Then you'll let me keep working here?"

"Keep working here?"

"I feared that you'd not want me to work for you, when you found out that I hadn't told you about my father."

"If I have my way, you will work here as long as you want. But have you thought about what your father may want?"

"What do you mean?"

"He's hoping you will go home with him. Who do you think he's built that big ranch for?" Elisha smiled at him as if he had revealed a secret. "You're his only son, his heir. Sam never lost hope that you would come home someday. That's why he never took any of the offers to sell the ranch. Before I ever met Susana, he told me he wanted to be there when you came home."

"I hadn't thought about that. I'd like to go visit, but I don't know that I can live there. There's a lot of bad memories there."

"Joe, I don't want to presume, but can you tell me some of what happened, so I can understand a little of what made it so bad?"

Joe looked at Elisha for a couple of minutes. He tried to get control of his emotions, but his Adams apple was going up and down making it hard to swallow as he fought his panic. He'd never told anyone of all that had gone on, and he didn't know that he ever could.

"I'll try. It wasn't only what she did, but what she said. Not once, but over and over. She was bad when my father was there, but when he'd ride out to spend a week with the herd, that's when it really got bad." Joe couldn't seem to get any air into his lungs.

"What did she say?"

"You shouldn't have been born. I hate even to look at you. You're evil. You don't deserve anything. Don't touch your sister, you'll make her evil. Why God even made something like you is a mystery . . . ." Joe fought to keep control. Her voice sounded so clearly in his mind, even now.

"I'm so sorry Joe, I—"

"And then she would beat me," Joe interrupted, as if he hadn't heard Elisha, "and put me in the closet in the bedroom. She would leave me for days with no food, and only a little water. She told me if I told my father she'd kill him. I believed her. The worst was when she'd come in the middle of the night, and make me lie on the cold floor naked while she read out of the Bible these horrible condemnations of God. Over and over and over and over. Hours and hours until I thought I'd go crazy.

"So when I got a chance to run away, after my father gave me a pony of my own on my fourteenth birthday, I took it. The day after my birthday, he went back to the herd. He'd be gone a week. If only he hadn't gone, or if he'd taken me with him . . . . I was old enough, why didn't he, Elisha? Why didn't he take me with him? He didn't and she beat me again with his belt, always with his belt. The buckle tore the skin, and my back was bloody and would hurt for days. I could have stopped her. I was big enough by then, but he said not ever to hit a woman. So I let her beat me." Joe finally stopped. He'd opened a door on that time of his life, one he had pushed deep down, and now it gushed forth like a dam breaking. And now he couldn't control it. Heavy sobs racked his body.

Elisha's hand rested on Joe's arm. A firm, warm touch. A safe one.

"Joe, you're safe from her now. She can't hurt you anymore." Elisha tightened his hold as if to protect him from such cruelty. "Joe, trust me. It's all over."

Joe found deep concern in Elisha's eyes. "I'm sorry Elisha, but you asked." Joe took his handkerchief out and wiped his face. "I must trust you, because I've never told another living soul all of these things."

"When I asked I'd no idea it was so bad, and I suspect that you've only told me a small part of it. However, you need to know that what your mother did wasn't normal. Something was wrong with her mind for her to act that way."

"How do you know that? Maybe it was something about me that made her act that way."

"I know you, and you're a good, kind man. I trust my children with you, and my own life. I wouldn't do that with someone who was evil. Your mother wasn't right in her mind. I don't know what to call it, but it was her, and not you. How old were you when you remember her first being so mean to you?"

"I don't remember a time when she wasn't. It went on all my life."

"No, not all your life, you escaped. It hasn't gone on for the last thirteen years. She's been dead."

Joe looked at Elisha without blinking. He'd been carrying his mother around with him all these years, and letting the effect of her cruelty go on, when all that time she'd been dead. A glimmer of light appeared at the edge of the dark cloud that had always been at the core of his being. She had been dead all these years. He didn't have to carry her if he could just find a way to put her down.

"Thank you, Elisha." Joe whispered simply. What else could he say to someone who had suddenly shown the way out of prison?

"You're welcome, my friend. You look so tired. You want to stretch out here on the couch and get some sleep? You need to take some time alone to think about all of this. Over the next couple of weeks, take the time with your father you need. It'll be fine with me if you decide to go back with him, but if you want to stay with us, that's even better."

"Thanks, I'll take you up on that." Joe was so tired, and didn't want to feel any more.

Elisha turned out the lamps except for one by the couch where Joe stretched out. Elisha picked up some throw blankets from the back of the couches, and handed them to Joe.

"Goodnight Joe. God's blessings on you, my friend."

"And to you."

Elisha left to retire to his bedroom.

Joe pulled his boots off, arranged the covers, and lay down on the couch with a sigh. He was wrung out, like a dishrag. Why he had shared so much with Elisha he didn't know. He had always been so good at holding it all in. Maybe it was all right if Elisha wanted him to stay, and didn't hold it against him that he had deceived him. He had heard that confession was good for the soul. Maybe his confessing to Elisha was what his soul needed in order to let go of the past, and move on to whatever the future held for him. He hoped so, because he couldn't go through many more days like the last two.

Chapter Thirty

Joe woke the next morning while the house was still dark and quiet. He got up and put on his boots. Even after a night of sleep, he felt exhausted. The moon lit the front room as he walked into the kitchen. There the moonlight streamed in through the windows. Joe lit one of the lanterns, and then worked to get a fire going in the stove. He put water into the pot and dumped some ground coffee in. When the coffee was made he poured a cup, and then sat at the table wondering what he should do first to help Cookie with the breakfast. On hearing a rustling sound from the loft, he glanced up and saw Cookie stepping down the ladder rubbing his hand through his hair.

"Morning Joe, what are you doing up so early?" Cookie yawned, and continued to scratch his head.

"I couldn't sleep." Joe rubbed his temple against the start of a headache.

Cookie poured a cup of coffee, and sat at the table. "You look awful. What's wrong?"

"A lot to deal with . . . all this with my father being here. I'm all right."

"You know I'm here if you need me."

"What can I do to help with breakfast?"

"Well, let's see. How about we make pancakes this morning since we're both up early?"

Joe got up and mixed the pancake batter and Cookie made biscuits. By the time the family wandered into the kitchen, they had the breakfast ready. Cookie rang the bell calling the crew in.

When Bob came in, he sat next to Joe and quietly asked. "You all right? You didn't sleep in your bunk for the second night in a row, and you look awfully tired."

"I'm all right. Thanks for asking. I'll be back at my bunk tonight." Joe told him.

"I know something is going on with your father being here. I don't need to know what it is, but I want to say all the hands are behind you. You need us for anything, you say so." Without waiting for an answer, Bob got up and went to his usual seat at the table.

Joe couldn't think of anything the cowhands could do to help him, but knowing they were behind him left him feeling less alone and as if they were his brothers.

After breakfast, Joe and his father went to the box canyon and spent the day working with the horses. Because he was more at ease with his father, Joe focused better on his work with the horses.

~

Elisha had declared Sunday as a day off unless there was work that had to be done such as milking the milk cows or tending to sick or injured animals. Everyone lazed around the bunkroom and house. At ten in the morning, those who wanted gathered in the front room with Elisha leading worship.

Joe took a seat near the kitchen door, but Vivian called to him and patted the couch next to her and his father. He got up and sat by her. As he listened to the others sing, Joe reflected on all that had come to pass.

Elisha started the service with a prayer. At Elisha's invitation, Joe's father got up to deliver a lesson. Sam spoke on joy and appreciating the blessings that the Lord provides.

As his father spoke, Joe tried to think when he had ever had much joy. Through the years there had been times of enjoyment, but few moments of joy. He wanted to experience that in his life. He knew he had to learn how to go forward, because that was the only place he would find any joy. He hoped he could do it.

Joe spent the afternoon relaxing with his father and Vivian. He liked his father's wife. There was just a nice quietness about her. He finally asked her what he should call her.

She laughed. "If I can call you Joe, you can call me Vivian. You know, I'm thirty-eight years old. That's only twelve years older than you."

"Well, that makes it easier to call you Vivian." He smiled back at her. She sure was easy to be around and attractive. Joe glanced over at his father. After life with his mother, he could understand the older man's wanting a loving, caring wife.

Joe appreciated that Elisha had not said anything about the conversation from the evening before, and trusted the man to keep confidential what Joe had shared with him.

That evening Joe made it back to his bunk. He felt like he had spent days working with the horses and just wanted to disappear into sleep, and he did for a few hours. Sometime in the middle of the night, Joe woke with Elisha gently shaking his shoulder.

"Joe, I need your help."

"Sure Elisha. What's the matter?" Joe sat up and reached for his pants.

"Susana is having the baby, and I need Little Sam and Christine away from bedrooms. Christine is upset, and she'll only go with you or me, and I need to be with Susana." Elisha shook his head. "You got to tell me someday your secret with children and horses."

Joe put on his clothes and thought about what he could do. "Let me go make up a bed in the chuck wagon, and I'll take them out there to sleep. I'll tell them we're playing a game, and going camping." Joe pulled on his boots and slapped on his hat.

"That's a great idea. When you're ready, I'll help you carry them out to the barn."

Joe gathered up his bedding and mattress, and carried it out to the chuck wagon. He made a bed in the empty wagon, and went back into the house to the children's bedroom.

Elisha sat on Christine's bed holding her.

The little girl saw Joe and reached out to him.

He lifted her from Elisha's arms into his own. He could understand Elisha wanting to protect these little ones from the fright of their mother's pain. Joe wanted to keep anything that would be hurtful away from these precious beings.

Elisha picked up Little Sam who was still in deep sleep.

They carried them out to the wagon and Joe climbed up then placed Christine on the bedding.

She protested being sat down.

Joe turned and took Little Sam from Elisha and put him down beside his sister.

"I'll bunk here with the children. You go on back to the house, and be at ease about your family. You can pay attention to Susana, now."

"Thanks. I knew you'd help me out. I'll let you know how it goes. I had better get back to Susana. Keep her in your prayers." Elisha called over his shoulder as he left.

Joe sat on the bedding next to Christine and Little Sam. He got the little girl to lie down next to her brother who was still sound asleep, then covered them up to their chins with a blanket. He talked to her like he did the horses, and in a few minutes she fell asleep. Joe soon followed, but not before he prayed for Susana and the baby about to be born.

Joe awoke to daylight. The children were still sleeping hard. The sound of gravel crunched beneath someone's footstep. Joe climbed out of the wagon to find Pa walking toward him, carrying clothes for the children.

"I wanted to see if you needed any help with the children."

"Not yet. How's Susana?"

"She's having a hard time of it. Vivian and Mara are both with her and Elisha of course. It may be a long day."

"Pa, we need to take care of these children. Let's take them on a ride and a picnic down by the creek."

"That'll be our job today." His father seemed pleased with the idea. "I'll go tell Vivian and Elisha what we're doing and get Cookie to pack us a basket of food."

"Ask Cookie to include some biscuits with jam and butter for their breakfast and some jars of milk. I'll get them up and dressed." As he turned back to the chuck wagon he heard a little voice calling, "Yoe, Yoe."

The day passed with lots of laughter and fun. Little Sam was delighted to have two adults to roughhouse with, and Christine was happy to ride around in the cart, and then on Joe's shoulder as they played along the creek. As it got toward dark, they drove the cart back to the barn where Elisha met them with a big smile on his face.

Sam asked. "What's the word, Elisha?"

Elisha lifted Christine out of the cart. "You have a new little brother. Mama is fine." He looked over at Joe and Sam. "Thank you, fellows, for watching out for these little ones."

Sam picked up Little Sam. "They wore us out. They've twice the energy that we have. But we had fun, didn't we, buckaroo?"

Little Sam nodded. "We sure did, Grandpa. Can we go see the baby now?"

"Sure. We haven't named him yet. I'm leaving that up to your mother."

They carried the two children from the barn to the house and then into the bedroom to see their new little brother. As soon as they entered the bedroom, Little Sam and Christine wanted to crawl up on the bed with their mother. But Elisha held them back. "Mama isn't feeling well. We need to be quiet and gentle."

"Hello, my precious ones. You want to see little Joshua Thomas Evans?" Susana smiled at Elisha as she held up the baby for them to see. "Is that all right?"

"That's fine, my love. Little Sam and Little Josh."

Christine quickly lost interest in the new baby who was sleeping quietly. "Yoe, let's go play."

~

The next two weeks passed quickly. Joe and his father worked with the horses every day. On days they had time, they rode out, Joe in the cart, and Sam riding along side, to look over the herd of broken horses. They talked about many things that had happened to each of them over the last years, but not what Joe wanted to talk about most.

Joe sensed that his father wanted to talk, and he wanted to talk to his father about what he planned to do. He chose a day, and after getting a lunch packed, he hitched his horse to the cart, and then saddled a horse for his father. By the time his father came out of the house, Joe had both horses ready to go. Joe led them down the valley to a trail that went up into the hills south of the valley. The trail flattened out for a bit, to a place where Joe came often. He liked to sit on the large rocks, and look out over the whole valley with the mountains beyond.

Sam sat on a big rock. "This is nice. Thanks for bringing me up here."

Joe knew that the valley spread out before them was like a picture frame for the ranch house that was barely visible in the distance.

"I've always found it to be a good place to think." Joe faced his father.

Sam looked at his son. "I'm glad to have this chance for us to talk. I know we've talked a lot the last couple of weeks. But we haven't talked about what happened when you left. You have some things you need to say to me, don't you?"

"Like what, sir?" Joe feared that he knew, but he didn't want to face it. Not yet.

"Anything you want to ask me. I'm ready."

Joe kept his gaze out over the valley. Yes, he needed to know about some things. "I'm not sure how to ask. I don't want to be disrespectful to you."

"Ask it, Joseph."

Joe tightly gripped his hands and made himself look his father in the eyes. "Did you know what she was doing to me?" There, he'd finally asked what he needed to know for years. "Did you know about the beatings, the starvation? All of it—did you know?"

"I knew some, but I still don't know all of it. I knew enough that I should have done something. I didn't protect you."

"Why? Why didn't you protect me? Didn't you care?" Joe could hear the anger in his voice. "I was a little boy. I couldn't protect myself. Why didn't you help me?" He hadn't known he had so much anger at his father.

"There are lots of explanations. I couldn't stand against her fury. I couldn't believe it was as bad as it was. When I look at myself now, I can only say that I was a coward. I can tell you, over and over, I'm sorry. I can ask you to forgive me. But what I can't do, is change what happened."

"That makes me so sad...and angry." Joe's dead calm voice had no warmth in it. "I don't know what to do about it. I love you, but I also don't know if I can forgive you."

"I want your forgiveness. I'll keep praying that you'll be able to give it to me some day. My only assurance is God has forgiven me, even if I don't deserve it." The warmth in Sam's voice made up for what Joe's lacked. "When I got home, and you were gone, I searched your room, and found my belt covered in blood. I confronted her, and she told me what she had done. I wanted to take that belt, and beat her. It took me years to forgive her for costing me my son. I was even angry at her for dying, and taking Christine with her. I don't know if you know that she was driving the wagon when the accident occurred. She was angry at me and whipped the horses till they went wild and ran into a gulch."

They sat in silence for a while each deep in their thoughts.

Joe took a ragged breathe. "If it's all right I want us to keep in touch, even if I'm angry at you."

"Yes, son, it's all right. I'd like you to come home. You always have a place at the ranch. Someday it'll be yours, if you want it." Sam waited for Joe's answer.

Joe thought out his words carefully. "I'd like to visit, but I don't think I could live there. She's too much there."

"What will you do?"

"Elisha says that if I don't go back with you he wants me to stay and work with him. I like this area, and I've friends here." As soon as he said it, he knew that it was true. He could be of help to Elisha and Susana, and his other friends such as Cookie and Billy. Yes, he would stay at the Rocking ES.

"If you're not coming home, then this is the place I'd want you to be. Elisha and Susana are good people. If you could come, and visit for a short time, you might change your mind. I'll hang onto that hope."

The sadness in his father's voice tore at Joe's heart, but he couldn't give him what he wanted, not yet. He wanted to, but he couldn't face going back into that house, into that room.

"You remember me talking about joy at the Sunday service a couple of weeks ago? That's what I want for you, son. I want you to have the joy in your life that you were robbed of as a child. I look at Little Sam and Christine and see their innocence and simple joy of life. I don't remember you ever being like that as a child. I realize you weren't allowed to have it. You deserve to get that now, and I plan to pray for you every day, son."

"Thanks, Pa. I don't mind you praying for me. I need it."

"Do you pray, son?"

"Sometimes, but not often."

"Then, you believe in God?"

"Oh, yes, I believe in Him. I'm not sure I trust Him."

"How do you mean?"

"I'm not sure I understand what He's up to."

"I can understand that. I hope that one day you'll figure it out," Sam said with a nod. "I'll pray that one day you can trust God, in spite of how I've let you down."

Joe had no answer. Back then, his father did let him down. He didn't know if he could forgive him. If his father had been stronger, Joe wouldn't have believed that his only choice was to run away.

Over the last twelve years, he could have had a home. A father.

And he might still be able to ride.

"We should get going if we want to be back at the house before dark," Joe suggested.

"I hate to start back. I don't know how many more opportunities I'll have to talk to you like this. Thanks again for bringing me up here."

"I'm glad we could come." Joe climbed up on the cart seat while his father mounted his horse.

Joe had mixed feelings as he watched Pa and Vivian leave later that week to return home.

He gotten used to Pa being there, but he couldn't relax. Their time together had been almost three weeks of constant strain. He hoped he could get some better sleep, and feel more settled now that they were gone. He went back to working as hard as he could, so that he was exhausted and could sleep at night.

Chapter Thirty-One

A week after Sam and Vivian left, Elisha asked everyone to stay seated after breakfast for a meeting. "I wanted you all to know that I've decided to gather two thousand head of cattle and drive to the rail at Cheyenne. We first have to divide the cattle. I want to start the herd toward the rail head four weeks from today." Elisha sipped his coffee.

"You want us to get the chuck wagon ready?" Cookie asked.

"Yes, I want us to plan to move out, as if this were a regular trail drive. Which it is—just not one like you all did last year coming up from Texas." Elisha smiled.

"How long do you think it will take? And how do you want us to plan the supplies for the drive?" Cookie asked.

"It should take us about a week and a half to get there with the herd, and then load the cattle on the train. Then it'll take only two or three days to get back home. Why don't you plan to take enough supplies for the first part of the trip, and then we'll get supply there and bring a full load back."

Joe leaned forward. "Fort D. A. Russell is only three miles west of Cheyenne. What would you think about taking the horse herd to the fort at the same time? I need to do another count, but I think we got three hundred horses broke. We could get both done on the same drive."

"Good idea. If we have the horses broke there's no reason not to drive them to the fort and make delivery. It's a couple month's early, but if we deliver now we can save some grass for the rest of the herd." Elisha swung his gaze to Bob. "How will that work as far as the number of men we have to make the drive?"

Bob stretched his arm and then rubbed the back of his neck. "If we can have Jim, Santo, and Billy handle the horses, the rest of us can handle the cattle."

Elisha turned to Jacob. "Would you mind staying here on the ranch with the women and children? I plan to go with the herd, but I won't leave the ranch without a man on it."

"Of course, I will do whatever needs done to help." Jacob gave a serious glance around the table at all the hands. "Of course, I do not know if you men can get the herd there without my great ability as a horseman."

Everyone laughed, Jacob being the worst rider on the ranch.

Joe wondered whether he should take his cart, or ride with Cookie on the chuck wagon. He didn't even consider not going.

Elisha drained his coffee cup, which made a hollow sound when he set it on the table. "Cookie, you get the chuck wagon ready. Call on any of the hands you need. Bob, the first thing we need to do is decide how to divide the herd. Joe, you do a count of the horse herd, and see if we have three hundred horses ready. How about we hold the horses in the square box canyon, and have them ready to go?" He then stood. "We'll go slow and let the cattle graze along the way. It will take longer but that way we will arrive with the cattle fat for better pricing in the sale. All right, men, let's get to work."

Elisha's ability to make decisions and get everyone working impressed Joe.

"Joe, come on into the front room. Let's talk about how to handle the horse herd."

Joe followed the rancher, and sat in the chair facing the desk.

"You want to take your cart, or ride the chuck wagon?" Elisha sat in the chair by his desk.

"I want the cart to get around, but that's a rough trip. I'd hate for something to happen to the cart. I need it too much here for my work." Joe rubbed the back of his head. "So I guess I better ride in the chuck wagon. If Billy helps with the horse herd, then Cookie will need someone to help drive the wrangler wagon."

Joe knew he would have to rely on the riders to deliver the horse herd. He sighed and rubbed his face. He hated to be faced with decisions ruled by the fact that he couldn't ride. He was comfortable with the routine at the ranch, and he almost didn't want to face the outside world. However, he would do it anyway.

The trail drive to the rails was a big undertaking for the ranch, but compared to the trail drive the cowhands had been on the year before, it couldn't compare.

It took them a month to get the herd divided, and branded with a trail brand.

Joe, with the help of Jim and Santo, made sure all the horses they were delivering to fulfill the army contract were sufficiently broke for riding.

~

On a cool August morning, Joe left his footprints on the graze of dew spread over the grass as he walked over, climbed up on the chuck wagon seat, and took up the reins. Cookie took the reins of the wrangler wagon, and they waited for Elisha's signal.

Elisha kissed his wife and babies, mounted his horse, and waved his hat. "Head'em out!"

The first full day of the drive was a struggle for the riders as they continually raced after cattle that didn't want to join the herd moving out of the valley.

Joe and Cookie drove the two wagons ahead of the herd to the first camp, only eight miles from the ranch.

Cookie pulled the wrangler wagon up behind the parked chuck wagon. Joe climbed down and surveyed the campground. It brought back a flood of memories of the year before.

They quickly unhitched the horses and led them down to the creek to let them drink their full. Then they staked them out in the meadow to graze.

Joe started gathering stones to ring the fires they needed to cook supper. "I'll get the fires going and the coffee."

"You sure you remember how to make coffee?" Cookie chuckled as he let down the worktable on the chuck wagon.

"I'll try to get it right. I don't want to get the boys mad at me." Joe grinned at Cookie.

"While you're doing that I'll get the worktable set up. I've already got roast and bread made that I brought with us and apple pies, so supper tonight won't be that much work."

Joe found the stones and made the usual three fires. He got the pots filled with water and made the coffee. Cookie had potatoes peeled and ready to boil by the time coffee finished making.

Taking two of the enamel cups Joe poured a couple of cups of coffee and took them over to where Cookie was working at the worktable. He handed a cup to Cookie, then took a sip from his own.

Cookie swallowed some of the strong brew. "How does it feel to be back on the trail?"

"You know me, I don't mind the work. But it's just a reminder that I can't ride." Joe hated the feeling it conjured up. As if, he was less somehow. He hadn't had the feeling so strong since the year before.

Cookie just nodded and didn't say anything.

Joe appreciated that he understood and felt no need to talk about it. He emptied his cup, heaved a deep sigh, and then he grabbed the wash-up tub to go fill it.

The slow pace of the herd that Elisha set made it easier for Joe and Cookie, as they could arrive at the next night's camp several hours before the herd caught up with them. With Billy working the horse herd, Joe and Cookie divided the more mundane chores such as the washing up after the meals.

Joe expected some ribbing from the riders about being back as Cookie's helper. None of them said anything except to give words of appreciation for the meals.

The days went by quick as they did their work. Eager to get back to the ranch, Joe didn't mind how fast the week had gone. He liked his work and routine at the ranch much more than his work on the trail drive.

When they were about five miles out from Cheyenne, Elisha rode up beside the chuck wagon. "Joe, I'm going to bed the herds just up ahead. Then I'm going to ride in and see about the sale of the cattle. I'm picking up a buggy I have on order. I'll bring that back and you use that to get around town."

"Thanks. That'll help." He tried to speak without clenching his jaw. Although thankful for Elisha's thoughtfulness, it stuck in his craw that he needed it.

"Then you and I can ride over to the fort in the buggy and see the Major to arrange delivery of the horse herd."

"I'll be ready." He watched as Elisha who rode back to the wrangler wagon to explain the plans to Cookie. Joe knew that Elisha could deliver the horse herd without him, but felt good that he wanted Joe to go with him.

They made camp along a creek two miles southwest of Cheyenne early in the afternoon. Supper came together easily for Joe and Cookie. The riders came into camp more often once they had the herd settled, so Joe was busy keeping the coffee pots full.

The riders hardly got the herd trail broke, and they were within sight of the railway. They'd taken seven days to get the herd to the rail yard at Cheyenne.

Joe and Cookie had already served the supper to the riders when Elisha drove back into camp in a new double-seated covered buggy.

Joe could see how it was more appropriate for Elisha's growing family.

Elisha handed the buggy and horses off to Jeff then strolled over to the worktable. "You got any food left?"

Cookie took a plate and filled it with beans, ham, and cornbread. "For you, we got food."

"Thanks, I'm tired and hungry. Joe, come sit a bit with me while I eat."

Joe and Elisha sat in the camp chairs to the side of the chuck wagon.

"I did well with the sale of the herd. I had paid Matt Barnes five dollars a head and I just sold them a year later for twelve dollars a head." Elisha scooped a couple of spoonfuls of beans and ham into his mouth. After chewing and swallowing, he said, "It didn't hurt that they're fat prime beef now and no longer trail weary beef from Texas."

"That's great. As hard as you've worked, you deserve to make a profit." Joe leaned forward to emphasize his praise.

"I know I couldn't have done it without all the crew at the ranch. Now, tomorrow morning I want us to ride over to Fort Russell together and get the horse herd sold."

"I'll be ready." Joe felt anxious about what the major at the fort would think of the horse herd.

~

In the cool morning air, Joe and Elisha rode together in the new buggy. The fort was located about three miles outside of town.

Behind them, Jim, Santo, and Billy herded the horses toward the fort.

The major met Elisha and Joe, as they rode up to the headquarters, and invited them into his office.

"Glad to see you men." Major Donaldson said. "We really need those horses now."

Elisha glanced at Joe and then back to the major. "Our agreement last year was for three hundred horses at twenty dollars a head. Does that still hold?"

"Depending on the shape the horses are in and how well broke they are." Major Donaldson said.

"They should be here in a couple of hours. I'm sure you'll want to have some of your soldiers ready to try the horses. You'll be able to judge whether they're properly broke." Joe suggested.

"Let me check that my sergeant has the men ready for that." The major stood and then opened the door to his office. "Sergeant Reynolds, we have a herd of Rocking ES horses coming in about an hour. Be ready to take delivery and have about fifteen soldiers ready to check the horses out."

"Yes, Major." Joe heard someone from the other room respond

~

An hour later Joe and Elisha leaned against the railings and watched the horse herd stream into the big corral where a bunch of soldiers waited. Joe stood tall and proud as he watched the product of his work running into the corral. They were delivering some excellent horseflesh. The fifteen soldiers were soon throwing ropes and saddling horses.

Jim, Santo, and Billy had dismounted and wandered over to where Joe and Elisha stood by the rails of the corral. Their job done and the soldiers were now responsible for the horse herd.

With eagerness, Joe watched the soldiers mount the horses and put them through various paces. A smile stretched over his face and he breathed a sigh of relief as none of the horses bucked, but responded to the signals of their riders.

Elisha slapped Joe on the back and looked at the other three riders. "Look at those horses. You boys did a great job." He grinned and his eyes glimmered with pleasure as he gazed at the horses.

"Thanks. I'm sort of proud of the work we did." Joe nodded and glanced at the other three riders to include them in the praise.

Elisha shook hands with each of the men. "You men ride on back to town and take the rest of the day off. You've earned it. Joe and I'll finish our business here then come on to town. I've reserved some rooms at the hotel for the crew for tonight. So go on into town and enjoy yourselves."

"Thanks, boss. We appreciate that." Jim spoke for all three. They mounted and rode off toward town.

The major sent word for Joe and Elisha to meet him in his office again.

After they were all seated, the major looked at Elisha and Joe from across his desk. "That is the finest herd I have ever taken delivery of. So far, every horse that has been ridden is well broke and ready for us to work with."

Joe couldn't help the grin that broke out across his face. He was pleased for the ranch, as well as for himself.

"You have to thank Joe here for that. He manages the horse business on the ranch and does all the breaking of the horses." Elisha said.

"Well, young man, you did a great job. Now, can you deliver another herd next year? In fact, I want to contract with you for any horses you want to deliver." The major looked from Joe to Elisha.

"That's completely up to Joe. If he agrees then that's what we'll do, but it is up to him." Elisha turned to Joe.

Joe felt his face warm from such a statement of confidence by Elisha. "I'm willing, but with the understanding that we'll try to deliver a herd of three hundred, but no guarantees. There's too many things that can go wrong, but we'll do the best we can."

Joe and Elisha in turn shook hands with the major to seal the contract for the next herd of horses to be delivered. It was with contentment that Joe drove them back to town in the buggy.

The crew spent the night at the hotel, which was a treat for the men. The next day they shopped for the ranch, then ate dinner at a restaurant.

A train had come into town that afternoon from the west, so Joe went to the post office to see if any more mail had came in from Sara. Joe had already collected the mail from her, Doc, and his father, and left the ones he had written. He didn't want to chance leaving town and missing a letter coming from Sara. When he got to the post office, he found he had received another letter. He sat down on the bench outside of the post office to read it.

Chapter Thirty-Two

Dear Joe,

I only have a little time to write. I have someone waiting to take this letter down to the train that leaves this evening, so I can get this in the mail to you. My father is very ill. The doctor says it is cholera. I am so frightened. If only you were here. There have been many people getting cholera, and I am afraid I will also.

Please pray for me. I feel so alone. What will I do if my father dies? And I am so afraid that he will.

You are a dear friend, and even though you are not with me, I feel the presence of your friendship. Don't forget me.

Give my love to all my friends at the Rocking ES. I miss you all.

God bless us all,

Sara

Sara's letter left him frozen in place. He looked at the date. She had written it only three days earlier. Joe read the letter a second time. He looked up through narrowed eyes. He didn't much notice what went on around him, but he'd made up his mind. He would go to her. His thoughts scrambled with plans for getting to her.

Joe went up to the ticket counter and learned that a train would come through at midnight. He could catch it, heading west. With that settled, he went in search of Elisha to ask for an advance in his pay as he had no money with him.

Elisha and Cookie had just stepped out of the large general merchandise store. Joe met them on the steps. Silently he handed the letter to Elisha.

He read the letter. "What do you want to do?" He frowned and handed it to Cookie.

Joe frowned. "I plan to catch the midnight train, and go to San Francisco. She needs me. I don't know what I can do, but especially if her father dies, I can't stand the thought of her being by herself to handle it alone."

"You're right. You need to go." Cookie said firmly before Elisha even had a chance to speak.

"Yes, you must go. Do you want someone to go with you?" Elisha's concern edged his voice.

Joe thought for a moment. "No, I can take the train to San Francisco, and hire a buggy when I get there."

"Have you ever been to California?" Cookie asked.

"No. I've been to New York, but this will be a first time to see the other side of the country."

"Come on back into the store with me," Cookie said. "We need to get you outfitted to go to the big city. You only brought along those rough ranch clothes."

"That's right," Elisha gave a nod to Joe, "and put everything on the ranch's tab. Now we have to decide how much money you need to carry. I'll get your ticket, and the money. Cookie, you make sure Joe has the clothes he needs."

Elisha turned back to Joe. "You got six hours before the train leaves. We have time to get you organized." When Elisha took hold, he took hold.

"What about getting the buggy back to the ranch, and the work with the horses?" Joe asked.

"I can get one of the hands to drive the buggy. Jim and Santo can do what they can do with the horses. You should be back in a couple of weeks. And I mean that, you don't have my permission to stay in California." Elisha grinned as if to soften his words.

"Don't worry. I've no interest in staying in California." Joe promised.

"Then you get what you need from the general store, and I'll meet you at the hotel in about an hour. We'll eat, and get you ready to head for California. Cookie, you might want to pack some food and a canteen for Joe to have on the train." Elisha waved to them as he strode off toward the bank.

Joe and Cookie went back into the store, and purchased Joe new clothes, including a broadcloth black suit with a white shirt and tie. He didn't want to get the suit, but Cookie insisted.

"When you get to the city people will judge a lot more by appearance. You want to turn up at Sara's door with the look of a prosperous rancher, and not a down-at-the-heels cowpoke. Now listen to me. I know what I'm talking about."

"Yes, Cookie." Joe smiled. Cookie must know what he was talking about.

Joe protested the new jacket and hat until Cookie made him take off his old hat, and look at it. Joe admitted it was poor looking.

When they left the store, Joe carried a valise packed with three sets of clothes and a suit.

Cookie sent Joe to the barbershop for a haircut and shave. He told Joe he'd go to the chuck wagon in the wagon yard and make up a packet of food and a canteen for Joe's trip.

An hour later, they met with Elisha in the hotel.

Elisha pulled out a money belt from around his waist, and gave it to Joe. "There's five hundred dollars in there. I don't think you'll need all of it, but in case you do, you have enough. If you need more you send me a telegraph in care of the bank, and I'll tell them to send you anything you ask for. Now here's your train ticket. It's to go and return."

Joe smiled faintly at Elisha. "You're determined that I get back here."

"I have to be. Susana would never forgive me if I didn't get you back. Not to mention Christine." Elisha chuckled. "Joe, I don't know what you'll find when you get to San Francisco. Cholera is bad. The worst thing you may find is that Mr. Barnes has died, and Sara is very ill, or worse. If Mr. Barnes has died, I want you to offer Sara a home with us."

Joe wanted to block Elisha from saying, 'or worse'. There couldn't be a worse...he couldn't even bear to think that Sara might be ill enough to die. He just needed to get to her.

"Thank you, Elisha. I know she'll appreciate the offer." Once again, the caring giving spirit of Elisha and Susana swept over Joe. "I'll do my best to see what I can do for her, and for Mr. Barnes."

"Here's my Bible, and a novel by Jules Verne called Five Weeks In a Balloon, to help you pass the time on the train." Elisha handed him the two books wrapped in a piece of tanned cowhide.

"Thanks. I'll need something to keep me busy if this trip takes as long as I think it does." Joe carefully placed the Bible and the novel on the top of his clothes in the valise.

Cookie handed him a big packet that Joe placed at the top of the now full valise.

"You'll have to carry your canteen until you eat up some of that food." Cookie nodded toward Joe's things. "I got the hotel to make up some roast beef sandwiches. I also put in some jerky. Save it for last."

"Thanks for the help, fellows. I'll let you know what I find in San Francisco." Joe put on his new jacket and hat. What with his new haircut and clothes he did feel worthy of approaching the home of Sara and Matthew Barnes.

"Let's have a prayer before we go down to the train station," suggested Elisha. The three of them stood in the room, and Elisha prayed very simply for the God to bless Sara and Mr. Barnes, and to keep Joe safe on his travels.

Joe appreciated Elisha's prayer as always, and Cookie's encouragement and support. He was blessed to have two such friends to whom he could turn to for help.

They walked to the train station, and Joe was surprised to see all of the riders from the ranch there. The word had filtered out about Sara's need, and the trip Joe was making to San Francisco. He didn't know what to say at such a show of support, so he went from one man to the next, shook their hand and thanked each one.

Elisha handed him a letter for Sara. Cookie also handed him a letter to give to her. Before he got on the train, all the men from the Rocking ES took their hats off, and stood in a semicircle around him. Elisha said another prayer, and then Joe boarded the train. The men waved goodbye as the train pulled out of the station.

It didn't escape Joe's attention that, as the train pulled away, the other passengers looked out their windows to the ten men on the station platform waving to Joe. More confounded than anything else, he didn't know how respond to such a show of solidarity and respect. However, he didn't think he'd ever forget that moment, or how blessed it made him feel.

~

The train made several stops along the way, with enough time for him to get off and get something to eat, but otherwise, he ate the food Cookie had sent with him. As the train made its way through the countryside, he thought about Sara. As long as the letters kept coming, he hadn't lost her completely, but if she died ... that he couldn't bear to think about or at least he tried not to think about it. To pass the time he read the novel Elisha sent, and most of the Bible. Impatient for the journey to end, he grew more anxious at each stop the train made.

~

Joe's train pulled into San Francisco in the late afternoon almost forty hours after he'd left Cheyenne. He found a buggy to hire to take him to the address that he had for the Barnes. When they pulled up in front of the large house on a street of similar large houses, Joe noticed a black buggy in front of the house. He ran up to the front door, and jerked the bell pull.

The door opened and a woman in her late twenties in a black dress, white apron, and cap stood there.

"May I help you?" The woman asked.

Joe held his hat in his hand. "My name is Joe Storm, and I'm a friend of Mister and Miss Barnes. I've just arrived in town. Would you tell them I'm calling?"

The woman suddenly began to cry, and covered her mouth with her handkerchief.

"Ma'am? May I be of help?" Fear ran through Joe. Sara...

"Mr. Barnes died, and Miss Barnes is ill until death." The woman cried convulsively into her handkerchief.

Chapter Thirty-Three

Joe's heart pounded within his chest, and a vise squeezed his temples. He couldn't speak; because of his throat was dry and his tongue seemed swollen.

He walked past the woman into the hall, and closed the door. He put his valise down on the floor, and guided her to a chair in the hallway. "Sit down, ma'am. Who's with Miss Barnes?" He wanted to tear through the house and find Sara, but he forced himself to calm down. With her father dead and Sara ill, she needed his calm strength now.

"The doctor is with her, and we have a nurse to take care of her. Oh, sir, it has been just awful. Miss Barnes is so sick, and I'm afraid she'll die like her father." The woman cried even harder.

"What is your name?" Joe asked gently.

"I'm Minnie. I'm the maid for Miss Barnes. Everyone else has left. They're afraid of the cholera."

"Minnie, can you make coffee or tea?" Joe asked.

"Yes sir, I can." Minnie still had tears running down her face, but she wasn't crying as hard.

"I would like a cup, and I think you better fix yourself a cup. Where is the kitchen?" He looked around at the fine furniture.

"It's down the hallway past the dining room."

"And where is Miss Barnes' room?"

"It's up at the top of those stairs." Minnie pointed to the large circular stairway that led up to the second floor of the grand house.

"I'm going to talk to the doctor. You go make some coffee or tea, and if you have cake, we can offer that to the doctor. All right?" Joe looked at her expectantly.

"Yes sir. Thank you, sir." Minnie got up, and moved toward the kitchen.

Joe went up the stairway to the second floor. Voices came from a room at the end of the hall. Joe pushed open the door.

An older man, Joe supposed him to be the doctor, stood on the far side of the bed. A woman in a uniform-like gray dress with a white apron and cap stood on the other side.

Sara lay in the big bed, looking small and fragile. Her eyes were closed, and her breathing labored. The harsh sound of it jarred on Joe's ears.

The older man turned when he heard Joe came into the room. "Hello, who are you?"

"I'm a family friend. I've come to help. Are you the doctor?" Joe stopped by the end of the bed. What he wanted was to rush in and take Sara into his arms.

"Yes, I'm Doctor Brown. This is Nurse Franklin."

"How is Miss Barnes?" Joe was afraid to know.

"She's very ill, but I'm hopeful she's turned the corner. Are there other family members you can contact? With Miss Barnes so ill and Mr. Barnes dying, we need instructions."

"I don't think they have any other family. Perhaps if I ask the maid she'll know Mr. Barnes' business partners or perhaps a lawyer."

"You said you're a friend?" The doctor's brows knit together.

"Yes sir. Miss Barnes and I are close friends. She wrote asking for help, and I took the first train. I'm only sorry I didn't get here before the passing of Mr. Barnes."

"Where are you from?"

"Northern Colorado. I came in on the train from Cheyenne. We got Sara's, I mean Miss Barnes's, letter two days ago. I came as soon as I could."

"We got her letter?"

"Yes, Elisha and Susana Evans are her good friends also, and want her to come stay with them if her father passed on." Joe had given this man about all the explanation he was going to. Now, he wanted some answers. "Tell me more about Miss Barnes' illness. What can we do to help her? How will we know she's getting better? What do I need to do?"

"Slow down, young man. It looks as if you're the only one here to help her. Nurse Franklin can stay tonight, but we've so many ill that I doubt I can spare her longer than that. You need to bring in another woman to help you. We'll know in a couple of days whether she's going to make it, and then another week or so before she starts to recover. Can you stay around that long?"

"Yes sir. I'm here for as long as it takes. I need to know what to do for her." Joe made up his mind. Sara needed him, and he would be there to meet that need.

"I'm glad to hear that. I'll stop in every day. I've called some people to come get Mr. Barnes' body, and you need to see about getting him buried," the doctor said in a matter of fact manner.

Joe was shocked. He hadn't understood that the death was so recent that the body was still in the house. Well, that was something he could do for Sara. Take care of the burial arrangements for her father.

The doctor gave the nurse some instructions about medicine, and then asked Joe to walk him downstairs.

Joe started to lead him into the kitchen, but noticed that Minnie had set out tea at the dining table. "Before you leave, Doc, let us offer you a cup of tea and some cake." Joe motioned him into the dining room.

"That'll be good, but first let me make sure that the maid boiled the water way I told her." The doctor, with Joe following, went into the kitchen where Minnie cleaned the kitchen table. "Minnie, did you do like I told you, and boiled the water?"

"Yes, Doctor. I boiled the water for twenty minutes, and washed my hands three different times, and then poured vinegar over them."

"Good girl. Now you have to be very careful. All the soiled linens and clothes ... well, best to burn it. Don't get any on your hands. Wear gloves, and every drop of water used in this house for any reason must be boiled for at least twenty minutes, if not more." Doctor Brown spoke to Minnie while he washed his hands in a basin with hot water and soap.

The doctor looked up at Joe. "Did you say your name was Joe?"

"Yes sir."

"You know anything about cholera?" Doctor Brown dried his hands on a clean towel, and looked at Joe over his glasses.

"No sir. Just that it's bad." Joe's stomach tightened, at what the doctor was getting at and what it might mean for Sara.

"It's real bad. I'd been hopeful that Mr. Barnes would make it. Most people who die from it do so within the first three days, but he lived for a week before he died. If Miss Barnes is to make it you'll have to keep her drinking lots of water, and I mean a lot. Every thirty minutes you must get a full glass of water down her. However, you don't touch anything that comes out of her. It can kill you. Are you up to helping her?" The doctor looked him up and down with a frown.

Joe remembered how kind and caring Mrs. Purdy had been to him. Because of his love for Sara, he could do that much and more. "I'm up for it. I need to know what to do."

"Minnie, are you willing to stay here, and help Joe care for Miss Barnes?"

She looked like she wanted to say anything, but yes. "Is there anyone else that can do it?"

"I don't think so. I can ask around, but I don't think I can find a nurse that will come."

Joe thought of the greenbacks in the money belt Elisha had given him. "If it's a question of cost, I'll pay whatever it takes."

"Well, I'll ask around. That's all I can say. Let me get a cup of tea, and then be on my way. I've other patients waiting." Joe went into the dining room, and poured a cup of tea for the doctor.

Joe's gaze fell on the doctor's untouched plate with cake. "Sir, is the food in the house safe to eat?"

"It depends on how it's handled. You don't want to eat anything that hasn't been cooked or boiled. Be careful. I have to go. I'll be back sometime tomorrow. Keep her drinking as much water as you can." The doctor picked up his bag, and left.

Joe returned to the kitchen. "Minnie, thanks for your help. We'll do what the doctor says, and we'll get Miss Barnes through this. I'll go check with the nurse, and see what we need to do. Is there a bedroom where I can leave my things?" Joe rested his hand on Minnie's arm to convey his support.

She still looked very shaken. "Yes sir, you can use the bedroom up the hall from Miss Barnes." Minnie sniffed, and then blew into her handkerchief.

"Call me Joe. I'll be back in a few minutes." He picked up his valise, and carried it upstairs. He found the empty bedroom, and dropped his valise, coat, and hat on the bed. The room was luxurious compared to what Joe was used to. The entire house was opulent. Joe closed the door as he slipped out of his room then visited Sara's room. He went in quietly.

The nurse poured a glass of water.

"Hello. I'm Joe. How is she doing?" Joe peered down at Sara's shrunken and ashen face.

"I'm Anna. She's holding her own, but it could go either way. I'm about to try to get another glass of water down her. Is there anyone else to help?"

"There's Minnie, but I'm not sure how much help she's going to be. I'm willing to do whatever needs doing. You just tell me."

Anna wore white gloves.

Did he need to have gloves on? He didn't know.

She frowned and nodded. "If you can get Minnie to keep water boiled, and get rid of the bedding. It would be better if we could burn the bedding, and put on new sheets and gowns."

"Then that's what we'll do."

"If you could hold her up, I'll get her to swallow the water." Anna said.

Joe gently propped the semi unconscious Sara up, sat on the bed behind her, and held her head up against his chest. He didn't know whether she was aware that he was there or not.

Anna held Sara's nose until she opened her mouth and then poured the water down her throat.

Joe's fingers wove through her hair as he held her head. She probably wasn't even aware of what was happening.

"There, that's all right then. If we can do that about every fifteen minutes, she has a chance. I'll speak to the doctor, and see if he'll let me stay. You do need the help." Anna wiped Sara's face with a wet cloth. "Poor little thing, first she lost her father, and now she's so ill. Are you her young man?"

Joe smiled at her. "I guess I am." He liked the sound of that, Sara's young man.

"You can lay her down for now. Thank you, that was very helpful in getting her to drink the water. It's hard for one person to do it."

"Don't worry, Anna. I'm here to help as long as needed. I'll go downstairs and talk to Minnie. I'll also see what's in the pantry. You and I will need to eat something this evening. The doctor said it was all right if we only eat what's been boiled."

"All right, bring us up some more boiled water. By the time you get back it'll be time to give her another glass of water."

"So soon? I thought the doctor said every thirty minutes."

"I don't want to contradict the doctor. I'm sure he knows best, but it's been my experience that every fifteen minutes has a better results. The other thing is to put salt and sugar in the water. If we can do that over the next three or four days she should be all right."

"Anna, somehow I think you may have more experience helping people get better than even the doctor. You tell me what to do, and we will do it your way. I'll be right back with more water." Joe didn't know why he trusted her, but he did.

He went back downstairs.

Minnie had cleared up the tea things from the dining table.

Joe found her in the kitchen boiling more water. "Are there several extra sheets here in the house?"

She looked puzzled. "Yes sir. We have a whole linen closet full."

"We need to keep Miss Sara clean, and we need to use fresh sheets. The soiled sheets need to be burned, without touching any of the soiled part. I'm sorry I need to tell you that, but we need to be careful, so we don't get sick. Tomorrow, I want you to go out, and buy Miss Sara more gowns and more sheets if we need them. And Minnie, for your loyalty in helping, I'll personally treble your pay for the duration of Miss Sara's illness."

"Thank you, Mr. Joe. That will be nice to have a bonus, but only if you can afford it."

"I can afford it." He patted her on the shoulder. She seemed to need his reassurance. "The doctor said that any food we eat here needs to be boiled. I'm saying that because we need to eat something. Do you think you can prepare some supper for us? I can, if you can't." Joe's gaze roamed the spacious kitchen. Under different circumstances, it would be fun to cook in such a well-equipped place.

"Oh no, you don't need to worry. I'll get supper ready." She put the tea things away.

"The nurse says we need more boiled water upstairs. I'll take it up when it's ready."

"Here, take this pitcher. I boiled it earlier and let it cool. The nurse said to put salt and sugar into it. Is that right?" She set a pitcher of water on the table in front of Joe.

"Yes, that's right. And the doctor is sending someone to get Mr. Barnes' body. Will you listen for the bell, and let me know when they come?"

"Yes, I'll be sure to let you know." She looked pained at the thought.

Joe took the pitcher of water up to Sara's room.

The nurse took the pitcher from Joe, and poured a glass of water. "You ready to help again?"

"Yes, I'm ready." He was ready to do whatever it took to save Sara. He sat her up, then leaned her against his chest. He held her head while Anna forced Sara to swallow the water.

Sara's eyes opened but she didn't seem to be aware of what was happening to her. Joe thought it was just as well although he longed to hear her voice.

The evening dragged into a long tiring night as they continually forced the water down Sara's throat every fifteen minutes. They took time to eat the boiled beef and rice that Minnie had prepared.

The doctor came by the next day about noon. He pronounced that Sara seemed to be better.

By the next night, she was much better, and even began to recognize Joe. She smiled weakly at him. "You came, Joe, you came." Her hand weakly clutched at him.

"Of course, I came. I got your letter at three in the afternoon, and by midnight, I was on the train. I got here as soon as I could. Now you rest, and get better. I know you don't want to keep drinking the water, but that is what you must do to get well. Anna stayed to help us." Joe rubbed her back and shoulder. He gently continued to massage her back. He felt her muscles loosen under his touch.

She drifted off to sleep for the ten minutes they gave her before the next glass of water.

Joe was exhausted, and knew that the nurse was also tired, but they couldn't stop. He woke Sara, lifted her up, and leaned her against his chest for Anna to get Sara to drink the glass of water.

Sara had a difficult time getting the water down and some of it spilled on Joe's arm.

He didn't mind. At least they did something to try to help her. He held her tenderly, as if she were a child that needed his help.

Joe couldn't imagine drinking that much water. He was so tired the second night that he dozed off, as did the nurse, during their short fifteen minutes between glasses of water.

Joe was concerned for Sara, as they couldn't leave her in peace for more than a few minutes.

Several times, she cried and begged to be let alone to rest, she was so exhausted.

As Joe wiped away her tears, his own slipped down his cheeks. He was so helpless to take away her suffering.

By the morning of the second day, Sara was better.

Joe was so tired he could hardly function, but pushed on heartened by her improvement.

The doctor came into the bedroom as Joe and Anna got Sara to swallow another glass of water.

"How is our patient?" He looked at her eyes, felt of her forehead, and listened to her heart through a tube with an earpiece.

"You tell us, sir." Joe wanted to hear that she was better and out of danger.

The doctor looked at the nurse. "What do you say, Nurse Franklin?"

"I think she's better, sir."

"I think you're right. In fact, I think this little girl may be out of danger. Continue to give her the water for another day and then gradually lengthen the time between."

Joe held onto the bedpost to keep his knees from folding. He was so relieved to hear what the doctor had said. Sara was better; he wasn't going to lose her. If he had had the energy, he would have hugged the doctor.

Minnie worked nonstop to keep water boiled, kept clean linens available, and prepared meals for Joe and Anna.

On the morning of the fourth day, Joe had Minnie heat some water. He carried it up to the bedroom to fill the bathtub that Minnie brought into the room. Anna and Minnie gave Sara a bath, and washed her hair.

While they helped Sara to bathe, Joe went downstairs to talk to Sara's lawyer who finally stopped by.

The lawyer was an older man named Horace Johnston.

"Can I offer you some coffee?" Joe escorted the man into the formal setting room.

"No, thank you, I'm in a hurry. I've other people to see this morning." Johnston sat on the edge of the chair as if he was about to bolt.

Joe understood. People had died in this house, within the past week, of a disease that anyone could catch. Joe probably wouldn't have wanted coffee either, except he knew the water had been boiled twice, first as water and then in making the coffee. He didn't try to change the man's mind, but got down to business.

"What do we need to do to take care of Mr. Barnes's affairs?" Joe asked

"Well, I've read the will again, and it is very straight forward. Everything goes to the daughter, Sara. By the way, how is she?" Mr. Johnston looked over his glasses at Joe. He held a bunch of papers he had taken out of his satchel.

"She's much better. The doctor said she is recovering, and seems to be out of danger." Joe was happier to say that than the man seated across from him could possibly understand.

"That's a relief. I can't tell you how shocked I was to hear of Matthew Barnes' death. I haven't heard of a service. Has the funeral been planned?"

"No, the doctor handled the instruction to the funeral director. They buried him the next day. With Sara so ill we had to make some decisions for her." Joe didn't know who should even be invited to a service, and Sara wasn't able to attend.

The lawyer frowned. "You don't have the authority to make decisions for her."

"The doctor has the authority to make the decision because of the nature of the death. What would it take for me to have the authority to make decisions for her?"

"You would have the authority if you were her husband, but you're not. The only other way is for her to sign a paper putting you in charge of her affairs."

"How would we do that?" Joe didn't want to be responsible for Sara's affairs, but someone had to help her.

"I'd write out the paper right now, and if she signed it in front of witnesses I'd file it with the judge today. It's fairly simple."

"Can you wait a few minutes while I go talk to her?" They may as well get it done.

"Yes, I'll wait if we can do it quickly. I do need to get going."

"I'll be right back." Joe took the steps two at a time, then tapped on Sara's bedroom door.

Anna opened it.

"I need to talk to Sara. May I come in?" He wanted to make sure Sara finished her bath before he entered her bedroom.

Anna opened the door wider, and motioned him to come in. "We have her back in a clean bed, and feeling better after her bath. She's very weak, so don't talk very long."

Joe walked over, and then sat down in the straight-backed chair next to the bed where Sara lay. She looked pale and fragile. He couldn't believe how much weight she had lost in the three days he'd been at the house. He took her thin hand in his and looked at her face. The skin pulled tight across her facial bones, and had a translucent look, as if he could see beyond the flesh.

"Sara, I need to ask you something if you feel up to it."

In a small voice she answered, "I'm feeling much better Joe. Just so weak...what do you need to ask me?"

Joe pushed back a curl of hair from her forehead that was still damp from her bath. "The lawyer is downstairs, needing some papers signed. Either you have to sign them, or you need to give me the authority to sign for you."

"Why don't you get my father to sign them?"

Joe took a deep breath and then slowly let it out. He opened his mouth, but no words came forth.

Chapter Thirty-Four

Joe shot a look up at Anna. The nurse stood mute, her mouth hung open a bit. He could barely breathe. She doesn't understand her father's dead.

He wondered whether they should tell her. She looked so fragile. "You know he's been ill with the same illness that you've had?"

"Yes, he was sick for several days before me. Is he still as ill?" Her voice sounded like that of a tired little girl.

His heart couldn't break any harder for her than right now. "He isn't able to sign any papers. I hate to bother you, but the lawyer says there are some things that are in need of being handled. He can come up here, so you can sign a paper that gives me permission to take care of your business for you. That's all you need to do. I'll handle the rest."

He didn't want to press her, but he could see that she was in no shape to handle her father's death yet, and some things had to be dwelt with. Joe looked up at Anna.

The nurse nodded as if she approved his not telling Sara about her father.

"Joe ... I don't feel like even thinking. You ... tell me what to do ... I'll do it." Even her voice was heavy with weariness.

"All right, I'll have Mr. Johnston come up, you sign the paper, and Anna and Minnie can be witnesses."

Sara nodded her agreement.

Joe went back down stairs, and told Mr. Johnston to prepare the paper.

"I brought one prepared, just in case. We can do it now, if Miss Barnes is ready."

"Let me get the maid. She'll be a witness, then we'll all go upstairs." After Minnie agreed, the three of them went upstairs.

The lawyer paused in the doorway of Sara's room upon seeing how ill she still was. He must have thought her to be further along in her recovery.

Joe understood his shock. She looked what she was, desperately ill.

Mr. Johnston cleared his throat, then moved into the room and sat in the chair next to the bed. "Miss Barnes, do you understand that if you sign this paper that Joe Storm will be able to manage your affairs for you? He will have legal authority to make decisions."

"Yes, I understand that, and I want him to make whatever decisions he needs to make." Sara spoke softly, but clearly. "I trust him."

"Then all you have to do is sign both these documents here and here."

Sara's hand shook slightly as she signed the papers.

Mr. Johnston stood, then walked over to Anna and Minnie and had them sign both papers as witnesses.

Mr. Johnston returned to Sara's side and took her hand. "I'll give Mr. Storm instructions as to what needs to be done. I hope that the next time I see you, you'll be well and strong."

"Thank you, Mr. Johnston." Sara looked limp with a mixture of relief and exhaustion. As soon as the lawyer left the room, her eyes slid shut.

With her resting, Joe followed the lawyer.

At the front door, Mr. Johnston handed Joe one of the papers. "This copy is for you to keep. You can now deal with the banks, or Mr. Barnes's company, and make any decisions necessary."

"Can my first decision be to instruct you to make decisions for the company until Miss Barnes can decide what she wants to do with it?" Joe would rather Johnston be in charge of whatever businesses Barnes had since, as Barnes' lawyer, the man would be more familiar with the business dealings.

"Yes, I can take over the management of the business affairs. I'll work up another document for you to sign, authorizing me to become the business manager for Miss Barnes under your directions. Will that work for you?" Mr. Johnston picked up his hat from the hall table.

"Yes, please do that today, if possible. Can I get some of their money out of the bank to pay household expenses? Minnie needs to be paid, and several other things should be handled."

"You have complete access to all of the money now."

"When will you be back with the other papers?" Joe wanted to get things in order as quickly as possible.

"I'll be back at four, if that'll be all right."

"I'll see you at four, and thank you for your help." Joe shut the door behind the lawyer then turned toward Mr. Barnes' old study. He wanted to find papers to figure out what should be paid, and even which bank to visit to attend to Sara's affairs. He searched through the desk and when he found what he needed, he decided to turn it over to the lawyer to sort the business papers from the personal.

As Joe left the study, he found Dr. Johnston in the hall about to go up to see Sara.

"How's our patient today?" The doctor asked.

"She's much better. With help, she took a bath. I've some questions for you, doctor."

"Sure. Ask away."

"First, when can she eat something? She's so weak. Also, she doesn't realize her father has died. Will you tell her, or do you want me to tell her?

And, should she stay here in the city with so much sickness about, or can she travel?"

"Well, young man. That's a lot of questions. Let me see her, and then I'll be better able to give you the answers."

"Fair enough. Do you want me to come upstairs with you?" Joe wasn't sure he should intrude. He wanted to give the doctor privacy for his examination of Sara if needed.

"Yes, I think so. You seem to be the only one in charge. You might as well know what's going on." The doctor led the way up the stairs, and into Sara's bedroom.

"Nurse Franklin, how's our patient?"

"She's much better, Doctor. We've not had to change the bedding since yesterday."

"Miss Barnes, you're looking better. Your skin is showing more color." The doctor listened to Sara's heart and felt her forehead. "You're doing fine. You now need to get your strength back." The doctor turned to Anna. "Nurse, you need to continue the water, but only every couple of hours."

"Doctor, should I give her some beef broth and tea?" Anna asked.

"Yes, that would be fine. Start out with small amounts. If there is any indication of problems then go back to the water. I'll be back tomorrow."

The doctor patted Sara's hand then left the room.

Joe followed close behind until they were at the front door. He wanted answers to his questions.

The doctor laid his hand on the door handle, but turned back to face Joe. "In answer to your questions, young man, I think Miss Barnes is out of the woods. Take it slow in giving her food. You need to tell her about her father. The sooner the better. It may set her back some, but she has to know. If you have the means, and a place to take her, I'd get her out of the city. But, as long as you are in the city do not, under any circumstance, drink any water without boiling it first."

Chapter Thirty-Five

Joe asked, "Is it the water that causes the illness?"

"It seems to be. Of course, I've no way of knowing for sure. But people who do not drink the water aren't sick." The doctor put on his hat, bid Joe good-bye then left.

Joe could only imagine how many patients he was attending.

He climbed the stairs, dreading what he had to do. From the hall, he motioned for the nurse to join him.

"Anna, I'm going to leave the house for a couple of hours. Can you manage?"

"Yes sir, I can manage now. When are you going to tell Miss Barnes about her father?"

Joe responded quietly. "I plan to tell her tonight. Let's give her a few more hours to recover." Joe waited for her eyes to meet his. "Anna, let me ask you something. The doctor said that it would be best if we left the city. What would you think about making the journey with us? Are you tied to the city?"

"Where would we go?"

"I want to take Miss Barnes by train to Cheyenne, Wyoming, and then on to the ranch of her best friends. They want her to stay with them. I'd like you to come with us as her nurse, stay as long as she needs you. You'll be paid good wages." Joe waited for her to respond to his sudden request.

"I couldn't afford the train ticket."

She hadn't said no. This gave Joe a bit of hope that she'd consider his offer. "You don't have to be concerned about your expenses. I'll take care of those. You may need to stay several months. If at any time, you want to come back to San Francisco, you'll be free to return. I'll pay your way. Think about it, and we'll talk more later."

Anna nodded then returned to Sara's bedroom.

Joe left the house to find the bank, and check on what other things he could see to on Sara's behalf.

Joe made it back to the house before dark. As he stepped through the front door, he smelled beef roasting. He strolled into the kitchen looking for supper. He hadn't eaten anything since the morning.

Anna and Minnie prepared a tray for Anna to take up to Sara.

"Something smells good. What's for supper?" Joe asked.

"I broiled a roast, and from the juices I made a broth for Miss Sara. I also boiled some potatoes and carrots. I made custard for Miss Sara, but we're going to see if she can take the broth and tea first. As soon as we get Miss Barnes settled, I'll serve your supper in the dining room, if that'll be all right."

Joe raised a brow. He hadn't heard Minnie speak so many words from the first day he'd arrived. Joe inhaled again to savor the aromas. Everyone's routine was returning to normal now that Sara was better.

"Joe, may I speak with you? Minnie can take this up, and serve Miss Sara." Anna passed the tray to Minnie.

"Of course, Anna, let's go into the sitting room." Joe led the way while Minnie mounted the stairs carrying the tray.

They sat in the big wingback chairs. Anna looked directly into Joe's eyes. "I've thought all afternoon about what you asked me, Mr. Storm, and I've decided to accept the job as long as I can come back here at any time. I'd want the price of a return ticket, paid in advance. And I have another request. I want Minnie to go with us. She doesn't have any family either. Between the two of us, we could take very good care of Miss Sara. Minnie wants to get out of the city also."

Anna looked at Joe as if she expected he would protest.

But, it was an excellent idea.

Anna was about twenty-five-years-old. Minnie seemed a few years older.

His arriving at the ranch with three single females would cause a stir among the riders. Perhaps it would be a blessing to both the women and the riders. Joe had the thought that only God knew the outcome of such a decision.

"That's a great idea. With both you and Minnie to care for Sara, I wouldn't be as concerned about her. There's a problem, and I want to be honest with you. The ranch is a two-day ride from any town of any size. It's up in the mountains."

"Who else will be at the ranch?" Anna asked.

"That's a good question, and shows sense on your part. Let me think ... there are about fourteen of us. No, that's not right. There's fifteen of us since Susana had another baby. Elisha Evans and his wife, Susana, own the ranch. They have three children. Then there's Santo Real and his wife, Mara. She helps with the children. Cookie is the cook, and Billy and I help with that. Then we have the cowhands. Bob Fife is the foreman of the ranch. Jeff Kingston, Will Ramsey, Jim Finely, and Jacob Blunfeld are the cowhands for the ranch. And, oh yes, me," Joe grinned.

"How would we get there?"

"I'll hire a salon coach from the railway. It's like a sitting room, and bedroom in a train car. It'll take us from here to Cheyenne. Then at

Cheyenne, I'll rent a wagon, fix it up with a bed for Sara. We'll drive slowly to the ranch. If we need to, we can stay a few days in Cheyenne to rest up before the trip. Anna, understand something. These are people who know and love Sara. They'll make a home for her as long as she wants. I promised Elisha Evans that I'd come back to the ranch as soon as I could. But, I can't leave Sara alone in this big house with no who cares for her."

"I understand, and I think she should go back with you. It's just that I've never been to Wyoming, or anywhere else. It's a little frightening." After a moment, Anna nodded as though she'd made up her mind. "I'll go, and Minnie will do what I tell her. When do you want to leave?"

"When do you think Sara will be able to travel?" Joe wanted to leave the next day, but knew that was too soon for Sara.

"You'll be amazed at how quickly she'll get her strength back once she can eat normally. I think she could be prepared to leave in three or four days with us to help her get ready. One problem is closing up the house, but I can give you the name of someone who could be left here as caretaker." Anna stood, then smoothed her white apron. "I'll go up now and get her ready for the night. Why don't you come up after you eat, and tell her about her father? I'll have the sleeping powder ready that the doctor left behind. After you tell her, I'll give it to her in a cup of tea. She'll be better able to cope with the news a little at a time. Tomorrow she can start her grieving."

"Thanks Anna. I don't know what we would've done without your help." Joe walked her to the bottom of the stairs where they parted, her upstairs, him into the dining room where Minnie had set a place for supper for him. It was strange sitting at the long formal table eating by himself. This would be Sara's experience if he left her here alone. No, he couldn't do that to her.

~

Sara sobbed deeply after Joe told her about her father. She admitted that she suspected something when no one would talk to her about him. Joe sat on the bed, held her in his arms, and rocked her for what seemed hours while she cried.

Joe encouraged Sara to sip slowly the cup of tea Anna made. Within fifteen minutes, she fell into a deep sleep. Anna had laced Sara's tea with the sleeping powder. He laid Sara back onto her pillow and then pulled the covers up to her chin. He hoped she'd sleep until morning.

He arranged with Anna for her to wake him at two in the morning so he could sit with Sara and let Anna get some sleep. He went into the bedroom and only took his boots off. He fell across the bed asleep.

The next three days were hard for Sara as she came to terms with the reality of her situation. She turned to Joe for every decision.

Joe made the plans for them to head back to the ranch. He sent a telegram to tell Elisha, and the others that he was coming, and bringing Sara with him. He didn't know if they would get the telegram before they arrived or not.

Joe was shocked at the amount of money in the bank account that the letter had gained him access to. The money was only a small part of what Sara had inherited from her father.

Joe withdrew a liberal amount of funds to pay for the trip back to the mountains, and to pay for the upkeep of the house. He hadn't even made a dent in the account balance. Not knowing how long Sara would stay at the ranch, he took out several thousand dollars for her to have on hand.

Minnie and Anna spent the time packing for Sara. They had Joe pull several trunks down from the attic storage room, and place them in a spare bedroom.

Sara lay on her bed, and watched all the activity with a wan ashen face. She had told Joe she didn't know enough about Mr. Barnes' friends and business acquaintances to bother with a funeral, especially since he'd already been buried for over a week.

Joe was sorry that they couldn't even have a funeral, if for no one else but her, but she hadn't been strong enough to handle it.

The day they planned to head for the mountains, Joe arranged for the trunks to be taken to the train earlier in the day. An ambulance, a small-enclosed wooden wagon, was driven to the house, and the men carried Sara out on a stretcher.

Anna rode in the ambulance with Sara, and Joe and Minnie rode in a carriage behind it. When they arrived at the train station, they transferred Sara to the train car Joe had arranged for. The car, leased from one of the owners of the railroad, boasted an opulence with every convenience one could wish to serve their needs for the journey. As they boarded the train car, people looked at them as if to wonder who these important people were.

Joe settled the expense with the ambulance drivers, and then went in search of the train porter. He paid the porter a big tip, to have food brought to the train car at meal times during the journey. He also insisted they be brought water that had been boiled for thirty minutes. They had some with them, but not enough for the whole trip.

Joe ducked into the little bedroom in the train car to check on Sara. She lay propped up on pillows looking almost ethereal in a white lacey bed jacket.

"How are you doing?" Joe sat on the edge of the bed since there wasn't a chair.

"I'm doing all right. I'm tired, but I think I'll be tired for the rest of my life. I want you to know that I'm so glad to go to Susana and Elisha. But, it is so hard to leave Papa." Tears ran down her cheeks. With the death of her father still so raw for her, she couldn't mention him without crying.

Joe couldn't stop himself. He took her in his arms, kissed her tears, and gently held her. She didn't seem to mind.

"It'll do you good to get up in the mountains, and away from the city. And you know Susana is going to take care of you." He stroked her back, and ran his fingers through the long waves of her long blonde hair.

"Oh Joe, what would I have done if you hadn't come?" She put her arms around his neck, and pulled him tight.

He looked into her eyes and found acceptance there. He gently kissed her on the lips, and felt her response. Gently, he laid her back on the bed, and stood up. He breathed slow and deep to try to clear his head. He hadn't ever felt anything as soft as her lips. The thought of Sara filled his mind, but he needed to get things done.

"I need to check that your trunks made it on the train. I'll come back later. Then we can visit until you're ready to sleep."

She smiled up at him. "You're always taking care of everyone. You're a good man, Joe."

"Well, someone has to take care of things, and it might as well be me." He gazed down at her for a moment. She was so precious to him. "I'll be back in a few minutes."

He turned and left, heading into the sitting room of the train car. There he found Anna and Minnie trying to figure out how the sofas became beds. "Don't worry about that. The porter will be in soon to do that for us. We need to figure out a schedule for sitting up with Miss Barnes. She may not need it, but I'd rather be sure that she's all right."

Joe verified that all of the trunks were in the baggage car, except for the one they kept with them in the train car. The train wouldn't pull out for three more hours, but Joe was glad they were settled in the train car, and would soon be heading for the mountains. The big city held no attraction for him.

Chapter Thirty-Six

The traveling wore on all of them, especially Sara. With the stops in towns, stops to fill up the boiler of the engine, and slow sections up the mountains it took them almost four days on the train to get to Cheyenne. Joe was impressed that the train could speed up to forty miles an hour on the flat land, but through the mountains, they did good to make ten miles an hour. Joe reminded himself several times of how long it took traveling in a chuck wagon with a trail herd.

When they arrived at Cheyenne, Joe asked at the telegraph office if anyone had picked up his telegrams that he had send before leaving San Francisco. No one had been to town to receive them from the ranch. He wasn't surprised. On Anna's advice, they stayed over in Cheyenne for a couple of days to let Sara rest. He bought a large covered wagon and four horses, and had it outfitted for the three women, and for traveling.

The morning they were to start out for the ranch, Joe carried Sara down from her hotel room, and carefully placed her on the bed he had made for her in the wagon. He told Anna to let him know when he needed to stop, otherwise he'd push to get to the ranch as soon as possible without it being too bumpy for Sara.

After two full days of travel, Joe drove the wagon through the gap, and looked out over the valley. The sun was about to disappear behind the craggy blue gray mountains to the west. He felt a tension drain from his body. Words could not express how glad he was to be home.

"Sara," Joe called to the back of the wagon. "We're here. The ranch house is in view, and you'll be with Susana and the others in a few minutes."

"Thank the Lord. I'm so glad." Her voice was stronger every day.

As they drove up to the house, Elisha and Susana stepped out onto the porch from the front room.

The riders filtered out from the bunkroom and the barn. Greetings of "Hey Joe," "Glad your back," and "Hey pard," were shouted as he stopped the wagon in front of the house.

"Hey, yourself," Joe shouted at the men.

He climbed down from the wagon and then Elisha's arms came around him in a bear hug.

Susana hugged him next and kissed his cheek.

"Sara is in the wagon. She's still very weak." Joe helped Minnie climb down from the wagon seat. "This is Minnie who works for Sara as a maid. And in the wagon is Anna, Sara's nurse. They'll stay with us for a while, if that's all right." Joe led them around to the back of the wagon and Elisha helped him lower the tailgate.

Susana immediately scurried up into the wagon before anyone could offer her assistance.

"Oh, Sara, honey. I'm so glad you've come." Susana gave Sara a gentle hug, and then she turned and hugged Anna. "Thank you so much for taking care of Sara, and coming all this way."

"Susana, which room do you want us to move Sara to?" Elisha asked.

Susana reached a hand out to Elisha and he steadied her to climb out of the wagon. "She'll stay in the guest room where she stayed before, but I need to go make up the bed."

"We'll carry Sara into the house." Elisha directed.

Joe didn't have to do anything but show Minnie and Anna into the house. He was tired of being in charge, and could now let down a bit.

When he entered the house, Cookie came from the kitchen and grabbed him in a bear hug before Joe could say anything. "Am I glad to see you! Elisha had decided that tomorrow someone would ride in and see if there was any news. We've been so worried." Cookie hugged him again.

Bob Fife carried Sara through the front door as if she weighed nothing at all. He took her into the bedroom, and laid her down on the freshly made bed.

Joe followed to make sure she didn't need anything and was comfortable.

"There, Miss Sara. Now you'll be all right." Bob said it as if to get her into the house was all she needed to be all right.

"Thanks, Bob." She smiled.

Bob's face reddened. He ducked his head and stepped back into the hall. He quickly headed for the front door. Others brought in the trunks and boxes and placed them in the corner of the bedroom.

Joe went back out to help take the wagon up to the barn, and unhitch the horses. The riders told him to go away. They would take care of the horses. He wandered into the kitchen.

Cookie put a cup of coffee on the table that was set for supper Then he encouraged Joe to sit down.

Elisha came in, got a cup of coffee, and sat down with him. "Tell me what happened, Joe." Elisha took a swallow of the hot coffee and waited.

"I got there in a little over two days, but Mr. Barnes had already died. Sara was real sick, and I believe that if Anna hadn't been her nurse, she would've died from the cholera. They had people sick and dying all over the city. I turned all of Sara's business over to her lawyer, rented a fancy

Pullman car, and got her back here as soon as I could. I needed help, so I got her maid, Minnie, and her nurse, Anna, to come back with me."

"Is Sara doing all right with the death of her father?"

"She's cried a lot and it wears her out. She's still very weak from the illness. But considering everything, I think she's doing as well as can be expected." Joe rubbed his face. "I'm glad to be here. I'm worn out."

"We're glad you're back. You're missed when you aren't here." Elisha said this with a grin. "Christine hasn't been happy with her Yoe being gone. The children are out for a walk with Mara and will be back soon for supper."

Joe grinned back at him. He looked forward to seeing the children.

~

The next few weeks went by quickly. Joe got back into the routine of breaking the horses.

Susana and Mara, along with Minnie and Anna, treated Sara as if she was fine china. She didn't resist for the first couple of weeks, she was too weak. However, with the clear mountain air, and the food Cookie prepared especially for Sara, she began to regain her strength.

Minnie and Anna made the work around the house that much easier for Susana and Mara. All four women took turns taking care of the children, and helping Cookie in the kitchen.

Joe found it amusing to watch the calf eyes the fellows threw Minnie's and Anna's way. It was soon apparent that Anna was settling on Jeff. It took a little longer, but to everyone's surprise, it was Bob Fife and Minnie that began to take walks together.

At the end of the third week, Joe found Anna sitting on the front porch. "How's it going?"

Anna smiled. "It's going well. Sara is almost fully recovered and I am thoroughly enjoying being here on the ranch."

"I'm glad you like it here and I think that a certain cowboy is also glad you're here." Joe noted the blush on Anna's cheeks. "I'd like to take Sara for a ride this Sunday and have a picnic. Do you think she is up for it?"

Anna nodded. "Sara would benefit from getting away from the ranch house for a while. I think it is a good idea."

"Great! I'll go ask Cookie to put together a picnic basket for us." Joe headed for the kitchen.

That evening he sat with Sara on the sofa. "How are you feeling?"

Sara glanced at him and smiled. "I'm doing fine. I still get tired easily but I don't have that sick feeling anymore. It will just take me a while to get all of my strength back."

Joe pushed a blond curl back from her face. "You think you might feel up to a ride in the cart and a picnic lunch Sunday afternoon?"

"Yes! I would love to get out and see more of the ranch. I have felt so cooped up."

~

After the worship service Sunday morning, Joe hitched up the cart and put the big basket of food Cookie had prepared along with a couple of blankets behind the seat. He then helped Sara up onto the seat, and then got up beside her. He drove down the trail along the south edge of the valley. He headed for the lookout where he had talked with his father. They didn't say much, but enjoyed the feel of the breeze as the red sorrel trotted along pulling the cart at a good pace.

Because of the small seat of the cart, Sara sat pressed up against him. She put her arm around his waist to hold on against the bouncing of the cart. A soft smile and her bright gaze as she looked out over the ranch land indicated her pleasure.

Joe didn't mind the ride at all. Just having Sara well and content next to him was a gift.

He stopped the cart at the lookout, and then helped Sara down. He spread a blanket out, guided Sara to sit on it, and spread out the picnic for them.

A sense of contentment filled him as he looked out over the valley and to the snow capped mountains.

"Joe, could we have a blessing for the food?" Sara asked.

"Of course, let's pray.

"Heavenly Father, we thank you for allowing us this time to gaze upon your handy work. Thank you for Sara's return to health, and be with her as she mourns her father. Give her your comfort always. We thank you for the bounty of this food. Be with us in all our decisions. In the name of Jesus the Christ. Amen."

Joe knew he was repeating phrases he had heard his father and Elisha pray, but was surprised that he felt that there was someone really listening to his prayer. When had he started to feel more comfortable with the thought of a caring heavenly Father?

They ate the food Cookie prepared while gazing out over the valley. It was good to sit together. He glanced over at Sara.

She wore a serious look.

He wasn't sure what it meant. He returned her look, and raised his eyebrows as if in question.

"Joe, this is a wonderful place, and to be here with you after all this time. What a miracle this moment is. If it weren't for the loss of my papa, I would be completely content." She turned to him. "Thank you for bringing me up here."

Joe brushed a blonde curl from her eyes. Her curly blond hair was continually escaping her effort to contain it. He didn't mind as it gave him an excuse to touch her hair. "I'm glad you're here with me. This is a special place. I feel closer to God from this view than anywhere else on the ranch. I wanted to share it with someone I care about." He wanted to say more, but didn't know if he dared. With the death of Mr. Barnes, he felt a barrier had been removed between himself and Sara. However, he was a poor ranch hand. And she was a wealthy young woman.

"Do you truly care about me?" Sara asked softly.

Her question surprised him. Could he take the risk and speak his heart? "I care a great deal for you. More than you could possibly know. But do I have the right to speak of it?"

"What do you mean? Of course, you have the right." She tilted her head, and reached out to take his hand with hers.

Joe moved closer to her. "I love you. I have for a long time. But you got to be realistic about it." He longed to take her into his arms, and hold her safe against him.

She slid her arms around his shoulders.

He felt free to slip his arms around her waist, and pulled her close.

As she gazed into his eyes she asked, "What do we have to be realistic about?"

He felt a tightness in his chest with her so close, but he needed to say some things to her.

"Sara, I'm crippled and always will be. I can't ride like other men." She couldn't possibly know how he hated to say the words.

She smiled, and placed her hand on his hip, below his belt. He didn't know what to do. Whether to pull her hand away or to let it rest there, the place that always hurt the worst.

"Joe, you aren't crippled unless you decide to be. You work harder and accomplish more than any rider on the ranch. I know you push yourself to prove you're as good as the next man. You're better because you're strong and gentle." She continued to press her hand against his bad hip.

"Don't you care that I can't ride like the other men?" He couldn't believe that she wouldn't mind that he couldn't ride. He minded so much he assumed that she would, too.

"I wish for your sake you could ride. But I don't care. I just want you to love me." She moved her hand from his hip and brought it up to rest gently against his cheek.

He tightened his arms around her. Then he buried his face in her hair and deeply breathed in the faint scent of flowers. "I do love you. But you need to know it all." He shuddered as he thought of what he needed to share with her.

She pulled back, and then looked at his face. "What is it? What's so terrible that you would look so troubled?"

He let go of her, and looked out over the valley. His last conversation with his father came to mind. Yes, he had to tell her about his mother. Joe wanted Sara more than he had wanted anything in his life, but not with secrets. She had to know. What would she think of him once she knew it all?

"Sara, I'm going to tell you about when I was a boy. It wasn't like your growing up with your parents, and it wasn't normal. I don't know how much it's still with me, nor how it will affect how I might live with a woman." He turned to find her looking up at him with a calm gaze. "How it might affect us if we decided to live our lives together."

Her eyes widened, and she looked as if she had something to say.

He put his finger on her lips. "Just hear me out."

He told her of his childhood, and his relationship with his mother. Nothing was left out, and by the time he was through telling her the full truth, she was crying.

"I'm sorry. I won't say anymore. Don't cry." He handed her his handkerchief.

"No, don't stop. Tell me everything. I'm all right. I'm just crying for that little boy."

Joe wanted to cry, but couldn't. Every time he talked about what had happened with his mother, it tore him up a little more inside. He ended by telling her about his father.

"He wants my forgiveness for what he allowed to happen, and I haven't been able to give it to him. That's my fault, my weakness. I can't get past it. He wants me to come home, and work on the ranch with him. He wants me to have the ranch some day, but I don't know if I can even face going into the house. I'm glad I don't have to see her again. It's not right, and I'm not sure what God thinks of me, but I'm glad she's dead. And I admit it, I'm a coward, still afraid of a dead woman. I've lived my whole life afraid of her."

At this Sara took him into her arms, cradled his head to her, and rocked him. "Shhh, you're not a coward. You're the bravest man I know. You don't have to go into that house. Not ever if you don't want to, just stay with me. I do so love you, Joe. I have ever since we rode all those days on the chuck wagon. We'll turn to God together, and He'll help us work it out."

Joe wanted to believe her, that none of it mattered anymore. Maybe he could bury his mother. He looked into Sara's beautiful blue eyes. He took her face into his hands, and gently kissed her cheeks, and then her lips. "We have another problem, Sara," he said softly.

"What is that?" She rested her arms around his neck, and then kissed him back.

"I'm a working ranch hand. I'll never make a lot of money. You're rich. Your father left you with a lot of money. You can go anywhere, and live anywhere. I only want to live here in the mountains, and work with horses. What kind of life is that to offer you?"

"Is it a life that I would get to spend with you?" She asked with a small smile as if she knew a secret.

"Is that what you want?" He barely dared to hope.

"Yes," she said simply. "I want to be with you, for the rest of my life. And if it's to be here in these mountains, that's all right. I love these mountains. But where will we live?"

"I'll build us a house. I'm sure Elisha and Susana will let me."

"Joe, if the money is a problem I'll give it away. It means nothing to me if it stands between us. Of course, I'd rather give it to you to use for us. If it is not a problem for me, please don't let it be a problem for you. I love that you're a ranch hand and work with the horses. You have a gift that I am so proud of. I only ask that we stay faithful to what God wants."

"I've come to want what God wants also, even when I don't know what that is. Elisha and my father have talked to me lately about who God is. I told my father that I didn't trust God, but look what He's done for you, making you well. I prayed and prayed for you, and God heard me. Maybe I can trust Him."

"Oh, you can trust because God cares for you, and loves you, Joe. Even with all that happened years ago, God has always loved you." She had such a look of serenity.

Her words gave him comfort, and he wanted to hear more about this God in whom she had such trust. However, there was something else he had to say to her. Harder in a way than telling her about his mother. He had it to do.

"Sara, what if I turn out like my mother, and I was cruel to our children?" A thought, a fear he couldn't bear to face, and had been unable to say to anyone.

"That's what you're afraid of, isn't it? That you'll be like your mother? Well, I don't believe it. It'd have shown up a long time ago if you were a mean, cruel person."

"But how can you know for sure?" He needed her to reassure him because the question went to the core of his being. From the depth of his soul, he wanted her to be right.

"Look into yourself, Joe. Are you mean? Could you be cruel to little Christine, or little Sam? Or even to baby Josh? Could little Christine be so wrong about you when she puts her arm around your neck, her little head on your shoulder, and goes to sleep with such love and trust in your arms? Could you hurt her? Could you?" She asked with an urgent, intense challenge.

He couldn't imagine himself hurting one of the children. "No, I couldn't hurt any of those children. I love them."

"So, there is your answer. If you couldn't hurt those children, how can you imagine you would love your own children any less?" She looked at him with a questioning gaze.

"I couldn't." He hugged her, threw back his head, and laughed. He shouted at the mountaintops. "I couldn't."

A ton of weight lifted from his heart. He stood up and pulled her up with him. Catching her by the waist, he swung her around. He set her feet down on the ground, and took her into his arms. He buried his head in her thick blonde hair that broken free from its ribbon. "Oh Sara, I couldn't." He whispered into her ear.

She laughed and cried at the same time. She slid her hands up the back of his neck, then pulled his head down until his lips met hers.

He wanted as many of her kisses as he could get in a lifetime together. He pulled away from her so he could see her face.

"Sara, will you marry me?"

"Yes, Joe, I will." She again smiled that small secret smile, as if she had known all along.

The End

A J HAWKE BOOKS AVAILABLE ON AMAZON/AMAZON KINDLE

CABIN ON PINTO CREEK (Cedar Ridge Chronicles) 2011

Elisha Evans is out of luck. By the age of twenty-five, he had planned to have his own ranch. Instead, he is forced to beg for a job, destroying his dreams of having a family he can provide for and protect. Betrayal and loss bring him to a cabin on Pinto Creek in the high Colorado Rockies. Just before winter hits, he finds a broken-down wagon in the snow with precious cargo inside. Perhaps, his luck is about to change.

Susana Jamison doesn't feel so lucky. Despite being rescued by Elisha, she is challenged to the limit of her strength, both physically and spiritually, when faced with the brutal conditions of frontier living and the dangers she encounters. Can she hold on to her faith in the midst of this desperate situation, especially when she's forced to marry a man she's doesn't love?

An inspirational historical western romance, CABIN ON PINTO CREEK is the first in the Cedar Ridge Chronicles. - An Inspirational Western Historical Romance

CAUGHT BETWEEN TWO WORLDS 2011

He comes from a ranch in Colorado; she comes from Upper Manhattan. He's struggling to provide the medical care his daughter needs; she has more money than she can spend in a lifetime. He has a strong faith to see him through; she is alone without a belief. They are caught between their two worlds. Widower Flint Tucker doesn't have the resources to get the medical treatment his three-year-old daughter needs. Stephanie Wellbourne has a chance encounter with Flint and she offers him a job that will enable him to earn the money. The only problem is the job takes him away from his life in Colorado and brings him to New York City. Drawn to the tall rugged Westerner, Stephanie can't understand his clinging to a belief that God will provide a way to help him with his problems. How can a man from a ranch in Colorado and an Upper Manhattan career woman find love as they are caught between their two worlds.
An Inspirational Contemporary Romance

MOUNTAIN JOURNEY HOME 2012

Rock   Corner,   Texas.   1877.

Life couldn't get much better for Dave Kimbrough. He has a beautiful wife in Jenny, a fine young son in Jonathan, and a small ranch with which to build their future. But when Jenny suddenly dies, the heartache is more than Dave can bear, so he leaves his son with his wife's family and rides off into the rugged Texas country alone. After several years Dave is wrongly accused of murder, and when he sets out to find the man who can clear his name, he runs instead into a posse that has set out to kill him. Wounded, he holes up for the winter in a cave. It is not time wasted, however, as he is given time to contemplate the mistake he made in abandoning his son.

Once spring arrives, Dave returns to make things in his life right. Things rarely go as planned, however, and Dave's plans are no different. Beset by a trip to jail, Jenny's spirited sister Rachel, and the heartache of taking away the only life and family his son really knows, Kimbrough makes a promise he thinks is the right thing to do. But a fateful winter followed by a deadly spring storm changes the course of their lives in ways that no one—least of all Dave—could have ever imagined. – An Inspirational Western Historical Romance

38558473R00153

Made in the USA
San Bernardino, CA
11 September 2016